THE BOBBI BLEND

By S.R. Bradford

1st Edition
Cover Design: S.R. Bradford and Kristin Campbell
Edits & Formats: Kristin Campbell at Pinnacle Pen & Proof

ISBN: 979-8-218-82171-5

Contents

CHAPTER ONE: DISCOVERY DAY

Saturday, January 2
Bobbi

As daylight surrendered to the Manhattan shadows on Saturday, January 2nd, Dr. Bobbi Wyatt stepped into a painting. By the time she returned from Rome, her life had changed forever.

After delivering a dazzling speech at the American Neurology Consortium Conference at Times Square's NYTSQ Hotel, Bobbi knew she'd knocked it out of the park. Bobbi was the youngest doctor—and the first woman—ever chosen to give the keynote.

She'd explained her groundbreaking work at the Brooklyn Women's Health Center, which had led to new concussion assessment protocols now used across New York, helping countless young female soccer players.

Bobbi was by far the youngest doctor they'd ever hired, and she worked hard to downplay her youth, height, and unmistakably striking looks. She typically wore flats, a lab coat over a plain top, and black dress pants, her long, honey-blonde hair tied back in a practical ponytail.

However, at cocktail hour following the conference's closing session, the stunning blonde in a knee-length cerulean dress reminded everyone that brilliance and beauty weren't mutually exclusive. The dress was flattering and feminine without being flashy. Paired with sheer stockings and low heels that subtly enhanced her height, her look was elegant and understated.

Confident and poised, Bobbi mingled effortlessly, sipping an Italian Pinot Grigio that she had watched the bartender pour. Many attendees asked for more information about her innovative study, while others requested her number—thinly veiled invitations for "private research" over drinks.

Bobbi was used to strangers hitting on her, assuming she was just another brainless blonde. If she couldn't politely deflect their advances, she'd shift the conversation to the intricacies of the limbic system, particularly the amygdala's role in the initial response to sexual stimuli and the generation of desire. Most quickly got the hint.

But surrounded by medical hounds, that tactic wasn't an option. Rather than reveal the truth—that she was a single mother with little time nor inclination for dating—she simply pretended to misinterpret their innuendos. Tactfully, she redirected their attention to her research, offering to send a PDF of her findings. It was a small price to pay to keep her private life separate from her professional one, especially as one of the youngest female neurologists in the country.

When an older, Jim Beam-swilling doctor with a sweaty toupee called her "Dr. Barbie" and remarked, "If your research has legs as good as yours, this is a game changer," Bobbi stifled a sigh and gracefully retrieved her hat and bag, ready to head home.

Bobbi glided across the polished marble floor, taking in the art deco splendor of the NYTSQ Hotel lobby. A boutique pop-up filled with exquisite leather purses and elegant watches, all from Italy, caused her to stop. She paused and silently vowed—again—that one day she *would* visit Italy.

Stepping outside onto the snowless sidewalks, she tugged her coat tighter and headed west on 47th Street. For the first time in months, she'd missed the gym, so a brisk twenty-minute walk to the new ferry terminal on the Hudson would help make up for it. The thought of circling Manhattan on the ferry, maybe even doing laps around the deck while breathing in the crisp afternoon air, felt like the perfect way to end the day.

Bobbi glowed, replaying the standing ovation after her presentation. Despite her reverie, she kept her gaze fixed ahead, focused on finding her way to the ferry.

The wind picked up, its sharp chill biting at her neck. Reaching into her bag for her scarf, she yelped as a sudden gust whipped her ponytail across her face, blinding her for a moment. She stopped abruptly, yanking her ponytail back with quick, irritated movements before wrapping the scarf snugly around her neck.

When she looked up again, disorientation hit her. She was convinced she'd ended up on the wrong street. She scanned for landmarks—a street sign, a familiar building—but nothing looked right. Bobbi couldn't shake the unsettling sense that something was off. The street ran only one way, yet she felt out of place.

Struggling to get her bearings, Bobbi looked to her left as if something unseen had prompted her. A small, unassuming storefront art gallery came into view, one she was certain hadn't been there moments before.

The dimly lit sign above the door read "*Fortuna's on 47th*," advertising an exhibition by a new Italian painter, Marianna Remi.

Bobbi's fascination with Italy had begun during childhood. She couldn't explain it—her Icelandic and Danish roots offered no connection—but Italian food, art, and language had always captivated her. Even now, the allure never failed to pull her in. Although not typically a movie lover, Bobbi couldn't resist Italian films, either.

Thanks to taking Italian in high school and college, she understood the language perfectly. She had even briefly dated an Italian-American real estate agent, and on one date, Bobbi had declined to hold his hand while watching a movie set in Positano. She hadn't been trying to be cold; just utterly lost in the beautiful cinematography.

When they had unexpectedly ran into his parents later at Coffee Corner, Bobbi had effortlessly switched to Italian, again ignoring him while happily listening to their memories of life back in Sorrento. Her date couldn't follow the conversation. He had soon stopped calling Bobbi. She'd thought he was nice enough, but romance wasn't her priority. Bobbi's thoughts about the future were always focused on her daughter's education and happiness.

Maybe after Sami's away at college, I'll get serious about dating. Not now. Maybe, someday, I'll find someone to explore Italy with.

Forgetting the ferry, she pushed open the heavy wood doors and stepped into Fortuna's. The city's cacophony evaporated, replaced by a hushed reverence. Muffled laughter and melodic Italian music, like warm sunlight filtered through wispy clouds, replaced the slush and car horns. The harsh geometry of New York dissolved, replaced by an embrace of soft angles and sun-bleached plaster.

A woman with a crown of silver coils pinned back by ivory combs greeted Bobbi in a feathery voice, "Welcome to Fortuna's. I'm Penelope. Please let me know if you have any questions."

Bobbi happily accepted the associate's offer to take her long checkered coat, tangled scarf, and leather bag filled with electronics and work. With each item she handed over, Bobbi felt a layer of New York's heaviness slip away, exchanged for a growing sense of lightness.

Gentle spotlights bathed the canvases like fireflies in amber glass. Each wall whispered a secret of Marianna Remi's soul.

Crossing the parquet floor and walking clockwise, Bobbi found herself in a labyrinth of rooms, each veiled by dividers, compelling her to weave in and out of separate viewing areas.

Each painting unveiled a new chapter, drawing Bobbi deeper into Fortuna's spell. As she wandered deeper, a yearning bloomed in her, a homesickness for a place that was not her home.

Was it a longing to escape the weight of being an only child, single mother, and young doctor? Or was it something more profound—a whisper of belonging, a return to a land of her heart that she'd never visited?

Fortuna's was nearly empty. New Yorkers were recovering from the holiday or watching football; tourists were dressing for dinner and Broadway. Her every step brought Bobbi a deepening sense of calm and tranquility. It was as if the exhibition existed only for her, each painting waiting its turn to speak only to her.

She loved Marianna Remi's graceful, unique style. None of the paintings depicted people, and traditional tourist sites like the Trevi Fountain, the Spanish Steps, and the Colosseum were nowhere to be seen. Instead, Remi's vision captured small, intimate moments: the reflection of a church steeple in a puddle after evening rain, or a weathered bench in front of a window. The warm, natural tones conveyed a sense of being within those places rather than merely observing from afar. Her blend of realism and impressionism created an evocative atmosphere that beckoned Bobbi to come closer, with the absence of human figures only deepening their beauty.

In the last gallery room, Bobbi felt an overwhelming magnetic pull toward a painting that was slightly larger than the others. Its beauty nearly stopped her heart—a serene side street.

A strange recognition crept over Bobbi as she stood mesmerized. *I've walked on this street before. But that's impossible ... I've never been to Italy.*

A sublime fragrance wafted over her. It seemed to be coming from ... the Italian flowers in the painting? Confused, she inched closer. The painting blurred; Bobbi rubbed her tired eyes. She glanced around to see if anyone else had noticed but found herself utterly alone. A warm breeze, as if from the Italian street, touched her face. The painting seemed to come to life, the beautiful street transforming into a three-dimensional scene.

Bobbi stepped inside, finding herself on the quiet, sunlit street of a Roman neighborhood. She squinted in the startling sunshine, unable to remember what had just happened.

She was in Italy.

Serenity flooded over her as Bobbi walked to an ancient bench in a lovely garden park. Comforted by its peacefulness and stillness, she gazed down a quiet street. The cobblestone road was worn and aged. The buildings on either side were tall and narrow, with ornate brick and stucco façades. As her green eyes adjusted to dappled sunlight coming through unfamiliar trees, Bobbi noticed most of the homes had window boxes overflowing with flowers, injecting vibrant colors into the tranquil surroundings.

Tall trees lined the peaceful road, their branches rustling faintly in the slight breeze. The air carried a fragrant aroma that Bobbi couldn't quite place. Drawn by the breeze, she rose to explore.

Benches and tables dotted the park. Pausing briefly, Bobbi took in the gentle mist rising from a graceful fountain portraying a couple in love. Curious, she walked comfortably in the shade of the elegant umbrella pine trees. Their slender trunks stretched toward the sky, topped by a beautiful canopy of delicate needles.

Ornate balconies and shutters graced the homes on either side of the cobblestone road. Bobbi imagined a different story behind each window and wanted to know them all. She wondered if the neighborhood residents were as peaceful and content as she felt.

Bobbi stopped in front of a lovely terracotta home, lifting her hand to adjust her ponytail—only to pause mid-gesture, realizing her long hair was down and loose.

The delicious aroma was more noticeable now. Examining the window boxes, Bobbi realized she smelled a hypnotic blend of lavender and jasmine. Breathing in deeply, she had no memory of the gallery or New York. Here, in the

Eternal City, she felt a sense of serenity and belonging. She took another deep breath, as if trying to hold onto the moment forever.

A hand-lettered sign in the lower window caught her eye:

*Appartamento soleggiato con terrazza in affitto—
perfetto per novelli sposi.*
*Sunny apartment with terrace for rent—perfect for
newlyweds.*

From the upper terrace, soft blue flowers—maybe morning glories—cascaded over the railing, mingling with sprigs of lavender and delicate white jasmine. The shutters were thrown open to the sun, and a single blue café chair sat beside a small table, as if someone had just stepped inside. The air was fragrant and still.

Bobbi stood motionless, drawn to the scene without knowing why. *If only I had someone to stay there with*, she thought. *In that apartment for newlyweds.*

The thought surprised her—small and wistful, gone as quickly as it came.

Standing before the terracotta home, a nagging, unavoidable thought danced on the edge of Bobbi's consciousness. She tried to grasp it, but it was like catching an individual snowflake falling out of a white sky on a windy day. Whenever Bobbi reached for it, the thought darted away. The solution, she decided, was to stand still and let the thought come to her.

She took another long, slow breath and closed her eyes. The answer arrived as a warm breeze brought more jasmine and lavender. It was one she had neither expected nor understood.

Bobbi felt completely at home. She wanted to fall in love and stay there forever.

The sudden clatter of metal on the parquet floor shattered her reverie. Bobbi jolted back to reality, finding herself in a Hell's Kitchen art gallery. It was January again, and the painting hung on the wall, still mysterious and inviting but now definitely two-dimensional. Penelope had dropped her keys.

Bobbi struggled to put her thoughts into some kind of logical order. She was a neurologist, an educated woman who didn't believe in New Age mumbo-jumbo. However, although she didn't remember stepping into the painting, Bobbi knew she'd stood on that precise street.

But how? I've never been to Italy ...

A man's voice, quiet and thoughtful, broke the silence. "It's almost as if you can smell the flowers."

Bobbi was startled by the sound of his voice but didn't shift her gaze from the canvas. "Lavender and jasmine," she answered softly.

"Yes, you're right. Each is beautiful, but I've never experienced them together. What would the combination smell like, I wonder." The instant they started talking, an invisible bubble enveloped them, shielding them from the world.

Still staring deeply into the painting, Bobbi murmured, "Serene. Heavenly. It smells like you're being energized and comforted at the same moment."

The man didn't immediately answer. Finally, he said, "Maybe when we think we're most in need of comfort, in reality, what we need is to be uplifted. Out of the contradiction of the scents comes the perfect balance for our souls."

Intrigued, Bobbi finally turned to look at him.

They'd never met, but he looked vaguely familiar. The man was taller than her, athletic, clean-shaven, and fair. She liked his dark sports coat and black, open-necked shirt. He looked about thirty-five, with no wedding ring. She spotted a brace on his left wrist, peeking out from beneath the coat. A black hat hid his hair color, but even tortoiseshell glasses couldn't disguise his striking blue eyes.

That was when another illogical revelation jolted her.

You, she thought. *I've walked down that street with you.*

A wave of icy air and the chime of a crystal bell above the door announced new visitors to Fortuna's. Bobbi barely noticed.

How could I have been on a street in a city I've never visited, with a man I've never met?

"The painting's beautiful but so empty," Bobbi continued. "This perfect street and park, yet not a person to be seen."

Moving his gaze back to the canvas, the man seemed to consider her words. She followed his eyes back to the painting. He was searching every window and every leafy area of the park for so much as a shadow of a person.

Finally, he said, "It's as if the painter welcomes us to create the life we choose to enter."

Bobbi was intensely curious about the man sharing the empty street with her. She fought the urge to look at him again while she mused, "Maybe ... Or maybe she's saying everyone is out of sight because even though they see their street every day, they don't want to spoil the intense beauty of this perfect moment."

The man nodded thoughtfully. "Do you think the title is a clue?"

Bobbi put a hand to her chin. "I've got to admit; I've been so mesmerized I never looked at the title."

"*2:29*," he explained, flicking his eyes toward the small handwritten sign beside the frame. "Maybe the kids are at school, people are at work, and the older folks are taking naps to avoid the summer heat."

Bobbi pretended to consider this, but she already knew there was another explanation. If she shared it with the handsome stranger, he'd probably think she was a lunatic.

Just as she started to comment on the unique hue of the roof of the terra-cotta home, a voice dented their bubble.

"Sorry, it's almost closing time." Penelope gestured at the painting. "Isn't this one exquisite?"

They nodded, the man muttering, "All her paintings are magnificent."

"So beautiful," Bobbi added.

Penelope looked at Bobbi and said, "It seems to speak to you. Would you like to buy it?"

Bobbi exhaled wistfully. "In another lifetime. I *do* love it but, unfortunately, art isn't my priority right now." Sami, her daughter, had her heart set on an expensive prep school and wanted to attend an Ivy League college. She glanced lovingly at *2:29* one last time.

Penelope then looked inquisitively at the man, who shook his head.

Following Penelope's lead, they moved away from *2:29* and walked toward the gallery entrance. While

11

Bobbi asked about Marianna Remi, the tall man remained quiet.

When the conversation paused, he asked Penelope, "Would you give us a moment?"

Bobbi looked up at him quizzically, noting his hesitation, as if he were deciding what to say. Meanwhile, Penelope discreetly stepped away, opening the front door wide enough for the blaring of car horns to spill in as she flipped the sign to "*Closed.*"

"I haven't introduced myself. My name is—"

The rush of traffic drowned out his quiet voice.

What is his name? Did he say Brian? Brad?

"I'm Bobbi Wyatt," she offered.

"I'd love to continue this conversation. I noticed a Chinese restaurant directly across the street."

Bobbi followed his gaze, spotting The Red Butterfly.

"I'm sorry if this is too forward, but would you like to join me for a quick meal?"

Her heart all but exploded. While Bobbi was the most rational, least impulsive person she knew, she was somehow sure they had walked down that enchanted street together. So, against her history, Bobbi decided she would walk across 47th Street with a man she didn't know.

"That's a lovely offer. Give me a minute; I need to call my sitter to let her know I'll be a little later than expected."

"Of course," he replied. "Take your time."

Just then, a second woman emerged from the office. Penelope introduced her as Graciela Fortuna, the gallery owner. Bobbi shook Graciela's hand, complimenting her on discovering Marianna Remi, then excused herself.

Stepping into the powder room, Bobbi felt dazed by what had just happened. *Did I just let myself get picked up?*

Something about the stranger made her feel safe. He wasn't overly familiar, nor had he made the conversation all about him. He had seemed genuinely interested in her reaction to the painting. They'd talked only for ten minutes, yet the conversation still oddly felt more deeply intimate than pillow talk.

Then a surreal thought jolted her. Could he have said his name was *BR*? As in, *BR Bradford*?

Quickly grabbing her flip phone, she called her cousin Gina, who was hanging out with Sami. "Pick up, pick up," Bobbi murmured. It went to voicemail. Bobbi tried again— the same maddening result.

As she brushed her ponytail, Bobbi faced a stunning print of a sunset on the Amalfi Coast. Beneath it, someone had written, "*I don't need therapy. I need to go to Italy.*"

I may need both, she thought with a sigh.

Bobbi called again. Gina finally answered.

"Hey, Bobs, how'd your speech go? Sami and I are watching *Singing in the Rain* for the three thousandth time. Dorkus Malorkus is trying to teach me the Charleston."

"Quick, Gina, what does BR Bradford look like?" Bobbi asked.

"What the actual—"

"Tell me."

Gina laughed. "He looks like what you'd get if Chris Hemsworth and Scarlett Johansson had an adult son—he's gorgeous."

"Details, please."

"Bobs, have you been drinking?"

"Seriously, I need to know—long story. Just tell me," Bobbi whispered.

"Okay. He's a little older than you, tall, with blond hair and blue eyes."

Bobbi quickly processed the information. It *might* be him, but she hadn't been able to see his hair color. "Wait—does he wear glasses?"

"No."

"You sure?"

Gina thought for a moment. "I'm looking at pictures online. It'd be a crime to cover up those amazing eyes."

Bobbi mused. Maybe it *wasn't* him. Then she remembered one detail that might be definitive. "Can you think of any reason he'd have a brace on his left arm?"

"If you had a modern phone, you could see his picture," Gina replied. "Hold on. I'll look it up. Maybe he has one because of that Chicago bombing last September."

Bobbi shuddered, remembering hearing about the incident.

Sami sang along with Gene Kelly, "*I'm fit as a fiddle and ready for love ...*"

Bobbi touched up her lip gloss while Gina read the highlights of an article from *People*. "Chicago bombing victim ... hero ... shoulder surgery ... liver injury ... long recovery ..." Gina paused. "And—wow—multibillionaire. First made a fortune as a rockstar then walked away to write and star in some of Broadway's biggest hits. The real money came when he was the major ground-floor investor in Coffee Corner and Jade Technologies. Seems to be a bit of a recluse now, though he spends a lot of time on his charitable foundation."

"Is he really that famous?"

Gina snorted. "Are you kidding me? I've downloaded every one of his pop albums. And whenever we're in the car, your daughter's belting out his show tunes."

"Quick—see if he's married? Kids?"

"Bobs, you're weirding me out. What the hell is going on?"

"*Swear jar!*" Sami yelled.

"Please, Gina. I promise I'll explain later."

"Okay, I'm looking at his Wikipedia. Never married. No girlfriend."

"Is he gay?"

"Doesn't seem to be," Gina snorted. "*New York Magazine* named him 'The Most Eligible Man in America.'"

Of course. Because today couldn't get any more surreal.

Bobbi made up her mind. She was actually going to do this—go to dinner with a complete stranger who might just be a celebrity billionaire.

Gina dropped a bombshell.

"Hey, this is weird. Apparently, he's got a daughter."

"What? How old? Who's her mother?"

"She's little. Not much is known about her. There's one picture of them at a park. I'm thinking she's adopted. She looks sweet."

Bobbi reached into her bag, retrieving navy heels. Slipping off her walking shoes, she asked, "Gina, would you be okay watching Sami for an extra hour or two?"

Sami warbled, "*All I do the whole day through is think of you,*" in the background.

"You want me to spend even *more* time with my favorite little nut bar in the whole world? You got it. What the"—she paused—"*fork* is happening, Bobs? Are you at the conference?"

Bobbi inhaled deeply. "One more thing. Can you give me an 'Aunt Mary' bailout call in twenty minutes? I'm still in the city. I'll be at a restaurant called The Red Butterfly on 47th."

"Wait—*what*?" Gina sputtered. "*You* need a bailout call? Don't tell me my beloved cousin, the dateless wonder of Brooklyn Heights, is hooking up tonight?"

Trying to keep her voice low, Bobbi chuckled. "No, I'm not hooking up, but I think I have a date with BR Bradford."

CHAPTER TWO: A DRAGONFLY IN THE SNOW
Bobbi

The man was finishing a conversation with Graciela Fortuna as Bobbi emerged. His hat and scarf still hid his hair color, but even the horn-rimmed glasses couldn't hide the powerfully blue eyes. He wore a smart midnight blue overcoat and black gloves, Bobbi's coat draped over his right arm. His brace was gone, though the way he held her jacket still seemed slightly awkward. His smile beamed as she approached.

Graciella's voice warmed. "There's something special in the air for you tonight at Fortuna's." She gestured toward where *2:29* waited. "I hope you'll visit again, Ms. Wyatt."

A gust of wind hit as the man opened the door. Bobbi didn't feel the cold; her heart leaped, her mind racing with another question: *Why would he tell her my last name?*

Under Fortuna's awning, the scarlet lights of The Red Dragonfly dimmed beneath falling snow. Mild weather had turned the sidewalks into a salty, slushy mess.

Bobbi pulled out a candy apple red crocheted hat—a handmade gift from a grateful patient—donning it over her golden hair.

"Everything okay with your sitter?" He smiled.

"Perfect." She reached up and gently adjusted his scarf.

Cars honked along 47th Street, slush spraying in every direction.

"Okay, I'm embarrassed," Bobbi confessed, nodding at the street. "I'm a Brooklyn native with a black belt in dodging traffic, but heels in the snow? Not so much."

"If we pull our hats down, we can pretend we're tourists and use the crosswalk," he joked.

Bobbi smirked and tugged her cap low. "I'm swearing you to secrecy. My family would disown me if they knew I wimped out at a crosswalk."

He crossed his heart.

Three steps later, Bobbi slipped. Without a word, he offered his arm, and she took it, leaning in slightly. The faint contact made her heart race.

As traffic paused, she laughed. "Now's our chance. Don't let me fall!"

They darted between two taxis, avoiding the despised crosswalk.

"My Brooklyn girl street cred is intact, thanks to you," she teased, leaning into him a little more.

On the far sidewalk, he gently brushed snowflakes from her cheeks. She instinctively tilted her chin up, daring him to kiss her. *Calm down. If anyone else tried this, you'd slug him. You don't even know his name.*

Deeply confused—and vaguely disappointed—she slipped her arm through his again. The restaurant, just three doors down, seemed distant. The bubble between them blurred everything else.

He pushed open the door, and she slid around him, careful to stay on his right side.

The restaurant had a polished, modern Chinese design. Red paper dragonflies floated around lanterns above the tables while servers in black silk shirts with red accents moved gracefully through the room. The mouth-watering aroma drew them in, a unique blend of spices and flavors. The Red Dragonfly wasn't just another takeout spot—they'd stumbled upon a hidden gem.

Bobbi glanced at the empty host station while the man wiped his glasses and looked for someone to seat them. She spotted an open high school AP chemistry book and a homework sheet left behind. A moment later, a slim, harried teenager returned to her position. Her name tag read, "*Grace*."

Without looking up, she asked, "Can I help you?"

Before the man could respond, Bobbi said, "Hi. Maybe I can help *you*. I'm sorry; I wasn't prying. I was looking for a menu and noticed you're having trouble with your homework. It looks like you're stuck on question nine. If you'd like, I could help you. I know a bit about chemistry."

Grace shot her a puzzled look. "Really? That'd be great. This homework is impossible, and I'm the best student in the class."

"Why don't you read the question?"

Grace read, "*During a chemical reaction, a colorless gas made of one nitrogen atom and three hydrogen atoms (Compound X) reacts with a pale yellow solid made of one sulfur atom and four oxygen atoms (Compound Y), resulting in the formation of a pale yellow, clear, oily liquid known for its instability and explosive nature. What is the chemical name for Compound Z?*"

Bobbi barely paused before answering, "Okay, the answer you're looking for is a unique substance that can save someone having a heart attack or blow up a building."

The teenager narrowed her eyes in concentration. "Nitroglycerin? I didn't think of that."

The man looked at Bobbi with astonishment. "Nitro? The answer to the question is a bomb?"

Bobbi laughed. "Like everything in life, it's about balance. In one configuration, nitroglycerin can blow a hole in a mountain. But a small dose, properly prepared, can save the life of someone having a cardiac attack. So, it's a delicate dance between creating and averting explosions."

Grace scribbled furiously. "How'd you know that? Are you a teacher?"

"No, I'm a doctor. I've taken tons of chemistry." She scanned Grace's homework sheet. "Tough questions, but you nailed them."

Smiling, Grace said, "That's so cool. I want to be a doctor … if I survive Mr. Black's class. I don't know where to apply, though."

Bobbi pulled a card from her bag. "Here, email me if you need anything. My phone's on its last leg—it can barely handle texts—but I'll be glad to help if I can."

Grace carefully tucked the card into her pocket then remembered her job. She looked at the man standing next to the sweet doctor for the first time. Her jaw dropped. "Oh my God, you're *BR Bradford! Time and Love* is my favorite Broadway show *ever*! I've seen it twice. Every time Laura sings 'Falling Back,' I cry."

Holy ravioli! Bobbi drew a deep breath. *He really* is *BR Bradford! Gina's going to scream. Sami will be out of her mind.*

Nonetheless, Bobbi was unfazed. His celebrity and wealth were much less interesting than the bigger questions— *How did BR Bradford enter my bubble, and when did we walk down that Roman street together?*

CHAPTER THREE: THE BEST WOMAN
BR

BR recoiled and glanced at Bobbi, who seemed unfazed. He scanned the area and was relieved to see no one taking pictures or videos.

Grace struggled to compose herself. "Let me show you to the corner table by the window. It's the best in the house."

"No, thank you. Dr. Wyatt is my chemistry tutor; an out-of-the-way table would be better."

The teen gathered menus before ushering them to a table in the back. "My parents own the restaurant. I can't wait to tell them you're here."

"Please, Grace, don't make a big deal about it. We're just having dinner and want to talk privately."

BR pulled out Bobbi's chair for her while Grace made a beeline to the kitchen, bursting with the news.

Bobbi laughed. "Okay, BR, I have to confess. When you told me your name, I didn't hear it or know who you were."

"I'm actually delighted to hear that," he replied with a touch of whimsy. Then he looked at Bobbi more seriously. "Why'd you agree to dinner? I was scared to ask you, but I had this overwhelming feeling I couldn't leave the gallery without knowing you."

"Is my knowledge of Italian art really that impressive?"

"Any explanation I give you for my behavior tonight wouldn't make sense, even to me. I felt the painting bring us together, and I almost seemed to hear a voice telling me I needed to talk with you. Nothing like this has ever happened to me before. The urge to talk with you was overwhelming but inexplicable."

Bobbi's eyes locked on his; she said nothing.

The restaurant wasn't crowded, but he wouldn't have noticed even if it had been as packed and noisy as Times Square on New Year's Eve. The sounds and movements of others seemed distant and muted. To him, there was only one other person in the world. He was in a bubble with Bobbi.

Grace returned, pretending to check if they were comfortable.

"Yes, thanks for asking." BR said warmly, keeping his hands resting calmly on the table.

"Can I take a selfie with you?" she asked, barely containing her excitement.

He nodded. "Sure—but just a quick one. And please, no pictures of Dr. Wyatt."

Grace agreed with a quick nod.

"Promise me: no posting anything until after we've left. I'd really appreciate it."

"Of course!" she said, already raising her phone.

She leaned in from the side and snapped a single photo. BR didn't move—his hands remained folded on the table.

"Thank you so much," she whispered before walking away, glowing.

"Do you get that a lot?" Bobbi asked.

"Sometimes," he sighed. "Not as often as you may think. Back when I was a touring musician, I couldn't walk down the street without being mobbed. I've stayed out of the public eye for a while now, so it's gotten better. New Yorkers normally just catch my eye and nod. Fans and tourists can be more aggressive, but they're usually nice. Tell me; when you're running errands, do you ever bump into patients who stop to thank you for helping them?"

"Sure, once in a while," she answered as a busboy brought them water in beautiful, clear red glasses.

"Do you like it when they say thanks?"

"Sure, but I keep it short."

BR nodded. "Same with me. My job's just that—a job. I always try to be polite, and I'm happy when people say nice things, but then I like to move on. What's your specialty?"

"I'm a neurologist. I work at Brooklyn Women's Health Center."

"That's fascinating. I read an article about Brooklyn Women's in the *New York Times Magazine*."

She raised her dark eyebrows. "That was four years ago."

BR shrugged awkwardly. "I've got a pretty good memory. The founder's an African-American doctor, right? They described her as a legendary hero for civil rights and women's health. She recruits only the most talented female doctors."

"Dr. Caroline Thibodeau." Bobbi glowed. "She's my mentor. We keep hearing *60 Minutes* is planning a profile on her."

"And she recruited you? That says a lot about your talent and commitment. Where'd you go to med school?"

"University of Chicago, undergrad. Then I moved home and went to Weill-Cornell."

"Wow," he exclaimed, "two of the best schools in the universe." BR leaned in, dazzled as much by Bobbi's humility as her accomplishments. Most people tried too hard to impress him. Bobbi didn't. She was just ... herself, and that was rare.

A waiter appeared, gingerly placing two aromatic, beautifully prepared appetizers before them. "Compliments of the house. Mr. and Mrs. Li asked me to thank the pretty doctor for helping Grace. This dish is tea-smoked duck, and that's Sichuan spicy cold noodles."

"What a nice surprise," Bobbi said. "Please tell them I said thank you. It looks and smells amazing."

With a half-bow, the waiter walked away.

"Don't I feel special?" Bobbi grinned. "I thought only celebrities got free food."

"It's pretty obvious who the real rock star is tonight," BR said admiringly. "I was pretty good in science, but I'd never have gotten that chemistry problem."

"You *should* be impressed," she teased. "And you should also be grateful. Apparently, I'm a cheap date. Think of all the money I just saved you with two free appetizers."

BR wiped his brow with an exaggerated movement. "Whew. Thanks, Dr. Wyatt. Now we won't have to split an entrée."

He adored how her slim nose crinkled when she smiled.

"This presentation looks like something out of a magazine. It's a shame to eat it," Bobbi cooed.

"Are you going to let that stop you?"

"Fat chance, buddy. Dig in, or there won't be any left for you."

They split the plates. Each bite surprised them—nothing like typical Chinese-American fare. They exchanged glances and quiet moans of delight.

A small woman in a dark pantsuit and an even smaller man in a crisp white chef's toque approached the table.

"Welcome to our restaurant," the man said. He addressed BR directly, gesturing that he shouldn't stand. "I am Mr. Li, the chef, and this is my wife. We are honored you are with us tonight."

"Thank you, Chef. We're delighted to be here," BR said warmly.

Mr. Li nodded. "Perhaps you would honor us with a picture for our wall?"

"Dr. Wyatt and I would prefer to enjoy your cooking without drawing any attention. But if you'd like, I'll have an autographed headshot, thanking you, delivered tomorrow."

Mrs. Li's eyes widened as she got the message. She'd make sure none of the waitstaff bothered their celebrity patron.

After a nudge, her husband caught on. He spoke to Bobbi for the first time. "Thank you, Doctor, for helping our daughter. She works very hard in school."

"It's my pleasure. Grace is very bright. Thank you for the appetizers. I've never tasted such perfectly blended flavors."

BR loved the warmth of her happy tone. He nodded in agreement.

"My husband was the best chef in Dalian," Mrs. Li crowed. "Do you know it?"

They both shook their heads.

Mr. Li explained, "We come from Liaoning Province, on the northwest coast. It's called the Seafood Capital of China. I attended the Culinary Institute of China."

"Is that why you have two menus, one in Chinese and the other in English?" BR inquired.

A slight nod indicated Mr. Li's pleasure. "Yes. I've learned to make food the way Americans like it. However, The Red Dragonfly is very popular with Chinese expatriates here on the Lower West Side. They like to order authentic cuisine."

Bobbi's lustrous green eyes twinkled as she focused on BR. "Since I'm throwing caution to the wind tonight, what do you say we go on an adventure? Let's let Mr. Li choose our dinner and make it in the real Chinese style?"

The Lis looked delighted, clearly wanting to impress BR. One positive mention by him could put The Red Dragonfly on millions of people's "Do Not Miss" list.

"I'm in." BR was swept up in Bobbi's adventurous, playful spirit. "Tonight's definitely the start of a new adventure. Bobbi, what would you like?"

"Chef Li, since seafood is your specialty, I'd love to try your personal favorite fish recipe."

As Bobbi chatted eagerly with the chef, BR found himself staring at her—not her beauty, but the open, effortless way she connected with people. When she turned back, their eyes met. She gave him a small, knowing look that made his stomach flip. Her easy chuckle followed, but it didn't help; he couldn't risk driving her away. Then she pushed a stray lock behind her ear, and something inside him went warm. He forced himself to concentrate on what she was saying.

"What does your heart desire?" Mr. Li asked BR.

He opened his mouth, ready to say, *"Bobbi,"* but caught himself just in time.

"I love anything with shellfish or mushrooms, but not too spicy."

The Red Dragonfly was slowly filling. Obeying her mother's strict instructions, Grace carefully left a space around Bobbi and BR's table. Many of the guests chatted in Mandarin.

"You mentioned a sitter," BR started once the Lis walked away. "How many children do you have?"

"Just one. Although, sometimes it seems like seven. My daughter, Sami, is a bundle of energy. She's eleven going on eighteen, and maybe thirty-five." Bobbi's eyes danced.

"Sami sounds like a blast."

Bobbi seemed to be mulling over how to answer. Then she looked BR square in the eyes. "Sami's the love of my life. I know every mother thinks *she* has the world's most wonderful kid, but *I* really do. She's had a positive aura around her since she was born. Sami's so open, optimistic, and filled with wonder. I didn't plan to have a child while I was in medical school. It was hard—believe me—but it's the greatest thing that's ever happened to me."

The server refilled their waters, giving BR a moment to think.

Bobbi brushed a stray strand of hair behind her ear.

BR looked again and saw no wedding ring. He realized that the sparkly, gorgeous blonde must have somehow been in medical school at twenty.

"It's amazing, isn't it?" he responded. "You've accomplished so much and helped so many people. But seeing the person your Sami's becoming, that's what gives the real meaning to your life, doesn't it?"

"Yes, exactly. I love my job and want to be the best possible doctor, but I love Sami so much it makes my teeth hurt. You'd love her." Bobbi looked down, flushing.

He already knew he'd love Sami.

"I have no doubt. What's Sami into?"

"What *isn't* she into?" Bobbi rolled her eyes. "Sami's mind works a mile a minute. She loves writing, sings like an angel, and adores Broadway. She's a big fan of yours."

BR folded his fingers in front of his lips. "That means so much to me." His voice was shy and genuine, not the one he'd used to deflect praise from Grace and her parents.

As if on cue, Bobbi's phone buzzed. She held it up, giving BR a cute this-is-silly shrug. "Sorry. My cousin Gina with my bailout call. She's as whacko as Sami."

"Are you bailing?" he asked, only half-kiddingly.

"After my vast medical experience provided you with free appetizers? You're not off the hook that easily, sir." Bobbi held up a finger, indicating the call would be quick and BR didn't need to excuse himself.

"Hello, Aunt Mary," she answered, sounding extremely clinical. "I checked all the test results, and the diagnosis is perfect."

BR chuckled into his hand.

Bobbi's shoulders shook with suppressed giggles as Gina replied. Catching BR's amusement, Bobbi put the call on speaker.

The connection was crackly, but he could hear Sami's exuberant voice say, "Mom? Is it him? Aunt Gina said you're having dinner with BR Bradford. I told her she was joking. We made a bet."

BR bit his hand to keep from laughing.

"What'd you bet?" Bobbi asked.

"Ten unprotected tickles to the loser," Sami responded.

"Uh-oh." Bobbi snickered. "One of you is in *big* trouble."

BR scribbled furiously in a small notebook he always carried. He handed a sheet to Bobbi.

Bobbi looked at it, and her eyes twinkled merrily. She read, *"Would you like a hint?"*

"Yes!" they bellowed in unison.

BR was writing more notes.

"Are you *really* with BR Bradford? Can I talk to him, Mom?"

BR shook his head and pointed to another note. *Keep them guessing.*

Bobbi nodded conspiratorially, eyes twinkling. He handed her another note.

"Do you know the musical The Best Woman?" she read.

"Every line!" Sami shouted.

"Of course," Gina added. "The cast album sold like a gazillion copies."

Another sheet. "This clue is for Sami. *What does Morgan sing after Timothy says, 'This isn't what it looks like?'"*

In unison, Gina and Sami sang the famous lyric, *"You better run!"*

"Sorry, Sami, looks like you lost the bet," Bobbi chirped.

Gina growled in mock malevolence, "You're gonna get it! Come *here*, Dorkus Malorkus!"

"You can't catch meeeeeeee!" Sami shrieked, followed by the sounds of a playful struggle, punctuated by hilarious howls of girlish laughter.

Bobbi disconnected the call. "You see what I have to put up with?" she asked, sliding the phone into her clutch.

"Sounds pretty terrific to me."

"How about you, BR? I think I heard that you have a daughter?"

The seemingly simple question hung in the air.

BR drew a deep breath and looked down. In that instant, BR's future with Bobbi hung in the balance.

CHAPTER FOUR: ULTIMATE TEST
BR

A busboy cleared the table of the appetizers. The phone in Bobbi's clutch beeped incessantly.

"Sorry." She shrugged. "My lunatic cousin probably let my weirdo daughter take over the family chat."

The server approached. "Dinner will be out shortly. Chef Li would like to present it himself. May I get either of you something from the bar?"

"I'll check out the wines," Bobbi said. "Want a glass?"

"No, thanks. I don't drink, but I live on Pellegrino."

BR watched her walk to the bar, savoring the moment to gather his thoughts. If a fan asked about his daughter, he'd dodge the question. Reporters? His team would issue the usual line: "We never comment on Mr. Bradford's personal life." But Bobbi was too perceptive for deflection. And the connection? Unmistakable.

BR prayed silently, "You brought her to me for a reason. Help me trust her. Give me the words."

Bobbi returned with a small bottle in hand. "I realized I don't know if people in China drink wine," she said lightly. "The bartender recommended Changyu Golden Ice Wine—grapes harvested after freezing on the vines. Apparently, it's very sweet and pairs beautifully with seafood."

BR placed his hands flat on the table to steady himself. He dropped his voice to a near-whisper. "Yes, I have a daughter."

Bobbi's eyes widened with curiosity. She leaned in, waiting.

"I adopted Cassie at birth. She's almost five."

Bobbi didn't hesitate. "Sounds like you've got a heart full of love. She's lucky to have you."

"I'm really trying. Most of the time, I have no idea what I'm doing. And the rest, I'm probably doing it wrong."

Bobbi covered his hand with hers. Electricity raced through his body.

She nodded, her voice warm and understanding. "Every parent feels that way. Especially us single parents. Is Cassie happy?"

"Yes, very."

"Then you're doing it exactly right."

Neither noticed Mr. Li approach the table. With a flourish, he revealed Bobbi's meal. The fragrance made her mouth water.

"For the good doctor, I've prepared braised whole snapper in a ginger and scallion sauce with stir-fried mixed vegetables."

"I can't decide which is more beautiful—the presentation or the aroma," Bobbi gushed.

"For you, Mr. Bradford, this is stir-fried geoduck and black mushrooms in a savory soy, garlic, ginger, and rice wine sauce."

BR nodded, impressed. "I've never had geoduck. It's a large clam, right?"

Mr. Li nodded. "I hope you both enjoy your dinners." He needn't have worried—both were moaning with delight.

"If I show you a little more leg, will you let me try yours?" Bobbi teased. With a playful flick of her wrist, she raised the hem of her dress a quarter of an inch.

BR almost choked with laughter, blushing the color of her red bell pepper garnish.

Bobbi smirked. "Okay, the show's over. Pay up."

He fed her some of his delicacies.

Bobbi rolled her eyes with pleasure. "That's fabulous, although a smart businessman like you could've negotiated a better deal."

Looking Bobbi straight in her hypnotic green eyes, he said, "I think I already got a pretty fabulous deal tonight."

The conversation flowed easily as they discussed Italy. BR asked Bobbi about her love of the country, and she asked about where he'd traveled. Neither wanted the evening to end, but The Red Dragonfly was as full as their stomachs.

It was time to go when Mrs. Li checked in on them again.

Nervously, BR said, "Bobbi, thank you for a wonderful evening. I know you need to get home ... but instead of taking the ferry, I have a car and driver nearby. Ronnie's a retired Army captain who led an MP battalion overseas, and he's a fantastic driver. You'll get home quicker and warmer."

"Oh, that's so sweet but completely unnecessary. If you want to work off that dinner, you can walk me to the ferry."

"Please, let me do this for you. If I drove, I'd happily take you myself. I know your cousin's probably waiting to get home. Where does she live?"

"Williamsburg."

"Perfect. Ronnie can take you back to Brooklyn Heights, and then drive your cousin home. It puts him right on track to head home himself."

"She'll love that. But you don't have to do this."

"Hey, I owe you. You did score me free appetizers, after all."

Bobbi laughed. "Fair enough. You win—thank you. It'll be a nice treat."

Though she protested, BR insisted on paying the bill and silently left an extremely generous tip.

"Ronnie will be here in five minutes," BR said, looking up from his phone.

"Let's wait out front," she suggested. "I need some fresh air after that unbelievable meal. I'm stuffed."

BR held her long, checkered coat as Bobbi gracefully slipped her arms into the sleeves. She freed her ponytail, letting it glide down her back with effortless grace. The simple gesture captivated BR more than he had expected.

The snow still fell lightly, the cold air refreshing them as they sat on the steps of a brownstone a few doors down.

"Thank you so much for dinner," Bobbi said, breaking the silence. "It was wonderful to meet you."

"Bobbi, there's something I want to ask you."

"Sure," Bobbi managed, her voice light.

"I was thinking about something you said. When I told you the picture was titled *2:29*, it resonated with you; why?"

"How long till your car arrives?"

Reluctantly, BR checked his phone. "Two minutes."

"It's complicated," she said, tucking her hands deeper into her coat pockets. "Ask me another time."

"Could you do something for me?" he asked softly. He handed her a small page from his notepad, his voice shy as he told her, "This is my private cell number. Would you text me when you get home so I know you made it back safely?"

Bobbi's explosive laughter echoed off the quiet brownstones. "Seriously, Mr. Bradford? *That's* all the game you've got? This has to be the lamest way I've ever heard to get a girl's number."

BR grimaced ruefully, his ears turning red. "I'm not very good at this, am I?"

"Not even a little," she teased, holding out her hand. "Give me your phone."

He passed it over, and she caught a glimpse of the lock screen—a little blonde girl beamed back at her from a photo.

"Okay," she continued, removing her mittens. "I don't know how to use one of these fancy JadePhones, so just set up a new contact card for me."

Within a minute, she entered her cell number, work number, and birthday.

BR pocketed the phone just as Ronnie's sleek, midnight-blue limo pulled up to the curb.

Ronnie, a towering Black man with the build of the West Point linebacker he'd been, greeted BR warmly. The introductions were easy.

"It's a pleasure to meet you, Dr. Wyatt," Ronnie said, his voice deep and kind.

"*Bobbi*," she corrected. "If you call me Doctor, I'll have to call you Captain Tompkins—or give you a neurological exam."

Ronnie grinned. "Yes, ma'am."

"*Ma'am*?" Bobbi tittered. "I know you're trained in combat, Captain, but call me *ma'am* again, and you'll need to protect yourself."

Both men laughed as Ronnie opened the car door for her.

Bobbi moved toward the front passenger seat, but Ronnie gently stopped her.

"Please, Bobbi, it's easier for me to do my job if you sit in the back," he said kindly.

She hesitated, clearly more comfortable riding up front like she was catching a ride with a friend.

As she turned toward BR to say goodbye, he only offered a faint smile and a soft, "Good night, Bobbi."

"Good night," she replied, a note of confusion in her voice.

As the car disappeared around the corner, BR mumbled to himself, "Smooth."

Within seconds, BR's phone rang, and his spirits leaped in anticipation of hearing Bobbi's voice. However, it was just his security team checking in.

"Sawyer here. I know Tompkins is heading to Brooklyn Heights. I'm just a couple of minutes away. I'll pick you up."

"No, thank you. I'll walk back. I'm in that sweet spot where no musicals will be let out while I'm walking up 51st. I'll be careful of crowds in Times Square. My shoulder will be fine."

BR walked home in a daze. What had just happened? And what was he supposed to do now?

He tried to remember every detail, but his mind kept wandering back to how bewitching Bobbi had looked with snow on her cap and how his heart had raced when she'd leaned into him crossing the street.

Before he realized it, the private elevator opened into his home. It was the same penthouse, the same city skyline, but none of it felt quite the same now that she'd been part of it.

CHAPTER FIVE: ALL THROUGH THE NIGHT
Bobbi

Ronnie seemed to find every green light and non-crowded street. More quickly than she could've imagined, Bobbi was on her way out of Midtown and heading toward the Manhattan Bridge.

"Is the temperature okay? Want some music?"

"Everything's perfect, thanks. Play any music you like." The ride was incredibly comfortable, though Bobbi couldn't see much of the interior in the dark. "Do you mind if I call my cousin? I don't want to distract you."

"Go ahead. I'll put up the privacy screen." Soft R&B filled the car, fading as the screen rose.

Gina answered on the first ring. "Bobs, what the ... fork is going on?"

Bobbi smiled, guessing Sami was nearby. "I'm on my way home. Is Sami still up?"

"Dorkus Malorkus was writing the last time I checked, but she's about to conk out."

"Good. We've got an early day tomorrow," Bobbi whispered.

"Blah, blah, blah," Gina grumbled. "Tell me *everything.* You had dinner with BR freaking Bradford?"

"Yes, and it was great. I'll spill all the details tomorrow, I swear."

"Shut the … front door!" Gina roared. "What's he like?"

"Well, I'm on my way home in the back of a limo."

"*You*? *In a limo*? I don't believe it. If you were in labor, you'd take a bus instead of calling an Uber."

They both laughed.

"His driver's dropping me off, and then he'll drive you to Williamsburg. Pack your stuff."

"Now you're talking. I'm made for limos. I'll be ready."

Bobbi glanced out the window as the light snow, caught in streetlights, created a hypnotic strobe effect. The streets of Manhattan blurred—scaffolding, bodegas, high-rises, restaurants—all melting together in an endless carousel.

The rush of the presentation, the unexpected encounter with a mysterious painting, the handsome, enigmatic man, and the wine had lulled Bobbi into something rare—relaxation. She didn't realize she'd fallen asleep.

Her overtired brain slipped straight into REM sleep. Bobbi's dream was vivid—she wore a lab coat over a pale blue sundress, examining a patient speaking Italian. When the patient left, an Italian nurse announced it was lunchtime.

Bobbi stepped into dazzling sunlight. A man greeted her, holding a picnic basket with a loaf of bread and a bottle of wine peeking out from under a checkered cloth.

In Italian, she explained she couldn't drink during the day.

He answered in English, his voice both familiar and strange. "You look beautiful, Bobbi. I've been waiting all day just to see you."

A blaring siren jolted her awake.

Disoriented, Bobbi rubbed her eyes and checked her watch—she'd been asleep for nine minutes.

First the painting, and now this? I'm losing my mind. I either need to get laid or sleep for three days. Or BR and I could just cuddle in each other's arms for three days of sleep before he bangs me silly.

Bobbi found the control to lower the privacy screen. Ronnie's music filled the car, and her mind cleared. He turned it down when Bobbi struck up a pleasant chat that carried her over the river.

~~~

"Ronnie, I've loved talking with you. Thanks so much for bringing me home. I'll get my cousin. She'll be right out."

"No hurry. It was my pleasure, Bobbi. I really enjoyed our talk, too."

The moment Bobbi stepped inside, Gina hugged her. Then Gina smacked Bobbi's butt—hard. Bobbi yipped, the slap echoing in the empty vestibule.

"What's that for?" Bobbi asked, rubbing her rear.

"The hug's 'cause you look so happy. But you *deserve* a spanking for making me wait for all the details."

"I love you, Gina, so much. Real fast—BR's sweet, a little shy, brilliant, and I loved every second with him. He charmed the panties off me."

"*Panties?*"

Bobbi slapped a hand over her mouth so hard that she almost bruised her lip. "*Pants!* You *know* what I meant."

Gina narrowed her eyes, a playful smirk forming. "I *know* what you said."

41

Bobbi squirmed, embarrassed.

"I hope you were wearing pretty panties, at least." Gina gathered her things. "Seriously, you look terrific tonight. You better tell me *everything* tomorrow."

"I can't wait to tell you."

"And I'll teach you all about your new boyfriend. While I was waiting for *my limo*, I started reading everything about him online."

"He's *not* my boyfriend."

Flinging her backpack over her shoulder, Gina chirped, "Makes sense—he's using you to get to me. Ta-ta, Bobs. America's most eligible billionaire sent a chauffeur just for me. It'd be rude to keep him waiting."

As Gina left, Bobbi texted BR:

Home safe and sound. Ronnie is very nice.
Gina's in her glory. Thanks for joining me in
Rome (and China). Bobbi.

She debated adding a second, flirtier text, but her ancient phone died. There was only one person she wanted to talk to, anyway, and he was in Manhattan.

Plugging in her phone, Bobbi yawned as she walked down the hall to check on Sami.

Her daughter slept sprawled in every direction, dirty blonde hair covering her face. Bobbi gently removed Sami's headphones, placing them on the dresser. She grinned when she noticed Sami wearing a T-shirt with the poster from BR Bradford's musical, *Time and Love*.

A muffled voice surprised her as she kissed Sami's forehead.

"Mom?"

"Yes, baby. Sorry I woke you."

Half-asleep, Sami mumbled, "Did you really have dinner with BR Bradford?"

"Mmhmm."

Sami was asleep again before Bobbi could say another word.

~~~

BR

BR was despondent.

After thanking his niece, Anna Maria, and her partner, Siobhán, for watching Cassie, he listened to their report on Cassie's playdate. They were tired and eager to head downstairs to their apartment and left soon after.

BR puttered around, trying to kill time until he heard from Bobbi. He couldn't focus on anything. He briefly considered googling, *Dr. Bobbi Wyatt, Brooklyn Women's Medical Center*, but it didn't feel right.

Finally, he got her cute text. He immediately wrote back:

Thanks for such a fantastic night. Would it be
OK if I called to say good night?

He'd sent that text forty-five minutes ago, and Bobbi still hadn't responded.

Silence filled him with dread. What if she thought he was a creepy stalker? Or if she was on the couch with her boyfriend, laughing about her strange dinner with a famous oddball? Ignoring the obvious explanation—that she'd gone to sleep—BR's mood darkened by the minute.

~~~

Bobbi

Bobbi tidied up the living room and kitchen. Both rooms were in shambles after Gina and Sami—slobs, even under the best of circumstances—had their great tickle war.

Exhausted but oddly energized by the unexpected day, Bobbi scrubbed her face, put her hair in a messy bun, and then changed into a tank top and plaid pajama pants. She couldn't think about anything but BR.

Her oasis awaited. Tucked upstairs in her Brooklyn Heights two-flat, Bobbi's bedroom was a serene retreat, designed by her best friend, Megan "Red" O'Malley, to look and feel like a modern Italian bedroom. The walls, painted in warm golden hues by her father under Red's direction, evoked the soft light of Tuscany. An oversized, jet-black comforter, which Gina affectionately named "the shroud," dominated the bed, adding a bold contrast to the room's soft tones.

A beautiful lithograph of the Bridge of Sighs in Venice hung on one wall. Bobbi had bought it just for its beauty, but she looked at it with different eyes tonight. Catching her breath, she remembered the legend of that bridge—if you kissed someone under it at sunset while riding in a gondola, you'd find forever love.

Staring at the print one more time, she sighed. *Maybe someday I'll kiss BR in a gondola at sunset under you.*

She dimmed the lights and lit an Italian candle, enjoying the soft scent of the Mediterranean. Bobbi just wanted to lay in her comfy bed and remember every moment of her date with BR.

Wait—was it a date? Why am I thinking about kissing him in Italy? He didn't even hold my hand.

Before letting her brain relax, she remembered to set an alarm. Sami wanted to get to the Rye Book Fair at ten; the drive would be an hour.

Bobbi bumped her head on the nightstand, searching for her phone. When the phone powered up, she saw five messages from Gina.

Memo to self: The next time BR Bradford sends a hot driver to take me home, I must repeat 100 times, "I'm a married woman. I'm a married woman ..."

Please tell your boyfriend I'll need the driver and car to go to the yarn store tomorrow. Have them pick me up at nine. I'll leave my breakfast order with you.

I'm a married woman. I'm a married woman. I'm a married woman. He's hot. I'm a married woman ...

I called the restaurant and told them to look for your panties. If they can't find them, I'll have Ronnie drive me to BR Bradford's penthouse, and I'll search for them. If I'm not back in a week, don't come looking for me.

Laughing, Bobbi scrolled past several messages of congratulations on her presentation before spotting BR's unexpected text.

Bobbi gasped. He wanted to call her.

Crap. BR sent it almost an hour ago. He probably thinks I'm ghosting him.

Overly anxious to respond, Bobbi dropped the phone, bumping her head again in the process. Cursing under her breath, she quickly texted back:

> *SORRY. Phone died. I JUST saw your text. If you're still up, call.*

Immediately, her phone rang.

Bobbi's heart pounded; her mind raced.

"Hi, Bobbi," he began, sounding nervous.

As she tried to grab extra pillows, Bobbi dropped her phone again.

Finally sitting up comfortably, Bobbi squeaked, "Hello?"

"Um, it's BR Bradford. You got me free appetizers earlier, remember?"

Bobbi snorted. "I think I remember you. Tall guy I tutored in chemistry? The one who set up my daughter for tickle torture?"

"You *do* remember."

"I'm glad you called. We said goodbye kind of awkwardly, and I wasn't ready for our night to end."

"Oh, Bobbi, I felt the same way. Do you have a few minutes to talk?"

"Nothing would make me happier." *Unless you were lying next to me while we talked ...*

"How's Sami?"

Touched, Bobbi answered, "Sound asleep. She lost the great tickle war. I went in to kiss her, and she's wearing a *Love and Time* T-shirt as part of her PJs."

"Really? Did she like the show that much?"

Bobbi blushed. "Confession time. Sami knows every word by heart, but she's never seen it. Don't nominate me for the Evil Mother of the Year Award, but Sami's never been to a Broadway show."

BR said matter-of-factly, "If you and Sami want to see it sometime, I know the writer. I'm sure I could get you tickets."

Again, Bobbi found him hard to read. On the one hand, he was thoughtful and generous. Yet he hadn't mentioned himself in the offer. *If he isn't interested in me, why are we even talking?*

Bobbi decided to shift the topic. "Thanks again for having Ronnie drive me. How was your walk?"

"It gave me time to think. Mostly, I thought about you."

His warm voice sent a flutter through her chest.

"I hope that's a good thing," she said, trying to keep her voice even. "What were you thinking about?"

"To begin with, you should always wear blue. That color is amazing on you."

"Thanks. I'll make a note of it." Bobbi was joking, but she made a mental memo. It was the first time he'd mentioned her looks. She'd remember he liked her in blue. If there was a next time.

BR's voice grew more serious. "If I'm not boring you, I wanted to explain a few things I found hard to say in the restaurant."

"Okay."

His tone had made it clear this wouldn't be a flirty pillow-talk conversation, so Bobbi sat up straighter, bracing herself.

"Bobbi, I just really like you. Every moment at the gallery, and then at The Red Dragonfly, was very special to me."

"Me, too," she whispered, relieved.

"Because of who I am, the public sometimes thinks it knows me or has a right to know me. There are parts of my life I never talk about. I'd like to tell you."

"I'd love to know you better," Bobbi whispered. "You don't know me yet, but your celebrity status is the least interesting thing about you to me. I'm happy you're so successful, but that's not why I want to know you."

Emboldened, BR continued, "First, about Cassie. There's almost nothing about her online or in any gossip magazine. That's intentional on my part. Cassie's biological mother is a distant relative of mine. She was a teenager who couldn't care for an unexpected baby. We arranged for me to adopt Cassie at birth. I'm the only parent she's ever known." His voice faltered. "I love her so much."

"I saw her picture on your phone. She's adorable."

"Cassie's such a great kid, but she'll go through a lot as she grows up and wonders more about where she came from. I worry about her. Being adopted and having a celebrity parent might make it harder for her to have a normal childhood. Sometimes, I go overboard with security because I don't want the public bothering her."

"There's no perfect solution," Bobbi replied gently, "but when a little girl grows up with a daddy who's already thinking about her needs and responding out of love, she's starting life better off than many children who grow up in dysfunctional two-parent households."

"I've never thought of it in those terms." She heard BR choke up. "That helps. Thank you."

"What's Cassie like?"

BR's voice brightened. "She's wonderful. Cassie's scary smart. She's not even in kindergarten and reads at almost a third-grade level."

"Wow. That's amazing," Bobbi said.

"Cassie is shy around new people and a little too serious, but she's delightful. Very even-tempered, open to new experiences. She puts up with a father who's completely over his head. Right now, she's into reading, princesses, and tea parties."

"A brilliant princess who loves to read? I'm guessing she loves Belle."

"Her favorite." BR chuckled.

"Good choice, A self-reliant, independent princess … with a nerdy father she loves."

"Hey, I think I resemble that remark."

In their darkened rooms, separated by a river, Bobbi and BR shared another easy laugh.

"Speaking of princesses, you may have ruined Gina by offering her a fancy carriage and driver. Listen to this …" Bobbi then shared Gina's wacky text messages from the ride with Ronnie.

BR chortled. "She's hilarious."

"Gina's nuts, but she's cheap, and Sami adores her." Bobbi decided to take a gambit to gauge BR's interest. "I should warn you—Gina told me I have to date you so she never has to take the subway again."

BR laughed but didn't respond. For the first time in their conversation, there was a lull.

Finally, he asked, "May I tell you one more thing?"

"Tell me anything. I'm all ... ears." Bobbi caught herself just before saying, *All yours*.

"Something strange happened when I saw the painting."

Bobbi's languor instantly turned to full attention. The candle seemed to stop flickering. The room was absolutely still. Her breath caught, and her nipples hardened. Had BR felt the bubble? Did he know they had walked down the street together?

"Please," she whispered, "BR, please tell me."

He took a moment before he began. "I'd never noticed Fortuna's before. It was like some mysterious force was drawing me there."

Bobbi used the hem of "the shroud" to stifle a gasp.

"When I walked in, I started from the right and went through the gallery counterclockwise. All the paintings were beautiful, but then I saw *2:29*, and I stopped. I couldn't take my eyes off it. I couldn't move. You may have already been there, but I saw the painting before I saw you."

Bobbi's eyes moistened, a mixture of relief and awe swirling within her. Whatever had happened had happened to them both. She wasn't crazy. Or they were both crazy.

"Go on," she croaked out.

"I don't know how long I was staring at the painting, but there was a moment when I blinked and, out of nowhere, you were standing in front of me, lost in *2:29*. This may sound strange ... but I swear I heard a whisper. It was soft, almost like a breath against my ear, telling me I had to talk to you. It wasn't because you're beautiful—of course, you are—but I didn't notice that. It was like the painting was pulling us together in some way."

Bobbi's emotions were in overdrive. Her logical brain and naturally calm demeanor failed her. Maybe it was the physical exhaustion, the excitement of the conference, or the potential spark of romance, but she was a mess. At the heart of it all was their mysterious walk in Rome.

Her voice strangled with inexplicable emotions, Bobbi whispered, "BR, I'll call you back in five minutes." She hung up, holding her head in her hands as she struggled to get her feelings under control. It all felt surreal, and scary, and wonderful.

Am I falling in love with a man I don't know because of a mysterious bubble and a magic painting?

~~~

BR

BR waited eleven agonizing minutes until his JadePhone chirped with a text from Bobbi.

I'm calling now. We're fine.

"Sorry; I needed to deal with something. Tell me about where you live?" Bobbi's voice was cheerful and composed.

His answers were brief and self-effacing; BR was far more interested in hearing about her than discussing himself. He then asked Bobbi to explain her conference presentation, asking sharp questions and not hesitating to ask her to clarify concepts he didn't understand.

For over two hours, they talked about kids, work, and dreams. The tone was light, but their connection deepened. BR didn't want to say goodnight, but Bobbi needed sleep.

The call ended quietly, amidst yawns from both sides.

After the call, BR opened the contact card Bobbi had created. He stared at it as if it would somehow make her appear.

Then he saw it. In the field for her birthday, she'd written February 29.

2/29.

It was the rarest possible birthday.

And, written another way, the title of the mysterious painting that had brought them together—*2:29*.

CHAPTER SIX: HAPPY SUNDAY
Sunday, January 3
Bobbi

After Bobbi reluctantly found the strength to hang up, she checked the time—two a.m. They'd talked for three and a half hours.

Everything BR had said had touched her heart, made her laugh, and filled her with hope. She didn't want to forget a word.

Her bedroom was inky black; Honey Street below was silent.

Bobbi opened her laptop and fired off an email to Megan "Red" O'Malley, her ride-or-die best friend. Red was the one person she could talk to about anything—especially sex. Unfortunately, just as Bobbi was getting swept off her feet, Red was off the grid, deep in an extended holiday cruise in the South Pacific with her mother and aunt, completely disconnected. Before she'd left, Red had made Bobbi promise to write an email every day. Bobbi giggled as she typed.

Subject: He Ate My ...

Red,

How was New Year's Day? I hope you found a hot international date to celebrate with on the international dateline.

Get this: I'm not 100% sure, but I think I had a date tonight.

Confused? Me, too. But I refuse to clarify until I get one of your amazing hugs. You owe me.

If it was a date, he's a PPD*.

Fill in the blanks:

He ate my juicy __1__ with gusto while I moaned in delight because he put his big, hot __2__ in my mouth. I'm worn out in my bed because we __3__ all night.

Text me the second you're back. I miss you.

Blondie

P.S. PPD = Potential Panty Dropper

Quiz answers: 1 = appetizer sample. 2 = appetizer sample. 3 = talked.

Get your mind out of the gutter!

Bobbi yawned and laughed. Her brain was fried after two weeks of long shifts, holiday events, and late-night prep for her keynote. Now, despite the fatigue, she was too restless to sleep.

She lit a new Murano candle, its colors reminiscent of a Venetian sunset. Rosemary and citrus filled the air, stirring memories of her "trip" to

Rome with BR. Wrapped snugly under the shroud, she let her thoughts drift to him.

Drowsy, she closed her eyes and pictured them on the weathered bench from *2:29*, their fingers intertwined. She imagined herself in a flowing indigo sundress, matching the deep blue of his eyes. BR released her hand and cradled her face, his kiss both gentle and insistent. The heady fragrance of flowers and the reddish glow of the fading sun wrapped around them as their kisses deepened. She kissed him back with growing urgency, their tongues teasing, tasting, sending heat coursing through her body.

Bobbi's breath hitched as the fantasy blurred the line between longing and need. In her fantasy, BR reached under her dress, touching the bare legs he loved. Involuntarily, Bobbi's nipples poked through her tank top, and her hand slipped beneath the waistband of her pajama pants. She spread her legs for him, and a moment later, a decade of tension melted away in an unending tremor of relief.

Bobbi was still catching her breath when a fleeting thought crossed her mind: open the laptop, find BR videos, keep going.

Instead, she reached over and blew out the candle—a small act of willpower.

A rare calm settled over her as she sank into the bed, the shroud's weight cocooning her. Sleep came instantly.

Deep in a dreamless sleep, she didn't stir when Sami crawled under the covers beside her. On lazy Sunday mornings, they often cuddled for an extra hour.

When Bobbi finally awoke to use the bathroom, she was stunned to see it was almost nine o'clock—she hadn't slept this late in ages.

Didn't I just say goodnight to BR fifteen minutes ago?

Her heart warmed as she gazed at Sami, peacefully asleep. Carefully, she tucked the shroud under her daughter's chin and kissed her forehead, featherlight.

Sami's growing up too fast. Bobbi's soul ached for more moments like this.

Sleep tugged at her again, but her mind was already racing—plans for the day, lingering thoughts of the night before. It was time to get up.

She tickled Sami's nose with a stray strand of hair.

"Last night, Aunt Gina kept teasing me, saying you had a date with BR Bradford," Sami mumbled, snuggling closer. "Even when we called you, I thought you guys were playing a joke. Then I dreamed you told me it was true."

Bobbi brushed Sami's hair back gently. "Sweetheart, that wasn't a dream. I *did* have dinner with BR Bradford. Honestly, it feels a bit like a dream to me, too."

Sami's eyes flew open. "For real, Mom?"

Bobbi nodded, their faces inches apart.

As Bobbi recounted the highlights of the extraordinary evening, Sami listened in amazement, firing off questions. She especially loved that BR had written out clever clues just to make her laugh.

Sami snorted. "Since you don't know anything about Broadway, I thought it *might* really be him. But Aunt Gina's pulled off way crazier pranks, so I wasn't sure."

"He asked me to give you this." Bobbi rolled over to grab the slip of paper from her nightstand.

Sami's eyes widened at seeing BR's unfamiliar handwriting. Beneath the last clue, BR had added a note:

P.S. Sami, don't forget what Casey says at the end of Act 2: "Make your reality as beautiful as your dreams." – BR, January 2nd

For a moment, Sami just stared. Then, as if her brain had short-circuited, she let out a strangled squeak. Her head snapped up, eyes darting between the note and her mother. "*BR Bradford* wrote *me* a note? Like ... the actual *BR Bradford*?" Sami reread the paper. "He knows my name?"

Bobbi barely had time to nod before Sami let out a high-pitched shriek and flopped dramatically onto the bed, kicking her legs.

"I have to call Hunter. This is the greatest moment of my life!"

Bobbi burst out laughing.

"Mom, you have such a pretty smile," Sami said in wonder. "I love seeing you smile."

"I smile all the time," Bobbi protested.

"Not like this. You look really happy."

Bobbi squeezed her daughter close. "Maybe that's because I have the most wonderful daughter in the world."

Sami wrinkled her nose. "You *always* have the world's most wonderful daughter. But you don't always have a date with BR Bradford." She clutched the note tighter. "I know all his songs by heart. When do I get to meet him?"

Bobbi hesitated. She had to be honest, even if it wasn't what Sami wanted to hear. "I don't know, baby. It was a special night, but I'm not sure what'll come of it." She shrugged. "He might ask me out again … or maybe that was it."

"It sounds like he totally likes you."

Bobbi replied gently, "I think so. But he has a lot on his plate. Did you know he has a little girl? She's almost five and sounds adorable."

Sami's face darkened. "Wait—he's *married*?"

"No, never. He adopted Cassie. They live in a penthouse overlooking Times Square."

"He sounds amazing, Mom!" Sami practically bounced with excitement.

Smiling softly, she ran her fingers through Sami's hair, still processing everything herself. *Handsome, brilliant, and kind of mysterious. First time I've met a man I couldn't read in five minutes. He's different. He's famous and private … but with me, he was so down-to-earth, open, and easy to talk to. And I'm still not sure why he's interested in me.*

Sami clamored for details, but Bobbi glanced at the clock. "I'll fill you in on more in the car. Now, get moving, goofball. It's cold, so bundle up. There's a breakfast spot near the fair with great reviews. Plus, Sunday dinner at Grandma's tonight, so you're safe from my cooking today."

Sami chirped in a playful British accent, "Thank you ever so much for sparing me from potential food poisoning, most kind mother."

Bobbi shooed her away. "All right, let your most kind mother take a shower. Be dressed and ready to leave in thirty minutes."

Sami scrambled out from under the massive black comforter, clutching the note from BR as she headed to her room.

After her shower, Bobbi, still wrapped in her thick Italian towel, made a beeline for her phone—she'd avoided it, not wanting Sami to see how anxious she was or risk disappointment if there was nothing from BR. A flood of messages awaited.

The first was from her mother:

> *Is my silly granddaughter pulling my leg, or did you have a date with BR Bradford last night?*

Then Gina:

> *DETAILS!*

Five more texts from Gina followed, each more insistent, threatening massive retaliation if Bobbi didn't spill. She sighed. There'd probably be five more before they even left the driveway.

Dinner tonight will be … interesting.

She scrolled mindlessly through her messages, barely paying attention, until her jade eyes landed on the one she wanted.

It had arrived two hours ago.

A mix of excitement and nerves coursed through her. Would he ask her out, or say, *It was fun meeting you, but …?*

She took a steadying breath and opened it.

> *Good morning, Bobbi.*
> *I woke up thinking about you. I hope I didn't wake you by texting too early. Did Sami like*

her note? Tell her I said hi. I know you'll be out for the day. If I'm not being too pushy, could we talk after you get home from dinner? Have a beautiful day. I already miss your voice. — BR

Bobbi released a long breath, her feet stamping out a victory dance on the damp carpet. Her old phone made texting a chore, but she couldn't wait to reply.

Good morning, sweet man.
You've already made my day beautiful. Of course, I'd love another goodnight conversation. Give Cassie an extra hug today. That one's from me.

She hovered over the keyboard, debating *XOXO.* Second-guessed. Deleted it. Regretted it immediately. Still, her joy swelled.

Bobbi dressed quickly—maroon University of Chicago hoodie and black jeans—then pulled her long hair into a loose ponytail. Catching her reflection, she gave herself a once-over. *Would BR think I look cute today?*

Bobbi blanched, scolding herself. She'd never dressed for a man's approval and wasn't about to start now. What kind of role model would that be for Sami?

And yet …

She rummaged through a drawer and grabbed a blue scrunchie.

He likes me in blue, she thought, securing the navy tie around her hair. *This isn't about dressing for him—he won't even see it. I just like feeling connected to him.*

And yes, I do look cute.

She bounded downstairs, eager to share BR's hello. Their smiles lingered as they climbed into the ice-cold car and set off for Rye.

CHAPTER SEVEN: THE HARD TRUTH
BR

Have fun at the book fair. We had a guest speaker at church. It was a total snooze fest. I can't wait to hear what books Sami picked out.

BR's congregation, FOR Church, met in a West Harlem high school. He loved its focus on justice, love, and service. The diverse congregation—primarily young people and families—reflected New York's cultural mix. Cassie adored the preschool room, *Coat of Many Colors.*

After church, BR left her with Siobhán, who was making breakfast.

After texting Bobbi, he walked the five slushy blocks along Broadway to Dr. Jennifer Melendez's home office in Morningside Heights. It was still Broadway, but a world away from the blinding marquees of Times Square, where his name lit up the night. Here, the cold settled in his bones, and the silence was a kind of comfort.

He stopped at Coffee Corner, picking up a Crescendo Chai Tea for her and a Beautiful Rhythm Hot Chocolate for himself.

As he walked, his thoughts drifted.

The explosion in Chicago last September had left his body broken and his emotions raw. Anna Maria and Siobhán had moved in to care for Cassie while BR had faced an excruciatingly slow recovery, physically and emotionally. Withdrawn, BR had cut himself off from all but his closest circle.

His doctor, Max Stein, had urged him to start therapy, but BR had resisted. Raised with a churchgoing, self-reliant ethos, he believed he'd recover on his own once his appetite and mobility returned. Instead, he had withdrawn further, ignoring emails, work, and the world around him.

His charitable foundation carried on without him. His books sold, shows thrived, investments doubled ... and BR barely noticed.

By late November, he'd hit rock bottom.

Since his days at Columbia, when he had first bonded with Ed Johnson and Sabrina "Bree" Trice, Thanksgiving Week in Maple Meadows, Illinois, had become the cornerstone of his year. Ed's parents hosted this tradition. Over the years, the joy of these gatherings grew with the addition of Bree's wife, Chrissy, and Ed's longtime crush-turned-wife, Liz. Cassie had been part of this tradition since infancy.

But this last year, BR hadn't been able to bring himself to go. Just eight weeks after the explosion, he'd stayed alone in his penthouse, drowning in pain, while Cassie had spent the holiday at the horse farm with Siobhán's family—her favorite place in the world.

Alarmed by his decline, Bree and Ed had staged an intervention. The Sunday after Thanksgiving, they arrived—

spouses, Anna Maria, Siobhán, his lawyer, Alex Halifax, and even Mrs. Smith, the housekeeper.

Their raw emotions had shattered his defenses.

Shaken, BR had made the call before they'd left.

Dr. Stein had referred him to Dr. Jennifer Melendez, who had seen him the next morning.

For the past month, they'd met every Monday and Thursday while Cassie was in school. Dr. Melendez saw him in her home office, far from the public eye. Their sessions peeled back the layers of BR's complex life—his past, pressures, and isolation.

Arriving five minutes early, he scanned the warm waiting room. A terrarium sat on a table beneath framed photos of New Mexico landscapes—a nod to Dr. Melendez's heritage.

Woven tapestries in rust, terra-cotta, and deep turquoise adorned the walls, and the air carried the faint scent of sage from a diffuser. Though BR had grown up in a ski town in northwestern Colorado, the Southwestern décor felt inexplicably comforting.

He handed Dr. Melendez her tea before positioning himself on the couch, draping a soft woven throw over his lap.

She clinked cups against his. "Happy New Year, BR."

"Happy New Year. Thanks for seeing me on a Sunday. Tomorrow, I'm the guest reader at Cassie's school, but I need your help and didn't want to miss our session."

"I'm glad the timing worked out. Cassie's probably anxious to show you off. How was your holiday?"

BR shifted, meeting her eyes. "I met a woman." His voice was quieter than before. "She's wonderful. I'm not remotely in her league, but I can't stop thinking about her."

Dr. Melendez kept her expression neutral, but BR could tell she was processing. He had never mentioned dating before. Not once.

"When did you meet her?" she asked.

"Last night." He exhaled sharply, as if saying it out loud made it more real. "Her name is Bobbi. Dr. Bobbi Wyatt. She's a neurologist and a single mother from Brooklyn."

"I don't know her personally," Dr. Melendez said, "but I met her briefly at a mentoring seminar for women physicians. She made a great impression when she urged more of us to actively mentor young women doctors."

BR nodded slowly. That sounded like Bobbi.

"Now, start from the beginning."

BR launched into the story, barely pausing for breath as he recounted everything—their first conversation in front of the painting, the inexplicable pull he felt toward her, the way the world seemed to shift around them.

When he finally paused, she asked, "Are you going to ask her out?"

BR hesitated. "Maybe. I need your help. I haven't asked a woman out in over a decade. And never someone like Bobbi."

Dr. Melendez leaned back. "I see two things we can talk about. One's practical—it'll help with your nerves. The other is deeper—it might help you understand why Bobbi feels different."

BR clasped his hands together, bowing his head, a gesture indicating he was processing. "The first time I came here, you said the hardest roads lead to the most beautiful destinations," he murmured.

She nodded.

"You called therapy a journey from isolation to connection. I want Bobbi to be where that journey leads."

"The goal is *happiness*, BR." Dr. Melendez's voice was warm but steady. "Maybe Bobbi will be part of that. But go back to why you spoke to her. That's not like you."

BR swallowed. "Bobbi's stunning, but that wasn't what struck me first. It was her presence. And then the painting and the bubble. The combination felt ... magical."

"You've described the painting but not what it meant to you."

"Safety," BR finally whispered. "Belonging." His body trembled.

Dr. Melendez passed him a tissue. "You'd feel safe on that little street in Rome with Bobbi?"

"Yes." His voice cracked. "I barely know her. It makes no sense. But I'm sure I'm right."

Dr. Melendez studied him. "Why? Why her? Why now?"

The words hung in the air between them, raw and unguarded.

"I guess introverts make lousy therapy patients," he stammered. "I'm a fraud. I write great love songs, but I'm thirty-seven and have never been in love. I'm raising a child and running a charitable foundation built on family values, yet"—he folded his hands in front of his mouth, again—"I never even knew my birth parents."

He spoke slowly, as though he were assembling each thought for the first time. "Truthfully? I'm scared of the world. I've nearly died twice, and I've lived with uncertainty my entire life."

He raked a hand through his hair. "My adoptive parents were good people, but we were never especially close. They didn't know me or see my talent—not really. And their kids—my stepsiblings—were much older." A rare burst of anger flashed in his indigo eyes. "They resented my adoption. Superficially, they were polite when I saw them, which wasn't often. But I was never part of their family. I spent my childhood feeling like an outsider, never knowing where I fit."

He tapped his fingers against his knee—not restless, but rhythmic, as if composing a rhapsody only he could hear. "I found comfort in books, especially history. And maps—I loved maps. One day, I found a place in New Zealand called Doubtless Bay. Just the name—Doubtless—I still catch myself thinking about it. Like if I could just go there, dive under that water, let it wash over me ... maybe then I'd finally feel certain about something."

Dr. Melendez let a moment pass before softly asking, "What's the connection to Bobbi and Rome?"

BR's gaze drifted, distant. "I feel like all the answers I need are on that street in Rome ... with her."

"What would it mean to be there together?"

His throat bobbed as he swallowed hard. "I'd have a partner. A family." His eyes filled with tears. "I've been lonelier than I realized."

"Are you seriously considering asking her to go to Italy?" Dr. Melendez asked.

BR flushed slightly. "In that moment, I wanted to."

She smiled knowingly. "That might be jumping the gun. Let's focus on something smaller. What's stopping you from asking her out?"

He exhaled sharply, tightening his hands into fists before relaxing. "I'm afraid she'll say no."

Dr. Melendez arched a brow. "She agreed to have dinner with you, gave you her number, spent hours talking with you, and texted you the second she got home—what part of that suggests she's not interested?"

BR chuckled. "Points taken."

"Ready for the easy part? Just ask her. Tell her you like her and want to get to know her. I'll bet you a bizcochito she says yes."

BR exhaled, the weight of uncertainty lifting just a little.

When he left, his heart was pounding, hands unsteady. And yet, for the first time in a long time, hope felt stronger than fear.

CHAPTER EIGHT: PLANS AND MEMORIES
Ingrid

Sundays made Ingrid happy.

Before church, while her husband, Whit, slept in, Bobbi's mother brewed a cup of tea and settled into her cozy kitchen, flipping through cooking magazines to plan dinner. But after yesterday, she already knew what to make.

Sunday dinners were sacred—her one guaranteed night with all her girls at home. No matter how busy life got, Bobbi and Sami never missed one, despite having their own place in Brooklyn Heights. Gina, now married in Williamsburg, always made her way back, because Sunday dinner wasn't just a meal. It was home.

Surprise was part of the ritual. Sometimes Ingrid made their favorites; other times, she surprised them with something new. But if there was a big celebration, her legendary lasagna was a given. She always made extra—one for dinner, the rest to satisfy Sami's inevitable plea for leftovers.

When seven-year-old Bobbi had inexplicably fallen in love with all things Italy, Ingrid had made it her mission to perfect lasagna. It had become their tradition, a staple for celebrations—Bobbi's science fair wins and perfect report cards.

By the time Sami came along, it wasn't just a family favorite—it was a way of marking the most important days— Christmas Eve, Gina quitting smoking, Bobbi getting the clinic job, Sami's first day of school each year. Lasagna meant celebration, recognition, and love, all in one dish.

Ingrid and Whit had dreamed of a house full of children. High school sweethearts, they had stocked shelves and bagged groceries together after school. Two hardworking kids from blue-collar families. Weeks after graduation, they'd married, eager to build a life together.

But that dream hadn't come easily, as Ingrid had suffered two devastating miscarriages. When a doctor had coldly told her to give up, Ingrid had refused. She'd fired him on the spot, found a new physician, and prayed harder than ever.

Dr. Dawn Gerstein had been the answer to those prayers. Warm yet relentless, she had refused to let Ingrid lose hope.

After endless tests and treatments, the miracle had happened—Ingrid was pregnant again.

At twenty weeks, Dr. Gerstein diagnosed her with severe preeclampsia, a life-threatening condition. She monitored Ingrid weekly, not just out of duty but because something about Ingrid and Whit had moved her—their quiet courage, their unwavering hope. She wasn't just fighting for a baby; she was fighting for them.

At twenty-six weeks, a worrisome test result put Ingrid on bedrest.

At twenty-eight weeks, Dr. Gerstein sat them down for a painful conversation. No matter how this pregnancy ended, it had to be the last. With their consent, she scheduled a tubal ligation after delivery or if the unthinkable happened.

Whit squeezed Ingrid's hand. "One healthy baby is all we've ever prayed for."

And so, they waited.

On the eve of her next appointment, Ingrid needed a distraction. Bracing for the news that could determine the fate of her pregnancy, she escaped into a marathon of Frankie Avalon and Annette Funicello beach comedies.

One actress, a stunning blonde with Ingrid's spunky energy, fair coloring, and busty figure, kept catching her eye. Curious, she looked her up.

Her name was Bobbi Shaw.

When Whit walked in the door, Ingrid greeted him with her long blonde hair brushed to perfection, her mood radiant. The way she kissed him left no doubt she was feeling fantastic.

"Wow. What a welcome home." Whit grinned as he took her in. "You look incredible, sweetheart. How are you feeling? Need anything?"

With a playful purr, Ingrid patted the bed. "Come cuddle with me. I have something wonderful to tell you."

Safe in his arms, Ingrid declared, "I already know what's going to happen tomorrow. Dr. Gerstein will say everything's perfect. We're going to have a beautiful, healthy daughter. And tonight, I picked out her name—Bobbi Dawn Wyatt."

Whit didn't question her. "I love the name. I love you." Gently, he kissed Ingrid's belly, whispering, "And I love you, Bobbi Dawn Wyatt."

When labor began, a fully briefed neonatal surgical team, a chaplain, and a crash cart stood ready. Determined to minimize risks to her baby, Ingrid refused an epidural. Her three-hour labor was grueling, but Whit never left her side.

When the baby finally arrived, the room fell eerily silent. Ingrid and Whit froze, straining to hear a sound. The seconds stretched endlessly as the pediatrician swiftly conducted the crucial APGAR test. Clutching each other's hands, they held their breaths.

Then, at last, the doctor's eyes twinkled above his mask, his voice breaking as he announced a perfect score—10 out of 10. A heartbeat later, a thin wail pierced the silence. Bobbi Dawn Wyatt had arrived.

Relief crashed over them as they cried and laughed all at once. Lost in the moment, they barely noticed the tears streaming down the faces of the doctor, nurses, and chaplain.

The first time Ingrid held Bobbi, she knew total love. She had the answer to her prayers in her arms.

Bobbi resembled her mother and had her father's height, but the source of her extraordinary intellect was a mystery.

By second grade, she'd been placed in a gifted program and skipped a grade. In junior high, she skipped another. Her teachers, astounded by her reasoning skills and ability to synthesize complex information, had never seen such talent in someone so young.

Bobbi gravitated toward science, winning award after award for her projects. By the time she graduated high school—three years ahead of her peers—she'd exhausted every AP science, math, and Italian course available.

Bobbi's maturity often made Ingrid and Whit forget how young she truly was.

The phone chirped with a call from Gina, bringing Ingrid back to the present.

Without giving her a chance to speak, Ingrid said, "Good morning, Gina. And no, I won't forget to make the garlic bread—extra crispy, just the way you like it."

Gina cackled. "Your ability to read my mind saves me so much time. I was calling to check in and see if you needed anything. I thought I'd bake Bobbi's favorite Italian lemon cookies."

"Perfect. She'll love them."

"Great. I'll get there early to help you set up." Gina's voice turned conspiratorial. "Can you believe she went out with BR Bradford?"

Ingrid chuckled. "I'm still wrapping my head around it, but I can't wait to hear more."

"Me, too! Okay, I need to go to the produce market to get fresh veggies for my fabulous hubby's restaurant, then crush this project for class. Love you!"

Ingrid smiled as she hung up. *Gina is married, happy, and thriving—just as I always prayed she would be.*

But hearing Gina's voice sent Ingrid hurtling back in time to the night she had first come home.

Ingrid's pretentious half-sister, Jill, and her volatile husband, Kevin, had always kept their distance. Too busy, too many excuses. Ingrid had sensed something was off, but she hadn't seen it. None of them had. Jill had made sure of that.

At twelve, Bobbi had been the first to see through the façade. She'd begged Aunt Jill countless times to let her babysit Gina, but the answer had always been no ... until one night when Jill had finally relented. It wasn't out of trust or a change of heart. It was desperation. She and Kevin were too eager to get to a cocktail party to bother with their usual excuses—she just wanted to go out.

It had been a mistake because Bobbi had seen everything.

She came home shaking, tears in her eyes, and ran straight to her father.

Whit gently guided her to the couch, Ingrid beside them, their hearts hammering. Bobbi never cried.

After a long, shaky breath, Bobbi's entire demeanor shifted. Ingrid would later recognize it as her daughter's "doctor voice"—calm, steady, composed.

"Daddy, I think Uncle Kevin and Aunt Jill are hurting Gina."

Whit kept his voice even. "Did Gina say that?"

Bobbi shook her head. "No, but she told me they don't feed her." Despite her outward calm, Bobbi's hands curled into fists. "I made mac-and-cheese, and when I put the box in the recycling, it was full of whiskey bottles. And in the garbage, I saw shots."

Whit's jaw tightened. "Shots?"

Bobbi swallowed. "Um ... syringes."

Her voice never wavered as she continued, "Gina was starving, Mom. I made two whole boxes, and she ate every bite. I don't think she'd eaten all day. Maybe longer."

Ingrid's nails dug into the couch; she fought to keep her composure. "Did Aunt Jill or Uncle Kevin say anything when they got home?"

"They were fighting." Bobbi pressed her lips together. "Then Uncle Kevin told me to say I had a good time. He gave me this." She pulled a folded hundred-dollar bill from her jeans pocket and handed it to Whit. "I think they were drunk, Daddy," Bobbi whispered. "I was scared to let Uncle Kevin drive me home. I begged him to let me call you, but Aunt Jill just ... just shoved me into the car."

Ingrid reached out, threading her fingers through Bobbi's hair. "Oh, baby, I'm so glad you're okay."

Bobbi shook her head. "Mom, we have to help Gina." She closed her eyes, her head dropping. "She didn't have anything clean to sleep in. All her clothes were dirty, and they smelled bad."

Ingrid's heart clenched. "What'd you do?"

Bobbi finally met her mother's eyes. "I had a T-shirt on under my hoodie. It came down to her knees. She said she'd wear it forever."

"Sweetheart, you did exactly the right thing by telling us," Whit spoke, his voice reassuring. He pressed a kiss to the top of her head. "Mom and I are proud of you. Now, go finish your homework. We'll check on Gina."

As soon as Bobbi was out of earshot, Ingrid called Jill. The conversation was short. Her half-sister sounded dazed, unfocused—stoned. Kevin shouted in the background, his words thick with alcohol.

When Ingrid hung up, her hands trembled. "Honey, I'm scared. Poor little Gina."

Whit's expression hardened. He grabbed his phone, his fingers flying over the keypad. Holding the phone up to his ear, he said, "Marissa, it's Whit. I need your help."

Marissa, a former coworker who'd become a police detective, didn't hesitate.

Within minutes, Whit turned back to Ingrid. "Tell Bobbi to lock the doors. Get your coat. Marissa's sending a squad car and Child Protective Services. We're going now."

They didn't wait for the police. They stormed inside, finding the house a wreck—furniture overturned, Kevin and

Jill shouting and swearing, the stench of alcohol suffocating. Whit took charge while Ingrid ran to Gina's room.

She found the girl trembling under the bed, a pillow clutched over her head.

Ingrid dropped to her knees, keeping her voice soft. "Gina, sweetheart, it's me. It's Aunt Ingrid."

No movement.

She gentled her tone even more. "You're safe now, baby. But I need you to be brave and come to me."

A long silence. Then, slowly, the pillow lowered. Gina's wide, terrified eyes flickered to Ingrid. It took everything she had, but she crawled forward.

Ingrid scooped her up, feeling just how small, how weightless she was. She whispered, "Gina, would you like to live with Uncle Whit and me?"

A tiny hiccup of breath. "And Bobbi?"

Ingrid pressed a kiss to Gina's hair. "Yes, sweetheart. Bobbi loves you. So do I."

She carried Gina into the hallway. The living room had gone eerily silent, the kind of quiet that felt unnatural. Whit had somehow managed to calm Kevin and Jill.

Ingrid bent her head, her voice barely a whisper. "Close your eyes, baby. Just lean into me. Don't look. Can you do that?"

Gina nodded, squeezing her eyes shut and pressing her face into Ingrid's shoulder.

By the time sirens filled the air, Ingrid was already pulling out of the driveway.

Gina never saw her parents handcuffed and arrested. They went to rehab then jail. She never saw them again.

Uncle Whit did everything to make Gine feel safe. Aunt Ingrid surrounded her with motherly love, ensuring she had therapy, stability, and plenty to eat, especially on Sundays when family dinner became a ritual. And Bobbi? She became her big sister, protector, and heroine, sharing her heart and room.

Despite studying nonstop, Bobbi always had time for Gina. When Gina's night terrors hit, Bobbi would climb into Gina's bed to comfort her.

Gina was happiest in Bobbi's hand-me-downs. The family juggled a steady stream of legal, medical, and therapy bills, and Whit secured legal guardianship with the help of a lawyer. To ease the financial strain, Bobbi tutored and worked part-time as a bagger in her dad's store, while Whit and Ingrid lived frugally, denying themselves vacations and luxuries. They saved every dime because Bobbi would be the first in the family to go to college. By the time she entered high school, she was determined to be a doctor.

Years later, they sat at the kitchen table, staring at the acceptance letters spread across the counter, their thick envelopes bulging with scholarship offers. Every Ivy League school wanted her. So did Stanford, Duke, and MIT. Her "safety schools"—NYU and Johns Hopkins—had accepted her without hesitation.

Whit picked up the offer letter from Northwestern, flipping it over as if searching for an answer. "You loved Yale when we visited," he said. "And Harvard hasn't stopped calling. How do you want to narrow this down?"

Bobbi spoke with certainty. "Mom, Dad, I'm going to the University of Chicago." She handed her father the scholarship letter. "They're offering a full ride—tuition, room, board. The recruiter even promised me a mentor and a job on campus so I'd have money to fly home. I don't want you to worry about paying for anything."

Ingrid fidgeted, pressing her fingers to her temple. "Honey, we saved for this. You don't have to make your decision based on money."

"I know, Mom. But it's different now." She hesitated then added gently, "Gina's here."

Ingrid's chest tightened. Bobbi was right. Gina had arrived with nothing but the clothes on her back. They never called her a burden, but stretching every dollar had become second nature.

Bobbi glanced around the kitchen, her gaze settling on the stairs leading up to the room she shared with Gina. "Columbia would be amazing. I'd love to stay home." She hesitated. "But this makes the most sense."

Ingrid swallowed hard. "You're only sixteen. Chicago's far."

"I know." Bobbi traced the university's crest at the top of the letter. "But I'll come home for every break. And I'll call every day. Gina will probably get sick of hearing about my life." She smiled faintly, trying to lighten the moment.

Ingrid shook her head. "That girl idolizes you. She's going to be heartbroken."

"I know," Bobbi said. "That's the hardest part."

Whit met Bobbi's eyes, pride shining through. "She's made up her mind."

Ingrid picked up the housing packet. "Then I guess we better get you some warmer clothes. Chicago's a lot colder than Brooklyn. And you'd better get used to deep-dish."

Bobbi laughed. "Okay, that part I can handle."

After Bobbi left for college, Gina began to unravel. Insolence turned to withdrawal; defiance replaced cooperation. Night terrors returned, and school became a daily battle. Ingrid doubled down, smothering Gina with motherly affection no matter how much she resisted.

Despite years of therapy, Gina's turning point came when Bobbi needed her most. From that moment, she blossomed.

Then, after years of dating losers, Gina finally met Marco. The charming, talented chef adored his wild, unpredictable wife. Now twenty-seven, Gina was back in school but still as lively as ever, with a different hair color every month.

Whit and Ingrid had welcomed Marco with open arms. Bobbi had been especially thrilled—an Italian chef in the family? Perfection. Sami, meanwhile, had delighted in escaping her mother's pathetic attempts at cooking, indulging in endless breadsticks at Marco's cozy trattoria.

Though Ingrid's home had felt empty when Gina had moved in with Marco, their bond never wavered. As Sami's adoring godmother, mischief-making sitter, and closer-than-a-sister to Bobbi, Gina never missed a Sunday dinner, even when Marco had to work.

Ingrid smiled as she checked the pantry. Her three girls would be home soon. And she'd be serving lasagna.

CHAPTER NINE: LASAGNA AND LOVE
Bobbi

Bobbi and Sami stomped their boots on the porch, knocking off the snow. The unmistakable aroma of lasagna wafted out as Bobbi reached for the door. They whooped and broke into their well-rehearsed dance of joy.

Sami dropped her bag of books, shrugged off her coat, and dashed into the arms of her beaming grandfather. "Grandpa, I love you," she cooed as Whit kissed the top of her head.

Emerging from the kitchen with a broad smile, Ingrid hugged Sami. "Since you love him so much, you're both setting the table tonight."

"Of course," Whit replied joyfully. "More time with my favorite girl."

With mock suspicion, Bobbi asked, "Mom, not that I'd ever complain about lasagna, but please tell me this isn't to celebrate my date with BR Bradford."

Whit shot Ingrid a look, prompting her to roll her eyes. "And there it is"—Whit chuckled, checking his watch—"our first 'Bobbi Being Blonde' moment of the new year." Though brilliant, Bobbi's occasional ditzy moments were a long-standing family joke.

"My dear Dr. Daughter," Whit said warmly, "this *isn't* about a man; it's about your recognition by the top professionals in your field."

Bobbi blushed. "I almost forgot that was yesterday."

Whit kissed the top of her head. "If that guy helped you forget about work, maybe that's worth celebrating, too."

"Bobbi, you're glowing," Ingrid said, hugging her taller daughter. "That's before even having the lasagna. I made extra for you and Sami."

"Thanks, Mom. You're the best."

"I'm just happy to have all three of my girls home."

Dinner unfolded in familiar, joyful patterns. Sami excitedly shared her latest adventures, giving Ingrid a cookbook and Whit a book about Ebbets Field.

"Aunt Gina," Sami said, handing over tie-dye bookmarks, "I figured you'd need these for all your school books."

"Nothing for your mom? No Italian medical texts from the Renaissance?" Gina teased.

Bobbi glared playfully as Gina and Sami fist-bumped.

"Mom, I saved the best for last," Sami announced, handing her a beautifully wrapped gift.

"I saw you being all sneaky by the gift wrap table," Bobbi teased, unwrapping *The Total Beginner's Guide to Dating* and *Ten New York Minutes: How BR Bradford Revolutionized Music*.

The table erupted with laughter.

Whit clinked his glass for attention. "A toast to the woman of the hour. Explain your presentation so even we can understand it."

Bobbi kept it short, but Sami and Gina dramatically faked snoring halfway through.

"Sami," Ingrid scolded gently, "aren't you proud of your mother?"

Sami straightened. "Of course. Mom"—Sami straightened—"I'm proud that you said stuff I don't understand to people I don't know ... because we got lasagna."

Gina high-fived her. "Nerd power at its finest."

"Enough." Ingrid laughed. "Now, tell us about BR Bradford."

"He's terrific," Bobbi said, smiling. "A little shy, smart, and thoughtful. Also, funny—ask your granddaughter about the tickle takedown."

Sami proudly showed everyone the handwritten note from BR, even impressing Gina.

"Why'd you agree to dinner with a stranger?" Ingrid asked.

"I had a secret weapon—Gina and the 'Aunt Mary' emergency code."

Gina flexed dramatically. "I had her covered."

"What's Aunt Mary?" Sami asked, eyes wide.

"Your mother helped me dodge a few bad dates before I met Uncle Marco," Gina started to explain.

"A *few*?" Bobbi arched an eyebrow. "Try a hundred."

"To men of questionable intellect and dubious intentions," Whit groused.

Bobbi smirked. "Tell Sami about the blind date with the punk-rock puppeteer who sang songs about serial killers."

Sami's jaw dropped. "No way."

"True story," Gina said. "Your mom bailed me out by pretending she had 'Exploding Head Syndrome.'"

Sami wrinkled her brow. "That's not real."

Bobbi nodded. "It is. Fortunately, it's mostly harmless but causes loud noises as you fall asleep."

"And then there was the time Aunt Mary got a disease that made her pee purple," Gina added.

Sami snorted in disbelief. "You're making this up to trick me, right?"

"Porphyria," Bobbi confirmed. "Look it up if you don't believe me."

"Grandpa," Sami asked imploringly, "are they serious?"

Whit leaned in. "Never bet against your mom when it comes to medicine."

Ingrid interrupted with a laugh. "All right, you two con artists, clearing duty is all yours."

~~~

In the kitchen, Gina playfully swatted Bobbi's behind. "Nice job steering the conversation away from you. Now, tell me *everything*."

"I don't have time to get into all of it right now, but I've been dying to talk to you. I didn't want to get Sami's hopes up, and I didn't know what to tell my parents. I'm not sure where BR and I stand."

Bobbi washed the dishes while Gina dried. She kept an eye on the kitchen door as she told Gina about the mysterious painting and the magical bubble. Gina seemed to believe every word, and a wave of relief flooded over Bobbi. Gina's affirmation meant Bobbi wasn't entirely off her rocker.

"I've never met anyone like him," Bobbi admitted, almost to herself. "He called again last night after you left. We talked for hours about everything—the painting, our lives, our kids. I've never had a man just … get me like this."

"Wait," Gina interrupted, astonished. "BR Bradford talked about his kid? I scoured articles about him after Dorkus Malorkus hit the sack, and they all said he never discusses her. There's almost nothing about her anywhere on the internet. Even Wikipedia had nothing much."

"He told me a lot about her. I saw her picture. She's precious. BR adores her. I think it's just that he's very private and keeps his personal life out of the public eye," Bobbi explained, glancing nervously at the door. She then shared a brief overview of Cassie and Anna Maria.

Gina listened, eyes sharp. "Bobs, if he opened up to you like that, it wasn't just some throwaway dinner with a rando. Quiet guys don't spill their secrets unless it's real."

Bobbi nodded. "That's what I think, too. He told me about his little Cassie during dinner. You should've seen him, Gina. His whole face lit up. And remember, I didn't even recognize him when we met. We talked for what felt like minutes, but it was two hours. The rest of the world just faded away. It was only BR and me. I've never felt anything like it."

Gina leaned in, lowering her voice. "That sounds like some kind of magic, Bobs. Too many coincidences. Feels like fate's sending you a message."

Bobbi sighed. "I know, right? I don't believe in magic. I'm not some hopeless romantic. Or maybe I wasn't until yesterday."

After a thoughtful pause, Gina's eyes twinkled as a smirk spread across her face. "So, you're telling me this guy was with you for almost three hours and didn't even notice you look like you should be captain of the Swedish bikini team? For the sake of all that's holy, tell me he's not a monk. I mean, he's a guy, right? Seriously, Bobbi, you looked fantastic last night. I bet he's totally hot for you."

Bobbi giggled. "He loved my dress and told me blue was definitely my color ... so maybe he likes my legs? I don't know—I'm just guessing."

"Now we're getting somewhere." Gina leaned back, eyes glinting. "Look, I know you live in pants, but next time? Wear a blue skirt. See what kind of reaction you get."

Bobbi sighed. "Gina, I don't even know if there *is* going to be a next time. He hasn't asked me out. We talked until two in the morning, and then the whole thing ended so ... open-ended. We texted all day, but nothing about another date." Shyly, Bobbi recounted the end of their dinner when he said goodbye without a handshake, hug, or kiss. She uncharacteristically opened up, sharing details of their late-night conversation.

"Did you make it clear you were available?"

"Gina, I did everything but wear a sign around my neck saying, 'Ask me for a date now, idiot.' It's not something I've ever had to think about before. I don't know what he's thinking."

"Joke's on you, Bobs. You've never had to work for a guy's attention—half of them can't even form complete sentences around you. And now, for the first time, you're wondering if one actually likes you?" Gina stared at her then burst out laughing. "Oh my God. You really don't know how the rest of us live. Welcome to the struggle."

Bobbi scowled. "Easy for my happily married cousin to say. Not helpful."

Gina wiped a tear from her eye. "Bobs, listen to me. He *likes* you. You're just not used to a guy taking his time instead of falling at your feet."

Bobbi shrugged. "Maybe."

"He texted today?" Gina asked, holding out her hand.

Bobbi nodded, handing her phone over.

Gina's expression brightened as she scrolled through the messages. Looking up, she winked. "He's calling you later. Trust me; you'll have a date by tomorrow morning. He's totally into you."

CHAPTER TEN: NO QUESTION
Bobbi

Stuffed, happy, and laden with leftovers and book bags, Sami and Bobbi arrived home on Honey Street, thoroughly exhausted.

Before heading to their rooms, Sami mimicked Bobbi's "mom voice," wagging a finger as she scolded playfully, "Now, young lady, don't you stay up all night on the phone with your friend. Remember, you have work in the morning."

Bobbi responded with an exaggerated eyeroll. "Yes, ma'am."

They hugged goodnight, but halfway down the hall to her room, Sami turned back.

"Hey, Mom?"

"What is it, baby?" Bobbi asked.

"Would it be okay if you told BR I said hi?"

"I'm sure he'd love that," Bobbi replied with a smile.

After scrubbing her face, Bobbi chose an apricot top and black dress pants for the morning. She lit a lavender-scented candle then turned off the lights, wishing she had something prettier to wear to bed. Settling under her covers, she sent a text:

Finally home. Sorry it's later than expected.
If you're still awake, call me.

Her phone rang almost instantly.

"What took you so long?" Bobbi teased.

"At least you remembered who I am tonight," BR shot back with a chuckle.

"About that," Bobbi said, her tone shifting, "I have a question."

"Ask me anything."

"What's your name?"

"What?"

"What does BR stand for?"

There was a pause, longer than she had expected, before BR replied, "I don't know. Nobody does. On my birth certificate, under 'first name,' there are just two letters: BR. I have no idea what my birth mother was thinking."

Taken aback, Bobbi asked, "Did you know her?"

BR hesitated. "Are you sure you want to hear this story?"

Her chest tightened. They'd only known each other for a day, yet everything felt so intense, so real. She didn't want to push too far without knowing if he felt the same, but she needed to understand the connection and hear it from him.

She steadied herself, her voice soft but sure. "I do. But before you tell me, I need to ask you something." As the flickering candlelight cast shifting shadows across her face, Bobbi felt a surge of courage. The moment had arrived to ask the question that had haunted her since their poignant moment in front of the enigmatic *2:29*. "BR, do you feel like something is pushing us together?"

He responded immediately. "I believe that with one hundred percent certainty. My mother used to say coincidence is what happens when God wants to remain anonymous. I believe we were always meant to find each other. We've been in a bubble. Do you feel it, too?"

Bobbi's pulse quickened. "I'm not religious, like you. I'm not even sure there is a God. But from the moment we met, I felt something … like *the Universe* was directing us. It sounds crazy, but I believe it."

"Well, if a scientist and a poet see it the same way, we must be on the right track," BR said, his voice softer. Then he hesitated before admitting, "Bobbi, I haven't stopped thinking about you since that moment."

"Same," she murmured, her heart pounding.

"Here's the thing: people often ask me personal questions because I'm famous. But the public's only entitled to my work, not my life. Strangers wouldn't ask someone they don't know about their relationship status—it's rude. Yet, that's my daily reality. I never imagined my career would lead here. I thought I'd be teaching American history."

Bobbi sat up slightly. "Hey, I get it. Ask any woman how often she's hit with questions no one would ever throw at a man. Some guys act like they have a right to comment on what you wear, how you live, even your career. It's exhausting. I want to get to know you for who you are. And whatever happens, anything you tell me stays between us. No one will ever hear it from me."

BR's voice was steady but warm. "If I didn't trust you, I wouldn't have told you about Cassie. My birth story, however, is a bit of a saga."

Bobbi smiled, sensing the closeness building between them. "I'm not going anywhere."

"My birth parents were Brielle and Brock Bradford. I never knew them, and I've only found a few people who did. They were teenagers from Northern England with family issues, so they eloped and came to America to explore. Brielle and Brock were free spirits, going wherever the moment took them. I was born in Steamboat Springs, Colorado."

Bobbi's stomach tightened. She knew BR was adopted but hadn't known the details. She could sense the story taking a darker turn.

BR's voice grew quieter. "This is hard for me to talk about. You may not believe it because of my job, but I'm really an introvert. But this crazy Bobbi Bubble makes me feel so close to you that I want you to know."

"Thank you," she whispered. "I want to know you."

BR asked gently, "I'm curious—you didn't know who I was when we met. Have you googled me?"

Bobbi's tone turned self-mocking. "No, not even a little. Though, my cousin has read enough about you in the last twenty-four hours to write a biography. I want *you* to introduce yourself to me."

BR chuckled. "I'm sure your cousin could do a better job than the ones already out there. You already know things about me that Wikipedia doesn't."

"You mean about Cassie and Anna Maria?"

"Yes."

"My turn—have you looked me up?"

He laughed. "No. But I confess I don't have your level of self-control. I really wanted to, but it felt like stalking.

Besides, I'm already overwhelmed by you. What am I going to find out next? That you graduated at the top of your class?"

"As a matter of fact, I did," Bobbi replied lightly. "But only in medical school. A couple of impossible history classes in undergrad dropped me all the way to number three. Where were you when I needed you? You could have tutored me. Those two A-minuses still bother me."

She could hear the grin on BR's face as he said, "I'm not sure if I would've been a help or a distraction."

She laughed. "Probably both. But don't worry; I don't even have Instagram. There's nothing embarrassing about me online."

Her voice softened. "Now, tell me the story about your parents. I want to know."

BR's sigh said this was trying for him. "They'd been in America for about ten months, moving from place to place. Brock scraped together money doing odd jobs. From what I've pieced together, they rented an apartment near Steamboat when it became clear I was about to be born. Why they ended up in that remote corner of Colorado, I have no idea.

"Brock somehow rented a car to get my mom to the hospital. Two days later, on the way home, a drunk driver blew a stoplight and totaled it. They died instantly. I didn't have a scratch. The next day, I was in foster care. And not long after, Michael and Connie Palermo adopted me—that's another story. They kept my birth name."

Bobbi's heart ached for the child he'd been, an orphan before he even knew his parents. She ached to know everything but held back, hoping the stories would come on their own.

"Let me ask you: what's your name? Is Bobbi short for something?"

"Nope. I'm just Bobbi Dawn Wyatt."

"*Dr.* Bobbi Dawn Wyatt," he said admiringly

As he asked about her family, the mood lifted. Laughter bubbled as Bobbi shared stories of her wonderful parents and the hilarious chaos of Sunday dinners.

Hours slipped by. It was after midnight when she stifled a yawn.

"I know you've got an early day," he said. "I should apologize for having you up so late."

"Oh, BR, you could have me any way you want."

The second it slipped out, she slapped her forehead. *Did I just say that?*

"Sorry," she sputtered, face flaming. "I meant, you could have me all night if you wanted."

Worse.

He chuckled. "Either offer works for me."

She was sure he could hear her blushing.

"Bobbi, there's one more thing I want to ask you …"

Her heart pounded. She knew the question she wanted to hear.

"I know you're busy with Sami, your family, and work, but would you'd go out on a date with—"

"Yes!" Bobbi cut him off. She was grateful he couldn't see her enthusiastic fist-pump—it made the candle flame flicker.

"Really?" His voice was a mix of surprise and delight.

Bobbi rolled her eyes. *And Gina thinks* I'm *clueless about dating?*

"Are you kidding? The Universe basically threw us together. We had that amazing dinner and talked for what— six hours in two days? Now it's almost one in the morning, and I still don't want you to say goodnight. So, Mr. Mensa Member, yes, of course I want to go out with you. How could you even question that?"

He let out a relieved, happy sigh. "Every time you texted me today, my heart jumped. After I put Cassie to bed, I kept looking at the clock, waiting until I could hear your voice again."

Then BR's tone shifted, becoming more serious. "There's something I need to mention. I'm used to people asking for selfies or sneaking pictures when I'm out. If the paparazzi catch us, it could end up online. I've kept Cassie and Anna Maria out of that spotlight, and I don't want you to feel uncomfortable. It's our first date. I just want you to feel safe."

Bobbi paused, turning his words over in her mind. She hadn't considered the implications. The idea of a single mom from Brooklyn walking a red carpet felt as likely as vacationing on the International Space Station. And yet ... this man had awakened something thrilling, something long dormant.

She shifted to her logical doctor's mindset. *I want to go out with him. But do I want to end up on the front page of the Daily News?*

"I've got an idea," she said. "I'm working Friday. Remember I told you about Gina's husband's restaurant near the Promenade? Let's meet there. I'll get us a quiet booth. The food's fabulous, and Marco will make sure nobody bothers us.

And if you play your cards right, I might even let you walk me to my favorite gelato shop for dessert."

"Perfect. I can't wait to see you again," BR said.

His warmth melted her. "Oh, sweetie, that feeling is more mutual than you could imagine."

No! Did I just call him sweetie? Don't scare him off!

To her relief, BR's voice was just as tender. "It's a date. And if I'm not pushing my luck, could we make a standing goodnight call until then? I'd love for your voice to be the last one I hear before I sleep."

After six hours of conversation, Bobbi's heart felt full. "I'd love that," she responded joyfully.

Then a funny thought struck her. Now that she and BR were on the same page, she felt relaxed enough to share it.

"I just realized we might have a problem with our date. I'm not worried about the paparazzi—you can handle that—but we have a much bigger challenge."

"What's that?"

"I might have to lock Sami in a tower to keep her from joining us."

"If her hair's as long as yours, she might escape," he teased.

"Of course you know the story of Rapunzel—you do have a five-year-old." She laughed. "Not to worry, good sir. My daughter's hair is but shoulder-length. I'll make sure the tower is high and the moat swarming with slimy, disgusting eels. You're all mine on Friday." Then, more softly, she told him, "Sami asked me to say hi."

"Wow. Tell her I said hi back. She sounds like a great kid."

"I like her."

"I'm sure I will, too."

Bobbi yawned again, still smiling.

"I hope I dream about you tonight," BR said gently. "I'll text you in the morning."

"I look forward to it. Goodnight, sweet man," she whispered.

"Goodnight, my brilliant, beautiful brainiac."

After hanging up, Bobbi stared at her phone then placed it beside a smiling photo of Sami on her nightstand. Morning was only a few hours away, and she'd need to sleep fast.

Too sleepy to put her hair up or email Red, she happily curled up under the shroud.

One word echoed in her mind.

He had called her "my."

CHAPTER ELEVEN: BRAIDS AND BOUQUETS
Monday, January 4
Bobbi

Bobbi was rudely awakened from a deep, dreamless sleep when an excited eleven-year-old pounced on her. With sparkling blue eyes and boundless energy, Sami straddled her mother, firing off rapid questions.

"Did BR call? Did he ask you out? When do I get to meet him?"

Still groggy, Bobbi couldn't muster any real frustration. Sami was her world.

With a sly grin, she played possum for a moment then pulled her daughter into a playful bear hug. "No 'good morning, Mom?'" she teased.

"Good morning, Mom!" Sami squealed, squirming. "Now spill—did he call? Did he ask about me? Are you going on a date?"

Bobbi groaned, rubbing sleep from her eyes. "What kind of weirdo wakes up early on the first day back from break to ambush her mom? Go back to bed."

"You slept through your alarm. I'm your snooze button."

Bobbi chuckled as she sat up, Sami flopping beside her, still grinning.

"Okay, Little Miss Snooze Button, when exactly did it become *your* job to track *my* love life?"

"Mom, you said *love*! Do you love him?" Sami's words came faster now, fueled by excitement.

Bobbi laughed. "You're such a goofball. It's way too soon for love. I just met him." Her tone softened. "But yes, BR called. He always asks about you, my most beloved daughter." She raised an eyebrow. "And for the record, yes, he asked me out. We're going on a date Friday night. Can you hang at Hunter's? Pizza and a movie with your bestie sounds like a win."

Sami practically bounced off the bed then paused to pout. "Why can't I come with you?"

"Seriously? Let me check *The Total Beginner's Guide to Dating* and get back to you."

Sami rolled her eyes. "Mom, don't you always say *I'm* your best feature? Let me come."

Bobbi leaned in. "Okay, I'll make you a deal. You can come with me on one condition ..."

Sami blinked. "Wait—what?"

"The day you turn twenty-nine and I finally let you start dating, you have to let me tag along."

"Come on, Mom," Sami groaned dramatically. "I *really* want to meet him."

Bobbi glanced at the clock. "What kind of mother takes her nutty eleven-year-old on a first date?"

"The kind who wants her most beloved daughter to meet the greatest, most wonderful Broadway star and composer of all time."

Bobbi knit her brow in mock deliberation. "Hmm. Good point. Let me think."

Sami closed her eyes and clasped her hands in mock prayer.

Bobbi seized the moment to whack her with a pillow.

"Not cool, Mom!" Sami squealed through giggles.

Bobbi kissed her daughter's head. "When I get home, I'll tell you all about it. And if things go well, maybe you'll meet him someday."

She smiled, giving Sami's arm a playful nudge. "Now, my most beloved daughter, get that pretty little rear in gear and get ready for school. I've got to shower."

As Bobbi slid off the bed and stretched, she never saw the flying pillow until it hit her squarely in the head. Sami's mischievous laughter echoed down the hallway as she darted out of the room.

Before stepping into the shower, Bobbi instinctively checked her phone. Her heart skipped a beat when she saw a text from BR waiting.

> *Good morning, my brilliant, beautiful brainiac. You have the most wonderful smile. If you knew how much I can't wait to see you, you'd definitely be smiling this morning.*

Beaming from ear-to-ear, Bobbi quickly typed back:

> *You ALWAYS make me smile. Remind me to tell you about the lunatic daughter ambush I survived this morning.*

Her phone chirped before she could even set it down.

Have a great day. I love that you spend your day helping others. Tell Sami I said hello, but no more ambushing her mother before 8 AM.

Bobbi laughed, shaking her head.

Oy—Sami will take that as permission to ambush me AFTER 8:00. TTYL.

Still grinning, she set her phone aside and turned on the shower. After staying up late two nights in a row, she made the water colder than usual, hoping the chill would help shake off the lingering grogginess. But no amount of cold water could drown out her thoughts of BR. As she scrubbed her hair, Bobbi realized she couldn't even remember if she'd already used shampoo.

Focus, Bobbi, she scolded herself, rolling her eyes.

As she pulled on a lightweight sweater, she sniffed her armpit just to be sure. *Well, at least I remembered deodorant.* She sighed in relief.

Recalling how BR had complimented the way she looked in blue, she reached for a pretty turquoise hair clip and tied her long, damp hair into its everyday ponytail.

Her mind wandered as she headed downstairs. She imagined BR helping little Cassie with her shoes and coat, gathering her backpack, and walking her to preschool. The thought of him being so hands-on with his daughter warmed her heart, even as she tried to focus on her hectic morning routine.

Sami was already perched at the kitchen island, headphones on, bopping along to the cast album of *Sock*

Hop—BR Bradford's first big musical. Lost in her own world, she munched on granola and a banana, oblivious to her mother's approach.

Without a word, Bobbi handed over her phone. Sami's eyes lit up as she scanned the texts, squealing with delight. They shared a conspiratorial smile.

Moments later, they were out the door, both grinning, both excited for the day ahead.

~~~

BR

"Daddy, it's still not right." Cassie frowned at her reflection. "Can't you fix it?"

BR sighed. Despite several valiant attempts with YouTube tutorials, the art of French braiding her sunny hair remained beyond him. Growing frustrated, he gave up and brushed it straight. Cassie winced—a small but potent reminder of the rough edges of single fatherhood. He settled for his fallback: a simple ponytail.

As she eagerly dug into her fruit cup, BR's mind wandered back to the stunning neurologist. Why hadn't he kissed her? Or even hugged her? He'd walked her to the car—the connection had been electric—and then … nothing. Not even a handshake.

Fear of rejection? Maybe.

But that wasn't really it.

The truth was riskier: he'd nearly asked her to come to Rome. The words had hovered on his lips. His crew could've readied the jet in an hour. Instead, he'd barely gotten her number.

"Daddy, are you listening?" Cassie's voice broke through the spiral. "I said: will you come to the reading circle when you pick me up?"

BR smiled. "I wouldn't miss it for all the gold hidden on Jackson's Island." They'd been reading *Tom Sawyer*.

She clapped at the reference then tugged on his hand impatiently. She hated being late.

Hand in hand, they left the penthouse, her ponytail bouncing as they walked.

~~~

Bobbi

Claude, the dashing barista with a voice fit for the stage, beamed as soon as Bobbi entered Corner Coffee. Without missing a beat, he launched into an impromptu serenade—a special "walk-on music" routine reserved for his select few favorite customers. To the tune of "You'll Be Back" from *Hamilton*, he sang:

"Bobbi's back,
Soon, you'll see,
That she cures the world,
But belongs to me.

The Bobbi Blend,
That's her fix,
And I'm the only one,
Who knows the mix—
Bobbi's back."

The shop erupted in applause and laughter. Regulars knew Claude never missed a chance to audition for Broadway, but few knew how deeply he admired Dr. Bobbi Wyatt. His serenades masked a lasting gratitude.

Years ago, when his grandmother had suffered a massive stroke, Bobbi's compassion had comforted his Bahamian family. Though she couldn't save his nana, Bobbi had kept visiting her in hospice and was the only White attendee at her memorial in East Flatbush.

Claude delighted in making the doctor smile, especially since she rarely recognized the songs.

"One Bobbi Blend coming up!" he sang with flair. He knew her precise requirements: a caramel macchiato with an extra pump of vanilla syrup and a drizzle of chocolate syrup, a concoction she credited with powering her through medical school and residency.

Bobbi lived for this delightful mix of sweetness and creaminess, enriched with robust coffee flavor and accents of chocolate and caramel. It was well-known to every barista near her home, her parents' house, and each Coffee Corner location near Weill Cornell Medical College and her clinic.

"Happy New Year, Claude. Great song this morning. You should be on Broadway," she said, beaming.

"You know it, and I know it. If you could just mention that to BR Bradford, I'd be all set. You don't happen to know him, do you?"

Bobbi laughed. "Believe me; if I knew BR Bradford, I'd be dating him."

The Coffee Corner buzzed with energy. A few regulars waved as Bobbi waited for her drink.

Claude's dreadlocks swayed to the jazz playing as he handed her the steaming cup.

This Coffee Corner, like the others, was a cozy neighborhood hub—free book exchange, open mic nights, tempting pastries, and strong Wi-Fi.

"Go get 'em, Doc," Claude said, grinning.

"Thanks." She dropped a generous tip in his jar. "Any auditions this week?"

"Tomorrow. Off-off-Broadway. If I land it, your tip might be worth more than the gig."

"Break a leg," she said warmly.

The northern wind bit through her coat as she walked toward the clinic, clutching her coffee. As much as she wanted to linger in daydreams of BR, Monday's demands pulled her back to reality.

Inside her office, Yolanda Ruiz, her manager, greeted her with a sly grin.

"Did you get a New Year's boyfriend I don't know about?"

"Wait—what?" Bobbi asked, blinking.

Yolanda pointed dramatically and launched into her trademark rapid-fire, Havana-born staccato. "Because if those flowers aren't for you, I've got a secret admirer who's gonna get very lucky later."

Bobbi turned. A stunning bouquet sat on her desk.

When she didn't answer, Yolanda huffed and walked off, clearly disappointed not to get the gossip first.

Most doctors kept a professional distance from the staff, but Bobbi was different—young, warm, and genuinely popular with the nurses. She and Yolanda sometimes grabbed drinks or met up at happy hour, so her secrecy about the flowers only deepened the mystery.

Bobbi closed her office door and opened the card tucked inside the bouquet.

To remind you of our first trip to Rome.

Smiling, Bobbi carefully placed the card into her wallet, a keepsake she intended to cherish.

~~~
## BR

When Bobbi's number flashed on his caller ID, BR excused himself from chatting with Mrs. Smith and slipped into his home office, closing the door.

"I have a quick question, you crazy man," Bobbi teased before even saying hello. "Are you planning to send me flowers after every dinner?"

"Is that what your other guys do?"

"Oh, absolutely," she replied. "My office is overflowing with bouquets from all my gentlemen callers."

"Uh-oh. I better up my game."

"You better," she sassed then softly said, "They're the most gorgeous flowers I've ever received. When did you even have time?"

"Saturday night. Right after I walked you to the car."

"Only you could get lavender and jasmine delivered on a Monday morning in January. Thank you. I love them."

"I'm glad they made you smile."

"I won't be able to text or call during the day, but I'll be thinking about you."

"Mind if I send you a note or two? I don't want the other guys to get a leg up."

She laughed. "Smart move. Talk to you later."

Still smiling, BR wandered upstairs into the vibrant thirtieth-floor workspace. The walls were painted the pale pink of Bermuda sand, with plush seafoam chairs giving the space a boutique-retreat feel—an atmosphere designed for calm collaboration.

Visitors expecting sleek minimalism were often surprised. Beyond security, twenty-five employees had personalized their desks with kid art, succulents, and travel mementos—a reflection of the company's deeply held belief in work-life balance. BR loved it, relishing everyday chats about hobbies and family.

But today, he bypassed the small talk and headed straight to the office of his longtime personal secretary, Mrs. Lincoln.

Her desk was immaculate, as always. Mrs. Lincoln scanned the room with her trademark sharp eye then rose to greet him.

"Good morning," Mrs. Lincoln chirped as BR entered. "Did you have a nice weekend?"

"I did, thank you. How are your husband and son?"

"They're doing well," she said, pleased by the question.

"I'm downstairs today unless someone needs me here," he added.

Mrs. Lincoln gave a knowing nod—he was writing and preferred not to be disturbed.

"Before I head down," he said, "I need a favor. Could you send bizcochitos to someone in Manhattan before Thursday?"

Her brow lifted slightly.

"They're the state cookie of New Mexico. I'll email you the address and note. I have no idea where to get them."

"I'll handle it," she said, already typing a reminder on her JadePad.

"Thanks. I'll check in later."

BR usually maintained strict writing discipline, but today was different. His focus kept slipping, his thoughts drifting back to Bobbi. Instead of sitting at his computer, he pulled out a sheet of manuscript paper and began sketching a tune. On a whim, he titled it "Blonde in Blue." The book would have to wait—his muse had steered him in a different direction today.

~~~

Bobbi

After ending the call, Bobbi inhaled the sweet scent of the flowers again then reread BR's note. She giggled mischievously to herself.

Oh, BR, no need to worry. The only one getting a leg up on you will be me.

She admired the bouquet, even as Yolanda coughed and announced the morning's first patient. Bobbi's thoughts lingered on the card, her pulse racing.

So you were already smitten with me, you sly man. Why didn't you tell me? The things we could have done ...

With a final glance at the flowers, Bobbi stood and prepared to tackle the day ahead, her heart lighter than it had been in weeks.

~~~

Later that night, after Sami had gone to bed, Bobbi began her familiar nighttime ritual, her thoughts already drifting toward her call with BR. She scrubbed away the day's stress, twisted her hair into a messy bun, and slipped into a white tank top and flannel PJ shorts. Before settling in, she lit the candle by her bed, its soft glow adding warmth to the room. With the shroud draped across her lap, she smoothed it affectionately, finding comfort in the peaceful order of her space.

"I swear I kept my promise—I haven't googled you," Bobbi said. "But that didn't stop my cousin. She's very protective."

BR laughed. "Did I pass?"

"Are you kidding? Gina's officially obsessed," Bobbi teased. "In a good way. I told her to keep her opinions to herself, but she knows me really well. There was one thing she wanted me to know."

"Yeah?"

"She said your main focus now isn't music or Broadway—it's philanthropy. That means a lot to me."

"Gina's right," BR said simply. "I'm not into what money can buy. I care about using it to make a real difference."

"She mentioned your foundation. That it's all about grassroots solutions—helping schools, training teachers, getting books to kids, things like that."

"That's the idea," he said, his voice warm. "We fund programs that don't just throw money at problems but actually change things long-term."

"And BR's Brigades?" she asked. "Turning fan clubs into volunteer groups? That's brilliant."

"I had fan clubs everywhere—hundreds. But I didn't want them to be about me. Sitting around dissecting lyrics or speculating about my life? No, thanks. But I saw something deeper. People wanted connection. I figured: why not build something that does real good?"

She leaned in, curious.

"So, we organized," BR said. "I wanted fans to connect—not just with me, but with each other. We created a network where they could take action in their own communities. No red tape. Just people pitching in. Lonely theater kids started mentoring; others rebuilt libraries, ran food drives, cleaned up beaches. Now there are Brigades in every state, doing real work and building real friendships. It's way more than I ever could've done on my own. And none of it can be bought. That's what makes it matter."

Bobbi exhaled, shaking her head. "I'll be honest; when I heard BR Bradford, I thought pop star, Broadway icon. I had no idea."

"Maybe it sounds idealistic, but I want to leave the world better than I found it. We're building our new headquarters in Harlem—not just an office, but something that honors the neighborhood and helps the people living there.

"Local businesses will benefit. We're working on food access—bringing in affordable grocery stores but making sure we don't push out local bodegas. We're creating jobs, mentoring students, building the most sustainable HQ in the city. There'll be on-site childcare and healthcare for our staff."

He paused. "Fame was never the goal. I just wanted to do something that mattered."

And there it was—the thing that made him different. He had every reason to be self-absorbed, but he wasn't. A perfect match for her values.

"That's incredible. Really."

He brushed off the compliment with a soft laugh, steering the conversation to her choice of working at a clinic for working-class women instead of joining a high-paying practice.

Talking to him felt easy, as if they'd known each other for years. Their conversation stretched into the night, deepening a connection she hadn't expected but already trusted.

When they finally said goodnight, the bond lingered, a bridge between two worlds growing smaller with each call.

Bobbi's last thought before sleep overtook her was simple: *I'm happy*.

~~~

BR

High above Times Square, BR's bedroom was austere, a stark space transformed by his surgeries. To ease the stiffness in his recovering shoulder, BR had put the phone on speaker and eased into the recliner by the window—the only chair in the room, and his bed, since the accident. Outside, a postcard view of Midtown Manhattan stretched before him.

When the call ended, he skipped the mild sleeping pill Dr. Melendez had prescribed. Instead, he picked up his JadePad and searched: *Dr. Bobbi Wyatt, Brooklyn Women's Health Center*.

He clicked on a photo of the smiling neurologist and stared at it until, for the first time since the surgeries in September, he fell asleep without the pill.

CHAPTER TWELVE: BR AND PT
Tuesday, January 5
BR

"Your nine o'clock is here; shall I have Ronnie bring him down?"

"Yes, please, Mrs. Lincoln."

Clad in a black and gold University of Colorado tee and sweats, BR waited in his home gym, now a physical therapy studio. The faint scent of antiseptic lingered in the air, softened only by the distant hum of Times Square traffic. Despite the city's constant motion, the room felt still and heavy with solitude and stalled progress.

For two months, he'd fought through grueling PT sessions here, battling slow gains and mounting frustration. His frozen shoulder refused to improve. The room had become a quiet witness to his lowest moments.

But after Sunday night's conversation with Bobbi, something had shifted. Just the idea of building a future with her had sparked something new—purpose.

The next morning, he sent a generous bonus and a respectful note to Tim, his former therapist. It was time to start over.

Ronnie appeared in the doorway, his broad frame backlit by hallway light.

"Good morning," BR said, rising.

"Morning," Ronnie replied. "This is Rex Yee, your new physical therapist. Rex, meet BR Bradford."

Rex stepped in with military precision. He was shorter than Ronnie by almost a foot, but his presence filled the room. His shirt strained over his biceps as he offered a firm handshake.

"Nice to meet you, Rex," BR said.

"I'll leave you guys to it," Ronnie said before disappearing down the hall.

Rex set down a backpack and pulled out a thick folder. "Mrs. Lincoln gave me a cubicle this morning. I've been reviewing all of Tim's records," he said crisply. "I can help you, if you're willing to work. I'm not here to *fix* your shoulder. I'm here to help you understand how to get better. But first, I need to understand *you*. Now, please sit down."

As BR took a seat, Rex shuffled through papers then looked up.

"Why aren't you getting better?"

BR bristled. "I ... I've been trying."

Rex didn't blink. "You're paying me. I can nod and say you're doing great, or I can tell you the truth. Which do you want?"

BR hesitated. The instinct to withdraw was strong. He'd spent a lifetime hiding the deepest parts of himself. A cold childhood had made him private and withdrawn. Fame had made him guarded. He never shared anything real in interviews, never trusted easily. His silence was a wall, and the world mistook it for mystique.

Rex wanted the truth, and after trusting Bobbi, BR realized maybe he *could* do this. Maybe he *had* to.

The decision surprised him by how quickly it had come.

"I feel like a failure," he said quietly. "I have a daughter to raise, a company that bears my name, and people I'm letting down. I'm in pain all the time. I'm not healing, and I don't know if I ever will. I'm only thirty-seven, and I've almost died twice. I can't live like this. I need help."

Rex nodded, steady. "You've accomplished more than most people do in ten lifetimes. That strength got you here. Let's use it to help you heal."

BR swallowed hard. "Yes. I want my life back."

"Good," Rex said. "Then let's set some goals. Tell me three things that'd make you feel like you're getting better."

BR took a breath. "I want to pick up my daughter again. Right now, I'm scared I'll drop her."

Rex nodded and took notes.

"Second … I *need* to sleep. Most nights, I stay in a chair because I'm afraid of rolling over wrong. If I could sleep, maybe I'd heal faster."

"Definitely," Rex said. "Third?"

BR thought of Bobbi. "I want to hug someone without wincing. Without worrying about the pain."

Rex met his eyes. "Why are you wearing that brace?"

BR blinked. "It supports the shoulder. Keeps the strain off."

"No," Rex said evenly. "It's a security blanket. It restricts movement and slows recovery. It might make you feel safer, but it's not helping."

BR stared at him, taking in the words. Then, without a word, he removed the brace and handed it over.

"Very good. I'll evaluate you now," Rex said. "Keep those three goals in mind. Eventually, you'll get full use of that arm back, and every benchmark you hit will remind you that your life *can* return to normal."

Exhausted and aching, BR didn't complain once during the grueling assessment. Then Rex made a few final notes and looked up.

"I've got good news. I know what's wrong, and it's fixable. You've healed from the original surgery, but you've developed a frozen shoulder."

"That's *good* news?" BR asked skeptically.

"The best kind," Rex said. "It's completely treatable. After major surgery, scar tissue can cause adhesions. You haven't worked through them enough, so your shoulder's locked up."

"That's it? I thought I might need another operation. How do we fix it?" His voice held both relief and urgency.

"That's what I want to hear." Rex nodded encouragingly. "I'll confirm everything with your doctor, but you've got two options. One is the standard route—physical therapy a few times a week. If you stay consistent, you'll likely have full range of motion in about three months."

"What's the other option?"

"If you're willing to push harder, I can work with you here every day for the next few weeks. It's more intense, more expensive, but it could get you there faster."

"Let's do it. I don't care about the cost."

"I'd also like to bring in some other modalities I use with athletes—hydrotherapy, electrical stimulation, and VR-assisted rehab."

"VR?" BR raised an eyebrow. "How does that help?"

"Virtual reality retrains your brain while you rebuild strength. One of your goals is to pick up your daughter. We'll simulate that experience—fifty-pound weight, her voice, her image. The goal isn't just physical; it's confidence, coordination, and connection. When your mind believes it, your body follows."

BR swallowed hard. "I miss holding her so much. It kills me that I can't comfort her the way I want to."

"Then let's get you there," Rex said. "And I want you to see someone else, as well—Lacey Rose. She's a board-certified sports acupuncturist. Her work helps speed up recovery, and I think it'll support everything we're doing here."

BR's voice rang with determination. "Let's get started."

~~~

Two hours later, drenched in sweat, BR placed a speakerphone call.

"Mrs. Lincoln, Rex Yee is coming up to see you. Prioritize his daily visits, as long as they don't interfere with taking Cassie to and from school. Reschedule everything else."

As soon as he hung up, Rex spoke, his tone firm but encouraging. "You were a beast today. I'll see you tomorrow. Follow my lead, put in the work, and I promise you'll get better. I got you."

When the door closed behind him, BR turned to the window. He thought of Cassie. Of Bobbi. Then he drew back the shades and let the winter sun flood the room.

CHAPTER THIRTEEN: RECONNECTIONS
Wednesday, January 6
Bobbi

Top o' the evening, Blondie. I'm back! How 'bout we grab a pint after work? The craic will be mighty! XX Red

Bobbi's nervous system was buzzing with anticipation for her date, now two days away. A drink with her best friend, Megan "Red" O'Malley, was just what the doctor needed!

You're BACK! Can't wait! 6:00 at the Inkwell? XX Blondie

An instant 👍 confirmed their plans.

For ten long days, Red had been off the grid, cruising around Tahiti with her parents. Despite the holiday chaos, Bobbi had missed her like crazy. Unlike Gina, whom she adored like a kid sister, Red was her equal, her confidante. Whip-smart, bold, and hilarious, she was the yin to Bobbi's yang. They always had each other's backs and never sugarcoated the truth.

Bobbi couldn't wait to see her reaction to the whirlwind turn of events.

As she packed up for the day, her mind drifted back to a Friday night two years ago—the night she'd met Megan ...

The clinic break room buzzed that afternoon with talk of weekend plans. Bobbi was well-liked, approachable, and warm, but as the youngest doctor by more than a decade, she often felt like an outsider. The older physicians were all married, and the younger nurses and PAs partied together after shifts. As a single mom, she didn't quite fit into either world.

With Sami sleeping over at her best friend Hunter's house and no desire to return to her empty home, Bobbi felt adrift.

Gino's was unassuming from the outside but boasted the most authentic gelato this side of Venice. The nearly empty gelateria exuded a nostalgic charm, with retro diner-style booths, polished chrome accents, and walls adorned with black-and-white photographs of old Brooklyn. And tonight, to Bobbi's delight, eighty-year-old Gino himself was working the counter.

Since losing his wife of fifty-three years, he'd started coming in more often, flirting shamelessly with Bobbi, who looked Scandinavian but spoke flawless Italian, even if he never quite remembered her name.

His eyes lit up when he saw her. "*Ciao, mia bella amica. Mi sei mancata. Perché non fai felice un vecchio e sposi mio nipote?*"

Bobbi replied playfully, "*Non sarebbe mai felice con me perché avrebbe saputo che tu sei l'unico uomo che potrei mai amare.*"

Gino clutched his chest dramatically. "Ah, if I could give you my heart, I would. But for tonight, how about a big cup of lemon gelato on the house, Blondie?"

Behind Bobbi, a slender redhead waited patiently, smirking. She tapped Bobbi on the shoulder. "Hey, *Blondie*, think you could bat your eyelashes at the silver fox and score me some free gelato, too? Pistachio, please."

Bobbi leaned in, laughing. Tilting her head, she rested it on her folded hands, blinking up at Gino like a cartoon princess. "Oh, *Signor Gino*," she cooed, "won't you please be nice to my new friend?"

The redhead added her prettiest smile for good measure.

Gino, basking in the attention, gave an exaggerated sigh. "Red, since you are a friend of my Blondie, how can I refuse?"

As Gino turned away to prepare their order, the redhead leaned closer to Bobbi. "What were you two saying in Italian? It sounded charming."

"He begged me to marry his grandson. I told him no because no man could ever compare to him."

Bobbi discreetly slipped twice the cost of their gelato into the tip jar, knowing Gino would pass it along to the high school kids he hired.

As they gathered their desserts and bags, Bobbi turned to her new partner in crime. "Care to join me?"

They slid into a retro Formica booth.

"Hi," Bobbi said, extending her hand. "Apparently, I'm Blondie."

"Which makes me Red. Nice to meet you."

"So, Red, why's a gorgeous girl like you eating gelato alone on a Friday night in Brooklyn?"

"Obviously, I was looking for a hot blonde to wrangle me some free gelato and ask me to sit with her," Red quipped.

Bobbi laughed. "Mission accomplished."

She studied Red—impossibly slender, effortlessly chic. A brick-red chignon, cat-eye glasses, and a polka-dot dress gave her a vintage-meets-hipster aesthetic.

They dug into their gelato. Red moaned in delight.

"What do you do, Red?"

Red's golden eyes twinkled with mischief. "Nope! I just moved to Brooklyn. You're the first person I've met, and this is the best gelato in the galaxy. Let's agree to be friends forever and never talk about work. I spend way too much time thinking about my job. But first, I bet I can guess what you do."

"Deal," Bobbi replied, clinking gelato cups. "It'd be wonderful not to think about work. But go ahead, take your best guess."

Red polished her glasses, dangling from a chain of shimmering pearls, and then appraised Bobbi coolly. "Lingerie model, but that's too obvious. You're tall, toned, and gorgeous. You're a professional wrestler!"

Bobbi snorted gelato out of her nose. She could barely speak as Red handed her a napkin from the dispenser.

"You got me," she managed to say, wiping her nose.

"I *knew* it," Red gloated. "You look like a babyface, but you're completely evil, right? You beat up a friend of mine. Thanks! *She* never got me free gelato. Now, see if you can guess what I do before we swear off talking about work forever."

"Okay," Bobbi replied. "You're smoking hot and unbelievably chic. You could be Manhattan's highest-paid escort, but I think you're the strictest Catholic school kindergarten teacher in Flatbush." Bobbi mimed a whip crack, complete with sound effects.

119

Red threw her head back and cackled at the ceiling. Bobbi pumped her fist triumphantly.

"Absolutely right, Blondie. I was Sister Red before the other nuns discovered my penchant for Fendi bags and five-inch stilettos. Now I'm *Miss* Red, 'The Terror in the Aisles' at Our Lady of Prada School."

They bantered about Red's recent move from Manhattan and their mutual passion for weight training and yoga. Their laughter and smiles lit up the room like bursts of lightning on a dark Brooklyn night.

After a while, Red sighed. "Boy trouble. Isn't that why girls eat ice cream alone on a Friday night?"

Bobbi shrugged. "Want to talk about it?"

Red hesitated then nodded. "I just went through a terrible, shattering breakup and started a rebound guy. I call him NQ."

"What?" Bobbi blinked.

"I give guys nicknames based on initials." Red noticed Bobbi's confusion and elaborated, "After my second Josh and third Tyler, it made sense to keep them straight. *NQ* stands for '*Not Quite*,'" Red explained. "Not quite good enough to be a keeper, but not quite bad enough to dump. Should I give it more time or move on?"

"Which is hurting you more: the breakup or the rebound guy?"

Red poured out her feelings, and Bobbi listened intently.

They hadn't noticed they were the last customers until Gino started wiping down the counters.

Bobbi scribbled her number on a business card.

Red grinned. "Impressive. Gorgeous Italian-speaking lady doctor by day; kickass wrestler by night? You're the total package, Dr. Bobbi." She fished a funky mother-of-pearl case from her designer purse and handed Bobbi a crimson business card embossed in Art Deco font.

Megan O'Malley, Interior Design

"That's so cool!" Bobbi exclaimed. "I'm useless at anything aesthetic. Do you run your own business?"

Red waggled her finger. "No work talk, remember? But my job is great. I handle interior design for an amazing company—sometimes offices, sometimes executives' homes. My boss is phenomenal."

As they reached the door, Red hugged Bobbi tightly. "Let's do this again soon," she whispered.

Their friendship deepened into what is was today.

Now, racing home to change, Bobbi followed Red's strict "no ponytails" rule. She twisted her hair into an elegant halo, swapped her plain top for a soft sweater, packed her potential date-night outfit in a bag, and hurried downstairs to meet her Lyft.

They arrived at The Inkwell at the same time.

Bobbi flew into her arms for a long hug. "Oh, Red, I missed you."

"Same! I haven't seen you since *last year*. Ten days without you? I went through withdrawals. How's Rugrat?"

"She's awesome. Said to say hi. Dad's helping her build a diorama."

They linked arms and found a cozy table. When they removed their coats, a dozen men turned to stare. Megan looked incredible in a winter-white wool dress and faux ruby jewelry that looked anything but fake.

"I want to hear all about your cruise," Bobbi said, "but I'm bursting with news."

Megan's perfectly arched brows shot up. "You're absolutely glowing. And wanting wine on a Wednesday? You definitely met a guy."

Bobbi's beaming smile was her answer.

"Yes!" Megan cheered. "Tell me everything. But first, let's toast. Asti Spumante on me."

"I'll get it." Bobbi walked to the bar.

She returned with two glasses and leaned in. "Cute guy, maroon sweater, table under the poster to your left. Totally checking you out."

Megan flipped open her mother-of-pearl compact to "check her lipstick." Her eyes sparkled. "Nice. But right now? I want to hear about *your* guy. What do we call him?"

"I knew you'd ask. He's 'MP.'"

"MP ... MP ..." Megan mused. "Let me guess ... because he has a massive—" She spread her hands far apart.

Bobbi flicked her. "I don't know. I haven't seen it—"

"*Yet*." Megan grinned. "What does MP stand for?"

"Maybe Perfect."

She told the story, carefully omitting his name and profession. Bobbi had promised BR she'd protect his privacy, and she meant it, even with her best friend. Megan would understand, but the rest of the world might not. It was too new. He was too big.

Red beamed. "I'm so happy for you. You've listened to *me* talk about guys for years. It's definitely your turn."

When Bobbi finished recounting their latest text exchange, she returned to the bar.

"A second drink on a work night?" Megan teased. "What's this man done to you?"

"That's why I took a Lyft. I wanted to drink wine and tell you everything. I missed you so much."

"So, let me get this straight—MP is hot, employed, sweet, smart, loves kids, and completely focused on you. Just tell me he's rich, and I'll go pick out a bridesmaid dress."

Bobbi wrinkled her nose and gave a bashful smile.

Megan's jaw dropped. She crossed herself dramatically. "Saints be praised."

"Red, I've got the whim-whams."

"The what now?"

"The whim-whams—that's what my mom calls it. When your head's dizzy, your heart flutters—"

"—and your lady parts start chiming in?" Megan added with a smirk.

Bobbi nodded, lips twitching.

Megan's laugh bounced off the walls. She raised her glass. "Happy New Year, love. And happy love in the New Year."

"To us both," Bobbi said. "Happy New Year."

They clinked glasses.

"I need your help," Bobbi admitted. "Since you weren't around, I had to pick my first-date outfit on my own. I started with a skirt of Gina's—it might be too short—but I tried to channel you for the rest. You're the only one who'll tell me the truth about how I look."

"You read my mind. I figured we'd need a shopping trip. Did you bring a picture?"

"No, I brought the outfit." She patted her bag. "I'm going to try it on. Tell me if it's too much."

"Perfect!"

A few minutes later, Bobbi stepped out of the washroom wearing a stunning blue top, tweed miniskirt, stockings, and heels.

"What do you think? Too short? Too tight?"

Megan grabbed a napkin and wrote a giant *10* in lipstick, holding it high like an Olympic judge.

A few men applauded. Bobbi blushed, smiling despite herself.

"Blondie, that's not an outfit—it's a *weapon*. You wear that to dinner, and you'd better pack a toothbrush and fresh panties."

Bobbi didn't object when Megan stood and undid another button, revealing more cleavage.

"You'll need a prettier bra. Black underwire. Smile!"

Bobbi posed; Megan snapped a photo.

"I'll use this to pick out perfect accessories. I'll bring them tomorrow. We'll skip yoga; get mani-pedis. Bring Rugrat. I got her a little present from Tahiti."

They sat again. As Bobbi settled into her chair, her skirt inched higher. She reached to tug it down, but Megan playfully slapped her hand away.

"You said he loves your legs. Blondie, he'll be so obsessed you two might skip dessert. Better plan to send Rugrat to your mom's."

CHAPTER FOURTEEN: ALMOST
Wednesday, January 6 – Thursday, January 7
BR

On Wednesday, Bobbi shared a story from early in her career about a man she'd dated who'd asked her to work less so that she'd be more available to him.

"I'd never put you in a position like that," BR promised.

"Sweetie, you can put me in any position you want," she murmured, her voice warm and sleepy.

BR snorted.

A beat passed, and then there was the sound of her lightly smacking her forehead. "That's not what I meant."

He waited.

"I meant, I'd always want to know what position *you* wanted me in."

He laughed again.

"I'd say goodnight," Bobbi mumbled, "but it's hard to talk with my foot in my mouth. I'm getting a mani-pedi tomorrow, so at least next time I stick my foot in there, my toes will look pretty. Goodnight, sweet man."

~~~

BR woke up with a jolt of energy. After praying, he sent Bobbi a good morning text, checked his email, showered, shaved, and woke Cassie with a song. He then utterly failed at another attempt to braid her hair before dropping her off at school.

Rex was already waiting in the PT room for a double session.

Two exhausting hours later, both men were covered in sweat.

"You're blowing me away, man," Rex said. "I've never seen anyone work this hard. You've already crushed the goals we set for the *first week*—and it's only day two."

After noon, Dr. Melendez greeted BR with a tray of bizcochitos and a warm smile.

"BR, I wasn't serious about the bet. But thanks for the cookies."

As BR bit into the star-shaped New Mexico treat, the crisp texture and warm cinnamon raised bittersweet memories of Alicia Rodriguez, his former singing partner, now retired and battling serious health issues in Sedona.

He set a voice reminder on his JadePhone: "Reach out to Alicia."

Settling onto the couch with a more relaxed posture, BR caught Dr. Melendez watching him with her usual keen eye.

"I assume the bizcochitos mean you asked Bobbi out and she said yes?"

"Yes. Tomorrow," he said, smiling. "I'm thrilled. But that's not what I want to talk about."

She clicked her pen and tilted her head. "Oh? What's on your mind?"

"I had a breakthrough this week. I think it's time we change how we're working together."

She adjusted the Navajo blanket on her lap. "Go on."

"You've been amazing, Dr. M. When I first walked in here, I was a mess. Thanks to you, I understand more about my relationship with the family who adopted me. I've made progress on my claustrophobia and agoraphobia. But ... I haven't dealt with the hardest part.

"There's a part of me I've kept hidden. I care too much about how people see me—even you—so I've avoided being completely vulnerable. We need to talk about the bombing and my near-death experience. I'm terrified."

Without a word, Dr. Melendez handed him the Kleenex box.

"I can't stay stuck," he said quietly. "How do I live with nearly dying—twice? I've been lucky and successful, but I'm still ... unhappy. And I hate myself for it. I feel ungrateful."

"It's *not* ridiculous," she said gently. "If money solved everything, there wouldn't be therapists working overtime on the Upper West Side. You've got to accept the pain along with the progress. You've built a foundation that changes lives. Your work brings people joy and comfort. That matters. You're not done yet. We've still got work to do, but you're smart, compassionate, and full of integrity. I'm here. You're safe."

BR took a few moments to steady himself. "Thank you," he said at last. "I never meant to be famous or rich—it just happened. Maybe it was God's plan for me to give away a billion dollars. But I've made so much I can't give it away fast enough. And I still feel empty. Saying that makes me sound like some 'poor little rich boy.'"

127

"BR," she said softly but firmly, "you're not defined by your wealth *or* your awards. I think we've reached a turning point. Over the last few months, I've seen a man trying to be a light in the world. Your family didn't nurture your talent or your emotions. Things fall apart, but they can be rebuilt. Let's work on that."

They talked through changes to the rhythm of their sessions. Then BR added, "My new physical therapist is phenomenal. I'm making real progress. I'm starting to feel hopeful."

"That's wonderful. You look better. No more brace?"

"No more security blanket," he said with a small smile. "I didn't talk about Bobbi much today because ... honestly? She's the *least* stressful part of my life. We talk every night, and the connection keeps getting deeper. I could rave about how amazing she is, but anything I say would be an understatement."

Dr. Melendez smiled and softly clapped. "BR, I hope the date is everything you're hoping for. Just remember: be generous. Not with your money—that's easy for you. Be generous with yourself. Let her see *you*."

As soon as he got home, BR finished the intense exercises that Rex had prescribed. Pushing himself so hard was precisely what BR needed to pull out of the emotional funk. Rex knew what he was doing—not just with physical therapy, but with treating BR's wounded spirit.

Cassie's high spirits after school reflected her father's joy. Despite her gentle shyness, she was popular among her peers and adored by her teachers. Miss Sarah Jane discussed Cassie's placement for the next year with BR, explaining that she was researching kindergartens with programs for advanced students.

At four forty-five, Bobbi texted:

Wow! So exciting that Cassie's teacher is finding accelerated programs for her. Sorry for the late reply; swamped at the clinic, as usual. Off to get my mani-pedi. Still trying to get the taste of my foot out of my mouth. XX

Then, at five forty-five, Anna Maria sent a text.

Hey, Unc. Confirming tomorrow. Siobhán and I will get Cassie from school and take care of her.

Thanks, kiddo. Cassie's excited. I appreciate it.

Going out on a weekend night twice in one week? Hot date?

For all she knew, her uncle had never been on a date in the seven years since she had moved to New York.

Yes. 👍

Anna Maria replied with a 😊

Cassie and Howard, her beloved moose, teamed up to beat BR at several rounds of Concentration. Without hesitation, BR scooped them both up and carried them to the library for their reading hour. All the VR practice with Rex had paid off—BR was elated to his core.

"Daddy, we like it when you carry us like you used to," Cassie squealed in happy surprise, snuggling closer.

"I'm always happy to give you both a lift," BR replied, his heart swelling at her joy.

"Will you read more from *Tom Sawyer*? Howard and I wanna hear more about the treasure on Jackson Island."

Later, with Cassie and Howard sound asleep, BR iced his shoulder and awaited Bobbi's text. Soon enough, she texted:

> *We just got home. Sami and I went for gelato after our mani-pedis, so my toes look pretty, and my tummy's happy. I'm not sure when I'll be free to talk on Friday; I have a date.*

~~~

Bobbi's Day

Exhaustion overpowered Bobbi. She'd meant to text Red about her scandalous slip of the tongue, but she'd fallen asleep with the lights on. Two hours later, she jolted awake when a car backfired just below her window. Groaning, Bobbi pulled the shroud over her head. She vaguely realized she'd been dreaming something about Cassie.

~~~

"Why are you humming?" Yolanda asked as Bobbi pored over her first chart.

"Was I humming?" she responded absentmindedly.

"You were. Where's your coffee? Was your cute barista off duty?"

Bobbi looked up, shocked. She'd been so immersed in her thoughts of BR that she hadn't stopped for a Bobbi Blend for the first time in forever.

~~~

With Sami navigating, Bobbi drove to Red's new favorite salon, Nice & Naughty Nails.

"It looks cool, Mom. Thanks for letting me get a manicure!" Sami exclaimed.

"Thank Red. It was her idea," Bobbi replied.

"She's the best, even though she calls me Rugrat," Sami said with a smile.

The salon buzzed with vibrant colors and lively chatter, its eclectic décor a testament to the creative flair of the Mongolian sisters, Katie and Noreen, who ran it. Nice & Naughty was a funky haven for self-expression and bold beauty transformations.

As Bobbi checked in, Megan swept inside, hugging Sami. Instantly, Noreen excused herself from a client to greet them.

There's more than one superstar in my life. Bobbi chuckled to herself.

"Noreen, meet my best friend, Dr. Bobbi Wyatt, and her daughter, Rugrat."

After shooting Megan a death stare, Sami corrected, "Hi, I'm Sami."

"Nice to meet you, Sami. Daisy will take care of you now." She then looked at Megan. "Katie and I will be with you and Dr. Bobbi shortly," Noreen chirped before returning to her client.

Sami happily followed Daisy to her station. Watching them, Bobbi sighed deeply, struck by how mature Sami seemed. *Please stop growing up so fast.*

Megan and Bobbi settled into a loveseat in the waiting area. With a flourish, Megan produced three small gift bags. "This coral one's for Rugrat. Since she loves Hawaiian shirts, I got her a bracelet made from shells I found. I even took a picture as the artist made it right in front of me on the beach in Tahiti."

"She'll love it," Bobbi cooed, touched.

When four women sat near them, Megan discreetly lowered her voice. "This bag's for you. I know the most fabulous lingerie boutique in Soho. It's a deep-cut, black push-up bra for tomorrow night. The gift receipt's in there."

"Red, you're amazing. I'll try it on tonight and Venmo you the money."

Megan ignored the remark. "Blondie, I missed you so much. The cruise with my mom was great, but I kept thinking of all the fun we'd be having. You and I, sharing a cabin, relaxing in bikinis by day and dancing the night away? Heaven."

Bobbi sighed wistfully and nodded in agreement.

"I got you these blue Tahitian pearl drop earrings. Talk about good karma—they'll complement that stunning blue silk top perfectly."

Bobbi gasped then quickly swapped out her plain earrings for the pearls.

Megan clucked with approval. "Perfect."

Bobbi hugged her. "*Of course*, they're perfect—*you* picked them out."

Finally, Megan handed Bobbi a small, velvet-lined box. "I got one more present for you," she said, her voice intimate.

Bobbi opened the box to find a delicate antique gold chain with a mesmerizing emerald pendant.

"Your mother's gorgeous necklace," Bobbi said, astonished.

"It's always brought me good luck."

Bobbi's eyes welled up. She lifted her hair as Megan carefully clasped the necklace around her neck.

"The emerald matches your eyes perfectly." Megan adjusted the chain so the jewel dipped into Bobbi's cleavage. "I love how it accentuates the girls. This'll seal the deal. Now, how do you plan to wear your hair?"

Bobbi rolled her eyes. "Does it matter what *I* think? I'm sure you've already got a plan."

Megan showed Bobbi a photo on her phone. "You clip your hair up at the back, add a few waves, and let it cascade over one shoulder. Add some wispy bangs to frame your face. The effect will make you look long and lean while framing your world-class rack. What do you think?"

"I think you're a genius. That'll look fantastic."

"Great. Are you nervous?"

"No. We've talked every night for hours. It doesn't feel like a first date; it feels more like the tenth. Strangely, I'm only worried about one thing."

"What's that?"

"I'm crushing hard. But what if the sexual chemistry is just in my head? Like, what if I see him in person and there's no spark?"

"That's easy."

"*Easy*? In what universe is that easy?"

"Blondie, within two minutes, you'll know if you have major league whim-whams or not. If you do, full speed ahead. If not, you develop a convenient headache. Text me. I'll scoop you up, we'll go to Gino's and order our weight in gelato, then eat it at my place in our comfiest pajamas, watching a rom-com and booing every time they kiss."

~~~

After dropping off Red, Bobbi returned home, exhausted. She called Gina, who was uncharacteristically too tired to chat much.

"I can't wait to see how gorgeous you look tomorrow night, Bobs. I reminded Adriana to reserve that quiet booth in the back corner for you. Are you *sure* I can't just *accidentally* drop by the restaurant to meet BR Bradford?" Gina snickered.

"It's hard to tell who's worse: you or your nutty niece. She keeps threatening to do the same thing." Bobbi laughed.

After she brushed her teeth, Bobbi was distracted by one last nagging task. She pulled out her date night outfit and slipped it on, including the bra and jewelry from Megan. After checking herself in the full-length mirror, Bobbi yipped and dove for her phone.

"Blondie, everything okay?" Megan's voice came through muffled.

"Red, I just tried on the outfit. It's a killer, but there are two *big* problems."

"What's wrong?"

"The bra isn't fully lined. My 'wind chill indicators' are poking through the top. What do I do?"

Megan guffawed. "Tell Marco to crank up the AC!"

"That won't help," Bobbi muttered.

"Your date will think otherwise." Megan crowed triumphantly.

For the first time, Bobbi noticed the background hum of a bustling bar. "Wait—where are you?" she asked.

"I'm having a drink with the maroon sweater guy from the Inkwell," Megan revealed.

Bobbi's cheeks flushed. "I'm so sorry. Get back to him *right now*! Text me with a report."

"Will do. Have fun tomorrow. Don't do anything I wouldn't do."

Bobbi giggled. "That doesn't exactly limit me much."

"Not a lick," Red teased before she disconnected.

After she crawled into bed, Bobbi texted a goodnight note to BR.

> *I can't wait to see you! But if you want your date to be a fun, chatty, pretty girl who doesn't ruin her makeup by falling asleep in her minestrone, she MUST sleep tonight. Please just leave me a voice message and tell me you're thinking about me. Sweet dreams, sweetie.*

Bobbi's phone chirped almost immediately. She let it go straight to voicemail. Drowsy, burrowed deep under the shroud, she listened to BR's message.

"If I called every time I thought about you, your voicemail would be full, and I'd be unemployed. You've made this week one of the happiest of my life. Tomorrow will just be a continuation of our conversations, except that I'll see your beautiful smile. I can't wait. Sleep now, and not in your minestrone."

BR's beautiful baritone echoed in her ears, and warmth spread through Bobbi's chest, soothing her tired mind. After a contented sigh, she immediately fell into a deep sleep.

CHAPTER FIFTEEN: DATE DAY
Friday, January 8
Bobbi

Marco's jaw dropped when Bobbi removed her checkered wool overcoat and fluffed her hair. "Bobbi … you look *hot*. Maybe I shouldn't say that since you're basically my sister-in-law, but you're a total babe."

"Thanks." Bobbi beamed. "Your opinion means a lot. After all, you managed to bag and tag my hottie cousin."

"The best thing that ever happened to me." Careful not to smudge her makeup, Marco warmly hugged Bobbi.

Bobbi loved Luna Azur. Marco and Gina had sunk every dollar they had and every dollar they could borrow into the cozy, rustic restaurant. The decor was simple, but the food was fabulous. The exposed brick walls, warm Edison bulbs, weathered wooden tables, and wax candles created an inviting atmosphere. The air carried the tantalizing scent of fresh bread and simmering sauces.

Despite seemingly being just a neighborhood hole-in-the-wall near the Brooklyn Heights Promenade, the glowing reviews from local influencers, Google, and Yelp kept the place busy. Against all odds, Luna Azur consistently made a small profit.

"I've gotta get back to the kitchen, but my wife threatened me with ice cubes down my shorts in my sleep if I didn't send her a picture of you."

Bobbi shivered in solidarity. "Not Gina's Glacial Gambit! I've been the victim of that more than once. Save yourself; take a picture." She posed against an interior brick backdrop, which beautifully complemented her long, golden hair.

Before Marco returned to work, Bobbi gave him Megan's number, asking that he send the shot to her and separately to the Wyatt family group chat. Almost instantly, Bobbi's phone started chirping.

Red's text was first.

> 🙊 *Sex on a stick!* 🙊 *If this guy isn't blind, he'll be blown away!* 👗 100%

Bobbi responded:

> 💜 *He's not blind, just nearsighted.* 👀 *Guess I'll have to get closer to make an impression.* 😊

> 🤩 *If you get too close, your high beams will definitely make an impression on him.* 😵

Next, Gina texted:

HOME RUN!! Marco said the temperature in the restaurant went up 10° when you came in. Have fun!

The next text came from Sami's best friend's, Hunter, phone.

Aunt Gina sent us the picture. You look so beautiful! Are you SURE I can't come over to meet BR Bradford?

I'm 100% sure, baby. Have fun at Hunter's.

The last text contained the greatest compliment.

Dr. Daughter, you look so much like your mother that it takes my breath away. Have a wonderful time tonight. Love you, Dad.

Bobbi was so engrossed in her phone that she hadn't realized Adriana was escorting BR through the restaurant—she'd reserved a rear corner table, hoping to keep BR Bradford out of view—until he was suddenly standing right in front of her.

The awkwardness of their in-person parting last Saturday evaporated. Without hesitating, he opened his arms, and Bobbi melted into them.

The "Bobbi Bubble" was back, stronger than before.

The hug felt like it went on forever, but it was over too soon, as far as Bobbi was concerned.

Marco walked over to the table to shake hands with BR before they were even seated.

Surreptitiously, Bobbi texted Red:

WHIM-WHAMS!

She heard BR respond, "The pleasure's all mine. Bobbi's raved about you and your fantastic food."

"Anything she told you that was positive is one hundred percent true."

"What's your specialty? What should I absolutely not miss?" BR asked.

"Bobbi said you had the Chinese chef cook special for you the other night. I'd love to do the same. Just tell me what ingredients you like, and I'll go off the menu."

"I know exactly what I want," Bobbi cheered. "Do you remember that amazing fish you made for Gina's back-to-school dinner?"

"Great choice. That was *Salsa di Acciughe e Capperi.* I've got some beautiful sea bass. And for you, BR?"

"My mind's racing. I love shellfish and pasta. What do you suggest, Chef?"

Marco smiled. "How about *Spaghetti alle Tre Delizie del Mare*?"

Bobbi translated, "Spaghetti with three seafood delights."

"*Perfetto*, Bobbi." Marco beamed.

"*Grazie*, Marco."

"How does this sound, BR? Shrimp, scallops, and mussels sautéed in garlic, cherry tomatoes, and white wine, tossed with spaghetti, parsley, and parmesan. I think you'll love it."

"Sold."

Bobbi desperately wanted to be alone with BR, but there was something she needed—a quiet way to see where they were at.

"Would it be okay if Marco took a picture of us? Our first official date?"

"Absolutely. We *have* to have that."

Bobbi sat at the table, right arm resting on the linen, eyes twinkling, hair cascading dramatically over one shoulder. BR stood behind her and, to her surprise and delight, reached down and held her hand. Marco took the photo at that exact moment, capturing the forever smiles of a couple falling in love.

"Please, send it to me." BR gave Marco his number.

Bobbi added, "*Only* send it to Gina and Dad. Ask them not to share it."

When Marco stepped away, BR turned to her. "Bobbi, you look sensational. I'm a writer, but words are failing me."

She winked. "This old thing?" She glanced down at herself with a smirk. "Had it forever. Just threw it on."

Their server, Jacqy, arrived and took their drink orders. Bobbi asked for a glass of Marco's hand-squeezed lemonade. BR requested San Pellegrino.

Finally alone, Bobbi asked, "So, when did you learn to tap dance?"

BR held a hand to his chest as a deep laugh escaped. "That may be the weirdest first date question ever."

"It's not our first date. It's our *next* date. We probably know each other better than couples who've gone out for months."

"True. Meeting Marco felt like reconnecting with someone I already knew. You're right; this *is* our next date. And I'm already looking forward to the one after it."

"Me, too. Tonight, I just want to sit across from you and enjoy it. It's been less than a week, but it feels like a year since I saw you. So, how'd you learn to tap?"

"I picked it up at work. Do you like dancing?"

"No way, pal." She wagged a finger. "You did this all week. I ask a question, and you turn it back on me. Not tonight. I want to know everything about *you*."

BR smiled. "Sorry, reflex. I'd much rather listen to you, but I promised to be open.

"When my first musical, *Sock Hop*, was rehearsing, one of the supporting actors had to drop out. The character had a big song and several dance numbers. The director asked me to step in until they could recast. I already had rhythm from playing music, so I worked nonstop with our associate choreographer.

"There was a moment when my character spontaneously joins his love interest in a tap routine. It brought down the house every night. I worked my butt off to learn it. My partner was incredible. We kept pushing to make the number faster and more exciting. Audiences loved it—totally unexpected in a 1950s rock musical. Now tell me: do you like to dance?"

"Red and I go out dancing all the time—for fun—but I don't really *know* how to do it. Someday, I'd love to learn ballroom. It's so romantic."

Jacqy laid out a trio of appetizers: a shrimp cocktail, crab-stuffed mushrooms for BR, and a caprese platter. Knowing Marco's sense of humor, Bobbi was relieved he hadn't sent oysters.

When Bobbi excused herself to go to the ladies' room, BR stood. She wobbled slightly in her heels, and BR placed a hand on her hip to steady her, though the effect was just the opposite.

Bobbi's phone had been vibrating nonstop. The only text she looked at was from Red. Her response to Bobbi's note about having the whim-whams was:

Bobbi responded:

Their salads arrived. Around them, the restaurant buzzed with a dozen conversations, but Bobbi didn't notice. The bubble had closed around them.

Between bites, the conversation moved effortlessly from Bobbi's intense workout routine to BR's uncanny gift for playing anything by ear.

Marco's soups were sensational, but nothing compared to the entrées. BR fed Bobbi a bite of his pasta—garlicky and rich—and her eyes sparkled. The sea bass was perfection.

Marco checked in briefly. "My sous chef's covering so I could cook your dishes myself."

BR smiled. "I've eaten all over Italy. I've never had anything this good. You should put it on the menu."

Bobbi added her own praise, but Marco was already racing back to the kitchen.

Meanwhile, her phone buzzed constantly—Marco, no doubt, updating the family group chat.

"BR," she said, "this feels so natural … and somehow surreal. I haven't even told Red you're my date. Only my immediate family knows. They can't believe I'm dating you."

"I understand why."

She raised an eyebrow. "*Really*? And why's that, Mr. Bradford?"

"Because you're so far out of my league we're not even playing the same sport, Dr. Wyatt. You're major league MVP. I'm JV cross-country at a middle school. I still don't know why you said yes."

He looked at her, steady now. "You dazzle me. You're brilliant. An amazing mom, daughter, cousin, friend. I bet your patients adore you. You spend your life making people's lives better. I can't say the same for myself."

"You're sweet," Bobbi murmured. "But I'm just a single mom from Brooklyn with a good job and a great family."

She hesitated then added, "I don't know much about your career. Gina mentioned that you're … close … with Alicia Rodriguez and Aurora Bellucci—two of the most glamorous women on the planet. I imagine lots of women throw themselves at you. What am *I* doing here? You could have anyone."

He didn't flinch. "Ask me anything, and I'll tell you the truth. Alicia and Rory are friends and collaborators—nothing romantic. Ever."

The way he said *ever* eased her doubts.

"I've never been married. Never been in love. I haven't been on a date in seven years. I'm here because I want to be with *you*." His voice shifted. "People obsess over celebrities. It's all surface. What *you* do actually matters. My work's just … visible."

Bobbi didn't respond right away. She studied him, this man who could command stadiums and stages, now speaking to her with quiet sincerity. No flattery, no pretense.

Men noticed her. BR *saw* her. And instead of being intimidated by her intellect, he admired it. And he was offering her something rare: presence. Honesty.

Bobbi reached out and brushed his cheek. He swallowed hard.

"I don't see a rock star billionaire," she said. "I see a man taking on the world with so much love in his heart. Not many guys would take in their niece after what she went through. You say you worry about being a good parent, but Cassie is clearly surrounded by love. Your career's impressive, but it's who you are that brought me here tonight."

Nearby, Adriana could no longer keep the nearest table empty. Jacqy arrived with dessert menus, but Bobbi declined.

BR insisted on picking up the check. Bobbi didn't protest—being on a real date felt glorious. She smiled as he scribbled a thank-you on the receipt and left a massive tip.

"The weather's so warm for January," she said. "Want to walk along the Promenade with me? I'm dying to be alone with you."

"I can't think of anything I'd enjoy more. Did you drive?"

"No," she replied, brushing hair from her face with a playful smile. "I took a Lyft. I think I can trust you to get me home safely. But not just yet."

CHAPTER SIXTEEN: WALKING TO THE FUTURE
BR

Just two blocks from Luna Azur, the Brooklyn Heights Promenade beckoned. Under a golden moon and a gentle western breeze, they relished the fresh air and the sheer joy of being together. The unseasonably mild night had coaxed couples from their post-holiday hibernation, and BR and Bobbi joined the quiet stream, her arm looped easily through his as they strolled down Orange Street.

BR hadn't expected tonight to feel this easy, this natural. After all their late-night conversations, he thought he knew her—her warmth, her wit, the way her mind worked. But this? Walking beside her, hearing her laugh, feeling the gentle weight of her arm tucked into his—this was something else entirely. It felt right.

She cooed, "I hope we can take a lot of walks like this. Especially if they include a stop at Coffee Corner."

"I should probably tell you ... I don't like coffee," he said matter-of-factly.

Bobbi stopped in her tracks, like he'd confessed to something criminal. She pulled her arm away, staring at him with mock outrage. "What do you mean you don't like coffee? How did I not know this? Honestly, I might not have gone out with you if you'd told me." She planted her hands on her hips, eyes sparkling. "How can you *not* like coffee? I'm so serious about it I've taught the barista at *every* Coffee Corner I've ever visited how to make the Bobbi Blend.

BR's heart felt light. This side of her—the playful indignation, the sparkle, the energy—he hadn't seen over the phone. Standing here now, watching her pretend to be scandalized over something so small, so perfectly her, he realized just how completely he'd fallen for her.

"If it helps, I like hot chocolate," he offered, fully aware it wouldn't.

She didn't miss a beat. "Grab a ladder," she said. "You've dug a deep hole for yourself. Hot chocolate is to coffee what lemonade is to champagne. You'd better explain—*now*."

"I *love* the smell of coffee. I just can't stand the taste. Anything coffee-flavored makes me gag. But I'll happily buy you coffee anytime you want."

"I'm an open-minded woman," she said with mock solemnity. "I could date someone from another country … maybe even, if he were truly extraordinary, a Yankees fan. But *no coffee*? That might be a dealbreaker."

"Chicago Cubs, actually," he added, bracing himself.

She threw up her hands. "This is too much! Do you have any other disgraceful secrets before I agree to walk any farther with you?"

"I don't like olives," he admitted, laughing. "Shall I leave now?"

Her reply was swift and affectionate—she reconnected their arms. "No, you just helped yourself. More for me when we share a salad."

They stepped onto the promenade, pausing to take in the breathtaking Manhattan skyline.

"This view never gets old," Bobbi whispered, leaning lightly against him.

BR smiled, his gaze drifting toward the horizon. "I love it here. My first book, *The Winter Crossing*, about the Battle of Trenton, has a chapter on the Battle of Brooklyn Heights." Earlier that week, he had mentioned how he'd once planned to be a history teacher—a goal that had led him to start his doctorate at Columbia and one he'd quietly kept alive. "Brooklyn Heights was one of my favorite spots to research."

Bobbi turned to face him, her eyes glowing with curiosity and a bit of wonder. "Do you ever think maybe we crossed paths before? You know, before Rome?"

He tilted his head, considering. "I've thought about that. I played gigs with Alicia at a club near the University of Chicago, and I stayed in Chicago for a month when *Sock Hop* had its tryout run." He took a long, thoughtful pause. "But somehow, I think the Universe always meant for us to meet in front of *2:29*."

Bobbi sighed dreamily. He wondered if he should kiss her but realized they were in the way of a couple trying to take a selfie.

"Back to coffee," he nudged, curiosity piqued. "How'd the Bobbi Blend come to be?"

Bobbi smiled at the memory. "Funny story. During undergrad in Chicago, Coffee Corner became my second home. I lived on caffeine, Cap'n Crunch, and bananas while studying. One super cute barista was always looking for a reason to chat me up. One day, they got creative and made a drink just for me. I wanted something special. That barista spent the whole afternoon perfecting it."

"And? Did his move work?"

She flicked an imaginary speck from his jacket, eyes gleaming. "I never said the barista was a guy."

BR's laughter was immediate. He muffled it with his hand, trying not to disturb a nearby hipster couple mid-kiss. "Seems I'm not the only one full of surprises tonight."

"Gina mentioned you're the main investor in Coffee Corner. If you don't even like coffee, what's the appeal?"

"Janelle Christiansen's vision. Organic, responsibly sourced coffee. A welcoming space for the community. Fresh pastries from local bakeries. Support for women entrepreneurs. I couldn't say no."

Bobbi raised a brow. "So, you're a hands-off investor? Any chance I can get a discount?"

"I'm sure I could make that happen." He laughed. "Janelle handles operations. I just shaped the ethos—no stomping on local businesses, strong environmental policies, and every store includes a free lending library to support reading and writers. All my profits from Coffee Corner go straight to my charitable foundation. Every Bobbi Blend helps make the world a little better."

"I like that."

"I also insisted we serve the world's best hot chocolate. Next time you're there, check the board for the Beautiful Rhythm Hot Chocolate. That was my little touch. Beautiful Rhythm—BR. Get it?"

Bobbi's laughter lit up the night. "We both inspired secret menu items? That's just perfect."

At the end of the promenade, they stepped into the park, where benches basked under the glow of overhead heaters. Nearby, a street singer strummed a guitar, covering "Not This Time."

Bobbi applauded when he finished. "Wow, that's a fantastic song."

"Thanks. It won me a Grammy."

Bobbi groaned and dramatically hung her head.

The singer launched into another song.

"Did you write this one, too?" she asked.

"Nope. This was written by John Lennon and Paul McCartney. Early 1960s."

Bobbi cracked up. Her laughter rang through the crisp air. She held out her hands, palms up. "Please, lend me your ladder—I'm the one who's dug a hole now."

When she caught her breath, Bobbi asked, "Do you like the singer?"

BR whispered, "His guitar's a little out of tune, and he's not singing in the same key he's playing in. But he's got something. He just needs training." He waved and dropped a twenty into the open case.

They took a seat under one of the heaters.

Bobbi rubbed her hands together. "That was a generous tip, considering you weren't impressed."

"He's trying. Playing in the cold's tough, and it never hurts to encourage someone. I know it's getting late, but I have an idea—"

"That's Hunter's ringtone, so it's Sami," Bobbi said, reaching for her phone that had interrupted him. "I'm sorry."

BR gestured toward a nearby table. "Want me to …?"

"Don't you *dare*. I want every minute with you I can get. I'll be quick."

BR could only hear her side of the call.

"Everything okay?"

"Yeah, he's okay ... I guess." She winked at BR. "I've had worse dates, believe it or not." A pause. "I'll call you later when I'm on my way." Another pause. "Don't worry; I'll tell him."

She hung up. "Sami's so sorry for interrupting. She and Hunter are taking a safe babysitting class tomorrow morning. Her mom can't take them, so I'll swing by after you drop me off and scoop them up."

"Got it. Actually, I was about to ask if your favorite gelato place is still open?"

"Gino's? Yes! It stays open all winter. Can your driver take us there? Gelato with you sounds perfect."

"What if Ronnie drives us to pick up Sami and Hunter and we all go together?"

"Stop." Her voice was soft, but the shift was immediate. Her hand came to rest gently on his chest. "Can I say something important?"

"Of course," he said, surprised.

Bobbi sat a little straighter on the bench, folding her hands loosely in her lap. The lightness in her voice was gone, replaced by calm seriousness. Not cold—just focused. "You were being considerate and sweet—I love that about you— but meeting Sami tonight would change things for me. We've been calling this our first 'official' date, and I had so much fun getting dressed up just for you. But I think it's more than that. We've already spent—what—almost twenty hours talking since we met six days ago. You wouldn't be doing that unless you believed this could be something real."

"I do," he said quietly. And he meant it.

"Neither would I."

Her response allowed him to breathe again.

"Sami's my whole world. She's *never* met anyone I've dated, not one. If she meets you tonight, she'll assume you and I are serious." Her voice stayed even, but he heard the weight behind it.

"It's not that I don't want you to meet her—I do, more than you know. But, for me, meeting her isn't casual. It's a big step in my relationship with her. And I want you and I to be sure what that means—that we're on the same page."

He took her hand. "I trust your instincts. When it comes to parenting, you lead. I understand. I can't wait for our next date, and the one after that. Just … consider where I'm coming from?"

She gave a tiny nod.

"You know I take parenting seriously. But if I were just after fun with a gorgeous genius, I'd have suggested a little adult time after dinner, instead of gelato with your kid."

That got a laugh.

"We're new. But this is real. I think about you constantly. Sami's the biggest part of your life. I just want to start the clock on knowing her, too."

Bobbi covered her face with her gloved hands then buried her head against his chest and began to cry. "You really care about me," she whispered.

A policeman walked over. "Everything okay, miss?"

Bobbi sat up straight. Her eyes were red, and her shoulders were shaking.

A group of onlookers increased the chances that someone would recognize BR and take their picture, so she offered an inspired fib.

Barely audibly, Bobbi replied, "I'm fine. I've never been happier. He just proposed." She beamed at the policeman. "A bit of privacy, and I might just get my ring!"

The policeman clapped BR on the shoulder, making him wince. The cop didn't notice. He congratulated Bobbi and walked away.

"Are you okay?" Bobbi asked as BR squirmed in pain.

He ignored the pain and turned the question to the one he needed answered. "You tell me. Are *we* okay?"

"Did you mean what you just said?"

"Every word."

He quivered when her lips brushed close to his ear and Bobbi whispered, "I trust you."

CHAPTER SEVENTEEN: SAMI'S SONG
Bobbi

"Hi, Hunter. Can you put Sami on speaker?" Bobbi's voice was once again light.

"Hi, Mom!" Sami's cheerful voice came through Bobbi's old phone.

"Guess what? How'd you girls like a trip to Gino's?" Bobbi teased.

Two excited squeals erupted in response.

"Will tell us all about BR, Mom?"

"Well, you can ask him yourself. We're on our way to pick you up. Be ready in …" She glanced at BR.

He mouthed, "*Twenty*."

"… twenty minutes."

Hunter and Sami screamed so loudly Bobbi wasn't sure they'd heard the instructions. She hung up, and her phone immediately rang again. She put it on speaker.

"Mom," Sami said, suspicious, "is this one of Aunt Gina's pranks? Like we get to the car, and she tries to scare us?"

Without missing a beat, BR jumped in, perfectly mimicking Gina's Brooklyn accent. "Ya caught me, Dorkus Malorkus. I was aiming to put one over on ya. Since you figured it out, no gelato for you."

Bobbi quickly ended the call, howling as she sent Sami's attempts to call back to voicemail. Her eyes danced. "You only heard Gina's voice for five minutes last week, and you nailed it. And remembering her nickname for Sami? She's probably losing her mind."

Bobbi's eyes, already red from crying, now brimmed with laughter. She wiped them with a mitten. "Look what you've done to me."

"That was fun. I can't wait to see her face when she gets in the car."

"Are you sure your shoulder's okay?"

"It's sore, but being with you is the best medicine."

"I think you'll find I'm warmer than a heating pad ... Though, for your injury, Mr. Bradford, heat would be contraindicated. You need an ice pack, but you're not going to get a cold shoulder from me. You'll like my bedside manner."

He covered his mouth to stifle a guffaw.

"Let me get serious for just a minute, then we'll have fun with the girls. There's something I need you to understand. I'm loving and compassionate to a fault. But if you *ever* cheat on me, even *once*, you won't get a second chance. That might sound harsh, but being with you means facing the eyes of the world. Some people will think I'm taking you away from Aurora Bellucci or Alicia Rodriguez. There'll always be girls after you. Just ... don't break my heart, okay?"

He pulled her into his arms, his voice steady. "I promise never to disrespect you or our relationship. You'll never have to question your place in my heart."

She was sure he'd kiss her but, just then, a towering Black man appeared out of the darkness.

"Hi, Bobbi," he said. "Terrific to see you again."

"Ronnie, hi. Same back at you."

Hand in hand, Bobbi and BR followed Ronnie through the dimly lit park to the waiting SUV. Ronnie had rearranged the seats so they'd be facing the girls.

As they settled in, Bobbi told Ronnie, "You mentioned you have two boys, so I know you'll get this—respect matters to me. My daughter will call you Mr. Tompkins. Please call her Sami."

"I understand. You and my wife think the same."

Fifteen minutes later, they pulled up outside the building where Hunter lived with her mother. The girls were waiting on the steps, winter coats and backpacks in hand.

Sami wore her usual flair: a Hawaiian shirt, flouncy skirt over black leggings, and the shell bracelet from Red. Hunter, taller and curvier than her best friend, had her jet-black hair pulled back and wore an NYU sweatshirt and jeans.

Bobbi stepped out to heighten the suspense, introduced the girls to Ronnie, and then they clambered into the car.

"It's really *you!*" Sami shrieked, a mix of disbelief and thrill. She and Hunter looked on the verge of hyperventilating.

"Are you sure?" BR asked, slipping back into his "Aunt Gina" voice. "I could be Aunt Gina in disguise."

Sami's bright, uninhibited laughter filled the car. "No way! You're too tall. Aunt Gina's not much taller than me. It's awesome to meet you, Mr. Bradford."

Hunter offered a breathless hello.

"I'm so happy to meet you both. Sami, if it's okay with your mom, I'd love for you to call me BR."

Sami glanced at Bobbi, who nodded.

"BR," Hunter said shyly, "we're both huge fans. We listen to your music *all* the time. I've downloaded all your cast albums."

"Thanks, Hunter. Which one's your favorite?"

"I love *Sock Hop*. Sami's favorite is *The Best Woman*. But they're all great."

"Hunter and I are auditioning for a showcase at the final choir concert," Sami added.

"What are you going to sing?"

"'She Said/He Said,'" Hunter replied tentatively.

"Cool. Hunter, you've got a beautiful alto. Sami, you're a soprano. That song's a bold choice—it's traditionally a male/female duet, and the counterpoint sections are tricky."

Sami glanced at Hunter then back to BR. "Is it cool if two girls sing it?"

"Absolutely," he said warmly. "It's a love duet about communication and seeing someone else's perspective. I think it'll work beautifully. Can you sing a few bars so I can hear you?"

They didn't hesitate.

Bobbi watched in amazement as the girls "auditioned" for a Broadway legend with the confidence of seasoned performers.

Sami's soprano took the lead, lovely and light.

He said:
"The gold crescent moon
is mine to give,
Your love is
the reason that I live."

Hunter's alto followed, warm and resonant.

"She said:
I don't need the sky;
Give me your heart,
Don't let the moon
keep us apart."

Then, together, their voices intertwined in harmony.

"On a night of indigo and candlelight,
I heard everything you said,
My hopes are high, but my chances are slight,
In this strange land where our dreams have led."

Bobbi applauded. Out of the corner of her eye, she eagerly glanced at BR. He'd been candid when evaluating the singer in the park—she was curious what he'd say now.

"Okay, Hunter, let's try that high note again," BR said. "Sneak up on it—don't grab it. Think of it like a slide instead of a jump. That way, when Sami comes in, it'll sound like the two of you are flying together."

He turned to both girls. "When you blend, it's magic. Sami, try stretching a bit higher within your comfort zone. Hunter, find a slightly lower harmony. That balance will elevate the whole duet."

Bobbi beamed as the girls nodded, hanging on to his every word.

"Give it a try," BR continued, his tone warm but professional. "If you lock this in, the harmony will be unforgettable. That's the sweet spot—where your voices meet and lift each other up. That's what gives the audience shivers."

"Let's try again, Hunter!"

Bobbi was blown away by how much better they sounded. BR made a chef's kiss gesture.

Sami hugged Hunter. "That sounded amazing!"

"Let's practice after class tomorrow."

Caught up in the moment, Sami turned to BR. "Could we send you a recording after we've practiced? So you can tell us if we've got it?"

Bobbi froze. She was thrilled by how easily they connected, but this was supposed to be a quick first meeting. It was too fast for Sami to expect an ongoing connection.

Before she could intervene, BR smiled. "I'd love that. I'm sure you two will sound fabulous."

Ronnie interrupted. "We're at Gino's."

"Mom, they had a concert at Music Emporium—it must've just let out," Sami said. A line stretched down the block.

Bobbi turned to BR, concern creeping in. "The wait's not a problem—the gelato's worth it. But a line full of music fans? You're bound to be recognized. I'd hate for a social media frenzy to start. And we need to be careful with your shoulder."

"What do you suggest?"

"How about letting these two Energizer bunnies wait in line? We give them our order and eat in the car, if that works for you and Ronnie?"

"That sounds like fun," Sami said brightly.

"I'm in," BR added, pulling up Gino's menu on his JadePhone. After they chose, he handed it to Ronnie. "What's your pick?"

Bobbi insisted on paying—BR had treated dinner—and handed them cash. They dashed off, buzzing with energy.

Ronnie excused himself to "stretch his legs," subtly giving Bobbi and BR privacy.

"You're wonderful," Bobbi said, glowing. "Sami really likes you."

"She's terrific. It'd be tough not to like her."

"I'm biased, but I agree. You're setting an amazing example."

"What do you mean?"

"When you asked my opinion about the line, you modeled the kind of respect girls should expect from guys. And asking Ronnie what he wanted? That was a great example of how to treat people. Are you truly okay with them sending a recording? I don't want you to feel put on the spot."

"She's your daughter," he said simply. "That means I'll do anything I can to help her."

The line moved quickly. Soon, Sami, Hunter, and Ronnie returned.

Hunter passed out the treats as Sami exclaimed, "Mom, guess what? I saw Red! She was with a guy. Does she have a new boyfriend?"

"Red *always* has a new boyfriend," Bobbi joked, and then her voice sharpened. "Sami, did you mention BR?"

"No, she was talking to the guy. I waved; she blew me a kiss."

On the ride home, the car overflowed with laughter and warmth. BR enjoyed the gelato in between happily answering a million questions from the girls.

At Bobbi's house, Sami and Hunter thanked BR enthusiastically.

"You two head inside," Bobbi said. "I'll be up in a bit."

She and BR settled onto the porch loveseat. Ronnie found a quiet parking spot at the end of the block.

"How'd you know so much about that song?" she asked.

"Um … because I wrote it."

Bobbi groaned and did a facepalm. "So much to learn about you."

"Do you know who Gregory Isaiah Walker is?"

"Him, I *do* know." Bobbi brightened. "The handsome Black man from that lawyer series."

"Greg's also a huge Broadway star with an unforgettable voice."

"Are you sure you don't want to trade me in for a normal girl?" Bobbi sighed.

"Why would I want normal when I could have extraordinary? My biggest Broadway hits have starred Greg Walker and Aurora Bellucci. They did the song Sami and Hunter just sang."

"It was beautiful."

"*Tonight* was beautiful," BR said. "Being with you, meeting Sami—it's all been incredible. I love being with you. Thank you for trusting me with her."

Nestling against him, Bobbi whispered, "This feels like a dream."

And then it got even better.

BR slid his hand beneath her chin and gently tilted her face toward his. For the first time, he kissed her.

Given all the missed cues earlier, she'd expected something hesitant. But BR kissed her with passion, and with every touch, he promised love.

Bobbi wrapped her arms around his neck and kissed him back. She didn't want it to end.

After a long moment, he pulled back slightly. "Goodnight, my sweetest Bobbi."

"Call me when you get home," she whispered. "You kissed me, so I'm officially allowed to worry now. I'll be awake. I know I'm not sleeping anytime soon."

CHAPTER EIGHTEEN: DATING IN HYPERSPEED

BR

When BR got home, the soft glow of the colossal living room TV illuminated Anna Maria's tears. She dabbed at her eyes, moved by the sappy, romantic finale of a made-for-cable Christmas movie. Siobhán slept peacefully, gently snoring, her head resting in Anna Maria's lap.

"Hey, Unc," Anna Maria greeted softly. "How'd the 'hot date' go?"

"Hot date, indeed," came Siobhán's drowsy brogue. "More likely, you were at some history nerd-fest learning how they scaled fish during the War of 1812."

Their laughter was a welcome sound.

BR sank into his chair, wincing as he held a bag of frozen spinach on his shoulder. Nodding toward the TV, he asked, "Which one was it this time?"

"*Christmas Kiss in the Boston Bookstore*," Anna Maria sighed. "You know, Unc, you should make a Christmas movie."

"But not as a romantic George Washington or Abe Lincoln, if you please," Siobhán added, eyes barely open.

"How's Cassie?"

"Sleeping like the little angel she is," Siobhán purred.

"I might need you to watch her a bit more often."

Anna Maria pushed her chestnut bangs from her eyes. "What's going on, Unc? We love Cassie—it's never a problem."

BR took a deep breath. "I've started seeing someone." It was the first time he'd said it aloud. It felt liberating.

Their reaction was instant. Anna Maria jumped up and threw her arms around him, Siobhán right behind her. A flood of happy questions and congratulations followed.

Later, when they'd gone, BR called Bobbi.

He already missed her.

~~~

Sunday, January 9
Bobbi

Bobbi's car came to a stop at her parents' house for Sunday dinner. Sami leapt out, practically bursting with excitement, ready to share every detail of her mom's date with BR. Everyone was intensely curious, and Sami couldn't wait to spill.

As she held court for Whit and Gina, Bobbi quietly asked her mother if they could talk. Ingrid suggested they retreat to Bobbi's old bedroom for a heart-to-heart.

Usually composed—thanks to her medical training and naturally steady temperament—Bobbi was in unfamiliar emotional territory. She'd cried in front of BR not once but twice on Friday. Now she felt dizzy and exposed.

They sat on the bed.

Bobbi's eyes filled with tears. She gasped, "Oh, Mom."

Ingrid stroked her daughter's sunny hair, soothing her the way she had when Bobbi was little.

"Mom, I've got the whim-whams! He's incredible. And Sami adores him. What do I do? I've never been in love before."

"Honey, *are you* in love with BR? You've only known him a week."

"Eight days," Bobbi mumbled.

Ingrid gave a little tut and kept stroking. "It didn't take me eight days to know I loved your father, and I was a lot younger and less experienced than you. You know your heart, Bobbi."

"It's the first time I've said it out loud. I haven't told him yet. I love him."

"Honey, I believe you."

Bobbi's voice dropped to a whisper, amazed by her own words. "I'm going to marry him someday."

Ingrid smiled softly. "Honey, I believe you."

~~~

BR

Cassie was utterly exhausted after a full day—Sunday school, church volunteering, helping BR pack meals for the homeless, and a long visit to the library where she read, played, and exchanged a tote bag full of books. She'd had no nap.

That evening, BR set up a video call with his closest friends—Ed and Bree and their wives, Liz and Chrissy. Their friendship had begun in a cramped brownstone near Columbia and had only deepened through the years and across the miles.

After college, Ed became a respected attorney in Maple Meadow, Illinois. Bree earned national acclaim for her work-life harmony research from her Malibu base. Their marriages—Ed to Liz, Bree to Chrissy—had expanded BR's circle of love.

Ed and Bree had known BR before the world did. Before the fame, the money, the mystique. And though they'd never said it aloud, all four worried about him. BR, thirty-seven, had never had a serious relationship. They feared his dazzling life was also a lonely one.

At BR's urging, both couples had moved to New York to take major roles in his companies. None reported to him. Ed had launched an arbitration service, Liz edited the company magazine, Chrissy created content for BR's foundation, and Bree had become the youngest woman of color to serve as CEO of a major American firm.

After the usual catching up, BR cleared his throat.

"Guys ... something exciting happened. I met somebody."

Chrissy snorted. "You've already met everyone in the world."

"No," BR said, smiling. "I met a woman. We've had two dates. I'm already head over heels."

Tumult erupted. Bree—an atheist—made the sign of the cross and folded her hands in mock prayer. Chrissy shrieked loudly enough to be heard in Colorado. Ed kissed Liz then launched into a joyful, wild jitterbug.

"Tell us *everything*," Liz demanded. "Don't leave out a syllable. Who *is* she? Do we know her?"

"Her name's Bobbi. Dr. Bobbi Wyatt. She's a neurologist in Brooklyn. She's brilliant, and she has a fantastic daughter."

Chrissy, already googling, interrupted. "She's hot!"

A collective scramble ensued as everyone reached for their phones.

Bree zeroed in on Bobbi's LinkedIn. "OMG, she's already board-certified and doing national presentations, and she's only thirty-one?"

"And she's crazy hot!" Chrissy repeated. "Too bad she doesn't play for our team, Bree."

The group erupted in laughter until Liz scolded, "You two keep your gorgeous hands off her. We've waited years for BR to get a girlfriend. Let him enjoy it."

BR told the story, starting with the mysterious painting and ending with Bobbi's latest charming text. He raved about Sami.

"All jokes aside," Ed said sincerely, "she sounds amazing, man. We're thrilled for you."

Everyone echoed his words, smiling into their screens. What BR didn't see were the hands quietly clasped out of view. Both couples supported him unconditionally, but his three months of depression had frightened them. Now, watching him light up again, their fears eased.

BR was coming back to life.

CHAPTER NINETEEN: A ROSE IN BROOKLYN
Monday, January 11
Bobbi

"Don't even *try* to tell me you don't have a boyfriend," Yolanda snapped as Bobbi entered the clinic, Coffee Corner cup in hand.

"Mind if I take off my coat and go into my office?" Bobbi replied, stalling, puzzled by her office manager's onslaught.

The reason became obvious the moment she stepped inside. A stunning bouquet—a dozen red roses accented with white Shasta daisies and delicate greenery—perfumed the room.

"I don't suppose you'd believe they're from my mother?" Bobbi stuttered, cheeks flushing.

Yolanda folded her arms and gave her a look.

"Okay," Bobbi relented, "I just started seeing someone. It's new, so please don't say anything."

Before Yolanda could respond, Bobbi checked her schedule. "Could you bring the first patient to exam room two?"

Yolanda huffed and left in a snit.

Bobbi turned back to the bouquet and read the card.

May the colors of Italy brighten your day. Missing you.

Texting on her out-of-date cell was hard, but she pecked out a message for BR.

> *You don't have to send me flowers every time we have a date. Love them! XX*

BR's response was immediate.

> *Too late. I've already prepaid for the first one million dates.*

Bobbi grinned, replying:

> *ONLY a million dates? What happens after that?*

> *After that, I'll prepay for the NEXT million dates.*

CHAPTER TWENTY: THE NEW NORMAL
Wednesday, January 13
Bobbi

Sami finished packing her lunch as Bobbi bounced down the stairs, phone in hand, rereading BR's good morning message.

"Hi, Mom. I can see you're really excited to see BR today."

"Huh?" Bobbi looked up. "What makes you say that?"

"You're wearing a skirt."

Bobbi rolled her eyes, blushing. "I didn't raise you to be such a wise guy."

"Nope," Sami replied, zipping her parka. "That's Aunt Gina's job.

At Coffee Corner, Claude and the regulars noticed the skirt, too. And when she arrived at the clinic, Yolanda's eyes were wide.

"So," she started knowingly, "when do I meet this mystery man?"

~~~

That evening, a cold snap hit, and Bobbi changed their plans.

Originally, she and Sami were going to give BR a walking tour of the neighborhood. But with the wind chill in single digits, they opted for a cozy booth at the local twenty-four-hour diner instead.

Sami was in the mood for breakfast-for-dinner and didn't hold back—Swedish pancakes, Canadian bacon, and Swiss cheese on an English muffin. The adults watched, amazed, as she dug in.

She looked up and caught them staring. "What?"

BR gestured at her plate. "That's the most international breakfast I've ever seen. They should serve that at the UN."

"I think it comes with a side of an angiogram," Bobbi added, smirking. "Did you skip lunch?"

"Nope. But I had a lab in pre-physics, and that's a lot of work. I'm hungry!"

Bobbi traded a bite of her veggie burger for a taste of BR's spinach and mushroom egg-white omelet.

BR sat with his back to the door, unnoticed by the few patrons around them. To anyone watching, they looked like a happy family—laughing, sharing stories, and scrolling through a dozen photos of Cassie on BR's JadePhone. Sami sat between them. Bobbi couldn't help wishing she were close enough to hold BR's hand.

When he stepped away to check in with Anna Maria, Sami leaned toward her mom. "Cassie looks just like you."

"When we get home, I'll show you a picture of me at her age. Grandma and Grandpa are going to freak out when they see the resemblance."

Bobbi was shocked when, after finishing her enormous meal, Sami still asked if they could stop by Gino's. The most extraordinary part of the evening was how ordinary it felt.

On the porch afterward, Bobbi smiled. "Thanks for dinner. But you don't have to keep taking me out. I could cook for you next time."

Sami made a gagging noise. "Mom! Why are you threatening him? BR is nice. Don't kill him with your cooking."

"Hey!" Bobbi protested. "I can cook."

Sami rolled her eyes and headed inside.

"I can't wait for Saturday," Bobbi whispered, nestled in BR's arms. "It's freezing, but you should kiss me three times. One for tonight, one for tomorrow, and one for Friday, until I can kiss you again in person."

"Three kisses?" BR smiled. "You don't have to ask me twice."

He didn't stop at three, but with her heart fluttering and her head full of whim-whams, Bobbi wasn't counting.

~~~

Friday, January 15

Bobbi picked up Red on the fly outside her place. "Where's Rugrat?"

"Hanging with Gina. I'm glad we've got some girls' time, Red."

"Life's funny, isn't it? Six months ago, who'd have thought we'd be swapping styles for our dates—you hunting for something girly and chic, me trying to pull off white jeans and a Brooklyn Nets jersey?"

"Are we still calling him NG? For New Guy?"

"Right now, he's NG for Nets Guy. He's showing promise, Blondie."

Bobbi snorted. "I thought you were going to say it stood for Naughty Guy!"

Megan's golden eyes sparkled with mischief. "Oh, he definitely earned Naughty Guy last night. But seriously, there's a vibe about him. It feels different, you know?"

Bobbi sighed. "Wouldn't it be something if he turned out to be your Never-Ending Guy?"

Megan's arched brows made it clear she'd wondered the same thing. "Speaking of never-ending guys, if you're buying *another* blue dress to please MP, I'd say he's well on his way to becoming Mr. Permanent."

Bobbi's laughter mingled with the blush creeping up her cheeks. "Red, I hope you're Miss Prescient."

They pulled up in front of an eclectic Williamsburg boutique.

"I spotted a blue wrap dress in there that's perfect for you. With your hair and legs? Forget about it. MP will weep with gratitude."

Bobbi laughed, shaking her head. "If that dress has that much power, I might just have to buy two."

CHAPTER TWENTY-ONE: A KISS UNDER FAIRY LIGHTS

Saturday, January 16
BR

The fairy lights strung along the wooden patio overlooking the Atlantic cast a warm, irresistible glow on Bobbi's radiant smile. Despite the offshore chill, she and BR had stepped outside the Clam Digger Restaurant in the quaint town of Ocean Inlet, New Jersey, for a moment alone.

"You're a pretty good guy, you know?" Bobbi teased. "Taking me somewhere new, stealing kisses under twinkly lights, even giving me the jacket off your back. Aren't you cold?"

"Not with you in that dress."

She smiled. "Sweetie, promise we'll come back this summer, eat outside, and count the waves. If you need extra inducement, I'll wear a pretty sundress."

"It's a date. Now we have a place that's ours."

They kissed—to the present, and to the future.

Back inside, the menu left Bobbi indecisive. "Everything looks so tempting. You might have to bring me here a dozen more times."

"If it means seeing you in that dress again, I'm all in," BR said, half-joking.

"And here I thought you loved me for my sparkling personality and razor-sharp mind. Turns out, it's all about the dress," she said with a playful pout.

BR grinned. "It's absolutely your personality ... *and* the dress."

A bubbly server arrived. "Struggling to decide?" she asked, noting Bobbi's expression.

"Nope. I've narrowed it down to seven." Bobbi laughed.

BR nodded toward her. "Why not make it harder? Let's hear the specials."

In the end, Bobbi chose a special—Sea Bass Florentine. BR ordered the Lobster Bisque followed by the Ocean Inlet Shellfish Medley.

Seated by the panoramic windows, they watched the waves crash in the moonlight. Their conversation turned reflective.

"I've waited too long to find you," BR said softly. "I don't want to waste a single moment. Every minute I'm away from you, I'm thinking about you."

Bobbi met his eyes. "BR, I think it's time we take the next step."

His heart skipped. "What do you have in mind?"

She leaned in. "I think it's time for me to meet Cassie."

He blinked, caught off guard. "Really?"

Bobbi nodded. "Sami's old enough to understand dating. But Cassie's so little. If she meets Daddy's 'girlfriend,' she'll assume we're forever. Dating is unpredictable for adults. For a little girl, the concept could be very confusing."

"True. But when it comes to 'mom decisions,' I trust your judgment completely. Cassie will love you. You decide when the time is right."

"It feels right," Bobbi said, glowing. "I'll take Friday afternoon off. I'd love to see your place and meet her."

CHAPTER TWENTY-TWO: THE TALE OF THE MOOSE

Friday, January 22
BR

The late afternoon sun bathed the Manhattan penthouse in a warm, golden light. The tea party was turning out to be a tremendous success. In a pink princess dress, five-year-old Cassie charmed her guests, DeDe and CeCe, the Scottish twin dolls in green tartan plaid. She was so engrossed in their conversation that she didn't hear her father calling out to her repeatedly.

BR made his way over to the soirée. "Miss Cassie," he said, "when your guests leave the party, could you join me in the living room? I have happy news I want to tell you."

BR glowed as Cassie politely excused herself from her guests. DeDe and CeCe didn't seem upset by the end of the party.

Their home was a two-story penthouse occupying the 28th and 29th floors of the NYTSQ hotel. Hotel guests never knew about the celebrity occupant above them. BR had financed the hotel, and his security team took precautions to ensure his home and the office above it were inaccessible to strangers. The security team, all former federal agents, marshals, or MPs, had built a system, including a hidden private elevator requiring a special pass and code to go through security checkpoints. Once inside, the penthouse looked like an ordinary suburban home.

Few members of BR's organization had been in his home, and no member of the press had set foot there. He was adamant about keeping his private life private.

BR hadn't originally intended the penthouse to be his full-time residence. However, when his teenage niece, Anna Maria, had unexpectedly moved in six years earlier, BR had needed the extra space and convenience of the location to balance his work responsibilities with raising her.

For Cassie, adopted at birth, it was the only home she'd ever known. It struck the perfect balance between luxury and practicality, a calm and comfortable sanctuary in the heart of Manhattan. Specially designed windows protected their privacy and safety, muffling almost all the noises from Times Square. Nonetheless, BR planned to find them a house in a quiet neighborhood where Cassie could ride her bike to school.

A comfy brown corduroy couch and loveseat sat in front of the big-screen TV with a special spot for Cassie. BR waited while Cassie carefully cleaned up the remnants of the tea party, neatly put the toy tea cups away on a shelf in her dollhouse, and lovingly tucked the twins into their bed, their plaid dresses and tartan kilts neatly arranged.

Scampering onto the couch, cuddling up next to her dad, the green-eyed girl eagerly asked, "What's up, Daddy?"

BR caught his breath. He wasn't at all worried that Bobbi wouldn't like Cassie. She adored children and always wanted to hear all the latest about Cassie. BR's worries were more amorphous. Would bringing a new woman and her daughter into their lives confuse or upset Cassie?

"Sweetheart, something exciting's been happening to me. I'm so happy I want to tell you."

Cassie was already grinning.

"Three weeks ago, I met someone special. I started dating a wonderful doctor named Bobbi."

Cassie squealed. In her games, dating involved princes and princesses, weddings, castles, and happy endings.

"Is Bobby nice?"

"Bobbi's very nice. And if it's okay with you, Bobbi wants to meet you."

Cassie's joyful "Yes" echoed in BR's heart.

"You're the most important thing in my whole world, Cassie. Are you okay with me dating? I'd never date anyone you didn't like."

"Daddy, it's great. And it's okay that you're dating a boy. Miss Sarah Jane at school says *love is love*."

BR was befuddled. Slowly, he figured out the misunderstanding and laughed to himself.

"Sweetie, Bobbi is a girl. Her name is spelled B-O-B-B-I."

Cassie did a double-take. "*Bobbi* is a girl's name?"

"Yes, it is. Bobbi's a wonderful *woman*."

"Is she pretty?"

BR paused, picturing Bobbi's beautiful face.

"Daddy, your whole face is smiling."

"Bobbi's very pretty. She has blonde hair and green eyes, just like you."

For the first time, BR realized that Cassie looked like a miniature Bobbi.

Lost in the moment, he missed Cassie's question and asked her to repeat it.

"Daddy, I asked if she likes kids." Cassie's soft voice betrayed her growing impatience. She had questions, and lots of them.

"Bobbi *loves* children. She has a daughter who's older than you, named Sami. I met her, and she's very cool."

"*Sami*?" Cassie laughed. "That's a boy's name, like Bobbi."

"Let me explain. Sami is a nickname for Samantha. Like how your name is Cassandra, but everyone calls you Cassie."

"I got it. Dr. Bobbi is a girl, and Sami is a girl."

BR nodded.

Cassie's voice was a sing-song. "Dr. Bobbi, Dr. Bobbi, Dr. Bobbi," she chanted, getting used to the sound.

"Bobbi wants to came over for dinner. Would you like that? I thought we'd take her out to Golden Star. You can order your favorite Pad Thai."

Cassie could barely contain her excitement. She jumped up, saying, "Yes! Can I wear a princess dress?"

Almost trembling with joy, BR said, "Of course. You can wear whatever you'd like."

Cassie grew pensive. "Daddy, should I call her Ms. Bobbi or Dr. Bobbi? I want to be polite so she'll like me."

BR brushed a strand of hair from her face. "You don't have to worry about that, sweetheart. I've told Bobbi all about you, and she already can't wait to meet you. I know she's going to think you're wonderful." He smiled softly. "She's a special friend, so I think just calling her Bobbi will be okay."

Cassie's eyes widened—she always used titles for adults. Even BR's closest friends were "Uncle Ed" and "Aunt Bree."

"Can I show her my room?"

"I'm sure she'd love that—and meeting all your animals and dolls, too."

Cassie wrapped him in a tight hug. "I'll have a private tea party just for her. But Daddy ..."

Here it came.

"Can you please try a French braid *again*?"

BR sighed. The braid was his Everest. He'd tried videos, tutorials—even practiced on a doll—but every attempt had ended in tears.

"Maybe next time, sweetheart. I still haven't figured it out."

Cassie frowned, unconvinced.

"What princess dress are you going to wear?" he asked quickly.

Brightening, she darted off toward her room, already planning the next tea party.

BR texted Bobbi:

> *Cassie is VERY excited to meet you! I can't wait for you to get here. XOXO BR.*

BR was surprised when, two seconds later, her response came through. Bobbi's patient load was nonstop, and her outdated phone made texting difficult at the best of times.

Every so often, BR caught sight of a small whirlwind racing through the penthouse—setting up a tea set, rearranging dolls, and parading out of her bedroom in one dress after another.

His nerves started to settle. One of his drivers was already on the way back from Brooklyn Heights with Bobbi aboard.

~~~

Bobbi

She'd insisted she could take the train, but Bobbi's argument hadn't gotten her far. As BR had explained, his company employed a fleet of drivers, and there was no reason she needed to sit for an hour in a noisy subway car after a long day.

Fiercely independent but genuinely touched by the gesture, Bobbi had relented and was instantly glad she had. It was a luxurious treat for someone who'd grown up relying on public transportation. She actually liked the subway, aside from the occasional stockbroker hitting on her.

BR was the lead investor in a carbon-neutral car company founded by immigrant brothers from New Zealand. All of his corporate vehicles were state-of-the-art, with top-tier environmental and safety features.

Her ride today—a quiet, midnight-blue sedan—was supremely comfortable, with space to stretch out. Bobbi wished she had a newer phone so she could surreptitiously snap pictures for Sami and Gina. Her driver, former Federal Marshal Jo Ann Stewart, was professional but friendly.

Bobbi relaxed in the back seat, letting the stress of the clinic fade away. She hadn't even had time to go to the bathroom that day. Now, eyes closed, she savored the rare calm—no worries about stolen purses or missed stops.

She was excited to meet Cassie and see BR's home. They talked about his daughter constantly, and he had shown her countless photos. One in particular made Bobbi's heart ache: Cassie, in snowflake pajamas, sat cross-legged on a beanbag chair, reading to a stuffed moose. The little girl was adorable, but what moved Bobbi the most was the reminder of the quiet moments she'd missed with Sami while building her career.

When Gina had asked about Cassie, Bobbi had replied, "I'll have BR take a picture of me with her. You'll notice something interesting."

Cassie looked just like Bobbi had at that age: slender nose, forest-green eyes, honey-blonde bangs parted in the middle. In her school photos, she wore a low ponytail that mimicked Bobbi's clinic hairstyle. The resemblance was uncanny—Cassie could've been mistaken for her daughter.

Stewart's crisp voice interrupted her thoughts. "We're making good time, Dr. Wyatt."

"Agent Stewart, please call me Bobbi. I'm only Dr. Wyatt if you're my patient, or if I'm trying to get out of a parking ticket."

Laughing, the driver said, "Whatever you prefer." She caught Bobbi's eye in the mirror. "But please just call me Stewart. Those of us on Mr. Bradford's personal security team go by last names."

Bobbi considered this. "May I call you Jo Ann? Are you part of his security detail?"

"Yes, Dr.—Bobbi. I'm on Mr. Bradford's team. The transport division drives executives to meetings and ensures staff—especially women—get home safely after late nights. But I usually only drive him."

Bobbi raised an eyebrow as the car exited the Brooklyn Bridge. "Why not send a regular driver?"

"You'd have to ask him. But this is the first time I've ever driven anyone other than Mr. Bradford."

As Stewart expertly turned off Canal onto 47th, Bobbi marveled at her skill. She loved to drive, but never in Manhattan.

She pulled out a compact and checked her reflection. At the clinic, she wore minimal makeup—just a little eye makeup and lip gloss—but BR was used to seeing her dolled up for dates. She touched up her lips as Stewart announced their arrival. The ride had flown by. Maybe traffic was light, or maybe Stewart really was that good.

They entered through a hidden underground garage. Bobbi stepped out before Stewart could open the door. Waving off help, she slung her medical bag, gym bag, and purse over one shoulder. Then Stewart escorted her past the public lobby and into a discreet private elevator. They rode in silence to the 29th floor.

~~~

BR

BR finished lighting wall sconces, giving the room a faint aroma of Italian orange. Two minutes later, his heart jumped—security had told him Bobbi was in the building and on her way up.

She arrived fresh from work, wearing a teal sweater and a calf-length black skirt, her long hair in a sleek ponytail.

She'd barely set down her bags and hugged BR when a child's piercing scream shattered the quiet foyer.

Cassie was in full meltdown.

BR froze, stunned and mortified. This was *not* how he'd wanted Bobbi to meet his daughter.

Ten minutes earlier, everything had been fine. Cassie had been her usual cheerful, quiet self. He couldn't remember her ever losing control like this.

She stumbled into him, sobbing so hard she didn't even notice Bobbi. Her small body shook as tears streamed down her flushed face.

BR turned to comfort her, grabbing tissues from the entryway table.

Bobbi silently mouthed, "*May I?*"

He nodded.

She knelt to Cassie's eye level. Dabbing Cassie's eyes, she gently asked, "What's wrong, sweetheart?"

Cassie's sobbing slowed a bit.

"Try to catch your breath, Cassie. If you tell me what's wrong, maybe I can make it better."

Cassie stopped crying at Bobbi's gentle coaxing and wailed, "Howard is dying! I don't want him to die. I don't know what to do."

Bobbi continued reassuringly, "Cassie, sweetheart, who is Howard?"

Cassie produced her beloved stuffed moose. Howard's left antler was barely hanging by a thread. At the sight of him, Cassie's tears returned.

Bobbi was unfazed.

"Cassie, hi, I'm Bobbi."

The girl's wet green eyes flickered with recognition.

Looking tenderly at Howard then at the bereft girl, Bobbi asked, "Did Daddy tell you what I do for my job?"

Cassie's eyes widened, and her voice was hopeful. "You're a *doctor*. Can you help mooses?" It was as if Bobbi had flipped a switch.

"Yes, I treat girls and *mooses*. But I'm going to need *your* help."

Cassie's tear-streaked face softened; a glimmer of hope appeared. "What can *I* do?"

"I can save Howard's antler, but I can't do moose surgery alone. Will you be my nurse, Cassie?"

Cassie nodded solemnly.

"BR," Bobbi said over her shoulder, "would you please put a clean towel on the coffee table?"

He hurried off, completely mesmerized. When he returned with a crisp, striped towel, Bobbi was showing Cassie how to cradle Howard carefully, supporting his neck to protect the damaged antler.

"Did I do it right?" Cassie asked.

Bobbi smiled. "Perfect, Nurse Cassie."

She led the girl to the kitchen sink, where a stepstool waited. "Before we examine a patient, we wash our hands really well. I'll show you."

Bobbi demonstrated, and Cassie copied her every move.

BR watched in awe. She'd transformed a crisis into calm in minutes. *This*, he thought, *is what our future could look like.*

Back at the coffee table, Bobbi pulled a forehead thermometer from her medical bag.

"Let's take Howard's temperature. We'll also need his medical history."

Cassie answered solemnly, "He's never been sick before. He's a great moose."

BR was enchanted. Bobbi radiated warmth and calm. He now understood exactly why her patients adored her.

Next came the stethoscope.

Cassie backed away. "I don't like those. They're cold and feel yucky."

"It won't feel yucky the way I do it," Bobbi promised.

"Really?"

Bobbi rubbed the instrument between her palms and pressed it against Cassie's hand.

The little girl eased closer.

"Now I'll listen to Howard's heart." She leaned in, listened for a moment, then nodded. "It sounds strong. Is he a very loving friend?"

Cassie's ponytail bobbed. "He's the best moose. He sleeps with me and makes me feel better when I'm sad."

"Sounds like the perfect heart rate for a moose," Bobbi said. "Would you like to hear your heartbeat? If it's okay with Daddy?"

Cassie turned to BR with pleading eyes.

He nodded.

Bobbi placed the stethoscope over Cassie's dress, listened, then guided the earbuds into Cassie's ears.

Cassie's face lit up. "It's going boop, boop, boop!"

"Perfect and full of love," Bobbi said.

Cassie beamed. "Can I hear Daddy's?"

BR undid two buttons on his shirt. Bobbi placed her hand on his chest—his pulse leapt at her touch. She gave him a conspiratorial smile then listened before passing the earbuds to Cassie.

"What's so funny?" BR asked.

"Your heart's very loud, Daddy. It's going *boom, boom, boom*. And I know why."

BR raised his eyebrows.

Cassie said nothing. She scooted over near Bobbi. Then, cupping her hand so her father couldn't hear, Cassie whispered, "Because every time Daddy looks at you, he has hearts coming out of his eyes."

Bobbi's eyes twinkled merrily. She cupped her hand to Cassie's ear. "Every time I look at Daddy, I have hearts coming out of *my* eyes, too."

Cassie clapped with delight.

Bobbi placed her tools on the "exam table" with practiced ease. Cassie watched closely as she then pulled on latex gloves and reached for baby powder.

"Ready, Nurse Cassie?"

Cassie nodded seriously. "Ready, Dr. Bobbi."

As twilight fell, BR pressed a button that tinted the windows and dimmed the lights. The recessed lamps bathed the room in a warm, golden glow.

Bobbi explained the next step. "This is special moose powder to prevent infection." She sprinkled it over the damaged antler, turning it into a snowy mountaintop. She gently cleaned the area then reached for a syringe.

Cassie cringed. "I hate shots."

Bobbi paused. "What does Daddy do when you get a shot?"

"He holds my hand and tells me to look at him."

"And does that help?"

Cassie nodded.

"Then that's what you should do for Howard."

189

Cassie grabbed the moose's paw. "Be brave, Howard. Look at me."

Bobbi injected the "medicine" then told the moose, "Good job, Howard. You were very calm."

Cassie kissed his nose. "You were so brave."

Bobbi smiled. "That's because he had such a great nurse. Doctors and nurses always have to work together to make sure their patients get better."

Bobbi pulled out a sewing kit. BR and Cassie watched as she threaded a needle and began to stitch the torn seam with careful precision.

"See, Cassie?" she said. "Sometimes we get hurt. But with love and care, we can heal and be as good as new again."

CHAPTER TWENTY-THREE: CASSIE'S PRAYER
Bobbi

"Nurse Cassie," Bobbi said gently, "let's wrap Howard in the towel to keep him warm."

Cassie watched intently as Bobbi demonstrated how to swaddle a baby.

"Howard's going to be sleepy for a little while," Bobbi continued. "Can you find a special spot where he can rest?"

Carefully lifting her moose the way Dr. Bobbi had shown her, Cassie prepared a quiet bed on the tie-dyed beanbag chair in front of the couch. She kissed his antler then tiptoed back to the living room. Without a word, she ran straight into Bobbi's arms.

It was their first physical contact, and Bobbi could barely breathe.

BR and Sami already adored each other. Now the picture was coming into focus. The four of them ... this could be a family.

They'd only been dating a few weeks, but her heart was galloping ahead of logic. Would she scare him off if she said how much this moment meant?

Bobbi finally spoke. "Sweetheart, instead of going out to eat, I think Nurse Cassie and I should stay close, in case Howard needs anything. What if we order takeout and play a game? That way, we can be nearby if he wakes up. How does that sound?"

"Please, Daddy?" Cassie asked eagerly.

"That sounds perfect." BR headed toward the bright, modern kitchen. "I'll grab the menu."

"Do you like Thai food, Bobbi?" Cassie asked.

"I sure do. And Sami loves it. Her favorite is Pad Thai."

"Me, too! Daddy showed me a picture of Sami. He said she's funny and cool. Do you want to see my room?"

"I'd love that. And maybe, afterward, could I get a tour of the whole house?" So far, Bobbi had only seen the kitchen and living room. All week, she'd wondered what a billionaire's Manhattan penthouse looked like.

They walked off hand-in-hand, Cassie happily pointing out every detail.

~~~

BR

BR fidgeted in the living room then wandered into the kitchen to set the dinner table. Still restless, he checked on Howard who, fortunately, had no complaints. The stitches were invisible. Howard looked as good as new.

He was over the moon that Cassie was enjoying herself with Bobbi. He fought the urge to follow them, contenting himself with the occasional sound of their voices drifting through the apartment as they explored, room by room.

It had gone quiet for a bit when security buzzed to say the food was on its way up. BR turned on some soft Mozart then headed downstairs to find them in the library.

Before sitting down to eat, Dr. Bobbi and Nurse Cassie checked on their patient. Cassie tiptoed to Howard's bedside while Bobbi knelt beside her.

Bobbi gently felt the moose's neck and antler. "Nurse Cassie, the patient is recovering perfectly. He's going to be all better."

Cassie grinned proudly.

At the dinner table, Cassie insisted Bobbi sit next to her, while BR unpacked the takeout. Warm scents filled the apartment.

Bobbi noticed Cassie eyeing her basil shrimp. "Have you ever tried this before? It's one of my favorites." She held up a bite-sized piece for inspection.

Cassie leaned in, took it, and lit up. Bobbi fed her another, and Cassie happily accepted it without hesitation.

BR, watching the exchange, smiled and took another bite of his pineapple fried rice. The whole evening felt so natural, like something they'd all done a dozen times before.

After dinner, BR stood up and said, "Bobbi, just relax for a second."

He and Cassie cleared the table and began loading the dishwasher, Cassie humming under her breath like a girl with a secret.

~~~

Bobbi

As they cleared the table, Bobbi mentally organized her impressions of BR's home in the sky. She thought back to a mansion in the Hamptons owned by a wealthy doctor colleague—far more ostentatious than this warm, understated place. She loved everything about the design.

She hadn't seen any precious artwork, antique rugs, or gold trim. No Tonys, Oscars, or Grammys on display. Instead, there were Cassie's drawings on the refrigerator, a well-loved brown corduroy couch, and all the quiet trappings of a happy home.

Cassie's bedroom was tidy, accented with princess decor. The walls featured painted scenes of odd, talking vegetables paired with inspirational quotes. Bobbi had no idea what they were and was too embarrassed to ask. *I'll google them later*, she promised herself.

Framed photos on the mantle showed Cassie with Anna Maria and Siobhán, and with BR's best friends, Ed and Sabrina, and their spouses. Cassie had eagerly introduced each one. But there were no celebrity snapshots, no pictures of BR performing.

Bobbi remembered BR telling her the night they met that Cassie was reading at a second-grade level despite still being in preschool. She loved the cozy reading nook tucked into the quietest corner of the downstairs library. Colorful beanbags were scattered for joint reading time, and Cassie had a special chair of her own. BR's reading chair sat nearby, flanked by a small stack of history books.

The shelves were filled with nonfiction—mostly American history and politics—while the lower shelves overflowed with Cassie's storybooks. Bobbi smiled at how the bright, playful spines mingled with BR's serious tomes.

Soft, warm light spilled from overhead lamps, and each reading chair had its own reading light. Bobbi sighed. She could imagine countless hours of happy reading in that room. Sami would love this.

BR's voice gently interrupted her thoughts. "Okay, little one, time for PJs and a bedtime story."

Cassie frowned but was clearly sleepy after their late dinner.

Before the adults could talk, Cassie reappeared, pajama top buttoned, a colorful book in hand.

She led Bobbi to the living room couch. "Howard needs to hear the story, too."

"Of course," Bobbi said warmly. "I'm sure that'll make him feel even better. I promise he'll be good as new by morning."

As they settled in, Cassie explained, "If I read really well, Daddy reads me a story. He does all the voices. It's so funny!"

"Oh, I can't wait to hear that. He told me you're a great reader. What book did you pick?"

Cassie held up *Dr. Bryan Saves a Lion*. "It's about a doctor, just like you—but he's not a girl."

The cover showed an African man in a lab coat, using a stethoscope on a smiling lion. Bobbi glanced at BR, impressed, then turned to watch Cassie tackle the challenging text with ease. Bobbi led the applause for the stellar performance.

BR high-fived Cassie, and she nestled next to Bobbi as he began a chapter from a children's version of *Pride and Prejudice*. Mr. Darcy's nasal voice made them giggle, while Elizabeth's calm poise earned admiration. They gave him a standing ovation, and he took a theatrical bow.

"See, Bobbi? I told you Daddy's great."

Bobbi smiled. "He's pretty great, all right."

"Does Sami like to read?" Cassie asked.

"Sami loves reading. She wants to be a writer someday."

"Um, Bobbi?" Cassie said shyly. "Do you know how to do a French braid? Daddy tries, but it always looks funny."

"Of course, sweetie. I'd love to." Bobbi grabbed a hairbrush and ties from her gym bag. "Why don't you come sit on my lap?"

Cassie climbed up in a blur of excitement.

Bobbi gently found a few tangles BR had clearly missed. She spritzed detangler and ran her fingers through the golden strands.

"Mmm," Cassie sighed.

"I'll make sure Daddy uses this so it won't hurt next time."

Brushing went smoothly, and Bobbi began weaving a perfect French braid.

When she finished, Cassie turned and hugged her. "My hair smells so pretty, like yours!"

Bobbi examined her handiwork. "You're welcome, sweetie. Your hair is beautiful, just like you."

Cassie twirled. "How does it look, Daddy?"

"Perfect!"

"Bobbi, you're so pretty. I wish I had long hair like you."

Bobbi adjusted her bangs. "Your hair is just right for you. It's the same length as Sami's, actually. I still love doing braids for her. Would you like me to teach you how to do one?"

Cassie's eyes lit up. "Really? Can you show me?"

"Sure. The easiest way is for you to watch me braid someone else's hair. Should I try a French braid on Daddy?"

"Bobbi, you're silly! Daddy's hair's too short."

"Hmm. If only someone here had long hair ..."

"You do!"

"That's right! You can help me."

Cassie carefully removed Bobbi's ponytail holder and spritzed her hair with mist. She delighted in brushing it out while they chatted. Then, like magic, Bobbi braided her own sun-kissed hair while explaining each step to her fascinated pupil.

"Sit with Bobbi so I can take a picture of your matching braids," BR said.

Cassie beamed, climbing onto Bobbi's lap. BR snapped a half-dozen photos of the two of them giggling together. In one, Cassie flashed bunny ears, and Bobbi playfully returned the favor. He captured the perfect shot.

"Will you show me again?" Cassie asked.

"I think Daddy said it's bedtime," Bobbi teased. "Why don't you brush your teeth and check your braid in the mirror? Then tell me if I did better than Daddy."

Cassie dashed off, squealing.

Bobbi turned to BR, still smiling. "She's so sweet. You've done a wonderful job with her."

"You make it look easy. Not just the braid—everything. You're a natural."

"Well, I've had eleven years of practice," Bobbi said. "And my mom's amazing—I learned from the best."

BR smiled. "You know I love your hair." His voice softened. "But that braid ... that's totally hot."

She touched the braid, a little flustered. "Thank you."

Cassie bounced back into the room. "Bobbi, can Daddy video you next time? He needs another lesson."

"I think Daddy needs a bunch of lessons."

"Daddy, can Bobbi tuck me in?" Cassie asked shyly.

BR turned to Bobbi. "If you want to. Otherwise, we can wait until …"

But Bobbi was already taking Cassie's hand.

Bobbi made an elaborate, silly production of the tucking-in ritual—measuring the perfect distance between Cassie's chin and the blanket, fluffing the pillow just right, making sure the quilt was perfectly even.

"That always makes Sami laugh, too."

Clutching Howard, Cassie blinked sleepily. "Bobbi, will you lie with me?"

Bobbi lay on top of the covers, propped on one elbow. In the soft glow of the nightlight, the talking vegetables stared down from the wall. Bobbi was surprised she couldn't hear even a trace of Times Square.

"Time to close your eyes, sweet girl," she said gently.

"I have to say my prayers first. I know what I'm going to pray for."

Bobbi paused. She knew BR was religious but hadn't realized Cassie prayed. Religion wasn't part of her own life. She had been raised going to church, but God had always felt abstract to her scientific mind.

"I'm going to pray you and Daddy get married, and you'll be my mommy."

Bobbi felt her heart might explode. Only Sami had ever evoked such powerful feelings of absolute love in her, and she'd only known Cassie for two hours. Bobbi didn't know what to say. She'd assumed Cassie would pray for her daddy … and maybe for Howard's recovery. Tears trickled from her green eyes.

Bobbi wrapped Cassie in a maternal hug, enveloping the motherless girl in a cloud of love. She heard Cassie sniffle against her neck. Soon, their tears joined together on Cassie's cheek. The little girl fell asleep wordlessly in Bobbi's embrace.

Bobbi delicately lay Cassie back on her pillow, using her fingertips to wipe the tears away from Cassie's face. She noticed a tear stain on Howard's antler but let it be.

Almost imperceptibly, Bobbi kissed Cassie's sleeping forehead. Looking at the precious child, Bobbi mouthed, "*Me, too.*"

CHAPTER TWENTY-FOUR: AN UNDERSTANDING
Bobbi

Bobbi was unraveling.

Sitting on the floor outside Cassie's room, her back slumped against the wall, shoulders shaking, she buried her face in her hands.

I'm close to a panic attack.

She'd guided patients through moments like this. In chaos, she was the calm center—an NYPD on-call neurologist, the steady voice at disaster sites, the cool-headed physician in the aftermath of unspeakable accidents. She was famous for being unflappable.

Not now.

Not tonight.

Bobbi was a mess.

Just three weeks ago, she'd been content—single, stable, and in control. She had a fulfilling career, a daughter she adored, a great family, a best friend, and no plans to change anything.

Then BR had appeared, and her carefully ordered world began spinning at supersonic speed.

Love had swept in like a force of nature, their lives and emotions colliding with dizzying intensity.

I don't want him to see me like this.

Desperate for privacy, Bobbi slipped into BR's bedroom—the one room Cassie hadn't shown her. She headed for the ensuite bathroom, closing the door quietly behind her. Cold water splashed on her face brought a brief shock of clarity.

She thought about calling her mother, just to hear a voice that would ground her, but decided against it. That would only bring more tears.

I'm on my own.

Gradually, she steadied her breathing. She leaned on the tools that had always gotten her through—rationalization, compartmentalization, medical logic. The same mental shift she'd use when delivering a devastating diagnosis.

Name the symptoms.

Find the solution.

But in a quiet, rarely accessed corner of her heart, she felt something rawer: a deep, abiding loneliness. Bobbi was proud of her life, but she'd done it alone.

Her tears weren't just about tonight. They came from eleven years of silent longing—for the children she never had, for a partner to share her life with. Tonight's overwhelming rush of love—for and from Cassie—had cracked open something buried deep.

She could have had a date every night if she wanted. Men—and sometimes women—asked her out constantly. Megan used to tease her, "You need one of those deli-counter ticket machines just to keep track of everyone who wants a shot." But Bobbi rarely said yes.

She'd indulged in the occasional discreet hookup—something only Megan knew about—but she'd never been invested emotionally. Most men were drawn to her looks. Few ever got close enough to see her mind, her depth, her heart. And no one had ever captured her interest or her heart. She needed depth. Substance. Soul.

Then, one ordinary day, she got lost, stepped out of a painting, and BR had appeared. And with him, a love that felt bottomless. Not just for her. For Sami, too.

Bobbi knew what needed to happen next.

A life-changing conversation.

It's too soon. But it has to happen now.

She dried her face and, for the first time, took a moment to explore BR's bedroom.

Its simplicity surprised her. Unlike the artful elegance of the rest of the penthouse, his room was minimal, almost bland—no trace of other women.

On the nightstand were three framed photographs.

The first: Cassie, beaming on a pony, joy radiating brighter than Times Square.

The second: Anna Maria and Siobhán perched on a fence, spring sunlight and horses behind them.

And the third stopped Bobbi in her tracks: Marco's photo of her and BR. Not a portrait of her. A picture of them.

It was the only image of a woman in his most intimate space. The only clue to who held his heart.

The sight of it steadied her.

She calmed her heart rate. Then she turned and walked out of the bedroom.

Toward the living room.

Toward BR.

Toward whatever came next.

~~~

BR

BR sat quietly on the corduroy couch, lost in thought. He loved the feeling of Bobbi in his home. It felt as if it had always been meant to be.

But something tugged at him. Cassie had assumed there'd be a next time—another dinner, another story, another braid. She'd spoken about it with complete certainty. Yet Bobbi hadn't. She hadn't said no, but she hadn't said yes either. And BR had noticed.

While they were on the house tour, he'd remembered that Bobbi's older phone couldn't send or receive pictures. He pulled out his JadePhone and scrolled through the photos he'd snapped earlier. He chose his two favorites—one where Cassie was giving Bobbi bunny ears, and one where they were smiling and glowing with happiness.

He tapped the screen and printed them. From a drawer, he found two small frames and slipped the pictures inside. Then he tucked them into a gift bag, planning to surprise Bobbi before she left.

But as he sat with the bag in his lap, he hesitated.

Why *hadn't* she promised to braid Cassie's hair again?

Was something wrong? Had he missed a sign? Doubt crept in. Was he getting ahead of himself? Was she?

He didn't know. And that uncertainty gnawed at him.

~~~

Bobbi

Bobbi wandered toward the living room windows and drew back the drapes. From this lofty perch, the view of Times Square was mesmerizing—distant, glittering, unreal.

She felt BR wrap his arm gently around her waist, and she instinctively leaned into him, resting her head on his good shoulder.

"Did Cassie go to sleep okay?"

"Mmhmm," she murmured, savoring a few more seconds of his quiet touch. "Can you see the New Year's Eve ball drop from here?"

"Yes, right there." He pointed. "The crowds start early, and by four p.m., the area's completely locked down. No one gets in or out until well after midnight."

Bobbi sighed, picturing a future New Year's Eve here—just the two of them, candles lit, making love while a million people cheered outside.

Then reality returned.

They wouldn't be alone, not really.

Shaken from the daydream, she turned to face him. "Let's sit down."

She tucked her legs beneath her as they settled on the couch. "I'm feeling really emotional, so this might come out jumbled," she said softly, "but I need you to promise to listen—no interrupting—until I've finished."

BR nodded, worry written across his face.

Her voice caught. "I've fallen deeply in love with you. We've only been 'us' for three weeks—I get it if you're not there yet—but you need to know where I stand. No one's ever made me feel so seen, so valued. These have been the happiest days of my life."

He nodded again, silent.

"If it were just us—no kids, no responsibilities—we wouldn't even be having this conversation. We'd be in your bed right now. Honestly? After our first date, I fantasized calling in sick just to stay in bed with you. And I guarantee it would've been the best physical therapy session of your life." She gave a shaky laugh, trying to ease the intensity. They hadn't talked much about sex; they'd been too busy falling in love.

She could see him fighting the urge to respond, but he stayed quiet, honoring her request.

"But it's not just us," she continued, more composed now. "I trusted you enough to let you meet Sami on our first official date—that's how safe I felt with you. And watching how much you two adore each other fills me with joy.

"If this didn't work out, I'd be devastated, but I'd heal. Sami's different. She wears her heart on her sleeve. She'd be crushed."

Tears welled in her eyes. "That's why I was so cautious about meeting Cassie. I thought I could handle it ... until I met her. Oh, BR, she's precious. And I already love her. You saw it—she trusted me right away. She opened her little heart because she knew she'd be safe with me."

Part of her wanted BR to kiss her, to pull her close and promise everything would be fine. But right now, she needed him to be steady—to hold space for her pain.

"Imagine if we introduced the girls," Bobbi whispered, "and they loved each other, and then it didn't work out. How would you explain to Cassie why she'd never see me or Sami again?"

Tears rolled down both their cheeks.

"The easiest thing in the world would be loving that sweet child, braiding her hair, teaching her everything girls should know. But the *worst* thing I could do is break her heart. Sami might understand—at least conceptually—that sometimes relationships end. But Cassie would feel abandoned. I couldn't live with that. *We* can't let that happen."

BR closed his eyes. His shoulders shook.

Bobbi steadied herself, sliding into her more rational voice. "I see three options," she said quietly. "One, we acknowledge these past three weeks were beautiful. Maybe in another life, we would've had forever. We could end things now, and hold on to the memories."

"That is *not* an option," BR interrupted, his voice fierce. "Don't *ever* say that again."

She paused, surprised by the force of it.

"Two, we slow things down. We keep it just between us for now—no Sami, no Cassie. And third"—she took a breath—"we take a leap of faith. We keep going at this pace, with both kids in the mix. Sometimes, it'll be just us. Sometimes, it's the four of us. I'm open to that, but only if we both believe this is real and lasting."

Her expression softened. "I'm not angling for a proposal. Normally, we'd take our time—no rush, no pressure. Being with you makes me happy. I'd love to disappear with you for a weekend in Cape Cod or Bermuda. But as a mom, I don't get to think just about myself. I have to think about the girls."

She drew in a breath. "I love you, BR. And I owe you an apology. I didn't expect to fall for Cassie this fast. I'm sorry if it feels like I'm pushing or trapping you—that's not my intention. Most couples wouldn't have this talk so soon, but we're not most couples. We have to talk about what this means for them—for Sami and Cassie. Can you forgive me for bringing this up now?"

"Forgive you?" he echoed, voice breaking. "Bobbi ... I'm in love with you."

"You are?" she whispered, blinking back tears.

He kissed her. Softly. Completely.

And just like that, the last of her fears melted away.

~~~

BR

"I'm in love with you," he said again, his voice steady. "I've never said those words to any other woman, and I'll never say them to anyone else. It's always been you. There's only you. So, you tell me: are you fully committed to building a future with me, now and in the years ahead?"

Bobbi shifted so they were face-to-face. "I'm yours—heart, soul, and body."

They kissed through their tears.

"Okay then," BR whispered. "We're agreed—full speed ahead. I promise that my love for you and Sami will guide everything I do. I'll never make an important decision without you. We'll do right by each other, and by our kids."

Bobbi cupped his face, eyes shining with love. BR was intoxicated by the scent of her skin, the warmth of her hands.

"I'll spend the rest of my life proving you made the right choice," she vowed. "Cassie already chose me."

They sank into silence, wrapped in each other. Bobbi rested her head on his chest, her hair tickling his nose. He stifled a sneeze and brushed it gently away.

"Better get used to that." She laughed. "It comes with the territory."

She pulled back. "Wait—did we just get engaged?"

BR chuckled. "Oh, Bobbi … you'll know it when I propose. I'll make it romantic and unforgettable, so you'll know just how much I want you to say yes. Until then, there's a wonderful phrase from the 1800s we can use: *we have an understanding*."

"So, we're engaged to be engaged?" She grinned. "I love our understanding."

"You know what we have to do next?"

Bobbi kissed him fiercely, her body radiating unmistakable desire. He returned her passion, savoring the moan she gave as he kissed the curve of her neck.

Then he pulled back slightly, cradling her face in his hands. "There's something I want you to do for me."

"Anything. I'll do *anything* for you."

"Do you have plans after work tomorrow?"

"No," she whispered. "I'm yours."

He handed her the gift bag.

She peeked inside then gasped softly. Clutching the two framed photos of her and Cassie to her chest, she closed her eyes in gratitude.

"Bobbi, my love … how about you and Sami come here tomorrow? Let the girls meet. Let's spend our first day together as a family."

CHAPTER TWENTY-FIVE: FIRST FAMILY DAY
Saturday, January 23
Bobbi

Bobbi stood naked in front of her bedroom mirror, feeling pretty proud of herself. It wasn't even noon, and she'd already knocked out a hefty chunk of her to-do list.

Her day had started, as usual, by checking eagerly for BR's morning text, but an SOS from Red had derailed her plans. In a flash, Bobbi had been out the door, picking up aspirin, refilling Megan's prescription, and grabbing emergency feminine supplies. While waiting at the pharmacy, she had dashed into the adjacent bodega, returning with flowers and chicken soup for her best friend, who'd claimed to be "bedridden with cramps and existential dread."

After making sure Red took her meds, Bobbi had tucked her in with a heating pad, queued up a movie, and left strict instructions to *eat the soup.*

Next stop: Williamsburg to return a book Gina had left behind. Then back to Brooklyn Heights, where she'd requested a rush order from her favorite bakery. The pastry decorator—a longtime patient—had agreed to have the custom cake ready in an hour.

Her ancient phone was still hanging by a thread, but she'd managed to send BR a confirmation text about their plans. Then she'd squeezed in a brutal boot camp, led by Jolene Hex, a nationally ranked fitness competitor. By the end, only Bobbi and one other woman had remained standing; the rest had quit or collapsed.

Last night, Bobbi had told Sami about the plan for their visit to BR's penthouse. Sami had shrieked with excitement then came up with a plan to surprise Cassie. It involved a trip to a specialty shop in downtown Brooklyn, but she'd promised to be ready as soon as Bobbi returned from the gym.

However, the moment Bobbi had stepped through the front door, she'd known better. A bleary-eyed Sami had clearly just stumbled out of bed, pretending she'd been up and dressed for hours. One look from her mother had told her the act hadn't fooled anyone.

With their shopping mission complete, they'd made it home just as the snow had begun to fall. Bobbi had organized the bags, laid out her outfit, and taken a quick shower. Still wrapped in a towel, she knocked on Sami's door.

"Ten-minute warning," she called. "With this weather on a Saturday, the drive into Midtown will take a while. You should probably use the bathroom before we go."

"Mom," Sami groaned, rolling her eyes in classic preteen exasperation, "*I'm* not the one who's five."

A satisfied smile crept across Bobbi's face as Sami, after a beat, turned around and headed straight to the bathroom.

She was waiting downstairs when Bobbi came down, fully dressed.

"Mom, you're not wearing a skirt. BR won't recognize you."

Bobbi laughed. "It's time he learned that his girlfriend usually wears pants."

Sami grinned. "You look great, Mom. Those jeans make your butt look amazing."

~~~

Stewart had brought the big car, ensuring plenty of room to stretch out in luxury—a detail Sami thoroughly enjoyed.

"Baby," Bobbi said gently, "this is going to be new for all of us. Cassie's a doll, but she's so young. She might cling to me while we're there. I don't want you to feel neglected."

"Don't worry, Mom. BR's taking me to his music room to help with my audition. And I'm excited to get to know Cassie better. It's all going to be fine."

Bobbi nodded, watching Sami's excitement build.

"This car is amazing! Do you think he'll let me hold his Tony? What's his house like? Can you see Times Square from there? I can't wait!"

~~~

Stewart whisked them upstairs. As the door swung open, Cassie's excited shriek rang out.

"Bobbbiiii!" she cried, hurling herself into Bobbi's arms.

BR followed with a warm hug for Sami, making it feel like a true reunion.

"Hi, Sami! Wanna see my room?" Cassie asked eagerly.

"Sure!" The two girls disappeared down the hall, hand in hand, giggling.

"Don't worry," BR said, chuckling as he watched them go. "Give them a couple weeks—they'll start to warm up to each other."

"One less thing to worry about." Bobbi smiled, miming an invisible checkmark in the air. "Now, my next concern is when you're going to kiss me hello."

A tender kiss followed. Bobbi made another checkmark.

"You look so hot in those jeans," BR said.

She twirled, adding one more imaginary check.

"So ... you don't just love me for my legs?" she teased then leaned into him. "Do you really want to marry me?"

"Bet your hot, little, denim-covered butt I do. And I've got surprises for you."

After stashing the cake box in the fridge, Bobbi followed BR into a stunning corner bedroom overlooking Times Square. A hand-lettered sign on the door read, *"Bobbi and Sami's Room,"* decorated with a child's drawing of a woman holding hands with two girls.

"I want you and Sami to have your own space," BR said, gesturing to a private bathroom. "I don't want you to feel like guests. Bring clothes, toiletries—whatever you want."

Overwhelmed, Bobbi threw her arms around his neck and kissed him deeply. "I think this bathroom is bigger than Sami's entire bedroom back home." She laughed. "You treat me like a queen. Don't think I don't notice."

BR motioned for her to sit. "I got you another present." He handed her a turquoise gift bag. Inside, beneath layers of wrapping paper, was the newest model JadePhone.

Bobbi raised an eyebrow. "Sweetheart, that's really sweet but unnecessary. I have a phone."

BR laughed. "The *only* thing I don't like about you is your phone. You can't take or send pictures. I'm pretty sure a telegraph would be faster. This way, we can share photos, have a family calendar, even video call Cassie on her JadePad. Don't worry; it's all on my household account."

She'd needed a new phone for years but never justified the splurge. The phone was expensive. She didn't know the price, but she knew what it meant: he wanted them closer. And so did she.

"Thank you. It'll definitely make my life easier. And our goodnight calls can be a whole lot more fun ... if you know what I mean," she added suggestively.

He blushed. "One more thing; I got Sami the basic model. Her starter phone."

Before she could speak, he continued quickly, "I know you don't want her having a phone until sixth grade. I'd never go behind your back. You can put it away until fall if you prefer."

Bobbi studied the phone in silence.

"I may be overprotective," BR admitted. "But with her going between your house, school, your mom's, Hunter's, and now here ... I'd feel better knowing we could reach her. The phone has a feature where you can see where she is."

Bobbi looked up, her voice soft. "I'm getting a little choked up."

"Why?" BR asked, confused.

"I've never co-parented before. We'll have to trust each other—listen, communicate—as we raise our girls. You're right; the phone *will* help. I'll set boundaries, and she can have it now. But let's be careful. I don't want her getting used to expensive gifts and limo rides."

"Understood." BR nodded. "You're the mom; you set the rules. And I want Cassie to grow up grounded, too. I've got Dev upstairs. He's great with tech; he can set it all up for you."

Bobbi hugged him tightly. "You don't need to walk me up. Just tell me how to get there and how to find him. Can I ask him to set up Sami's, too, while you keep an eye on the girls?"

~~~

Bobbi returned forty-five minutes later to find Cassie and Sami giggling on the couch.

"What are you two up to?" she asked as BR waved from the kitchen.

Cassie burst into laughter. "Sami's showing me funny baby animal videos!"

Bobbi lingered with them for a few minutes, laughing along, then gave BR a subtle signal. Together, they slipped away to her room.

"Dev is amazing," she said, holding up her new JadePhone. "I can't believe all the features. He also gave me this." She handed BR a small packet with personalized codes and keys for the secure elevator and front door, including one for Sami.

BR smiled, his expression tender. "I'm glad Dev took good care of you."

Their eyes locked.

Bobbi's voice dropped, rich with emotion. "You take good care of me, too. I'm going to have a key made for you, for our place."

She stepped closer, her voice steady. "Our family's going to be beautiful."

~~~

Cassie reluctantly agreed to a nap after a story from Bobbi. While she slept, BR gave Sami a long singing lesson. And Bobbi stretched out on the bed, watching TV, but soon dozed off.

She woke to a dreamlike scene: Sami standing in front of the mirror, holding an Oscar and practicing her acceptance speech.

"Dr. Bobbi!" Cassie called from the hall. "Did you bring your doctor's bag? We have to check on Howard!"

Sliding into character, Bobbi got up and conducted a full medical exam.

"Howard has made a complete recovery," she announced. "He's cleared to attend the tea party." She pulled out her prescription pad and wrote:

> *Give Howard ten hugs and ten kisses every*
> *day for ten days. ~ Dr. Bobbi Wyatt*

Cassie read it aloud, stumbling on the final word. "What does this say?"

"That's my last name," Bobbi said, sounding it out. "It's Sami's last name, too."

"Dr. Bobbi Wyatt," Cassie repeated thoughtfully. "Am I Nurse Cassie Wyatt?"

Bobbi smiled. "No, sweet pea. You're Nurse Cassie Bradford—my *favorite* nurse."

Returning to the living room, Bobbi grinned. "BR, here's a sentence I've never said before: did you give Sami permission to play with your Oscar?"

"I did *not*!" BR said, feigning outrage. "That sneaky little thief. I'm calling security. They'll toss her in the gutter. Now, what do you want for dinner? I'm thinking pizza."

"You expect me to eat pizza after you have my daughter thrown out of the building?" Bobbi huffed.

He shrugged. "You've got to eat. Besides, you can always get another kid. But an Oscar? Those are hard to come by."

Cassie emerged in a princess dress. "Can we have our tea party now?"

"In a few minutes," Bobbi replied. "Why don't you start setting up?"

She whispered to BR, "Sami and I have a surprise for her. You'll want to take pictures."

"Great," BR replied. "Want me to use your phone?"

Bobbi's heart melted. "Cassie's face will be the first thing on it."

Before they changed, Bobbi handed Sami the starter phone. Sami nearly fainted with excitement and eagerly agreed to all of Bobbi's conditions, obviously.

When they reappeared, Cassie gasped with delight, and BR began recording.

Bobbi entered dressed as Princess Rapunzel in a flowing purple gown, her long golden hair cascading down her back. Sami wore a Princess Moana costume, complete with a flowered headband and the shell bracelet Red had brought from Tahiti.

The tea party wrapped up just as dinner arrived.

"BR," Sami begged, eyes wide, "can we eat by the windows so I can see the lights come on in Times Square?"

"Daddy, we can have a picnic!" Cassie added.

After Bobbi gave the nod, BR rearranged the furniture, setting the low coffee table in front of the windows. They sat on the floor—Cassie on Bobbi's lap, and Howard with Sami, who live-streamed the view for Hunter.

Dessert was Bobbi's doing: a lemon sponge cake decorated with a heart and the inscription:

BR + Bobbi + Sami + Cassie + Howard = LOVE

Later, BR filmed Bobbi braiding Cassie's and Sami's hair. As the evening wound down, she bathed Cassie and tucked her in with Howard, who received a precision tuck-in of his own.

"Bobbi, will you be here when I wake up?" Cassie murmured sleepily.

"No, sweet pea," she said softly. "But we'll video call tomorrow, okay?"

Cassie drifted off after a gentle back rub.

In the quiet that followed, Bobbi and BR curled up on the couch. "Could this have gone any better?" she asked, nestling into him.

Soon, Sami reappeared. "Is there any more cake?"

BR grinned. "If you and your mom want a little adventure and a treat, take the private elevator to the third-floor lobby. Ask the VIP concierge for three 'special deliveries for 2900.'"

Sami and Bobbi loved exploring the Art Deco lobby. At the desk, a smiling concierge handed them three warm walnut chocolate chip cookies. Glasses of lemonade awaited their return.

"Can I get extras for Hunter and Aunt Gina next time?" Sami asked.

"Of course," BR said. "They have them twenty-four seven. This is your second home now—help yourself."

Bobbi played along, eyes sparkling. "Wait—can I take what I want?"

"Absolutely."

"Good," she said with a grin. "Because I already did."

"Mom," Sami said, "while you kiss BR goodnight, can Ms. Sawyer take me to the lobby for more cookies? Meet us there?"

"You've created a monster," Bobbi said as Sami disappeared again.

"A very sweet cookie monster," BR replied just before they shared a long, joyful goodnight kiss.

CHAPTER TWENTY-SIX: BR IN BROOKLYN; CASSIE IN THE KITCHEN

Sunday, January 24
BR

Bobbi was incredulous. "You're not tired of us yet?"

"Not even a little," BR said without hesitation. "I want *more* of you."

"Typical man," she sighed.

"Is Cassie invited?"

Bobbi snorted. "Sweetie, if you think my parents would let you in *without* her, then you clearly haven't met the most kid-obsessed people in the world."

"Perfect."

Bobbi's tone shifted slightly. "Are you sure you want to come to Sunday dinner tonight? My family's dying to meet you, but there's zero pressure. I don't want Cassie to feel uncomfortable. Mom spontaneously offered last night—if it feels too soon, we can wait."

BR brushed off her concern. "Text me your mom's number. I'll coordinate with her."

~~~

"Daddy, what if they don't like me? Will Bobbi go away?" Cassie clutched Howard tightly on the drive across the Brooklyn Bridge.

"Sweetheart, what did Bobbi say when you asked her what to wear?"

"She said they'll love me."

"That's right. I bet they're just as nice as Bobbi and Sami."

Cassie scrunched her face. "Tell me their names again, Daddy."

"Mr. Whit and Mrs. Ingrid."

She repeated the names softly, growing more confident with each try.

A light dusting of snow danced around the bridge lights, casting a magical glow. BR's heart swelled. He couldn't wait to see Bobbi—for the third straight day.

Ingrid had told him not to bring anything, but he wanted to make a good impression. Remembering some of the details Bobbi had shared, he'd enlisted Cassie's help to plan two small surprises.

Cassie had loved their impromptu adventure. They'd trekked downtown to Little Italy to buy a box of Mr. Whit's favorite cannoli from a tiny mom-and-pop bakery. At the counter, Cassie had eagerly sampled each flavor, pausing after every bite to deliver her expert verdict. "The chocolate chip is so creamy," she declared. "The lemon tastes like a smile." After careful deliberation, she picked her two favorites.

At a nearby florist, she chose a bouquet of purple roses for Mrs. Ingrid, proudly pointing out the color.

As Ronnie guided the car over the bridge, BR's JadePhone chirped.

Sorry! We're running late. Mother Nature decided to visit. I had to stop by the store. Mom and Dad are waiting for you. We're ten minutes behind you. XX

Cassie clutched Howard. "I don't wanna go in if Bobbi's not there. Daddy, I feel shy."

BR gave her hand a reassuring squeeze. "How about I carry you and Howard in, then come back for the flowers and the cannoli?"

Cassie shook her head. "No. They'll think I'm a baby." She straightened her shoulders. "I'll be brave, but you have to hold my hand the whole time."

A tall, handsome man in a rust sweater, plaid shirt, and corduroy pants greeted them at the door with a warm smile. Beside him stood a petite woman with golden hair streaked with silver, her face glowing with welcome.

BR placed the flowers and package on a bench and extended his hand. "Hi, I'm BR Bradford."

Whit's smile turned sly. "Sorry, I didn't catch the name."

Ingrid and BR burst out laughing. He loved the twinkle in Whit's eye. People usually treated him with admiration, or at least caution. But Bobbi had bragged about her father's disarming charm and her mother's warm heart. In an instant, he knew he was going to love them.

Cassie didn't get the joke and clung tightly to her father's hand. Sensing her unease, BR had an idea, and he was sure Bobbi's dad would play along.

BR shifted into a cartoonish European accent and launched into a dramatic riff, mimicking the opening of one of Cassie and Sami's favorite shows.

"My deepest apologies, good sir. I am Heinrich von Wienerschnitzel, of the Des Moines Wienerschnitzels. May I present Her Most Serene Highness, Princess Cassandra Quinn von Wienerschnitzel of the Sheboygan Wienerschnitzels, and her noble escort, Howard, Duke of Moosylvania?"

Whit immediately clicked his heels and bowed at the waist.

Cassie dropped into a deep curtsy, her nervousness ebbing, earning smiles from all the adults.

"We're so glad you could join us, Princess Cassie. It's wonderful to meet you, and your father. I didn't realize how handsome Duke Howard would be," Ingrid said.

"Princess Cassandra, I'm Sami's grandfather, and this is her grandmother. Bobbi told us you're a wonderful girl and an excellent nurse."

BR was touched by how they were focused entirely on Cassie. He'd overheard Sami explaining that her grandparents were the best. She hadn't been exaggerating.

"I brought you flowers, Mrs. Ingrid. I hope you like them. I picked them out myself."

"Cassie dear, these are beautiful. Purple roses are my favorite; how did you know? I'll put them in water so we can enjoy them tonight."

Cassie handed Whit the box of cannoli. "These are for you, Mr. Whit."

Whit and Ingrid exchanged a knowing look—BR took it as a good sign.

"Did your dad let you taste them?" Whit asked, leaning in like it was a secret.

"Yes!" Cassie's eyes sparkled. "He said I had to taste them all to pick the perfect one for you."

"Well then," Whit said with a wink, "since *you* did all the work, I'll share them with you for dessert."

Cassie squealed with delight.

Gina swept past, turquoise hair shining, mouthing, "*Hello*," while pointing to the phone at her ear.

"Cassie, sweetheart," Ingrid said gently, "why don't you hang up your coat and put your backpack in the little cubby over there? Sami used it when she was your age."

Just then, Bobbi and Sami walked in. Sami ran to hug her grandfather, while Cassie immediately lifted her arms toward Bobbi. Bobbi scooped her up and kissed her forehead.

BR watched the scene, heart full. Everyone was blending together so naturally.

Sami gave her grandmother a kiss then hugged BR. Cassie wriggled out of Bobbi's arms and dashed over to Sami.

Gina reappeared, sliding her phone into the pocket of her black jeans. Her voice was gentle, which surprised BR— Bobbi always described Gina as loud and fast-talking.

"Hi, BR, I'm Gina," she said, waving quickly before turning her attention to Cassie.

Kneeling, she smiled warmly. "Hi, Cassie. I'm so happy to meet you. Can I say hello to Howard? I heard Bobbi fixed his boo-boo. How's he doing?"

Cassie hesitated before handing over her moose. "Howard's all better because Bobbi's a great doctor."

"Bobbi's the best doctor in the world," Gina said proudly. She kissed Howard's antler tenderly before handing him back. "And she told me you're the best nurse she's ever worked with."

Gina's phone buzzed again. She sighed and stood. "Sorry, Marco needs help with something at the restaurant."

Sami reappeared, now holding the roses in a vase. "Wanna see the room I stay in? I've got videos, and we can call Hunter!" she said excitedly.

Without a word, Cassie took off after her.

"I need to get back to the kitchen," Ingrid said. "Why don't you boys make yourselves comfortable?"

"Hey, Whit," BR said, "can I see your workshop? Bobbi told me you fix up old furniture until it's better than new and donate it through your church. I'm the least handy guy in the world; maybe you can inspire me."

"I'd love to," Whit replied enthusiastically. He looked to Ingrid. "Sweetheart, do you need anything from me?"

"I always need your help, but not at the moment. I'll put my girls to work."

Whit led the way, his easygoing manner immediately putting BR at ease.

The house reminded BR of a different Brooklyn—not the brownstone-lined streets of New York, but the tiny, working-class neighborhood on the edge of Steamboat Springs, Colorado, where he'd grown up. That Brooklyn sat in the shadow of one of the wealthiest resort towns in the country— a place known for ski homes, high-end boutiques, and exclusive restaurants.

But his corner of it had been another world. His family's house had been slightly larger than this one, but the warmth here ran deeper.

The smells from the kitchen, the distant laughter of Cassie and Sami, Whit's easy banter—it all wrapped around him like a soft quilt, whispering, *This is the world that shaped Bobbi. She comes from love.* And love, BR thought, impressed him far more than anything money could buy.

He was eager to see the dining room table that had hosted Sunday dinners since Bobbi was a girl. She'd told him her father built it, along with the banister, the hardwood floors, even the molding. BR ran his hand along the woodwork, appreciating the care in every detail.

The walls and shelves were filled with photos: Bobbi winning science fairs; beaming in her cap and gown at high school, college, and medical school; Gina, usually clowning for the camera; and Sami at every stage of life. Sami's crayon drawings still hung on the fridge—edges faded but lovingly preserved. A corner of the living room overflowed with Gina's craft supplies: a small sewing machine, spools of yarn, and half-finished projects.

BR noticed a small piano, its surface crowded with framed photos of Sami.

He thought, *This is the kind of home I want to create for Cassie.*

~~~

Bobbi

"Mom, what's wrong with Gina?" Bobbi asked the moment they stepped into the kitchen sanctuary.

"What in the world are you talking about?"

"When she was talking to BR and Cassie, Gina sounded … normal. Not like herself."

Ingrid shook her head, stroking her taller daughter's arm. "You underestimate her. If anyone knows what it's like to be a scared little girl coming into this house without a mommy, it's Gina. She's probably trying to make Cassie feel comfortable. You might also consider that she's trying not to embarrass you in front of your new boyfriend."

Bobbi's cheeks reddened. Mom was right, as always.

"What do you think of him, Mom?"

Before Ingrid could respond, Gina entered. Bobbi hugged her tightly, whispering, "You're really wonderful."

"I've been telling you that for years."

Bobbi didn't let go.

"Okay, weirdo, knock it off," Gina said in her usual staccato Brooklyn voice. "What are we gonna talk about first? The fact that he's even more handsome in person, or how much that adorable kid looks like a pint-sized clone of you, right down to your freaky green eyes?"

They huddled around the kitchen table, comparing notes.

The door swung open, and the kids burst in, giggling. Cassie climbed onto Bobbi's lap.

"BR's helping Grandpa in his workshop," Sami explained. "Cassie wanted to see the kitchen. When do we eat, Grandma? I could eat a whole lasagna by myself!"

"Soon," Ingrid said happily. "I made extra so you and your mother will have leftovers for tomorrow."

Sami whooped, making Cassie laugh.

"Cassie dear, Bobbi told me you'd like to learn how to cook and bake. Is that true?"

Cassie nodded shyly.

"If you'd like," Ingrid continued, "I could teach you."

"Like you taught Bobbi?" Cassie asked.

That sent Gina and Sami into fits of laughter, ignoring sharp glares from both Ingrid and Bobbi.

"What's so funny?" Cassie asked, tilting her head.

"The only things Mom knows how to make for dinner are takeout orders, reservations, and frozen pizzas," Sami said, barely keeping a straight face. She started to mime gagging, but stopped under Ingrid's look.

"Bobbi's the smartest person in the world," Gina added soothingly, "but she doesn't know how to cook."

"Is that true, Bobbi?" Cassie asked, eyes wide.

Bobbi chuckled. "I'm not a good cook. But Mrs. Ingrid is amazing. I'm sure she'd love to teach you."

Cassie turned to Sami. "Did she teach you?"

Sami's cheeks flushed as everyone looked her way. Gina and Bobbi tried not to laugh.

"Well, um ..." Sami stammered.

"Yeah," Bobbi teased. "You're always complaining about *my* cooking, but I never see *you* making dinner. Why is that?"

Sami scrambled. "Well, since Mom doesn't even know how to make toast, she'd probably make me cook every meal. I'm too young to have a full-time job!"

The room burst into laughter, Cassie giggling along.

Sami leaned into Gina, who wrapped an arm around her shoulders. "Aunt Gina's terrific in the kitchen. When I was little, she made all my food. She learned from Grandma."

"I could help Mrs. Ingrid teach you, Cassie," Gina offered warmly.

Cassie cupped her hand to Bobbi's ear, and they had a hushed conversation. Finally, Bobbi nodded. "You can ask her. It's okay, I promise."

Still unsure, Cassie asked softly, "Mrs. Gina, are you going to play jokes on me? Sami said you used to put icky pretend spiders in her slippers and ice cubes down Bobbi's back."

"Oh, Cassie, my naughty niece has been telling you all about me, huh?" Gina chuckled.

"She said you're always loud and silly and play tricks."

Sami said gently, "Don't worry; Aunt Gina and I tease each other all the time, but she watched me every day while Mom was in school. She made sure I always had fun and lots of good food."

"Sometimes I *am* silly and loud," Gina admitted. "And yes, I might play jokes on Sami and Bobbi once in a while, but I'd never do anything to make you unhappy."

Cassie studied her. "Then how come you're not loud and silly now?"

"Because I want you to feel safe and comfortable," Gina said softly.

Cassie furrowed her brow. "But Mrs. Gina, I want you to be happy and comfortable. Just be yourself."

Gina whispered something to Sami, who darted out of the room. Moments later, she returned and handed Gina a purple stuffed animal.

"Howard," Gina said sweetly, "meet Matilda the Mauve Moose. She used to live at Coney Island. Years ago, I won her for Sami at a carnival. We used to take turns snuggling with her. Now she lives here. When Sami or I stay over, she cuddles with us. But sometimes Matilda gets a little lonely during the day. Maybe you could be her new friend."

Howard bowed and kissed Matilda's hoof. Matilda hugged him. Soon, the two were seated side by side on a chair.

"Cassie," Ingrid said warmly, "Bobbi told me you love salads. Let's work as a team to make a super salad. You name the ingredients. Sami will get them from the fridge and wash them. If anything needs chopping, Aunt Gina will do it. I'll show you how to mix everything so it's balanced and pretty. How does that sound?"

Cassie's smile sparkled with joy. "Yes! But what will Bobbi do?"

"Maybe she can take the temperature of the tomatoes," Gina joked.

"Stay out of the way," Sami added.

Bobbi kissed Cassie's head. "They're only teasing," she whispered. "Gina and Sami like to be silly."

"You two are impossible," Ingrid sighed. "How about if Bobbi helps you wash your hands, then takes care of Howard and Matilda?"

The succulent smells of lasagna and freshly baked bread filled the kitchen as the team got to work. Bobbi watched Cassie bask in the warmth of so much feminine love, her delight shining through every moment.

When Ingrid called everyone to the table, Sami and Gina brought out the food.

"Ingrid darling, this all looks wonderful, but you forgot the salad," Whit said coyly.

"I didn't forget," Ingrid said proudly. "We had a special sous chef tonight. Please welcome … Chef Cassie."

With BR snapping pictures, Cassie entered, carrying the salad bowl, with help from Bobbi. She proudly placed it on the table.

Whit studied the salad with exaggerated seriousness. "Hmm," he said, nodding slowly. "This is a masterpiece. Well done, Chef Cassie."

Cassie glowed as everyone applauded. Then Bobbi helped her into Sami's old booster seat as the adults passed the dishes.

~~~

BR

BR, an introvert by nature, felt overjoyed when the conversation wasn't focused on him. Having spent most of his adult life with people clamoring for his attention because of his celebrity, his looks, or his wealth, he loved sitting back and watching Whit preside over the table.

Whit began by asking the children to share the highlight of their week.

Sami started, telling a lovely story about how she and Hunter had volunteered to eat lunch in a classroom every day with a new student with social anxiety.

BR's heart swelled with pride. Sami's thoughtful, matter-of-fact compassion moved him. It was the same quiet joy he felt when he saw Cassie being helpful or kind.

"The *other* best part of my week, Grandpa," Sami added, "was BR giving me a singing lesson! He played piano and helped me polish my audition for a solo at the end-of-year concert. It was so cool! He said I was doing great with my vocals."

"You have a beautiful voice, Sami," BR said. "You'll crush that audition."

"Takes after me." Gina crowed, grinning and jabbing a thumb at herself.

"You sing?" BR asked.

"I always tried to convince Gina to join the church choir," Ingrid said, "but she was determined to be a rock 'n' roll chick."

"Aunt Gina used to sing me to sleep with her go-to lullabies—songs from Green Day and The Ramones," Sami said.

BR rubbed his chin. "Let me guess ... 'Time of Your Life' and 'I Wanna Be Sedated.'"

He and Gina exchanged amused smiles. The image of teenage Gina rocking baby Sami to punk rock made him grin and made it easy to see why they were still so close.

"Daddy sings to me after prayers and when I wake up," Cassie said proudly. "Daddy's a great singer."

"I think I've heard that." Whit chuckled. "Cassie, what's the best thing that happened to you this week?"

Cassie put down her fork. "Bobbi saved Howard. I was scared, but she stayed calm and taught me how to be a nurse and clean his injury. I got to listen to Daddy's heart with a ..."

Bobbi leaned over and whispered.

"... a stethoscope, just like a real doctor. Bobbi gave Howard stitches. Now he's all better and likes Matilda. When I'm a grownup, I'm going to be a doctor and help people, just like Bobbi."

Whit turned to Bobbi, his voice catching just slightly. "I'm proud of you, Dr. Daughter."

Gina went next. "I get to be here tonight. Marco is short-staffed. I thought Bobbi and I were gonna have to jump in and help."

"You work at the restaurant?" BR asked, surprised.

"A few times I've filled in as an emergency server," Bobbi explained.

"That's the *only* time anybody lets Mom get near a kitchen," Sami cracked.

Bobbi made a face as Sami and Gina shared a fist-bump.

"If Bobbi ever gives up that whole doctor jazz," Gina said, "she'd be the world's richest server. We pool our tips, and let's just say every guy in the place was so busy staring at her that they couldn't throw money at us fast enough."

BR raised his eyebrows. Bobbi responded with a nonchalant shrug, implying, *What can you do*?

"Bobbi, what's your highlight?" Whit asked once the laughter died down.

"My whole week's been a highlight," she said. "Meeting sweet Cassie, spending time with BR, seeing Sami so happy, helping Howard, and having the world's best lasagna with all of you—I couldn't be happier."

"BR?" Whit asked.

"Being here. Right now."

Sami added, "And the other best part of my week was Mom letting me have a phone, and BR showing me where to get free cookies!"

Bobbi rolled her eyes. "BR, you're a bad influence."

"My highlight's easy," Ingrid said. "I have all my girls home for dinner tonight." She looked from Bobbi to Sami to Gina, and then she gently squeezed Cassie's hand. "And it was such a big help having Cassie's great work in the kitchen. That salad was beautiful."

Cassie beamed.

"BR," Whit said, "it's great to meet you. Did Bobbi tell you that Ingrid and I love your music?"

Bobbi's jaw dropped. "What? When did you ever go to Broadway?"

Whit chuckled. "Dr. Daughter, back in the day, your mother and I loved listening to music on a thing called a CD. We saw BR at Yankee Stadium during his big tour after *Snow in the River* came out."

"*You did?*" Bobbi's voice jumped. "You never went to a concert in my life. I don't believe it."

"It was after you left for Chicago," Ingrid said. "Your father worked extra shifts at the store and picked up weekends at the lumberyard to surprise me with tickets."

"I don't remember that," Gina said. She turned to Bobbi. "Who *are* these people?"

Bobbi shook her head. "No idea."

"You had your own things going on, Gina," Ingrid said gently. "It was a big transition—Bobbi was gone, and you were struggling, sweetheart. Uncle Whit knew how badly I wanted to go."

"You ask for so little, my love. I wanted to put a smile on your face."

BR smiled softly. "I'm humbled. I remember that night. The band was exhausted, but the crowd's energy was incredible. Afterward, we all said it was one of our best shows. I'm so glad you were there."

Ingrid's eyes glowed. "That concert was one of the greatest nights we ever had. BR, you were amazing."

Whit nodded. "Your energy was electric. I remember wondering: how can you do this much on the very last night of a tour?"

BR leaned back, gesturing like he was painting a picture. "It's something my father taught me. He was a huge Cubs fan and always dreamed of seeing a game at Wrigley. After years as a letter carrier, he finally got promoted to postmaster and went to a conference in Chicago. The Cubs were playing a meaningless, late-season game—last place, drizzly afternoon, nearly empty stadium.

"Late in the game, a batter hit a screaming shot down the third-base line. The third baseman dove into the mud, backhanded the ball, and threw the runner out from his knees."

BR noticed Bobbi leaning in, eyes wide.

"My first job was stocking ski gear after school. Nothing heroic. But my dad told me—no matter the job, no matter who's watching—you give your best. Like that player did. That's integrity."

Beside him, Bobbi slid her hand onto his arm.

He looked at Ingrid. "Before every show—tiny club, sold-out arena, or Broadway stage—I'd peek through the curtain, find a face or two, and think about how long they waited and saved for that ticket. I never wanted to disappoint them. So, when you say you enjoyed it, it means the world to me."

Gina asked, "Is it true you changed the setlist every night?"

"Absolutely. My band never knew what was coming next. Sometimes *I* didn't know. I let inspiration guide me. I wanted every show to be the best."

Dinner ended, and BR insisted on helping clear the table. He rinsed while Bobbi loaded the dishwasher, the two of them moving easily around each other in the cozy kitchen.

"I love your family," he said, handing her a plate.

"They love you, too," Bobbi whispered. She bumped his hip. "But fair warning—they might try to keep Cassie."

BR's heart swelled. Cassie, usually shy with new people, had been welcomed simply for being her sweet, curious self.

Bobbi leaned closer. "Don't worry; I won't let them. Sami and I already called dibs."

BR chuckled, handing her another plate. "And what about me?"

Bobbi gave a playful palm-down wobble—maybe yes, maybe no—her green eyes sparkling.

He laughed, warmth rising in him. *Home* didn't feel so far away anymore.

When they finished, they joined the others in the living room. Whit had the fireplace roaring. As soon as the kids polished off their cannoli and milk, they ran off to video call Hunter.

"She's a special girl, BR. You must be proud," Ingrid said.

BR looked at Whit. "You understand."

"I certainly do—times three: Bobbi, Gina, and Sami."

With Bobbi curled up beside him on the loveseat, her bare feet tucked against his thigh, BR sipped hot chocolate, soaking in the warm, easy atmosphere. Across from them, Gina lounged in an armchair, knitting.

BR tilted his head. "I wouldn't have pegged you for a knitter."

"Before Sami came along, I was in big trouble— smoking, drinking, making bad choices." She gave Whit a sheepish look. "Bobbi helped me quit, but I needed something to do with my hands. One day, I wandered into a craft store hosting a knitting demo. Walked out with needles and yarn. Aunt Ingrid just about fainted."

Bobbi grinned. "Gina's crazy talented. She can do any craft. She's got an Etsy store with a waiting list as long as the Brooklyn Bridge."

BR raised an impressed brow. "That's awesome."

"She used to make the cutest baby stuff for Sami," Bobbi added.

Sami and Cassie reappeared, hunting for more treats.

Ingrid glanced at the piano. "BR, would you play something for us?"

Though he typically refused such requests, he nodded. "On one condition—Sami sings with me. I want you to hear her audition piece."

Excitement buzzed as BR took a seat at the piano and played the opening chords. Sami stood beside him confidently.

"I'm Samantha Wyatt," she announced with poise, "and I'll be singing 'Dizzy Night.'"

Her voice filled the room. The adults exchanged glances—Sami always sang beautifully, but tonight, she was transcendent. BR played with restraint, letting her shine.

As the final note lingered, the room erupted in applause.

Gina hugged her tightly. "You're no Alicia Rodriguez, but you're not bad, kid."

"That song is gorgeous," Bobbi said. "Who did the original?"

Silence. Then every adult looked at BR.

Bobbi groaned and covered her face. "Just shoot me."

As Cassie yawned, the evening wound down.

At the door, Gina knelt and said, "Cassie, you're a great kid."

To everyone's surprise, Cassie ran into her arms. "I think you're great, Aunt Gina. I wish my hair was a pretty color like yours."

"Your hair is beautiful. It looks just like Bobbi's."

BR was moved by Cassie's openness and hearing her say *Aunt Gina.*

Cassie hugged Whit, who kissed her head and shook Howard's paw. "You did such a great job picking out the cannoli that I asked Mrs. Ingrid to wrap up the last one just for you."

He shot Sami a wink, letting her know one was waiting for her, too.

Ingrid and Cassie shared a warm hug.

"You were a wonderful helper," Ingrid said. "I packed extra lasagna. Daddy can heat it up for dinner tomorrow."

Outside, Ronnie buckled Cassie into her car seat as Bobbi wrapped her arms around BR's neck, making his heart flutter and his knees go weak.

She kissed him tenderly and whispered, "I'll be waiting for your call."

CHAPTER TWENTY-SEVEN: REVELATION DAY
Monday, January 25
Bobbi

After the whirlwind of a perfect weekend, Bobbi and BR shared a brief, sleepy phone call. Both were exhausted but still glowing from everything that had unfolded.

Just as Bobbi was about to hang up, BR surprised her.

"If I come to Brooklyn, can you have dinner with me tomorrow?" he asked, his voice softer than usual.

Bobbi's breath caught for a moment, her mind flicking to how much time they'd already spent together—three consecutive, magical days. "I'd love to," she said, warmth blooming in her voice. "I just didn't expect it."

"I loved every second of our family time," BR whispered, "but I never want to stop dating you. You're everything to me."

"I'm yours," she purred.

"I think we have a lot of good things to talk about."

~~~

Monday was nonstop at the clinic, and by the time Bobbi headed to the gym, she was ready for a reset. She dialed back her usual intensity—yesterday's cramps and lingering fatigue ensured that—but the familiar rhythm of work and exercise helped clear her mind.

She'd just finished stretching when BR walked in. Seeing him in her everyday world was rare, yet it somehow felt natural.

Before they stepped outside, Bobbi glanced down at her leggings and oversized sweatshirt. "Let's get out of here. I don't want someone taking our picture—I'm not exactly dressed for a date," she said, adjusting her messy bun.

BR chuckled. "You look perfect to me."

"Flatterer." She rolled her eyes. "How about we pick up a pizza and head to my place? Sami's at choir rehearsal. Afterward, she and Hunter are having dinner with their new friend. It'll just be us tonight, if you can handle me without makeup."

The pizza—extra tomato and basil for her; mushroom and spinach for him—hit the spot. Seated at her kitchen island, they fell into an easy rhythm, as natural and comfortable as a couple who'd been together for years instead of just a month.

"You're officially my parents' second favorite person I've ever brought to Sunday dinner. They absolutely *love* you."

"*Second* favorite?"

"Cassie's their all-time number one now. Sorry, the vote wasn't close."

BR shook his head. "I was ready to be defensive, but I can't argue with their choice."

They moved over to the couch to nibble on some grapes. As usual, Bobbi tucked her ice-cold feet under BR.

After kisses, Bobbi confided, "My parents were already prepared to love you because Sami and I love you. But you won their hearts all on your own. When you gave Sami her lesson on Saturday, I knew it was the first time you'd played piano in months. I saw you rubbing your left hand afterward."

"I'm out of practice," he admitted.

"So I was surprised when you agreed to play last night. My family saw how you made it all about Sami. You care more about her happiness, Cassie's, and mine than your own." She smiled teasingly. "Of course, you could've been the biggest slug in the world, and as long as you brought Cassie, you were in."

"You've always said your family's amazing. The way they welcomed Cassie, how they made her feel so at home and so loved ... your parents are incredible." He added, "Gina took me by surprise. I'm glad you explained why she was subdued. I was confused at first, but she's wonderful. And her knitting? Siobhán loves handmade clothes—I'll definitely place some orders for birthdays and Christmas."

Uncharacteristically, BR rubbed his temples and mentioned a slight headache, which he attributed to accidentally putting in his old contact lenses.

"Why don't you come upstairs and rest on my bed while I shower?"

BR stretched out, discovering the comfort of the shroud for the first time.

Bobbi grabbed clothes from her dresser, glancing at him sprawled on her bed. She shook her head and sighed ruefully. "I finally get you in my bed, and just my luck, I'm out of commission for a couple of days. Sometimes, a girl can't catch a break."

When she returned a few minutes later, her damp hair framed her face, and she wore flannel pajama shorts and a white tank top. She slid into bed beside BR, resting an arm across his chest and draping her leg over his.

BR stirred awake. He tilted her chin up and kissed her gently.

"Feel better?" she asked.

"I do. And I can't imagine a more wonderful way to wake up."

Bobbi smiled, tracing lazy circles on his forehead. "Why don't you leave an extra pair of glasses here, and some clothes? I want this to feel like your bedroom, too."

He nodded happily. "I don't get to see your hair down very often. It's so beautiful. Someday, I *really* want you to let me wash it for you."

"I'd love that." She sat up, brushing her hair back over her shoulders.

"Sweetheart," she began, "there are a couple of things I need to tell you about me. Can we talk seriously for a few minutes? This is going to be hard for me."

He sat up, fully alert now, and leaned back against the headboard. "I want to know everything about you—for the rest of my life."

"There are two things. I know the first one won't be an issue, but the second one's difficult."

"Okay," he said, calm and reassuring.

"First, you should know that I like girls."

BR tilted his head. "So do I. Just one more thing we've got in common."

Bobbi laughed, leaning forward to kiss him. "No. I mean, I've *been* with girls in the past."

"Me, too," he said lightly, eyes twinkling.

She smirked and shook her head. "I knew it wouldn't be an issue for you, but I needed you to know."

His voice turned serious. "Of course it's not a problem."

She smiled fondly. "It only seems fair to tell you that your girlfriend's sampled both sides of the buffet, so to speak."

BR stroked her hair, his blue eyes calm and kind. "My only question is whether it affects our relationship moving forward."

"Absolutely not," Bobbi replied emphatically. "You're the only person for me, now and forever. No one else."

"Then it's a closed matter."

"And don't ever get any funny ideas. I'm never letting any other woman get that close to you!"

After laughter and more kisses, BR lay back with a smile. After a quiet beat, he asked, "Do you have a lawyer?"

She blinked. "Do I need one just to make out with my boyfriend? If I have to sign an NDA for kissing you, you're going to need a whole team of lawyers for what I've got in mind," she teased, her voice husky.

"An NDA? Are you kidding? I want to shout from the rooftops, 'Bobbi is mine!'"

That earned him a passionate kiss, and a question. "Why do you ask if I have a lawyer?"

"I talked to Sam Halifax—you met him briefly. He's my head of legal and a good friend. I told him, in confidence, that we plan to adopt each other's kids when we get married. He brought in Juliana Tricocci, his top associate. She has a background in family law and helped with Anna Maria's conservatorship and Cassie's adoption. She's terrific. You'll really like her."

"She'd help us with the adoption process?"

"Absolutely. It's very important to me that you're not just Cassie's stepmother. I want you to be her mother—by choice and forever."

"That's exactly how I feel about you and Sami."

"I also wanted to tell you a little more about Cassie's background. Her biological mother is a distant cousin—Sophia. She lives in Bradford, England. A sweet, sincere kid. She got pregnant in high school and wanted her baby to stay in the family but have a better life. Technically, Cassie's my second cousin once removed. But I'm the only father she's ever known. And you'll be her only mother."

Bobbi ran a hand across his cheek. "There are a lot of reasons I fell in love with you. But that first night, at the Red Dragonfly, when you told me about Cassie, I felt like you were showing me your heart. You could've just sent Sophia money to raise the baby. But that's not what she needed, was it?"

"No," he said softly. "She didn't have money and, of course, I offered. But what she needed was peace. She believed her baby would find it with me. And somehow ... I believed it, too."

"Will she be part of Cassie's life? Will she object to me adopting her?"

"Juliana covered all of that with her. Sophia wanted a clean break and the certainty that her baby would be loved and never want for anything. She told me she'd never reach out again, to avoid any future confusion. I haven't spoken to her since the day Cassie was born."

BR held Bobbi close as her shoulders shook. "I love you, and I couldn't love Sami more."

That gave Bobbi the courage she needed. "I know. More importantly, Sami knows. And my family—especially Gina—wouldn't let you anywhere near her if they didn't trust you."

He smiled and nodded.

"You've never asked who Sami's biological father is."

"Of course not. I've wondered, sure. But I figured you'd tell me when you were ready."

She sighed. "You're so perfect for me."

"That first night, when Gina and Sami called you with that whole fake-emergency routine, I remember thinking, you're such an amazing mom. Your daughter adores you, and the two of you have so much fun. That only happens when there's complete trust."

Bobbi tapped his chest. "Exactly. I grew up with that, but I've never told Sami who her father is. Someday, I will, and having you beside me will make it easier. When she was little, I'd just say he wasn't part of our life. Now I joke that she's the second immaculate conception."

BR laughed. "I'd believe you."

"I want us to be a team, like my parents are. I want our girls to grow up knowing that their parents are best friends and always tell the truth. You deserve to know."

BR didn't speak. He folded his hands in front of his mouth, his calm presence helping her find the words.

"Do you want the long or short version?" she asked.

"Tell me what you need to say."

"Would you mind going downstairs and opening that new bottle of wine in the fridge? Bring me a glass?"

When he returned, she took a deep breath. "You know I graduated high school more than two years early. My parents saved every nickel from the moment I was born to make sure

I could go to college. It was a huge financial drain when Gina came to live with us—legal expenses, medical bills, therapy, rehab."

"I remember," he said quietly. "That's why you took the full ride at the University of Chicago."

"Right. There was an iconic professor there, Dr. Sam Rabinowitz. He was the longtime dean of the medical school and a legend. By the time I got there, his health was failing, and everyone knew he didn't have much time left. But his mind was as sharp as ever. He became my mentor.

"For forty years, Dr. Rabinowitz personally chose one student from each class to mentor—first-year undergrad through final-year med school. We call ourselves 'Sam's Kids.' We still have a network and look out for each other. I was the youngest, and the last. I'll always carry that with me. I'm the last of 'Sam's Kids.'" Her voice broke, and she sobbed.

BR wrapped his arms around her, holding her close.

"He was such a great man," she whispered. "I miss him."

When she regained her composure, she sat up to face BR. "I graduated mid-year at nineteen. Meanwhile, Gina was … struggling. Mom poured so much love into her, but she was on a self-destructive path. I felt so guilty because it started after I left for school.

"When Dad told me they were coming to my graduation, my first thought was, 'What'll you do with Gina?' Then I worried about the expense. I was so proud my college education hadn't cost them a dime, but I knew how much they'd spent on Gina. Dad said no power in the world could stop them from seeing their daughter graduate.

"The pre-med students elected me as a commencement speaker. It was the proudest moment of my life. My family sacrificed everything for me, and now they saw their faith in me justified."

She exhaled, her hands trembling as she fiddled with her hair. "That night, Mom and Dad insisted on taking Dr. Sam and his wife, Ida, to dinner. I worried about the cost and tried to pay, but Dad was offended—it was one of the few times he was ever disappointed in me.

"Gina looked like a wreck—an eating disorder, smoking, drinking, maybe worse. But that night, she sat beside me at dinner, with her blue hair and lipstick, trying so hard to behave because she loved me. Later, I learned Dr. Sam had called my parents regularly to update them on me. I felt so loved."

BR's voice was quiet. "The world needs more people like your Dr. Sam."

Bobbi nodded, tears pooling in her eyes again. "At dinner, Dr. Sam dropped the most life-changing news. 'Bobbi, I spoke with the university president and the board. They've agreed that you're one of the most talented and promising medical students we've ever had. They're offering you a full-ride scholarship to cover all of medical school. You'll graduate as a doctor without any student debt. You'll need to live on campus and occasionally work as a TA, but please know we all believe in you.'

"Mom and Dad were out of their minds with excitement and pride. I was in shock. On top of my undergrad scholarship, this meant they were handing me over half a million dollars to live my dream.

"But then I looked at Gina. While everyone else was celebrating, Gina looked devastated. She ran to the bathroom.

I was so worried about her that I followed. She wouldn't—or couldn't—talk to me. Gina had been counting the days until I came home to New York."

Bobbi's emotions were raw as she continued. "That night, Gina stayed at my campus apartment. We slept in one bed, like we did when we were girls. I told her I was scared for her, and she said, 'I'm scared for me, too, Bobbi.'

"I said, 'How about I leave Chicago and go to medical school in New York? I'll go to Columbia, get an apartment, and you can live with me. I'll help you. I love you more than anyone and can't watch you hurt yourself. I'll do anything to help you.'"

BR's hand was on his heart, as if to keep it from breaking.

"The next day, the three of them flew home. My emotions were a jumble. I was proud of my achievements, and I loved my job in the lab. But I felt guilty knowing my success was coming at the cost of Gina's mental health. I felt like she'd self-destruct if I didn't go back home to help.

"That night, there was a party on campus. I wasn't a virgin, and while I occasionally had a beer, I didn't drink much. I just had to relax."

Bobbi stopped talking. Her silence was heavy, her body motionless, like the pause before a storm. When she spoke again, her voice was flat and emotionless.

"The next morning, I woke up on my couch, wearing only my bra and socks. My clothes, underwear, and shoes were nowhere to be seen. And I knew I'd had sex.

"I was in shock. I became scared that whoever attacked me might still be in the apartment. I was terrified he'd kill me. I wasn't going to go down without a fight." Bobbi's tone remained detached, as if she were recounting someone else's story.

"Survival instincts kicked in. I crawled to the kitchen and grabbed my largest knife. When I realized the apartment was empty, I locked the door, sat on the floor, hugged my knees, and cried until I ran out of tears. I didn't know what to do. I had no memory of the night before, but it was clear someone had brought me a drugged drink. I was so ashamed and scared." She paused before whispering, "I'd been raped."

Tears streaked BR's face. She handed him a tissue.

"When I finally stopped crying, my logical brain kicked in. I went to the lab and ran an STD screen to make sure I was safe. After it came back clean, I thought I was in the clear. But you can probably guess the rest. A couple of weeks later, I missed my period. I was pregnant. I don't know who Sami's father is. All I know is that he's a rapist.

"That's why I've never told Sami—she's too young to understand. I've spent her whole life trying to protect her from the darkness of how she came to be. But I know that, one day, when she's older, I'll have to tell her the truth. She deserves to know, even if the thought terrifies me."

BR held her, and she nestled into his chest. He kissed her head, and Bobbi felt the depth of his love in his unwavering affection.

"I couldn't call the police—what could I tell them? I was too ashamed to call home. I'd never felt so alone in my life.

"Thinking the cold air might clear my head, I took a long walk and debated what to do. Having a baby would end my dream of becoming a doctor. I thought through every option. Eventually, I walked to the women's clinic and made an appointment for Monday to terminate the pregnancy."

She paused and stared into his deep blue eyes. She saw no judgment, only love. She knew BR's religious faith ran deep, but he wouldn't judge her—not for what had happened or what she'd considered.

"My father always said never make an important decision when you're upset or before you've talked it through with someone you trust. So, I showed up at Dr. Rabinowitz's house uninvited. He and Ida welcomed me and fed me. I only picked at my food, but somehow, they knew to wait until I was ready to talk." Her words were slow and measured, masking the immense effort it took to hold herself together.

"We talked everything out. Dr. Sam promised to stand by me no matter what I decided. But he asked me the most important question."

Quietly, BR asked, "What'd he say?"

"He said to consider my future relationship with my parents. Keeping this secret for the rest of my life might create a wedge between us, one that would hurt me.

"At that moment, I knew he was right. I needed my mommy and daddy. Dr. Sam convinced me they'd never turn away from me."

Bobbi took a deep breath. "I flew home the next day. Dr. Sam emailed my professors, saying I was under the weather. Even though I'd already graduated with my bachelor's, my scholarship covered another semester. I was taking extra classes to shorten my time in medical school."

BR shifted so that he could hold her. "I wish I could've met him. I'll always bless the memory of someone who cared for you so much."

"He would have loved you," she sighed.

"I took a bus to Midway, flew into LaGuardia, and was back in Brooklyn by early afternoon. I'd told Dad I was homesick. He was at work, and Mom was out when I got home, but Gina was there. She knew something was wrong the second she saw me. She smelled like pot and cigarettes, but she hugged me and said, 'No matter what, I'm here for you.'

"She skipped school that day. By the time my parents came home, she'd showered, changed, and was on her best behavior, doing everything she could to hold it together."

Tears slid silently down BR's cheeks. Bobbi reached over and gently wiped them away.

"We sat in the living room. I asked Gina to stay. I told them I was pregnant and that the father wasn't part of the equation. That was all I could manage. But they didn't press me. They just hugged me. That's the family you met last night."

BR's voice was quiet. "As if I couldn't love them more."

Bobbi nodded. "I'd rehearsed what I was going to say, but then I looked at my mom and remembered everything she went through just to have me. She nearly died giving birth. And in her eyes, I saw my answer. I was going to keep the baby. I was ready to drop out of med school, move home, and work in a lab."

She tucked her hair behind her ears. "But Gina changed everything. She'd barely spoken until then. And then she came up with this idea. She'd drop out of high school and be the baby's nanny so I could keep going to med school. Her decision to drop out made Dad *furious*. I told her not to sacrifice her future for mine, but Gina wouldn't back down."

Bobbi's voice grew softer. "She promised Dad she'd graduate with her class; said she'd take online courses, quit drinking and smoking, and prove she was dependable. It was like a light went on inside her. For the first time, she saw a way forward—for both of us."

She paused. "Mom broke down. She said she knew Gina would never hurt a baby. And when Gina turned to me with tears in her eyes and said, 'Let me do this. I love you, Bobbi. Let me help,' I finally let myself cry, too."

Bobbi folded her hands in her lap. "Then Gina apologized for everything—for the years of chaos and heartbreak. She told them if it hadn't been for their love, she wouldn't be alive. And she said something I'll never forget: that it was my destiny to be a doctor, and hers to grow up."

She drew a breath. "Dad was quiet for a long time. Then he said he and Mom needed to sleep on it. He sent us to bed but told Gina to be up on time, showered, dressed, and off to school. And to throw out every cigarette and bottle."

Her tone gentled. "That night was so still. I never heard him call her down for a talk. But the next morning, she was up early. Mom cooked a huge breakfast, but we barely touched it. Gina was drinking cup after cup of black coffee. Her hands shook, but she looked scrubbed and serious.

"Then Dad asked me if I was sure I wanted the baby. I said yes. He looked at Mom. She nodded. They're always a team.

"He turned to Gina and said, 'We believe in you. We'll help you get yourself together, help you finish school. But the rest is on you.' Then she left for class. And that was the beginning of everything.

"I emailed Dr. Sam and filled him in. He replied right away and set up a video call that evening. He was hell-bent on helping me in every way he could. I still remember all of us huddled around the computer.

'Bobbi,' he said, 'I've been working the phones all day. I've got strong contacts at the med schools in New York. After I sent them your records, each one admitted you on the spot. Then I spent the afternoon getting them to compete for financial aid. I know you were thinking about Columbia or NYU, but how would you feel about Weill-Cornell? They've offered to match our scholarship offer.'

"I could barely speak. Of course, I said yes. Dr. Sam gave me the name of a doctor to call the next morning to schedule an interview and get the paperwork going. They were even assigning me a mentor."

BR raised his eyebrows. "That's incredible. How'd he pull that off?"

"Dr. Luis Castillo, the one who opened the door at Weill-Cornell? He's one of Sam's kids."

BR clapped. "Love it."

Bobbi continued, "By the time I finished in Chicago, Dad had taken out a second mortgage and built two extra rooms—one for me, one for the baby.

"Quitting everything was excruciating for Gina, but she never smoked again. The smell of pot disappeared from the house for good. She still drinks, but responsibly.

"I moved home, got a job in a diagnostic lab, and gave birth to Sami."

BR opened his arms. Bobbi burrowed in. He didn't say a word. She knew she was safe.

"What was it like when Sami was born?"

The mood shifted. Bobbi lit up at the memory. "I was taking classes at Weill-Cornell and working in a lab connected to the hospital. Thirteen days before my due date, my water broke. I just waddled over and took the elevator to the maternity unit."

BR sputtered. "*You walked yourself to maternity?*"

Bobbi shrugged. "I felt fine. Waiting for help would've taken longer.

"The admitting nurse called my parents. Dad was at work, Mom was home, and Gina was yarn shopping. By the time they met up and made it to Manhattan, Sami was already asleep in my arms."

She smiled as she recounted the scene. "They all cried when they saw her. I was calm. I handed the baby to Mom and said, 'This is your grandmother. She'll teach you how to fill the world with love.' Then to Dad, 'This is your grandfather. He'll teach you how to fix anything.' Finally, Dad gave her to Gina. Before I could speak, Gina jumped in: 'Kid, I'm Aunt Gina. I'll teach you about boys, music, and makeup, so you'll be cool like me, not a big Dorkus Malorkus like your mother.'"

They both laughed.

Bobbi added, "To this day, Gina *swears* I was holding the baby in one hand and doing homework with the other. I don't know if it's true, but she's stuck to that story."

BR tilted his head. He clearly believed Gina.

"When Mom asked the baby's name," Bobbi said, "I told her, 'Samantha. But we'll call her Sami. I named her after Dr. Sam. Her middle name is Rose. Gina, I'm trusting you with the greatest love of my life—that's why I gave her your middle name.'"

"Samantha Rose … that's beautiful."

Bobbi picked up her wine and gently clinked BR's Pellegrino. She took a small sip then looked at him steadily. "That toast was a big moment for me. Have you noticed I never take a drink from a waiter or off a tray when we're out?"

BR nodded. "I have. At first, I thought maybe you were just particular about your wine. Now I think I understand."

"Since Chicago," she said quietly, "the only men I've trusted to bring me a drink I didn't see poured were my dad and Marco. It might not seem like a big deal, but BR"—she paused—"it means I trust you in every possible way."

BR's voice was low. "And you're trusting me to be Samantha Rose's father. I'll make mistakes, but I'll never let you down."

They clinked again.

"So," BR said, lightening the mood, "your cousin turned out to be a fabulous nanny?"

"Gina made Mary Poppins look like a slacker. She dressed like a punk rocker and swore like a sailor's parrot, but she loved my baby fiercely."

Bobbi chuckled. "Want a funny story to end with? Gina changed Sami's name. I meant to spell it S-A-M-M-I, but she taught her to spell it S-A-M-I. She claimed *Sami* made the switch herself, but I'm pretty sure it was one of Gina's tricks."

CHAPTER TWENTY-EIGHT: SCARS
Bobbi

The heavy talk had left them famished, so Bobbi zipped downstairs, returning with the rest of the pizza, plates, and more Pellegrino. They talked over pizza about the rhythm of their new life: weekly dinners with the kids, weekend date nights just for them, and constant calls and texts to fill in the gaps. Later, after clearing the pizza, dimming the lamps, and lighting three Murano candles, Bobbi returned to bed and curled up beside him.

"BR," she murmured, trailing her fingers along his arm, "you think I'm pretty, don't you?"

He choked on his Pellegrino, coughing as he set the bottle down. "If you were any hotter, they'd blame you for global warming."

She laughed softly, but her eyes stayed serious. "Then how come you haven't made love to me yet?"

He sobered. "Are you kidding? I've wanted to since the night we met."

Her voice dipped. "Then why didn't you ask me, instead of sending me home?"

"Because you'd have slapped me, stormed out, ghosted me, and I'd miss you for the rest of my life."

Bobbi shifted closer. "You should've read my signals." Her words lingered, tender and raw.

BR studied her face. "You're saying ... you would've said yes?"

She nuzzled into his neck. "Yes. I'm not like that, but with you, it felt *different*. That night, we were in the bubble from the painting. I didn't want you to say goodnight."

Bobbi tilted her head. "So, let me ask you again: Why haven't we slept together?"

"We've mostly been with the kids or in public," he said sheepishly. "There hasn't been a lot of chances."

She arched a brow. "*That's* your answer?"

"I—"

She cut him off, teasing, "Do you want to see what I *stole* from your place?"

Before he could reply, she hopped off the bed and pulled a T-shirt out from under her pillow. She slipped it on over her pajama shorts then turned away and peeled off her tank top, tossing it aside.

In the candlelight, her fair skin and pale hair made her look almost ethereal. When she turned back, she was wearing his thigh-length, black-and-gold University of Colorado shirt. "I wear this to bed to feel close to you."

BR swallowed hard. "Come sit with me."

She curled into him, warm and sure.

He brushed the soft skin below the hem of her shirt. "Some of it *has* been timing. But ... there's another reason."

Bobbi lifted her head. "Tell me."

"I have scars. From the bomb. They did a lot of surgery to save me. I'm ... not proud of how I look." He gestured to his chest. "You're so beautiful, Bobbi. I didn't want to turn you off. I've been scared."

She exhaled, relief washing through her. *This* she could handle.

"Sweetheart, you're lucky you got a hot girlfriend who can't wait to sleep with you, and she's a doctor who's seen plenty of scars. Maybe this is the wrong metaphor, but let's rip the Band-Aid off—take off your shirt."

BR panicked. "You first."

"Sure." Her voice was easy, playful. She reached for the hem of the T-shirt she'd claimed as her own.

"Stop," he said quickly, just before she bared her breasts.

She smirked. "First time anyone's told me to put my shirt *on.* Way to crush a girl's self-esteem."

"Of course I want to see you. But not like this—not as some kind of trade. I'm just ... embarrassed."

Her tone softened. "Want me to help?"

He stood up. The candlelight cast a warm glow around them both as, without hesitation, she lifted his shirt.

His body was strong, muscled ... and crossed with jagged scars.

Bobbi stepped in, wrapping her arms around his neck— her signal for a real kiss. Her mouth met his, melting his fear. Then she stepped back, her doctor instincts kicking in. She bent slightly, reading the story his body told. She recognized the telltale signs of emergency surgery—the rushed, desperate cuts meant to save a life.

She kissed him again then handed back his shirt. The love in Bobbi's eyes was unmistakable.

"You were afraid the scars would turn me off? That they'd get in the way of sex?"

257

He nodded.

She gestured for him to sit then reached into her bedside drawer, the hem of his oversized shirt rising just enough to reveal her toned thighs.

First, she applied coral lipstick. Then she swept her long hair into a loose bun and knelt in front of him.

BR blinked. "What're you doing?"

She smiled confidently. "I'm going to make you feel like the most desired man in the world. When I'm done, you'll know the scars aren't a problem for us." She reached for his belt—

"No—stop," he gasped, breath ragged.

Bobbi froze then stood, hands on her hips. "Okay, that's definitely another first. No man's ever turned *that* down."

BR laughed, exhaling hard. He grabbed her waist and pulled her onto the bed. She squealed as he rolled on top of her.

"That'll be the only time I ever say no for the rest of our lives."

Their kisses were interrupted by laughter, then more kisses, then more laughter.

"Honey," he murmured between them, "I'm aching to have you, but when we make love the first time, I want to worship you from head to toe … and all the way back down." He brushed her jaw. "I know how my sexy girlfriend feels. Now tell me what the brilliant doctor thinks."

Bobbi smiled. "Sweetheart, has Max Stein ever discussed plastic surgery? I've seen amazing results, and I know a few top surgeons."

"He has, but I shut it down."

She nudged his knee. "Talk to me."

He flushed. "I *hate* the scars. They remind me of the worst time in my life. I've been afraid Cassie would see them and get scared, or that you wouldn't want me, or we'd go to the beach and I couldn't take off my shirt. But I also didn't want to scare Cassie again by being in the hospital for so long."

Bobbi held his hand. "If you never do anything about the scars, it won't change how I feel. I love you just as you are. But if you want, I'll talk to Max. We'll recommend a great surgeon and see what's possible. And I'll take care of Cassie—you can trust me."

"I need to think and pray about it," BR said. "But I do trust you, and I love you."

Bobbi slipped her arms around his neck as their lips met in a slow, lingering kiss.

"Next time you start taking your clothes off," BR murmured, "trust me; I'm not stopping you. But before I sleep with the world's hottest neurologist, I might need a consultation with the world's best cardiologist."

Bobbi grinned. "Not a bad idea. You'd better take your vitamins before you try to take me on," she purred. "I want you like crazy, and I've got weeks of pent-up energy."

~~~

Tuesday, January 26

After Sami's newspaper club ended, Bobbi and Sami stopped by to see Whit and Ingrid. While Sami showed off her front-page article to her grandfather, Bobbi visited with her mother in the kitchen.

"How about we start Sunday dinner an hour earlier this week?" Ingrid asked. "That way, Cassie can spend more time here before heading back to Manhattan."

Bobbi flushed. "Um, BR and Cassie aren't coming."

"Why not?"

"Because ... I didn't know I was allowed to invite them?"

Ingrid buried her face in her hands, shoulders shaking with laughter. "Call BR. Put it on speaker."

He picked up right away. "Hi, this is a nice treat. Where are you?"

Bobbi squeaked, "You're on speaker. My mommy wants to talk to you."

"Hi, Ingrid," BR said warmly. "Thanks again for Sunday. Cassie was sad when we ate the last of the lasagna."

"You're very welcome. That's why I'm calling. I thought I'd teach you something new about your girlfriend."

"Always."

"Bobbi's the most brilliant and competent person you'll ever meet."

"I thought you'd tell me something I *didn't* know."

Ingrid gave Bobbi a look. "But since she was a girl, she's had occasional moments so ditzy that we call them 'Bobbi Being Blonde.'"

Bobbi's face turned the color of a Santa suit. She closed her eyes and hung her head.

"We just had one. Apparently, Dr. Wyatt thought she needed my permission to invite you to Sunday dinner. May I fix it?"

BR's laughter only deepened Bobbi's mortification.

"Please do."

"Just so we're clear, you and Cassie are invited *every* Sunday. Join us whenever you can."

The silence that followed made Ingrid glance at Bobbi, who shrugged.

Finally, BR spoke, his voice thick with emotion. "Thank you. Cassie will be thrilled. I didn't grow up in a warm household, and I've never been close to my adopted siblings. Being with you, Whit, and Gina made me so happy. We'll be there Sunday. Just tell me what to bring."

~~~

Wednesday, January 27
Bobbi

Bobbi was relieved to see BR's driver, Liam, waiting with the sedan. The freezing ferry ride from Brooklyn had left her hands numb, so she didn't protest when he took her bags.

Sami and Gina had long-standing plans, so Bobbi had insisted they keep them, wanting Sami's life to stay as normal as possible.

"So, you're the famous Dr. Bobbi," a graceful woman with coiffed silver hair said as soon as Bobbi walked into the penthouse. "Cassie hasn't stopped talking about you."

Bobbi hung up her coat. "Mrs. Smith, I presume? I've heard so many nice things. Sami says you make the world's greatest omelets."

Mrs. Smith smiled. "Your daughter's a doll—so polite! I wish I had her energy."

"We all do. Sami's the poster child for perpetual motion."

Cassie ran up, arms outstretched, and Bobbi scooped her into the familiar rhythm of a kiss and a carry.

Mrs. Smith said her goodbyes, and Cassie politely wished her goodnight.

Early in their relationship, BR had told Bobbi that Mrs. Smith was his only household employee. He'd hired her to cook and manage the apartment after Anna Maria had come to live with him unexpectedly and under challenging circumstances while he had been juggling a new Broadway show.

~~~

After dinner and reading time, Cassie asked Bobbi to help with bathtime.

Passing by the bathroom, BR heard splashes and giggles. Each burst of laughter filled his heart. Plus, Bobbi's gentle attention, expert hair-washing, and braiding skills meant Dad wasn't needed tonight.

Later, Bobbi stretched out on Cassie's small bed, cradling Howard as Cassie whispered her prayers, starting with Daddy, Bobbi, Sami, Howard, her teacher, and all the children without food or homes. Then she added, "Please help Bobbi fix all her patients so they won't be scared."

Bobbi blinked back tears as Cassie went on to pray for Aunt Gina, Mrs. Ingrid, Mr. Whit, Hunter, and Matilda Moose.

"Will you be here in the morning, Bobbi?"

"No, sweet girl."

Cassie yawned. "I like it better when you're here."

Bobbi kissed her forehead. "I like it better when I see you, too. But we'll video chat. And don't forget, Sami, Hunter, and I are sleeping over on Friday. They'll babysit while Daddy takes me on a date."

Cassie purred in contentment.

BR smiled. "Time for your goodnight song."

Cassie curled onto her side, hugging Howard. Bobbi wrapped her arms around them both.

"Daddy, will you sing 'Sleepy Cassie Moon?' I want Bobbi to hear it."

BR sang:

> *"The sleepy Cassie moon is shining bright,*
> *But now it's time to say goodnight.*
> *It's tired from the busy day,*
> *And so are you, in just the same way.*

> *Sleepy Cassie moon, it's time to close your eyes,*
> *Drift away to dreamland, where starlight lies.*
> *When morning comes, the moon will go,*
> *But tonight, we'll rest again in its gentle glow.*

> *The moon will fade with morning light,*
> *But don't worry, it'll be all right.*
> *It'll rise again, so high and true,*
> *And I'll be here to sing to you.*

> *Sleepy Cassie moon, it's time to close your eyes,*
> *Drift away to dreamland, where the starlight lies.*
> *When morning comes, the moon will go,*
> *But tonight, we'll rest in its gentle glow.*

So, close your eyes, my sleepy Cass,
The moon and I will guard your path.
Tomorrow night, we'll sing this tune,
Under the sleepy Cassie moon."

With Cassie asleep, BR led Bobbi to his office for a video call. "My friends are dying to meet you. Ed and Liz are back in Illinois, Bree and Chrissy are still in California, and a lot of our people work remotely while the Harlem headquarters wraps up construction."

Bobbi had seen photos of BR's closest friends. Bree, striking and serene, radiated quiet confidence. Her wife, Chrissy, a hilariously unfiltered filmmaker, always kept the group in stitches. Liz's sleek blonde bob and ballerina frame, paired with Ed's lopsided grin, made them look like the couple in every new picture frame at the store.

Bobbi burst into laughter as the screen lit up with couples in red, donning party hats and blowing New Year's horns.

"What is happening?" she asked.

"BR introducing us to a girl after all these years, that's cause for celebration!" Chrissy declared.

Ed gestured to their shirts. "It's a red-letter day! One minute, the big mope wanders into an art gallery alone, and—Bob's your uncle—Bobbi's his girlfriend!"

For twenty minutes, they talked and laughed. Bobbi loved watching Ed, Bree, and BR finish each other's sentences while Liz and Chrissy rolled their eyes in unison.

When BR excused himself, the conversation didn't miss a beat.

"How do you two put up with these three nutty Musketeers?" Bobbi asked.

Chrissy guffawed. "Liz and I have our own group chat. We call ourselves The Outsiders."

Bobbi hesitated. "There's so much I want to ask you two."

Liz elbowed Ed, who took the hint and left. Bree gave Chrissy a kiss and followed.

"Bobbi, are you okay?" Liz asked gently.

"I'd kill for a glass of wine right now. Just my luck—my boyfriend doesn't drink."

Chrissy laughed. "You're in a hotel! Hit star seven on the landline. Room service will bring you whatever you want."

Bobbi smacked her forehead then ordered a small, unopened bottle of crisp Italian white.

"I didn't mean to be rude to Ed and Bree," she said. "I'm just trying to navigate this relationship. Their loyalty is to BR, and I didn't want to say anything that'd make them uncomfortable."

"Ask us anything," Chrissy said. "The Outsiders have a solemn girl code."

Bobbi raised a skeptical brow. "Really?"

"Absolutely. Chrissy and I have been in your position. BR accepted us immediately—he loves us like he loves Ed and Bree."

As if on cue—or via separate text—BR, Bree, and Ed reappeared, each delivering glasses of wine.

Bobbi took a sip. "Okay, BR seems too good to be true. I'm madly in love with him but way out on an emotional limb. How is he this wonderful and still single?"

Chrissy leaned back. "He's never had a girlfriend since I met him."

Liz nodded. "I asked Ed the same thing when I met BR."

"After Liz played hard-to-get for five years," Chrissy said, "Ed had BR fly out to sing to her because she didn't believe he actually knew him."

Bobbi giggled. "That sounds like a great story."

Liz leaned in, eyes twinkling. "It is. I'll tell you when we meet. But to answer your question: once BR became famous, I think he worried women only wanted him for his money and fame. We've seen grown women do outrageous things to get his attention. One rushed the stage in a wedding dress during Rory's big goodbye number."

Chrissy snorted. "And don't forget the topless girl who wrote *Bradford or Bust* across her chest and posed in front of every theater marquee."

Liz added, "And it's not just fans. We've seen famous married women practically proposition him. And BR being BR, he just gently extracts himself. Ed said a national morning show host once handed him her number—and a pair of underwear—while Cassie was in a stroller."

Bobbi's jaw dropped. "What have I gotten myself into?"

"We heard you didn't even know who he was at first. You just liked *him*," Chrissy said. "That, and your independence, is part of your appeal."

"Plus, he's crazy about your daughter."

Bobbi set down her glass. "Straight talk. He's worked with two of the world's sexiest women and done *nothing*?"

"That's easy," Chrissy said. "I'm gay. Liz is married!"

Bobbi laughed so hard she nearly fell off her chair. "Then we'd have to include Bree!"

She composed herself. "Okay, seriously, can you put my mind at ease about Aurora Bellucci and Alicia Rodriguez?"

Chrissy threw up her hands. "Hang on. I'm getting Bree."

When Bree returned, she got right to the point. "I'll tell you about BR and Alicia, but we take privacy seriously. We *never* talk about BR outside this group."

"Understood."

"Alicia is gay."

"*What*?" Bobbi gasped.

Liz snorted. "That was my reaction, too."

"She's never said it publicly, and that's her choice," Bree said. "But if she were out, all the speculation about her and BR would've stopped years ago."

Bobbi hesitated. "You think she kept it quiet because—"

"She didn't want to risk her career?" Bree nodded. "Probably. Her family's traditional, and her fanbase is diverse. Some wouldn't accept it. She also made a fortune off her sex appeal."

"And BR?"

"He always shut down the rumors, but he'd never out her. He's loyal. Like to us. Like to you."

Chrissy added, "He got in trouble because of our wedding, but he didn't care. His love for us mattered more. That's a story for another day. Let's finish your question."

Bobbi traced the rim of her glass. "What about Aurora?"

"Rory? Definitely *not* gay," Bree said. "She's gorgeous, talented, and has the worst taste in men. BR and Greg Walker think of her as a kid sister. The three of them just work together."

"When are you all back in New York?" Bobbi asked, reassured and happy.

Bree perked up. "Ed and I have a Monday meeting. Maybe Liz and Chrissy can come in for the weekend? Let's all meet on Saturday."

Chrissy clapped. "Perfect! You're about to experience something BR swore would never happen—a full Outsiders evaluation."

Bobbi raised an eyebrow. "What?"

Liz smirked. "Years ago, Chrissy and I made BR swear if he ever got serious about someone, *we* had to meet her first. Because she'd be joining The Outsiders whether she knew it or not."

Chrissy crossed her heart. "We take it seriously."

Bobbi folded her arms. "And how exactly does one earn Outsider approval?"

Liz rubbed her chin. "BR should be nervous. Technically, he can't keep dating you unless we sign off."

"What if I fail?"

"No idea," Liz said. "You're the first. You're making history."

"A résumé and references wouldn't hurt," Chrissy said. "You're a med school valedictorian—you'll ace the written exam."

~~~

Curled up with BR on the couch before heading back to Brooklyn, she got the verdict.

"They loved you. Ed and Bree were tripping over themselves talking you up."

"They're incredible," Bobbi said. "They made me feel like I've always been a part of this."

BR kissed her palm. "Sorry about the wine. I used to keep a bottle here for the gang. But when Anna Maria moved in, I stopped. No alcohol in the house with a teenager. I kind of forgot."

Bobbi squeezed his hand. "You're the best." Her eyes sparkled. "What was that story Chrissy started about you getting in trouble at their wedding?"

BR wiped his glasses. "Bree's family disowned her when she came out. Chrissy's family is great—she's close to her dad—but Bree was heartbroken. So, Ed and I walked her down the aisle. Liz got ordained online and married them on the cliffs in Malibu."

Her heart clenched. "That's beautiful."

BR shrugged. "Not everyone thought so. Some fans were upset I was involved in a gay wedding. I lost followers. But I don't make personal choices based on that. My faith says people will know us by our love. How could I not be there for my best friends?"

They held hands in the elevator. Liam waited with the sedan.

Bobbi's mind swirled. She'd never said it aloud, but loving a man—and raising a child—who practiced faith still confused her. Yet, Cassie's prayer and BR's quiet conviction gave her plenty to think about on the ride back to Brooklyn Heights.

BR sat on the couch, smiling as the penthouse rang with laughter and joy. It felt like someone had turned back the clock—before the depression, the surgeries, and the pain.

Liz and Chrissy burst through the door and zeroed in on Bobbi. They'd already welcomed her into the tribe, complete with a spot in The Outsiders group chat and the larger one with BR, Ed, and Bree.

They immediately whipped out toy magnifying glasses and circled Bobbi like over-caffeinated detectives.

"Excellent shoe choice," Liz declared after an exaggerated inspection.

"Manicure's on point," Chrissy added, squinting at her hands.

Bobbi howled with laughter and didn't flinch when Liz handed her a manila folder labeled:

Confidential: Outsider Application &
Orientation Packet

Without missing a beat, Chrissy dragged a chair across the floor, climbed on top, and examined Bobbi's hair. "Just checking for signs of a bottle blonde," she said solemnly. "We have standards."

BR turned as squealing and footsteps erupted from the kitchen. Ed and Sami were pretending to search frantically for Cassie, peeking behind doors and inside cabinets, while Cassie clung to Ed's back, riding piggyback and giggling uncontrollably.

When Bree opened the refrigerator, Sami called, "Look in the butter dish! She's probably hiding in there!"

"Not there!" Bree reported.

"Check the bananas!" Ed called. "With her yellow hair, she might be pretending to be one!"

"Nope! I'll check the blender!" Sami shouted.

Bobbi caught BR's eye and winked. "Check the cookie jar. I'll bet she's in there."

Liz and Chrissy announced they were taking Bobbi to her room to apply "finishing touches" before dinner, drinks, and dancing.

Bree dropped onto the couch beside BR. "Three wild kids, two lunatics probably running a polygraph on your girlfriend, and you look like you won the lottery."

"I did," BR replied, taking a Pellegrino from her.

They toasted as Ed peered into the milk carton and Sami examined the salt shaker. Cassie, still clinging to Ed's back, bellowed with laughter.

BR smiled. "Feels like the old days," he said quietly. "Only better, because Bobbi and Sami are here."

"Cassie's happier than I've ever seen her. And your shoulder—no pain?"

"Life's worth living again."

The living room quieted as the whirlwind of footsteps faded.

Cassie wriggled free from Ed's playful grasp and plopped down beside her father, her little body trembling with exhaustion and happiness.

Ed entered, grabbed a throw pillow, and threw it in front of her. "Hmm ... still can't find her," he announced.

When Cassie popped up like a jack-in-the-box and threw her arms around him, he acted shocked then hugged her back. The game was over.

Liz and Chrissy reappeared, looking effortlessly chic, with Bobbi walking between them, radiant and relaxed, her hair down in an elegant halo.

Sami trailed behind them and immediately smiled at her mother. "Mom, you look so pretty," she said sincerely then glanced at Liz and Chrissy. "You all do."

Bree walked to the doorway, grabbing Ed's jacket. "We're heading out. Dinner with a few of Monday's keynote speakers."

The adults hugged goodbye, the front door closing behind them, their laughter lingering like an echo.

As the energy in the room settled, Cassie crawled into BR's lap, and Sami flopped onto the couch beside them.

"Hey, Cass, wanna do bathtime the fancy way tonight? I'll show you how to make bubble beards. Aunt Gina used to do it for me all the time."

Cassie's face lit up. "You have to wear a beard, too!"

BR watched them disappear down the hallway, their chatter fading into the distance.

He sat for a long while, content and still, his thoughts drifting, anchored by how much his life had changed since meeting Bobbi. The headlines, awards, and applause felt like another lifetime. Everything had shifted that night in front of the painting, when they had stepped into the "Bobbi Bubble."

It wasn't just Bobbi. Her family hadn't just accepted him—they'd wrapped both him and Cassie in the unconditional love he'd only dreamed of. And his strength had returned. For the first time in forever, he felt whole. More than that, he felt newly driven to ensure the foundation would leave a lasting mark on the world.

The sound of footsteps pulled him from his thoughts. Sami and Cassie reappeared in pajamas.

"BR, Cassie did a fantastic job on her reading," Sami reported proudly. "She loved the book I picked."

He smiled. He hadn't even noticed them heading down to the library.

"Daddy, Sami didn't tell you the best part!" Cassie said excitedly.

"What's that?"

"We video-called Hunter. She helped Sami read a book about a dog who gets wrapped in spaghetti. It was so funny! Hunter did the dog voice, and Sami turned the pages and pretended to be the spaghetti. Did you know Hunter wants to be a teacher?"

"That sounds wonderful. Did you brush your teeth?"

"No. I told Cassie she did such a great job that I'd ask if we could have goodnight cookies from the front desk."

He laughed. "It sounds like you both earned them. I'll go."

In the elevator, BR checked his phone. Chrissy had sent a series of photos from a fancy restaurant. The first showed her and Liz digging into elaborate meals while Bobbi sat, studiously filling out her questionnaire, with only bread and water in front of her. The photos got funnier: Liz timed Bobbi with a stopwatch then helped Chrissy grade the test. Bobbi still had no food. The final one showed all three of them with their arms around each other, smiling brightly enough to light up Manhattan. Bobbi's dinner looked delicious.

Sami had sent pictures, too—one from bathtime, the girls cheek-to-cheek with bubble beards, and another of Hunter helping Sami read on Cassie's JadePad.

When he returned with the cookies, Cassie sat cross-legged on Sami's lap, happily chatting while Sami braided her hair. He snapped a photo without them noticing.

After the cookies, it was time for Cassie to head to bed. BR stood, ready to step in, but Sami held up a hand.

"I have one more surprise," she said. "Cassie, after we brush our teeth, how about I tuck you in and sing a special goodnight song?"

Cassie was delighted.

"Want to watch a movie, Sami?" BR asked.

"I'd love to, but I can't. I promised Mom I'd finish my history homework. Will you check it later?"

"Any time."

Cassie kissed him goodnight then grabbed Sami's hand. "Come on! I wanna hear my song!"

They disappeared down the hallway, their giggles softening behind them.

This, he realized, was what life would look like now. Not headlines, or awards, or afterparties, but bubble beards and bedtime stories. A penthouse filled with love.

~~~

BR awoke the next morning with the scent of Bobbi's perfume in his nostrils. He rolled over expectantly. On the pillow next to him was a note in her handwriting.

Had a great time. Wish I was here. ⬇️

He dressed and walked to the living room, where the big screen TV showed cartoons. Sami and Cassie were sound asleep on the couch, their heads practically touching, wrapped up in their blankies. Sami was clutching Howard.

BR pulled their blankets up under their chins, took a picture, and then texted it to the Wyatt family text chain before pouring a glass of grapefruit juice and heading to his home office.

BR moved lightly through the apartment, buoyed by how easily Bobbi and Sami had blended into his world, as if they'd always belonged.

The warmth of last night still lingered, woven into the walls like laughter and light. It felt like home now, not just the place he lived in.

As he crossed into his office, thinking he might clear a few emails before the girls woke up, something on his desk caught his eye: a sealed, official-looking manila envelope.

BR BRADFORD'S EYES ONLY
CONFIDENTIAL

Inside, he found several sheets of paper clipped together. His eyes crinkled with delight as he read the first page.

To: BR Bradford
From: The Outsiders Membership Committee
Re: Membership Application for Dr. Bobbi D. Wyatt
Case: 0000001

Overview
Per the solemn directive mandating a comprehensive evaluation of all potential new inductees to the hallowed status of Outsiders, we, the undersigned, have conducted an exhaustive review of Dr. Wyatt's application.

Protocol
After carefully assessing Dr. Wyatt's responses to the written exam (attached), the physical/dexterity test (she's a great dancer), and giving due consideration to the references submitted by unbiased observers (Miss Samantha R. Wyatt, Miss Cassandra Q. Bradford, and Mr. Howard T. Moose), and after conducting a thorough interrogation of Dr. Wyatt over cocktails, dinner, dessert, and dancing, we feel confident in making our recommendation. Our vote was unanimous and irrevocable.

Recommendation

If you let her get away, you will be an equine posterior of interstellar proportions.

Signed,

Elizabeth Victoria Mercury Johnson
Christiana Marie Bales

Elizabeth Victoria Mercury Johnson
Christiana Marie Bales

BR snickered as he flipped to the next page. Attached to the formal "recommendation" were character references. He kept reading, his smile growing wider.

ADDENDUM: Character References

Samantha Rose Wyatt: *"She's the greatest mom in the world, even though sometimes she tried to make me eat disgusting Brussels sprouts. Fortunately, my aunt Gina usually protected me. Other than that, Mom's perfect."*

Cassandra Quinn Bradford: *"When I grow up, I want to be just like Bobbi. She's a great doctor and makes everyone happy."*

Howard the Moose: *"She saved my life. And she keeps me in stitches. Literally."*

And just when he thought The Outsiders couldn't possibly top themselves, there it was—the infamous written exam they'd threatened Bobbi with. He'd honestly assumed they were kidding.

Written Exam: Evaluation of Dr. Bobbi D. Wyatt

Q: What is the difference between nigiri and sashimi?

A: Nigiri is sashimi with a rice backpack. It's ready for school and 70 calories heavier.

Chrissy: Hot nerd alert. Bonus points for calorie awareness.

Liz: Accurate. Concise. Slightly ridiculous. Approved.

Q: Why are boys so dumb?

A: As a neurologist, I can tell you that male and female brains develop differently, especially in areas tied to language, impulse control, and emotional processing. That's what I learned in medical school. But in fifth grade, I learned that girls rule and boys drool.

Chrissy: Extra credit for scientific AND elementary school sources.

Liz: Well-supported.   Personal observation supports the data.

Q: Who is the prettiest member of The Outsiders?

A: If it's physical beauty, it's a tie between Chrissy and Liz. If it's emotional beauty, it's a tie between Liz and Chrissy.

Chrissy: Duh. Obviously.

Liz: Correct. No further comments.

Q: New York pizza or Chicago pizza?

A: Pizza!

Chrissy: Pizza is always the answer.

Liz: Evasive, nonresponsive … but still technically correct. More research is needed. Suggest numerous taste tests together to reach a definitive conclusion.

Q: If you were alone in the woods, would you rather be with a man or a bear?

A: There are several men on the Chicago Bears I would've loved to have been alone with.

Before I met BR, of course.

Chrissy: I'd prefer one of the cheerleaders.

Liz: The correctness of the answer depends on her willingness to share with the blonde Outsider.

Q: What makes life so wonderful?

A: Life is wonderful because it's produced by the same people who make Cap'n Crunch.

Chrissy: Sweet, crunchy, and completely valid.

Liz: Breakfast philosophy was unexpected. Approved.

Q: Why did you become a neurologist?

A: Because if I became a proctologist, I'd have to be a pain in the ass. However, I do like getting to the bottom of things.

Chrissy: Answered directly, no ifs, and, or butts.

Liz: Nicely played.

Q: What would you offer as a bribe to achieve membership in The Outsiders?

A: I would offer you each a tray of my mother's lasagna. On second thought, if I did that, you'd ditch me

*and make her an Outsider. She's
already happily married.*

Chrissy: *How happily married? We've
heard about this lasagna.*

Liz: *I suggest a Bylaws Committee
meeting to evaluate honorary
membership for Mrs. Wyatt!*

**Q: If one of our spouses was being a
pain, how would you, as a
member of The Outsiders, help us
deal with it?**

A: *I'm over 21, so I can bring wine. I'm
from Brooklyn, so I know all about
revenge. And I'm a doctor, so I'm
great at coming up with prescriptions
to take care of pain.*

Chrissy: *She had me at revenge.*

Liz: *Wine, revenge, AND a prescription
pad credentials? A triple threat.*

Q: What is the secret to happiness?

A: *Fall in love with your best friend. But
both of you already know that!*

Chrissy: *100%*

Liz: *The only acceptable answer.*

BR closed the folder. Only The Outsiders could turn a joke into a legal brief and a prank into a full-blown initiation ritual. It was absurd. It was over the top. It was perfect.

He set the file aside, still laughing as he left the office.

The scent of fresh coffee led him into the kitchen, where Liz stood at the counter, scooping grounds into the machine. She wore a white bathrobe over a faded Northwestern sweatshirt and pajama bottoms, her short hair tousled from sleep. Chrissy leaned against the island, similarly dressed, shielding her eyes from the light like it personally offended her.

Before BR could speak, Chrissy squinted and said, "Not so loud."

BR raised both hands. "I didn't say anything."

Chrissy winced. "No, but you were going to. And I've got a headache that could bring down a rhinoceros." She gestured toward the front door. "Thank all that's holy your girlfriend stashed good coffee up here. We gave Cassie twenty bucks and sent her down to the Times Square Coffee Corner, but she's been gone over an hour. We needed caffeine—bad."

BR laughed, and both women shushed him.

"Seriously, where's Cassie?" he asked.

Chrissy blinked. "I think she's gone hunting."

"Hunting?"

"Yeah," she said slowly, rubbing her temples. "She and Sami said something about calling a hunter to help them with something."

BR smiled. "Hunter is Sami's best friend."

Liz groaned into her mug. "Okay, okay, we were close."

"Right now, this coffee is my best friend. No offense, Liz," Chrissy muttered.

"None taken," Liz replied. "I love you like a sister, but I'd steal your wedding ring and hock it for a latte if I had to."

Both women weakly booed BR for showing up with grapefruit juice.

"Pathetic," Chrissy snorted. "Why a fabulous girl like Bobbi would settle for a loser who doesn't drink coffee or wine is beyond me."

"I'm sure she's only after me for my friends."

They clinked mugs, and then winced at the sound.

"Is Bobbi okay after your night out?" BR asked.

Liz gave him the stink eye. "Your lunatic girlfriend had the unmitigated gall to get up early and join my idiot husband and Chrissy's weirdo wife to work out. If reading texts wasn't so painful, I'd give you an update. I had to silence my phone before I smashed it."

"Bree's in the shower. The other two knuckleheads wanted *more* exercise, so they're walking to Zabar's to pick up everything for brunch." Chrissy drained her mug, took Liz's, and washed them in the sink. She told the water to be quieter.

"Okay, you'll have to excuse us," Liz grumbled. "We have to get cleaned up before our workout."

"*You're* going to work out? In your condition?" BR asked, incredulous.

"Absolutely," Chrissy replied. "We want to be clean when we lift our bagels and smear the cream cheese on them."

CHAPTER THIRTY: THANKSGIVING

Sunday, January 31
Ed

The NYTSQ fitness center boasted excellent facilities, and Ed, Bree, and Bobbi had made the most of it, rotating through weights, cardio machines, and core work with quiet focus and a few groans.

After cooling down, Bree gave Ed a wry smile. "Enjoy your walk, Ed, but be warned: Bobbi just smoked us and looks like she could've gone another hour. I'm off to shower then mock my wasted wife mercilessly."

They left the hotel just after nine, slipping out of Times Square and heading uptown on foot. The morning air was brisk, the city still rubbing the sleep from its eyes—street carts setting up, joggers weaving through scattered tourists, traffic still light.

A few blocks north, the noise thinned out and the sidewalks emptied, replaced by the quiet rhythm of footsteps and the low hum of their easy conversation.

By the time they reached Columbus Circle, Ed and Bobbi walked in sync past sleepy cafés and bundled-up dog walkers, the city slowly waking up around them.

Before Liz had passed out, she'd shaken him awake just long enough to mumble, "She's way out of BR's league. I'm not sure there's *anybody* in her league."

They stood on a corner, waiting for a green light, when Bobbi changed the conversation.

"May I ask you something serious?" she whispered.

Instinctively, as he did whenever discussing BR in public, Ed looked around. "Sure. The order won't be ready for a while. There's a Coffee Corner over there; why don't we sit down? I'd like to try this famous Bobbi Blend."

Bobbi lit up. "Ah, you had me at coffee. I'll have to teach them how to make it, but I bet you'll like it."

Ed watched in amazement as Bobbi slowly, methodically walked the barista through the recipe. He found a quiet corner, and she joined him with the cups. One sip convinced him she was a genius.

"I thought this might be too sweet, but it's the perfect balance."

"Told you." She sipped thoughtfully.

He nodded. Bobbi's looks had already drawn attention, and if anyone heard BR's name, it could spread fast.

"Ed, the girls have been so terrific, but I wanted some time alone with you because I need to ask something."

"Go ahead," he said, his trademark lopsided grin giving way to a more serious expression.

"He told me that you're the one who called the intervention." Her voice broke slightly. "I'll always love you for that. You saved him. I can't imagine my life without him."

Under the table, Ed clenched his hands.

"He's mentioned how much Thanksgiving with your family means to him. I get the feeling that's when everything turned. Would you tell me what really happened?"

"You might need another cup of coffee. Get me one, too, please."

She returned with fresh cups and sat wordlessly.

"When Bree and I moved into the brownstone where BR was renting, we hit it off with him almost as quickly as you did. A week before Thanksgiving, we were sitting on the stoop, and I was worried about Bree. You know about her family?"

"I know they're not happy she's gay."

Ed snorted. "That's the tip of the iceberg. Bree's family disowned her. They won't speak to her and return her cards unopened. It guts her."

"I can't imagine not loving your daughter no matter what. I always tell Sami that nothing could ever separate her from my love."

"Exactly. And I'm guessing your parents are the same. Mine, too. So, I asked Bree if she had Thanksgiving plans. She said she'd stay in the city, paint, and catch up on coursework. Then BR said he had no plans either and maybe they should grab dinner."

"Why didn't he go home to Colorado?"

"His stepsiblings didn't invite him. So, I called my parents. They immediately insisted I bring Bree and BR home. The only problem was I had this old beater of a car. I didn't see how we'd fit three people and luggage and drive over eight hundred miles to Maple Meadows. It's just on the Illinois side of the Wisconsin border, between Rockford and Lake Geneva.

"Then BR made a call. A friend at an airline got us three seats from JFK to Chicago. The catch was we had to fly back from Milwaukee. He brushed off how he got the tickets. We knew he was a history major and a musician, but we didn't know about Alicia Rodriguez or that he was writing *Sock Hop*. He always deflected."

"I know that tone." Bobbi sighed. "He downplays everything and just wants to talk about Sami or me. I'm working on him to open up. It's about the only thing I'd change."

Ed nodded then continued, "He said he had a gazillion flyer miles. JFK was a zoo, but he got us into a lounge. Bree and I had drinks. BR gave us the first-class seats and sat in the back. Typical. That night, we flew into Chicago ..."

He stopped when Bobbi shivered.

"What time did you land?"

"About six thirty. Why?"

"I was in O'Hare at that exact moment, flying back to New York. Ed, it's possible we passed each other. I might have boarded the plane you just got off."

Ed made a mind-blown gesture then laughed as he said, "Bree and I took full advantage of the champagne, and by the time my dad picked us up in his minivan, we were ready to crash. BR, of course, was as fresh as a daisy. He loved hearing my dad tell the story of every town, bridge, maybe even every tree between Chicago and Maple Meadows.

"Dad runs a hardware store. The Wednesday before Thanksgiving is his busiest day. Everyone stops in for decorations, trees—you name it."

"That sounds so nice," Bobbi said.

"You might not like it. We don't have a Coffee Corner!"

Bobbi gave a thumbs-down.

"My folks went overboard to make them feel welcome. Bree stayed in the guest room. BR fell in love with our wood-paneled basement and insisted on sleeping there. The next morning, Bree and I slept in. When we came down, BR had gone to work with my dad."

"To see the store?"

"No, to actually *work*. He stocked shelves as a kid and figured he could help. My mom embroidered *BR* on a vest, Dad made a name tag, and he put in a full day. Bree and I saw him carrying a big box to an older lady's car."

"I can't explain why, but that sounds exactly like him."

"That night, we picked up pizzas. At home, Dad was sipping a beer, Mom was prepping pies ... and BR was peeling potatoes and talking about his life. Bree and I stared. He almost never discussed his family."

Bobbi's expression said she understood.

"He said his parents adopted him late in life. His stepsiblings were grown, already had kids of their own, and they'd been against the adoption to begin with. He hated Thanksgiving. They'd sit around, swapping stories and inside jokes, while he sat alone in his room, playing music. Like he wasn't even part of the family."

Bobbi said nothing, but Ed could see the compassion and pain on her face.

"Our Thanksgiving was a blast. Friends came over after dinner. One recognized him. Turns out, she'd seen him perform with Alicia. She told us he wrote 'Not That.'"

"He wrote 'Not That?' Even *I* know it, and I don't follow pop unless it's dance music."

"We had no idea, either."

Bobbi grinned. "That's hilarious."

"Before we left, Mom asked if they'd return next year. BR got emotional, hugged my parents, and asked if he could work the day before again. Dad said his vest would be waiting.

"Until last year, BR never missed Thanksgiving and always did a full day's work. Soon, my dad locked the vest in a glass case—to keep it safe, not show it off. Word had spread that BR would be there, and it got so busy you couldn't get near the place. I swear my dad tripled his usual profit—every unmarried woman in two states needed hardware.

"When Liz realized she loved me, and Chrissy fell for Bree, they became part of Thanksgiving. Anna Maria came sometimes. Cassie started coming as soon as he adopted her. She only missed last year."

Bobbi's expression darkened. "And last year?"

"Last September, BR was in Chicago when terrorists attacked three buildings—community centers that served the poor, the homeless, and the immigrants." Ed's voice was low. "The FBI thinks they were targeted because they helped people like that." He paused then added, "It's a miracle no one died, but BR almost did."

Bobbi's breath caught. "That's when Anna Maria and Siobhán took Cassie to the horse farm, when BR was taken to the hospital?"

"Yeah, as soon as they got the news." Ed nodded. "I was in Maple Meadows when the FBI called. Bree threw together a bag and had Ronnie and Sawyer drive her all night from New York. I sped through every toll road in Illinois. I was there before he got out of surgery. Bree arrived the next day, jumped out of the car, and came straight to his bedside. We didn't leave him for a week."

289

They moved to sit on a bench nearby, the air growing quieter around them.

"When he came home," Ed continued, "he wasn't BR anymore. Max said his body would heal—liver, shoulder, all that—but his spark was gone. Except when Cassie was in the room. She was the only one he let in."

Bobbi nodded slowly. "You thought Thanksgiving would help."

"We all did, but he refused to come. My parents even offered to host here. Bree tried logic, Liz tried memories, I tried begging. Nothing worked."

He exhaled hard. "On the flight home, we knew we couldn't keep waiting. I called Max; Bree reached out to everyone else. That Sunday, Siobhán took Cassie downstairs while the rest of us confronted BR; told him how scared we were, how much we missed him. He hugged us and thanked us, but he was noncommittal."

Bobbi whispered, "What finally got through?"

"Siobhán." His eyes grew glassy. "Siobhán came upstairs and simply said, 'Cassie's worried about you, and she's been having nightmares.'" He paused. "I saw something break in him. That wall he'd built just ... cracked. He called Dr. Melendez the next morning. But the therapy didn't save him—you did. He started living again because of *you*."

They walked the rest of the way in thoughtful silence until Zabar's chaos swallowed them whole.

Ed grabbed a ticket. "Okay," he said, surveying the crowd. "Remind me again: how many kinds of cream cheese did your boyfriend order?"

Bobbi held up her fingers. "Six. And don't even think about skipping the cinnamon-walnut one, or we'll be banished."

Ed groaned. "I liked it better when he just wanted a vest and a name tag."

They reached the counter. Bobbi pulled out her phone to show the order.

The clerk squinted then raised an eyebrow. "Uh-huh. Sweetheart, unless your name is *Perfume on My Pillow*, I don't think that's your bagel order."

Bobbi frowned and glanced down.

> *Next time you sneak into my room in the middle of the night, you could at least say hello. I miss the smell of your perfume on my pillow.*

"Oh no," she gasped, fumbling for the real message.

The clerk grinned, eyeing both Bobbi and Ed. "Hey, I'm not here to judge what two consenting adults do with cream cheese in the middle of the night. Just don't perfume the bagels."

Bobbi stammered, "No ... not us ... We're not a couple."

"We're not?" Ed asked, feigning offense. "That's not what you told my mother."

"Stop it, or I'll tell your wife on you."

The line behind grew anxious as the clerk guffawed.

Bobbi finally found the right message and held up her phone. "Sorry. The order's under Bradford, Wyatt, or possibly Johnson."

"I'm not surprised you can't keep all your men straight," the clerk said, handing over three bags. "Already paid for."

They stepped aside, arms full.

Bobbi exhaled. "Okay. That was a classic Bobbi Being Blonde moment—Zabar's Edition."

"Perfect," Ed said, pulling out his phone. "I'm texting the group. Just want to make sure I get the title right."

"Sleep with one eye open, my friend. I'm officially an Outsider now. Liz will get you for me."

CHAPTER THIRTY-ONE: BOBBI'S BIRTHDAY WEEKEND

Friday, February 26 – Saturday, February 27
Whit

"Ingrid, you look lovely."

"It's not every weekend our daughter turns thirty-two and her boyfriend sends a limo. And look at you—still the most handsome man I know." She kissed him and straightened his tie.

They greeted Ronnie warmly and settled into the back seat.

"We've got a long ride to Jersey," Ronnie said, pointing out the amenities before raising the privacy screen.

Whit turned to Ingrid. "I figured BR had something planned, but I don't get why he didn't tell us. You think he's proposing tonight?"

"Did he say anything to you?"

"Not a word."

Ingrid held out her pinkie. Whit linked his to hers—their signal for conversations meant to stay just between them.

"I know it sounds crazy," she said quietly, "but do you think there's any chance BR is Sami's biological father?"

Whit blinked. "What?"

"She's never told us *anything* about Sami's father. BR was in and out of Chicago when she was in school. What if they had a fling and signed an NDA? Now he just shows up and instantly connects with both of them."

"They *are* close," Whit admitted.

Ingrid leaned in. "You didn't hear what happened the other day. Bobbi got home, heard voices upstairs, and thought Sami had snuck a boy in."

"Sami? I don't believe it."

"She rushed upstairs, only to find Sami on a video call with BR. He'd left a meeting to help with her poetry homework."

Whit laughed. "BR's not the type to walk away from a daughter. If Bobbi had been pregnant, he would've married her on the spot." He paused. "Honestly? If we didn't know for sure Bobbi wasn't pregnant five years ago, I'd swear Cassie was hers."

Ingrid tilted her head. "You think so, too?"

"She looks just like her. But it's more than that—it's the way she moves through the world. The curiosity. The empathy. I've only met one other kid who could read people like that at five years old, and we raised her."

"It's uncanny," Ingrid agreed. "Cassie understands things you'd never expect a little girl to grasp. Emotional things. Adult things."

Whit agreed. "She's got Bobbi's brain and her heart. Just … in miniature. And if BR does propose, that little girl will be our granddaughter."

"She already feels like ours," Ingrid said. "If this becomes official, I think my heart might burst."

The ride from Brooklyn took just over an hour. Whit and Ingrid held hands, enjoying the quiet luxury. Then the car pulled up in front of The Clam Digger, a waterfront restaurant Bobbi had mentioned from an early date.

A hostess greeted them. "Are you here for Dr. Wyatt?" When they nodded, she said, "Right this way."

Whit noticed a soft glow spilling from the back patio.

The hostess smiled. "Normally, we don't serve outside in January, but your host arranged a private dinner in our heated oceanfront tent."

Inside, candles flickered on a beautifully set table. Music played softly. Bobbi stood at the far end, checking her phone, radiant in a blue wrap dress.

"Hello, Dr. Daughter," Whit called.

"Mom? Dad?" She lit up with surprise. "What …? What are you doing here?"

Ingrid chuckled. "Your boyfriend's full of surprises."

Bobbi took them in. "Mom, that dress is gorgeous. And Dad, coat and tie? Dashing."

"You're not so bad yourself," Whit said. "You look radiant."

"I wore this dress the first time we came here. I can't believe you're here! When did BR invite you? We were supposed to meet Megan tonight. She doesn't know I'm dating him, and he only knows I call her Red."

"How's her mother doing?" Ingrid asked.

"Much better. Megan called after the ER released her without doing any tests. I got a colleague in Florida to see her. The news is good, but Megan's staying a few more days."

"Why isn't BR here?" Whit asked.

"He's coming separately. Sami and I are spending the weekend at the penthouse. He said I deserve four days of surprises since I only get a real birthday every four years."

Whit arched a brow. "All of you under one roof? Some kind of diagnostic test, Dr. Daughter?"

The curtain opened, and BR stepped in, escorting a regal, white-haired woman with a cane.

Ingrid gasped. Whit forgot to breathe.

~~~

BR

As Bobbi's parents rushed to embrace the woman, Bobbi turned to BR, looking stunned. "Who is that?"

"I love you, and I'm so glad you're here."

"I love you, too, but who *is* she? My parents look like they're about to faint."

The woman approached, smiling. "You're the spitting image of your mother, except for those long legs. I'd know you anywhere."

"Bobbi," Ingrid said breathlessly, "this is Dr. Dawn Gerstein."

Tears welled in Bobbi's eyes. She gently hugged the older woman. "Thank you for my life," she whispered.

"When BR called, I looked you up. You're working with Dr. Thibodeau! I read about your awards. I couldn't be prouder."

"I became a doctor because of you," Bobbi said, steadying her voice. "I try to be the kind of doctor you were." She leaned subtly into BR, and he felt her fingers tighten around his. She didn't need to say a word. He was her anchor.

"Let's all sit down," Whit said, helping Dr. Gerstein to her chair.

Bobbi pulled BR aside. "I need you to do two things for me."

"Anything."

"First, get me a glass of white wine."

"Done. And the second?"

"Don't ever leave me."

~~~

On the ride home, Bobbi held BR's hand, quiet but present. He recognized the look—she was absorbing it all. Not withdrawing, just processing.

Finally, she turned to him and whispered, "I've been sitting here trying to find the words to thank you, but there's no way to explain how loved I feel."

He kissed her palm.

They rode in silence a while longer. Then she asked with a playful smile, "Can I at least know tomorrow's schedule? And what to wear?"

"First surprise is at ten in the music room. Wear anything you want. Second surprise is in the afternoon."

"You didn't have to do all this," she said softly. "Just being with the three of you, this is already the best birthday ever."

"I missed all your last ones. I'm making up for lost time. And I want to be around for the next."

"You will be." She laughed. "A thousand percent." Then she leaned in, voice low. "Can I ask for one more gift?"

"Anything."

Her voice dropped to a whisper. "I want to go home and crawl into bed with you. But if I do, I'll beg you to make love to me. And I don't want our kids just down the hall the first time. I want to relax. Just us." She snapped her fingers. "I've got it. Remember I told you the clinic's closed Thursday through Sunday? Electronic records overhaul—HIPAA compliance, server migration, the whole deal. Nobody can log in or see patients until Monday. Could we go away? Just the two of us?"

BR smiled. "Say the word, and I'll make a reservation anywhere you want. Hamptons? Honolulu?"

"Honolulu might be a stretch if we're to be back for Sunday dinner," she teased. "Just take me somewhere and make me yours."

"Deal."

"I'll have to figure out the logistics with the kids," she said.

He brushed her hair back. "Don't worry about a thing. You're not allowed to worry this weekend."

~~~

Sami and Cassie tiptoed into the bedroom, tray in hand.

"Happy birthday!" they cried, clambering onto the bed.

Bobbi fed them strawberries and toast, beaming.

BR stood back, watching. *This*, he thought, *is happiness.*

At ten, he led Bobbi, blindfolded, into the music room. "Ready?"

"Are you going to sing to me?"

"Better. Take off the blindfold."

She gasped. Standing by the piano was Claude, the singing barista from Coffee Corner.

He beamed. "Happy birthday, Dr. Bobbi!"

"Claude? Why are you here?"

"Mr. Bradford invited me and swore me to secrecy."

BR nodded. "You've said he's got a great voice but needs a break. Let's see what happens."

Claude launched into "A Change is Gonna Come," rich and honest. His voice floated through the room.

When the last note faded, BR asked, "Ready for your second song?"

Claude grinned. "Up-tempo? I'll sing 'No Backing Up.'"

BR was impressed. The song had been a huge hit for him from his second album. Few performers had the confidence to audition with one of his classics.

He jumped into the rhythm, bright and bold:

"No backing up, we're moving ahead.
Burned the maps, can't go where we've been.
Feet on the gas, fire in our gut.
No backing up, no backing up."

His voice was agile and rich, riding the rhythm with style. His phrasing was crisp, his energy contagious.

"Big difference singing for commuters versus the greatest Broadway composer. What'd you think, sir?"

BR didn't answer. He tapped on his JadePad.

Claude's phone buzzed. He checked it, froze, then whooped. "I've got an audition Tuesday with Wanda Roberts!"

"She casts for all our shows," BR explained.

Claude rapped:

"I make her special coffee, so the doc got me a shot.
I'm auditioning on Tuesday, and I'm going in hot.
She believed in my sound, now I'm takin' my swing.
It's not a hobby, Dr. Bobbi, I'm gonna professionally sing!"

BR turned to her, visibly impressed. "That's not just voice—that's presence. That's what we look for."

Claude murmured thanks all the way to the door.

When he was gone, Bobbi said, "Claude won't need the subway to get to Brooklyn. He'll probably float home. Is he really good?"

"That's my favorite kind of audition," BR said. "There are parts of singing and presence that can't be taught. He's got them. I don't remember you mentioning how handsome he is, but that doesn't hurt, either."

Bobbi blushed. "I hadn't noticed." She batted her lashes coyly. "Think you could pull off dreadlocks?"

BR rubbed his chin. "I'll take it under advisement. By the way, Cassie's with Anna Maria, working on your birthday present," BR said. "Your next surprise is upstairs."

And what a surprise! Gina, Sami, and Hunter—all in dresses!

CHAPTER THIRTY-TWO: THE BEST WOMAN

Saturday, February 27 – Sunday, Saturday, February 28
Gina

The girls wore casual dresses with leggings, bubbling with excitement. But the real shock was Gina, in a retro plum A-line dress, her tattoos visible beneath a cropped cardigan she'd knitted herself.

"Gina! The last time I saw you in a dress was at your wedding. What's going on?"

Sami jumped in. "Mom, we're going to see *The Best Woman*! All four of us!"

"BR said he got us the best seats in the house!" Hunter practically shouted.

Bobbi still looked baffled.

"Don't you remember?" Sami said. "BR promised us Broadway tickets in exchange for babysitting."

"I forgot about that." Bobbi laughed. "But how does Aunt Gina rate?"

"At Sunday dinner, I overheard Dorkus Malorkus negotiating babysitting rates with BR," Gina said. "So I made him a deal—future Cassie coverage in exchange for a ticket. Your daughter vouched for my excellence."

Sami mock-shivered. "I knew if I didn't, she'd make me pay. But yeah, she's the GOAT of sitters. BR said he'd pay it forward."

Bobbi waggled a finger. "Your aunt is a great sitter, and an even better con artist."

Gina smirked. "He asked Sami if you were a good enough sitter to earn a free ticket."

"I'm guessing you, my beloved daughter, defended my honor."

Sami slunk behind Gina. "I told him you never babysat anyone, and if you did, your cooking might kill them. But since you're a great doctor, maybe you could save them."

Bobbi raised an eyebrow at Gina. "And *you* didn't stand up for me?"

Gina shrugged. "I couldn't lie to the man."

"I'm surrounded by traitors!" Bobbi huffed. "I used to sit for *you* all the time, Gina. I managed to keep you alive, though I'm questioning that choice at the moment. So, how'd I get a ticket?"

Gina grinned. "Turns out your boyfriend's a terrible negotiator. I told him I wanted a plus one. That's you!"

Once the laughter settled, Hunter added sweetly, "For what it's worth, Bobbi, I told BR you watched me all the time when Mom had to work, and you're the best."

Bobbi stroked her arm. "At least *someone's* loyal. As for you two finks"—she scowled—"we'll talk later."

Gina shooed her. "Blah, blah, blah. Get dressed. I'm not missing curtain because my plus one couldn't get her butt in gear."

~~~

Following BR's instructions, Sami led everyone to the will-call window.

"Hi, do you have tickets for Samantha Wyatt?"

The woman behind the window tapped at her keyboard then brightened. She pressed a button and slid an envelope toward Sami. "I just notified our house manager that you and Ms. Jensen are here. We're so glad you could join us today."

Bobbi stepped up. "Do you have tickets for Bobbi Wyatt? Maybe Dr. Wyatt?"

"I'm sorry, there's nothing under either name."

Gina stepped in front, laughing. "Try Gina DiNapoli, sitter extraordinaire."

The woman beamed. "Yes, welcome, Ms. DiNapoli. I have tickets for you and an unnamed plus one."

Sami snapped photos of them in the lobby, each holding a personalized envelope. Bobbi's simply read: *Gina's Plus One.*

Bobbi studied her ticket. "Sami, we're not sitting together."

A house manager approached. "Dr. Wyatt and Ms. DiNapoli? We've arranged special seating for you. Please head up to the mezzanine level—an usher will escort you."

Sami and Hunter headed down the orchestra aisle and out of sight as the sold-out theater filled.

Bobbi and Gina ambled up the plush-carpeted stairs into a luxurious private box. The seats were deep velvet, with plenty of legroom. The view was spectacular.

Gina sent a glam selfie of her and Bobbi to BR.

Front-row auntie perks. You're spoiling us.

Below them—fourth row, center—Bobbi spotted the girls. "Look at Sami—she's glowing."

"Of course, they gave her the best seats," Gina said smugly. "They know *I'm* tight with BR Bradford."

As if on cue, their phones buzzed with a flurry of texts. Selfies. Seat numbers. A handwritten note:

Ms. Wyatt and Ms. Jensen, enjoy an item of merch and any concessions on us (excluding alcohol), and please meet us after the performance to meet the cast.

A guest relations rep appeared at the box entrance and knocked softly. "Ladies, you're welcome to order anything from the lounge. It's all on the house. We're happy to bring it to your seats."

Gina practically swooned. "A Best Woman Bellini and truffle popcorn, please."

Bobbi stood. "I think I'll stretch my legs and check in with Megan. Maybe see what's at the bar."

Ten minutes later, Gina was mesmerized by the pre-show atmosphere. Onstage, twilight was giving way to morning as a city block subtly transformed into a modest New York apartment. The show hadn't begun, but the world of *The Best Woman* was already unfolding. She didn't notice when Bobbi slipped into the seat beside her.

"Are you going to meet the cast after the show?" Bobbi asked softly, making Gina jump.

"It'll have to be quick. Marco just texted—every table's booked through closing. No idea what caused the surge, but he needs me to serve tonight. I'm in demand; what can I say?" She squeezed Bobbi's arm. "BR arranged a driver for me and Hunter. He's really something, Bobs."

Just then, the lights dimmed and the overture swelled. Onstage, the apartment shifted into a bedroom. A pretty young woman climbed out of bed to thunderous applause and began to sing the opening number.

"I'm ready, world..."

Bobbi gasped. "Wait—I know this song. BR wrote this?"

Eyes fixed on the stage, Gina whispered, "He wrote the whole thing, dimwit—the music, the lyrics, the book. Now, hush."

After the final bow, Gina, Sami, and Hunter headed backstage for five whirlwind minutes and managed to take what felt like a million selfies in that short time.

~~~

Bobbi

Bobbi waited in the lobby, rereading a message from Megan. Her mother was responding well to treatment. Relief flooded through her.

When the others emerged—ecstatic, breathless, and carrying merch—Gina quickly hugged Bobbi, and then she and Hunter jumped into the waiting car and headed to Brooklyn.

As they wove through Times Square, Bobbi asked, "What was it like meeting the cast?"

Sami's face glowed. "Like I was dreaming, but I was awake. They were all so nice and signed my poster. I want to go to Broadway every week."

Bobbi laughed. "Are you kidding? I want to go back *tonight* and see it again!"

Sami lit up. "Really? Can we go? I can ask BR for tickets."

Bobbi whooped. "The two of us would have to babysit Cassie tonight to earn them, so maybe we aim for tomorrow."

Sami started singing, "*I'm ready, world.*"

Bobbi joyfully joined in, the horns honking in Times Square rising behind them like applause.

~~~

City lights spilled softly through the penthouse windows as Bobbi followed BR into his bedroom. She sat on the edge of the bed, quietly slipping off her shoes. He brushed her hair aside and kissed the back of her neck—a move that always sent her body into overdrive.

"I'm glad you liked the show," he murmured above her soft moan.

"Yeah." She shuddered. *That's* why my body's trembling." She looked up at him, her jade eyes shimmering. "Seriously, sweetheart—seeing your work, hearing your music—I felt so close to you. I've never been to Broadway, but I can't imagine another show being that amazing. I keep thinking about the characters, especially Morgan, and how you created something magical, funny, serious, and inspiring. That wasn't just a show; that was genius. And it all came from *you.*"

BR shook his head. "It's a team effort. It took an incredible director, choreographer, set designers—"

"Don't," she said gently, standing to face him. "*You* wrote that amazing story, that music. Those words came from you. Watching that today … I felt like I was meeting a part of you I hadn't seen before. And it took my breath away."

"I'm glad you liked it. But *your* work saves lives. I just make people clap."

Bobbi straightened his collar. "Sami and Hunter told me *The Best Woman* has changed lives. It's become a movement. People do unexpected, good deeds, and say, 'I do it for Morgan.' You have no idea how many lives you've touched."

She paused. "I once had a patient tell me I reminded her of Morgan. I didn't understand the reference until today. Since then, a few people—including Red—have said that 'I'm Ready, World' makes them think of me."

"They're right," BR said. "You lift people up. Like the night you saved Howard—you didn't just patch him, you built a forever memory of love for Cassie."

Bobbi's voice dropped. "I kept picturing you as Billy. I would've been in the front row for every performance."

"If you were in the front row, I'd have forgotten every line."

He handed her a garment bag. She raised an eyebrow and unzipped it.

Inside was a stunning dress—sexy and elegant, with a plunging neckline and a beautifully draped silhouette. A cropped jacket hung beside it.

"You got me a sexy red dress?" she teased, wrinkling her nose.

"Check the card."

Happy Birthday, Bobbi!
We flew in just for tonight. We're taking you
to dinner, and all Outsiders must look drop-
dead gorgeous. We picked this out for you.
Love, Liz and Chrissy

She laughed, carrying her dress and makeup bag into BR's bathroom to change. Without thinking, she leaned toward the mirror and wrote with lipstick: *Thank you for your love.*

~~~

BR

BR woke the next morning with a heaviness in his chest and a tickle in his nose. He opened his eyes and saw Bobbi sprawled out all over him. Her long hair was in his eyes, nose, and mouth. The weight of her breasts and the electric coolness of her skin stirred him deeply.

Before he could brush her hair away, he sneezed.

Bobbi opened one eye. "*No,*" she murmured. "I didn't wanna wake up. This feels *so* good." Her voice was dreamy, sensual.

He gently rolled her to her side and kissed her softly. "I can't believe I didn't wake up when you came in."

"You did, for a minute. You even complimented my nightie."

Bobbi wore a smile, kissing his chest. "Liz and Chrissy took me to a black-tie charity event. We had a fantastic time, but then I tossed and turned all night. An hour ago, I woke up and knew where I wanted to be."

He brushed her hair back and kissed her throat. That single move made her shiver.

Panting softly, she growled, "That feels *so* good. Every time you touch me, it's like electricity. Yesterday was incredible, but I didn't get to spend much time with you, and I hardly saw Cassie."

BR kept running his fingers through her hair. "I missed you, too. But you're surrounded by people who love you, and all of them want to celebrate. Here's what's happening today. You have time to work out, and then it's time for brunch."

"Just the four of us?" she asked. "Are we going to my parents' for dinner?"

"Brunch was Gina's idea. It's girls only—family only. Your mom and Gina are coming in from Brooklyn. The other guests are Cassie, Sami, Anna Maria, and Siobhán. Gina thought it was time both families met."

Bobbi smiled. "I love that. I'm crazy about your nieces." She paused. "Where was Cassie yesterday?"

BR whispered, "She spent the whole day with your parents. Ran errands with your dad, helped your mom bake the birthday cake, and even napped in your old bed. She had the time of her life."

Bobbi blinked, her eyes shining. "That's amazing. My parents really love her."

"That's why I laughed yesterday when you wondered about babysitters for our weekend getaway. Gina owes me for the Broadway tickets, your parents are on standby, and Anna Maria and Siobhán would love more time with their new 'cousin' Sami."

Bobbi smirked. "You've thought of everything. Except maybe giving me more time alone with you."

"I'm fixing that today. After brunch, I'm taking you on a long drive to show you a place I've been waiting to share. I won't tell you why I love it, not yet. I just want to see your reaction."

"Are you sure you only want to see my *reaction*?"

"For today," he murmured, kissing her collarbone.

She shivered, her body betraying her raw desire.

"Okay, before you make me completely crazy, one more question. What's happening after the drive?"

"We're going to your parents' house for the party. Apparently, Red picked the theme and coordinated with Gina, and it's hilarious."

Bobbi laughed. "I'm in trouble."

~~~

Bobbi

The party had been a blast. As everyone said their goodbyes, BR handed Bobbi her jacket and said softly, "Cassie wants you to carry her out."

Cassie had been barely awake, curled around Howard. The weekend had been fun but exhausting.

Bobbi knelt beside her. "Hey, sweet pea. Ready to go?"

Without a word, Cassie reached for her.

Outside, the sky had deepened to a velvet-blue. The air was still.

Bobbi carried a drowsy Cassie to the car, gently buckled her in, and brushed her hair back from her forehead. "I love you, sweet pea," she whispered.

Cassie's voice was faint but unmistakable. "I love you, Mommy."

Bobbi froze. Her heart stopped. It was the first time Cassie had said it. Probably just a half-asleep slip, but it filled Bobbi's soul with something enormous and permanent.

She kissed Cassie again then stepped back.

BR leaned in for a long, tender kiss.

She sighed. "Now the clock strikes, and Cinderella leaves the castle and has to return to work."

And then they were gone.

Now, Bobbi sat alone by the fire pit in her parents' backyard, wrapped in one of the blankets Ingrid kept stacked by the door. The pine logs glowed comfortingly. Bobbi let the quiet surround her.

The brunch had been more wonderful than she could have imagined. BR had arranged a private room at one of Manhattan's most impossible-to-book restaurants. She'd watched with quiet joy as two different worlds blended effortlessly. Reserved Anna Maria and brash, fast-talking Gina had clicked instantly—a bond forming between two women who had been broken, rebuilt, and made stronger. Siobhán's Irish-accented stories had Ingrid completely enchanted.

And Cassie—sweet little Cassie—had surprised them all.

Ingrid had bought her a new dress, and Anna Maria had done her hair. But what truly moved Bobbi was what Whit shared later. Cassie had visited his workshop the day before. After watching him refurbish a headboard for a family in need, she'd asked, "Could you teach me to help? You fix furniture for people who don't have any, and Bobbi fixes people when they're sick. I want to help people so they're happy and not hurt." Then she added, "Maybe when we bring the furniture, Mrs. Ingrid could teach me to make cookies, and we could give them furniture and food." Her father had nearly cried telling Bobbi.

As Cassie had stood beside Sami, making everyone laugh with her pitch-perfect imitation of Siobhán's Irish accent, her ribboned dress catching the light, something had shifted in Bobbi's heart.

I have two daughters.

The brunch had been meant to blend two families, but it had done more than that. It had brought her clarity. Her past and future now stood side by side, blended together in a way that felt joyful and true.

Then there'd been the drive.

BR had taken her to a quiet, beautiful stretch of land after wandering through a picture-postcard town in Westchester. He had just let her take it in. Maybe he'd chosen it because she loved hiking. Perhaps it reminded him of Colorado. Either way, it had felt like something more than just a walk.

The only thing missing from the weekend was Red.

Bobbi missed her deeply. They'd postponed their long-anticipated double date when Megan had flown to Florida to care for her mother. But now, after everything that had unfolded, Bobbi knew precisely what she'd do the moment they were face-to-face again.

She was going to tell Megan everything. About BR. About the weekend. All of it.

Still, Red's presence had been everywhere.

Since Bobbi had been born on Leap Day, this was technically her eighth real birthday, so Red had decided they'd throw Bobbi a birthday party fit for an eight-year-old. She'd emailed Gina and Ingrid a complete game plan: backyard games, face painting, juice boxes, chicken tenders, mac-and-cheese, a playlist of pop songs from Bobbi's childhood, and a pink princess cake Cassie had helped bake, complete with a sugar crown and far too much frosting. Red wouldn't be back for a few more days, but it looked like the worst of her mother's crisis had passed.

Bobbi swirled the last of her wine and leaned back. She thought about work. Monday and Tuesday would be brutal—fourteen-hour days prepping the clinic for the electronic records shutdown. Wednesday wouldn't be much better. But Bobbi wasn't dreading it.

Because next weekend, she and BR were going away. Just the two of them. No work. No kids. And the thought of it—finally—left her breathless.

She pulled the blanket tighter and looked up at the stars. She missed him already.

CHAPTER THIRTY-THREE: YES DAY
Wednesday, March 2
BR

BR fidgeted and rechecked his to-do list. It hadn't changed since the last time he'd looked—five minutes ago—but he wanted to be sure everything was in place.

A text from Bobbi interrupted the scan and sent his heart racing.

> *I'm about to get off the ferry. Can we PLEASE just have dinner at your place? I look haggard. Two and a half days with no sleep, no gym, no makeup, and no kisses from you have left me tired and frumpy. I don't want one of your fans posting a picture of the handsome Broadway star and his hideous, schlubby date to Instagram.*

He'd never said no to Bobbi before, not really. Not on anything that mattered. But tonight was different.

> *On your worst day, you look amazing. We'll have a quiet dinner then head back to my place.*

Three little dots appeared. Then disappeared. Then came back. Then vanished again.

Bobbi was probably surprised and trying to figure out how to respond. No message came through.

BR checked the tracker. The car had already left the 34th Street Ferry Terminal and was inching through midtown traffic.

Scrolling through messages and replying to some work emails didn't distract him. He just needed Bobbi.

She entered quietly, handing her coat to the woman at the door, and walked toward him. The first thing he noticed was how tired she looked. She was wearing a plain sweater and black pants with low heels. Her hair was in a limp ponytail, and her eyes didn't have their usual sparkle.

Before she could speak, he took her hand. "Happy anniversary."

"Anniversary?" She looked genuinely confused.

"Yes. We met right here at Fortuna's, exactly two months ago tonight."

She offered a wrinkled smile and rubbed her temple. "Now can you see how tired I am? I couldn't figure out why Ronnie brought me to Fortuna's. Happy anniversary, sweetheart."

"Graciella closed the gallery so we could take a private tour of her new show. All the paintings are by students from a prestigious school in Turin."

They walked the exhibit in silence. A few pieces were lovely, but none matched Marianna Remi's genius.

Bobbi paused and gently tugged BR's hand. "This is where *2:29* was," she said softly. "I called the gallery a couple weeks after we met. I knew it had sold; I just didn't expect to feel so sad. I hope it brings love to whoever bought it."

"I'm sure it does," he murmured. "After all, it brought you to me, and then wrapped us up in the Bobbi Bubble. But something else strange happened that night."

She raised an eyebrow.

"I know I have told you this, but I must have blinked or something, because one moment I could've sworn I was standing alone, looking at the painting ... and then—*poof*— you were just there."

Her breath caught. "This weekend, when I'm lying in your arms in bed, I'll tell you what I think happened."

"I want to hear it. That night was so mysterious and special. You've seen how introverted I am. It took every ounce of my willpower to ask you to walk across the street and have dinner with me. But I didn't ask you the real question I wanted to."

"What was that?" she asked softly.

BR took a deep breath. "I wanted to ask you to go to Rome with me—right then."

She didn't answer. Her jade eyes moistened.

"Honey, it's been two months. Everyone says we're moving too fast, but I feel we're moving too slow. I had so much success in my life before I met you, and none of it seems even a little bit important. Falling in love with you has been the part of life I didn't know I was missing. Everything feels sweeter, better, more meaningful—because of you. You're the most extraordinary person I've ever met. I don't know how I got lucky enough to earn your love, but I never want to be without it. I don't want there to be a day in my life that isn't with you."

He dropped to one knee, and Bobbi's hands flew to her mouth. He reached into his pocket and opened a small box.

"Bobbi, will you—"

"Yes!" she burst out, her voice muffled behind her hands.

He stood, laughing through his tears. "You didn't let me finish my question."

Bobbi's shoulders shook. "By all means, ask again. But my answer's never going to change. If you ask me ten thousand times, I'll say yes ten thousand times."

"Let's find out," he whispered. "For the second time: Bobbi, will you marry me?"

"Yes. Ten thousand times, yes."

They were both crying now, and the kiss that followed was sweet and salty with tears.

She finally looked down at the ring in the box. "Holy ravioli," she whispered. "Is that …? Is that a blue diamond? It's huge. And so clear. It looks like it's glowing from the inside." She blinked. "You must really love me in blue."

BR smiled and gently slid the ring into place. "The band is antique gold—real Italian gold. I tracked it down from a mine that shut down almost a hundred years ago. You love Italy, so I wanted the ring to carry something rare. Something with history."

He touched one of the green stones, his voice softer now. "There are six jades. Four of them are us—Sami, Cassie, you, and me. One is for us as a couple, and one is for the family we're building."

After she studied it, he added, "I chose jade for the green. It reminded me of the beauty in your eyes." Then he gently turned the ring on her finger. "Around the outside are twenty-nine white diamonds, for your birthday—the twenty-ninth.

And two small yellow diamonds tucked in between. Two. Twenty-nine. It's not just your birthday—it's the painting. It's how we started."

"I'll love it forever," she whispered. "I'll love you forever."

"Come with me," he said, holding out his hand. "I want to give you your engagement present."

Bobbi let out a wheezing laugh, both crying and laughing now. "I think this ring is present enough for ten thousand proposals."

He led her toward the front of the gallery. Ronnie had slipped in quietly and now stood off to the side, holding BR's phone—he'd recorded the proposal.

Wagging a finger at him, Bobbi chortled. "I should've known you were in on this." She pulled Ronnie into a hug even as he offered his congratulations.

Graciella Fortuna and her assistant, Penelope, emerged from the office. Graciella carried a large, beautifully wrapped rectangular box with reverence usually reserved for sacred objects. Penelope followed with two somewhat smaller boxes, wrapped in matching paper.

Bobbi glanced at the packages then turned back to BR and threw her arms around him. "Is that what I think it is?" she managed, voice shaking.

He nodded. "Yes. And the two companion paintings you loved—they were part of it. It's *2:29*. I thought we could hang it in our living room when we build our home someday."

Bobbi shook her head. "No, no. It belongs in our bedroom—to always keep our love safe." She pulled back slightly. "But when did you buy it? How'd you get it?"

Graciella handed her a gift receipt, carefully unfolded. The timestamp read January 3ʳᵈ—the day after they'd met. In loopy, flowery handwriting, it read:

Purchased by BR Bradford as a gift for Dr. Bobbi Wyatt.

Bobbi stared at it. "What would you have done if it turned out we weren't right for each other?"

"I'd have given it to you, anyway," BR said simply. "Nobody else in the world could ever own that painting. It was always meant for you."

She looked at him for a long moment, her expression unreadable. Finally, she said softly, "There's no way I'd have accepted it. You weren't buying that painting for *me*. On some level, you already knew—you were buying it for *us*. Without you, *2:29* wouldn't mean anything."

Emotion tightened his throat. "Would you like to walk to The Red Dragonfly and have a celebratory dinner?"

"I'm starving," she admitted, laughing through tears. "But there's something I'd like to do before we eat."

Ronnie and BR nodded at one another.

Then BR said, "I told your parents we'd be coming shortly. I figured you'd want to tell them in person."

~~~

As the car slowly crept through Midtown, BR loved watching Bobbi alternately smile at him, look at her ring, and wipe stray tears away from her eyes.

"My parents are going to be so surprised. Sami's going to lose it. I can't believe this is really happening."

"All three of them already know. They're expecting us," BR confessed.

Bobbi let go of his hand and sat up straight, her eyes locked on his. "What are you talking about?"

"I asked Sami for her permission a couple weeks ago. Remember, she was staying with me that Saturday you were working?"

Bobbi nodded but didn't divert her gaze.

"We went to a diner that has special meaning for me, and I asked for her blessing to propose to you."

"You did *what*? Why would you ask her? You know how much she loves you."

"It was important to let Sami know I wasn't just marrying you. I was saying she'd be my daughter forever, that she wasn't a *throw-in* on the deal."

"I bet she said yes faster than I did."

"Everyone in the diner—and probably people across the street—heard her scream of joy! Don't be mad; I swore her to secrecy."

Bobbi's eyes melted. "That was a lovely thing to do. Does Cassie know?"

"No, absolutely not. I think it's important you be the one to tell her."

Chest heaving and hands shaking just a bit, Bobbi said, "That'll be one of the best moments of my life. I love that girl as if I had carried her inside me for nine months."

Now it was Bobbi's turn to wipe a tear from BR's cheek.

They rode silently for a few minutes before Bobbi looked up with a jolt. "How do my parents know?"

"I talked to your parents while you were out with Chrissy and Liz and asked for their blessing."

"You asked my parents for my hand? Do you think we're living in the 1950s?" Bobbi chortled. "What'd they say?"

"Your mom applauded and said she knew it. I got a big hug. Your father said he couldn't agree unless he was sure I was the right person for you. His exact words were, 'Do you have the financial resources to keep my daughter in the manner to which she's become accustomed?'"

Bobbi bellowed with laughter. "I can just hear him saying that!"

"It gets better," BR said, smiling at the memory. "I told him, if it comes down to it, I'll sell my share of Coffee Corner just to build enough bathrooms in the house. I mean, I'll be living with three women—I'd like to get into a bathroom before noon. And based on the shampoo inventory alone, I know I'm in over my head. Your dad couldn't stop laughing. Then I negotiated a dowry."

"A *dowry*? We've gone from the 1950s to the 1850s. I don't know who's weirder: you or him. But just so I know, how much did he offer to convince you to take me off his hands?"

"He offered to build a dollhouse for Cassie. I was on the fence, but then your mom threw in two trays of lasagna, and I agreed. Your father and I shook hands on the deal."

"Seriously? You're getting an Ivy-League-trained MD with no student debt, a killer sense of humor, and her own car. I've taken so much yoga I can bend myself into positions you can't even imagine, and I go for a dollhouse and some lasagna?"

"I would've asked for more, but I was getting Sami in the deal. So, no matter what, I was coming out ahead. Plus, it's really great lasagna."

"True on both counts." Then, more seriously, she said, "You didn't have to ask them."

"I know. I wanted to. They're such wonderful people, and they've been so great to Cassie. It felt respectful and bonding. They are going to be my parents. You're an only child. Now you have a partner who'll help you care for them when the time comes. And who can beat fantastic babysitters who can cook and fix anything?"

"Our kids will be so lucky. You've seen the love Sami's grown up with. Now Cassie is theirs, too."

"Honey, we have to figure out where we're going to live," he said as the car came to a full stop in traffic. "I love your place, but it's too small for four of us. We have plenty of room in mine, but it's a terrible location for you to get to work and Sami to school."

To his surprise, Bobbi waved this away with a flick of her hand. "That's already been decided. Sami and Hunter came up with a plan."

"They did?" He chuckled. "Can you fill me in so I know where I'll be living?"

"Ever since Sami was little, we've had something we call pajama talks. When something's on her mind, we snuggle in her bed. I lightly scratch her back with my fingernails, and we talk through everything.

"A couple of weeks ago, she asked for a pajama talk. Without any preliminaries, she asked if you and I were going to get married. I couldn't lie to her, but I didn't want her to know everything we've discussed. I simply told her that you hadn't asked me."

"I'm sure that wasn't enough for her."

"Not even a little." She chuckled. "Sami asked if I'd say yes if you proposed. She told me it's what she wanted. When I brought up where we'd live, she laid out the plan: we'll move into the penthouse but keep our place in Brooklyn. You'll have dedicated drivers to take us to work and school. It'll mean going to bed earlier and getting up earlier, but we're both happy to do that if the four of us are together as a family.

"After school, she can come home or go to Hunter's or my parents'—her schedule wouldn't have to change. We'll need two drivers most days, since she and I won't always be coming back together."

"That part's easy," BR said. "But it doesn't sit right. You and Sami are making all the sacrifices. Weekends in Brooklyn are a start. When your tenant lease is up, we can renovate for more space. Most importantly, we'll start building a new home for the four of us, somewhere you can get to work and the girls can go to great schools. We'll make it work, as long as we're together."

Bobbi agreed then lit up. "Wait—does Gina know you proposed?"

"No. I knew you'd want to see her face when you tell her."

"I'm texting her to meet us at Mom's."

As she fired off the message, BR's mind was already racing. "When would you and Sami want to move in?"

"Is this weekend too soon?"

He couldn't tell if she was joking, but he started running through logistics while she smiled, thumbs flying.

When she looked up, Bobbi's eyes widened. The car wasn't moving, and there was a lot of noise from the car horns around them. But the bubble was in full force, and they felt completely alone and connected.

"I can't read your expression, BR. What're you thinking?"

"Would you really want to move in this weekend, or were you kidding?"

Bobbi didn't hesitate. "We'd move in tonight if it were possible. But a move would take months."

"Not necessarily," he replied. "You're off until Monday. I could have a meeting first thing in the morning with key members of my team. We could get you mostly moved in within a couple of days."

She looked astonished but also excited. "How?"

"I have painters, carpenters, trucks, drivers, and a great packing service ready to go. Since you're keeping the house on Honey Street, we wouldn't need all your furniture and clothes right away. The main thing would be to get your essentials moved in, flip Sami's room from a hotel suite to a homemade bedroom, get a bigger dining room table, a new couch, chairs for you both in the reading area, and redecorate the bedroom so that it's ours."

Bobbi's excitement grew. "Do you really think we could do all of that in a couple of days?"

"Say the word, and I'll make it happen—starting tomorrow."

"*The word*!" she said enthusiastically.

~~~

BR barely noticed as Sami, shrieking, leaped into her mother's arms. He was busy on the phone with Mrs. Lincoln, making sure she invited the proper people for breakfast tomorrow. Each was to give an omelet order so Mrs. Smith could prep. He gave several apologies but no reason for the late notice.

Gina's car pulled up and, to his surprise, she ran over and delivered a bone-crushing hug. He wondered if Bobbi had told her about the proposal.

Instead, she blurted, "Thanks to you, I haven't seen my husband in three days! That quote you gave to the Brooklyn foodie blog went viral. The minute you called Luna Azur your favorite restaurant and mentioned Marco's seafood pasta, people started retweeting it, posting nonstop, and showing up just to snap Instagram pics. The phone won't stop ringing, the reservation system's crashing, and the servers are drowning in tips. Marco says you've ruined his life in the best possible way."

"Glad it helped," BR muttered as they went inside.

Bobbi joined them.

"What's going on tonight?" Gina asked, squinting at Bobbi. "I was ready for fuzzy slippers and trashy reality TV to celebrate finishing my project, and then you tell me to come over. No explanation."

"Oh," Bobbi said, feigning nonchalance, "I just wanted to ask you something."

"You could've texted me. You're being weird. Why are you being weird?"

"How'd you feel about being my Matron of Honor?" She held up her left hand.

Gina's shrieks reached the level of a twenty-one gun cannon salute of joy.

Ingrid set out glasses of champagne and freshly baked lemon bars. Sami and BR received glasses of sparkling grape juice.

Whit raised his glass, his voice thick with emotion. "To love. To family. And to the man wise enough to see what we've always known—our Bobbi is extraordinary. BR, you've given her the kind of love every parent hopes their child will find. You've become the father we prayed Sami would one day have. And you've brought Cassie into our lives—that bright, sweet little girl who has only added to the love and happiness of this family. Congratulations, Bobbi and BR."

Everyone clinked glasses.

Despite Bobbi shooting her the classic maternal stink-eye, Gina even let Sami take a celebratory sip of champagne.

Gina waved her off. "That's your engagement outfit? You look like you shopped at Beige & Confused."

Bobbi scowled, but Gina laughed.

"Will Sami and Cassie be flower girls?"

"Nope," Bobbi said, eyes twinkling. "Sami, I'd like you and Cassie to be my Maids of Honor."

Sami's screams rattled the glassware.

"Look at that," Gina said, grinning. "Not even twelve, and this is her second time as a Maid of Honor."

"Second?" BR asked, still absorbing the whirlwind of the Wyatt family energy.

"I stood up for Aunt Gina," Sami said proudly.

Gina nodded. "Dorkus Malorkus here saved me; caring for her gave my life purpose. Your girlfriend also carried some flowers."

"My *fiancée*," BR corrected, setting off another round of cheers.

Bobbi tapped Sami. "Come on, baby; let's go to your room. There's something I want to ask you."

The two of them trotted off, giggling.

Ingrid was aglow. "How excited is Cassie?"

"She doesn't know yet. Bobbi will tell her when Cassie gets back."

"Where is the munchkin?" Gina asked.

"Cassie's up at the horse farm," BR explained. "Siobhán's brother took in a rescued wild mare—she's about to give birth. Cassie's been obsessed with her from day one. They're letting her help and even name the foal."

"Yes," Whit added happily, "it's all she's talked about for weeks."

BR answered questions about the proposal until Bobbi and Sami returned excitedly.

Bobbi clinked a glass. "I have a few announcements. First, we're keeping our Honey Street house but moving into BR's penthouse this weekend."

Excited, overlapping questions followed.

"We're working out the logistics in the morning," she added. "Mom, is it okay if Sami stays here for a few days?"

Ingrid's face lit up. Nothing would make her happier.

"We're not making the engagement public yet. But there's something we want you to know." She gestured to BR.

"I've asked Bobbi to legally adopt Cassie," he said. "She won't be Cassie's stepmother—she'll be her mother. And, with Sami's blessing, I'm adopting her."

The room erupted in hugs and happy chaos. BR felt overwhelmed by the sheer joy.

Sami turned to her grandfather. "Grandpa … would it be okay if I used BR's last name? I don't want to hurt your feelings. I'd be Sami Rose Wyatt Bradford."

Every eye turned to Whit.

BR waited. The name change had been Sami's idea. He'd never do anything to disrespect Bobbi's family.

Whit's voice was unwavering. "I think that's a beautiful name."

Sami flew into his arms.

Gina, never one to let a moment stay too emotional, raised an eyebrow at Bobbi. "What about you, Bobs? Changing your name?"

Bobbi looked genuinely surprised. "I've never thought about it. What do you think, sweetheart?"

BR didn't hesitate. "It's your call. But unless you really want to, I don't think you should change your name. It was Bobbi *Wyatt* who graduated early, won all those awards, served as valedictorian, and became the youngest female neurologist in the country. Dr. Bobbi *Wyatt*."

Whit applauded. "Maybe, Dr. Daughter, you keep your name professionally and use Bradford when it comes to the kids. Like for PTA meetings and pizza orders."

"Oh, Daddy, that's the best idea. Do you see why I love him so much? The only thing that matters to BR is supporting me."

"That's how your father is. It's kept us happy for almost thirty-five years," Ingrid cooed.

~~~

Bobbi

Back in the car, BR was already tapping out messages. A moment later, he glanced over. "I'm looping you into a three-way call. Your mom and a woman named Zoë. You'll love her. She and her sister Avery run a moving company called Z to A."

"*Z to A?*" Bobbi asked.

"They're an amazing packing service. You tell them what you want to bring, and they fold, pack, label, and move it like it's their superpower—fast, neat, and scarily efficient.

"While you were talking to Gina, I asked your mom to help supervise the first wave. Zoë helped Liz and Ed move. Since Sami's off from school on Friday, they'll get Sami packed. They'll organize your things so when you get to Brooklyn Friday night, the move will go fast." He squeezed her hand. "I've got trucks and drivers ready. Once redecorations are done this weekend, Zoë and Avery will unpack and get you settled."

"What about tomorrow?"

"You'll meet the design team—painters, flooring, design, furniture. They'll create whatever makes you and Sami happy."

The phone chimed, and Zoë's bright, energetic voice came through. Ingrid joined, and the three women immediately clicked. Within minutes, they were trading ideas and laughing at the absurdity of pulling off a move in under seventy-two hours. It should've been overwhelming, but it was fun.

"This is the synchronized swimming of moving," Zoë quipped. "High coordination, big smiles, no one sees the kicking underneath."

329

Ingrid laughed. "My daughter's a brilliant doctor who stays cool under pressure, and she learned it from me. We don't get stressed—we make plans."

Bobbi was swept up in the momentum. "I'll start a list of everything I want packed first."

"Perfect," Zoë said. "Avery and I are fast—tornado energy—but careful and color-coordinated."

When the call ended, Bobbi leaned back, still holding BR's hand, her eyes on the lights flickering past the window.

"I can't believe this is all happening so fast ... and it's all so wonderful."

Bobbi was seeing a new side of him. She'd fallen for BR the father, the artist, the romantic. But this ... this was BR the leader. Calm, strategic, quietly in charge, he didn't need to raise his voice; he moved people with quiet confidence. She was loving every second of it.

She was curious, though ... "So, who actually knows we're engaged?"

"Besides your whole family and Ronnie? Just the jeweler, the appraiser, and my insurance guy. None of them know your name. No one else. Not even Bree, Ed or The Outsiders."

Bobbi's face lit up. "Can we *please* tell them tonight?"

He was already sending the message. "We'll video call as soon as we're back."

By the time she'd used the bathroom and answered texts from Sami and her mom, BR was on the couch with his laptop, the screen crowded with Bree, Chrissy, Liz, and Ed all talking over each other.

They greeted her with a chorus of excitement.

Bobbi laughed. "Hi! I actually just needed to talk to Liz and Chrissy."

"Oh, we didn't know," Ed said. "BR just said it was a catch-up call."

"Do you want Ed and me to drop off?" Bree offered.

"No, stay. It's fine. I just had a question. You two put me through that weird Outsiders application to become a probationary Outsider. Is there a process to become a full voting member?"

Liz didn't miss a beat. "It takes a wedding ring."

Bobbi held up her hand, flashing the stunning blue diamond. "Am I *now* eligible to be an official Outsider?"

Chrissy leaned in. "According to the bylaws, an engagement ring moves you from probationary to provisional status. But we'll need to inspect the wedding band in person. Which means ... we're your bridesmaids!"

"Done," Bobbi said. "Wouldn't want it any other way."

Chaos erupted—cheers, hugs, teasing all at once. Bree finally cut through it.

"Okay, spill. How did he do it?"

"I'll tell you in person. You'll all be back in New York next week, right? Let's plan our own engagement party, just us."

She glanced at her phone. "I've got to go. My mom, Zoë, and Avery are calling."

"Zoë and Avery?" Liz asked. "You're moving in? They're magic."

"I already love them. And I love you guys. I can't wait to see you."

As BR finished the call with his friends, Bobbi finished making calls in her room while changing into one of BR's dress shirt, legs bare, hair in a messy bun. She started to carry a bin of toiletries, moving it from her room to theirs.

She gasped softly as she opened the bedroom door. Draped across the bed was a familiar sight—the shroud. It was brand new and for a king-sized bed. When she flopped onto it, she knew he hadn't just bought her a comforter—he'd replaced his entire mattress with the exact model she slept on at home in her queen bed.

She padded back into the living room and stood before him.

"What were you doing?" he asked.

"Nesting." She straddled him and kissed him, slow and hungry. "How'd you know what kind of mattress I use? Or my ring size?"

"Your ... parents," he managed. "Excellent spies."

"I need to ask something hard," she whispered. "There's a method to my madness."

"Anything. I'd do anything for you."

"I might be pressing my luck. You know how much I want you. But ..."

"But ...?"

"Can you wait one more day?" Her voice was soft. "I'm so happy, but I'm exhausted. I haven't shaved my legs, washed my hair, or packed anything sexy. Tomorrow, let me dress up for you. Take me out then bring me home ... and make me yours." She kissed him again then whispered, "I promise I'll make it worth your while."

BR looked dazed. "Does this mean you're sleeping in your room?"

She snorted. "Are you out of your mind? I'm sleeping in *our* bed. I want to be next to you every night, starting now."

"And you expect me to just ... sleep ... next to you?"

"You said you'd do *anything* for me."

"Honey, you're making this very hard."

"I'm glad to hear it." She slipped off his lap and held out her hand. "Let's go to bed."

"I love your left hand," BR said as she turned down the sheets. "Seeing your ring when you climb in ... I'll never forget it."

Bobbi scooted under the covers. "Well, you asked my father for my hand, so that's all you get. At least for tonight."

They curled up, BR's arm wrapped around her. Bobbi looked at the ring, smiling to herself. First, she hummed, then she giggled.

"What's so funny?" he asked.

"I was just thinking of that song—'*If you like it, then you better put a ring on it.*' You don't even know if you'll like it and you already put a ring on it. After tomorrow, you'll think you got the bargain of the century."

"I have no doubt," BR murmured, kissing her shoulder.

CHAPTER THIRTY-FOUR: THE WHIRLWIND
Thursday, March 3
Bobbi

Bobbi awoke with the familiar, welcome sensation of the shroud tucked under her chin and the completely unfamiliar but *highly* welcome feeling of BR's hand under her shirt. She lay on her side, back against his chest, and let out a long, contented sigh as she looked at her engagement ring.

Snuggling back into him, she tried to erase any distance between them.

He woke with a laugh, sputtering as he pulled strands of her hair from his face.

Bobbi wrapped her arm over the hand that was fondling her, letting out a little moan of approval.

Although she didn't want to move, she rolled over to face him, whipping her hair across his face again. They both laughed.

"Now you know what I'd look like with long hair," he said.

"I love you, sweetheart. Waking up next to you feels so perfectly right."

"I love you, too, honey. But I didn't get as much sleep as you! You were out like a light, yet I couldn't turn off my brain. I'm just so happy." He kissed her.

Bobbi gathered her hair and tied it back. His hand still rested on her hip, grazing the edge of her panties … and making her ache with desire.

"I want you to do something for me," she said. "Something I've never asked a man to do in bed."

"Anything," he said, eyes instantly alert.

She smiled, watching his expression shift. "I want to lie here like a queen while you do the thing that'll make me feel amazing … I want you to sing to me."

BR didn't laugh. He sat up and looked into her eyes. Then, softly, he began to sing one of the most beautiful songs she'd ever heard, about the unexpected joy of falling in love.

Bobbi nearly gave in. She almost pulled him down and gave up the plan to wait until tonight. But her resolve held.

"It's like you wrote that just for me, like you knew how I'd feel this morning. When did you write it?"

"Um … George and Ira Gershwin wrote it over a hundred years ago. It's called 'How Long Has This Been Going On?'"

Bobbi yanked the covers over her head. "That's it. I'm not coming out until I've memorized every song you've ever written. Just go on without me. I'll be under here, studying."

BR laughed. "That'll surprise Cassie. She loves to jump on my bed. But you've got a day and a half before she returns, and you're a quick study. Want me to have breakfast sent in?"

She peeked out to answer, but a small light near the bedroom door caught her attention. "What's that?"

"That tells us Mrs. Smith is in the house. She must've come early to prep for the team. They'll be here soon. I'll go check in."

"No, let me. You go shower. But while you're in there, I definitely don't think you should be imagining me naked and joining you in a few minutes."

"You really don't play fair, do you?"

Bobbi pulled on flannel pajama pants she'd tucked into a drawer the night before.

In the living room, she was secretly pleased by the unmistakable look of surprise on Mrs. Smith's face—confirmation that no women had been around in the mornings.

"Dr. Wyatt! What a lovely surprise. Can I get you anything?"

"Yes," Bobbi said, adjusting her ponytail. "May I have a minute of your time?"

"Of course."

They sat at the kitchen table.

"It's wonderful to see you," Bobbi began warmly. "And we're going to be seeing a lot more of each other. Last night, BR asked me to marry him." She held up her hand.

Mrs. Smith hugged her. "That's wonderful news! I'm so happy for him."

Bobbi laughed. "Aren't you supposed to say you're happy for the bride?"

Unexpectedly, Mrs. Smith giggled. "Of course, I'm delighted for you. But I've known him for years and never seen him like this. You and your Sami have transformed him. Cassie worships you, but BR, he's different. Happier. And that makes me very happy for him."

Bobbi hugged her back. "This morning's going to be hectic. The team's gathering because Sami and I are moving in this weekend. I'm sorry for all the extra work. I'll need your help—not just now, but going forward. I don't cook, I've got a full-time job, and I'm bringing a sweet little slob with me. I don't even know how groceries or laundry work around here. Please tell me you'll help."

"Of course, dear. I was wondering if you'd want me to stay on."

"*Stay on?* I'm going to make sure you get a raise!"

"That won't be necessary," she said gently. "Your daughter's a joy, and cooking for four isn't harder than for two. After the move, I'll show you how we do shopping, laundry—everything. Don't worry; I'll make it all go smoothly. Anything you need to know now?"

Bobbi nodded and fiddled with her ponytail. "Yes. I'd like to know your first name."

Mrs. Smith laughed. "Cynthia."

"And I'm Bobbi. Sami will call you Mrs. Smith, but you and I are on a first-name basis. Two women under the same roof need to be a team, or things can get tricky fast."

"Bobbi, I hope we'll be great friends. I love working here, and now even more so."

They stood and hugged again.

"Thank you, Cynthia. That means so much to me. I'm going to shower and change. I'll be out when everyone arrives."

BR was buttoning his shirt as Bobbi walked in. She grabbed the peach sweater Gina had made and a pair of pretty jeans. As she headed for the bathroom, she peeled off her pajama pants. His T-shirt barely covered her.

She glanced over her shoulder. "I know you care about the environment. Maybe tomorrow morning, we should save water by showering together?"

~~~

Feeling refreshed, Bobbi brushed her hair into a pretty ponytail, did her makeup, and dressed, ready to meet BR's team.

BR saw her coming and began, "Everyone, I'd like you to meet—"

"*Blondie!*"

"*Red!*" Bobbi flew into the arms of her best friend.

They shrieked over each other, shouting half-formed questions, none of it making any sense.

Grabbing Megan's arm, Bobbi dragged her straight to the bedroom, shutting the door on the stunned staff.

"Megan, me first," Bobbi gasped. "What are you doing here?"

"I got in last night and had a message from my boss asking me to attend a meeting. What are *you* doing here?"

Bobbi couldn't speak. Her logical brain felt like the circuits were overloaded.

Megan hugged her then spotted BR's dress shirt with lipstick on the collar and Bobbi's panties on the bed. "Bobbi, did you sleep with my boss?"

Swallowing, Bobbi squeaked out, "Who's your boss?"

"I'm the lead designer for the BR Bradford Company. Did you hook up with BR last night?"

Bobbi winced. "Not exactly." She held up her left hand.

Megan shrieked at the sight of the engagement ring. Bobbi screamed back. It quickly devolved into a mix of hugs, laughter, and accusations.

"This is *your* fault!" Bobbi said. "You and your stupid rules about not discussing boyfriends and jobs! I've been dating MP for two months. Apparently, you've been working for him for years! I love you, but I'm going to kill you for not telling me you work for BR Bradford!"

More insane laughter. Another round of crushing hugs.

"Never in a million years did I connect the dots," Megan said, breathless. "You're *engaged*? To *BR Bradford*? How could you not tell me?"

"He asked me last night. You were already on the plane! I wanted to tell you in person. How could *you* not tell me who you worked for?"

"Let me see that ring again." Megan gasped. "We can't go out there looking like this."

Like they had countless times at gyms and nightclubs, they retreated into the bathroom to do damage control.

As Bobbi gave the shortest possible explanation about the morning's meeting, she replied to BR's text, letting him know she was fine and would be out soon.

Megan undid Bobbi's ponytail and restyled it into a flattering half-up, half-down look.

Before they finally emerged, arm in arm, Bobbi texted BR to meet them outside the bedroom for a quick private word.

"Sweetheart," she said, "may I introduce you to my best friend in the entire world, the impossibly weird but totally wonderful Megan 'Red' O'Malley."

Megan stepped forward. "Boss, may I introduce you to the most amazing human I know, my best friend and your fiancée, Dr. Bobbi 'Blondie' Wyatt."

The women collapsed in laughter again. BR eventually joined in, piecing together the madness.

BR then introduced Bobbi to the team, announced their engagement, and asked everyone to keep it private for now. Megan explained that BR's staff was famously loyal—his company topped every ranking as the best to work for, with top pay, a culture of respect, and true work-life balance. No NDAs needed. Everyone treated him with the same consideration he gave them.

"I don't report to BR directly," Megan said later, "but when I had to care for my mom, the company booked my flights and had a rental waiting in Miami. That's the kind of man you're marrying."

They ate omelets made by Mrs. Smith and sipped freshly squeezed juice. Ronnie had even picked up a Bobbi Blend.

As BR served breakfast to his team, Megan got to work, coordinating with her assistant, Trish. First priorities: Sami's room and the master bedroom.

"Bobbi, I need to talk with you—privately," Megan said, coming over to her.

They walked into the bedroom and shut the door.

"Before you say anything, I need you to forgive me." Megan sputtered, "I'm the village idiot. I never meant to hurt you with my stupid rules."

Bobbi sat on the bed, motioning for Megan to join her.

"When I met you, I was at the lowest point in my life. The guy I was dating broke my heart. He betrayed and cheated on me. He stole from me. And he did something even worse."

Bobbi squeezed Megan's hands.

"The worst thing he did was he tried to use me to get to BR. That happened a couple of times, in different ways with different people, when they found out that I work with BR Bradford. I was hurt and embarrassed by what he'd done to me, and I was super protective of BR. My defenses were up. It had nothing to do with you. After a while, it just kind of became a joke between us. If I'd known you were dating him, I would've told you everything."

"I know. It's just the strangest situation ever!"

"Bobbi, *please* say you forgive me."

"Of course I do. But I intend to hold this over your head for the rest of our lives." Bobbi laughed, and any tension left the room. "Now, show me what we have to get done today."

Paint swatches and fabric samples soon surrounded Bobbi. Ingrid joined via video call and helped finalize Sami's room's palette and window treatments. Furniture shopping would happen on Friday after Zoë and Avery finished.

Using her JadePad, Megan created digital mockups. Trish moved quickly, already coordinating with the lead painter and carpenters from BR's theatrical team, who were quietly unloading tools and protective covers. Furniture was being removed from Sami's room before Bobbi and Megan finished their second cup of juice.

BR told them the master bedroom had an unlimited budget and his full blessing—he wanted the room to reflect Bobbi.

Later, with the door closed, Bobbi asked, "Megan, did you design the rest of the house? I've loved it since my first visit."

"Yeah. It was kind of empty until Anna Maria moved in. BR hired me right after grad school—over much more experienced designers—and gave me carte blanche. He said he wanted it to feel like a real home. The only room he wouldn't let me touch was this one. That's why it's so bland. But now? Now it's your Italian palazzo suite."

She moved to the windows, already designing aloud. "Creamy ivory walls—clean, soft, and classic. A terracotta-toned carpet, plush and sun-warmed like the clay streets of Trastevere. Everything we choose will be here to showcase *2:29* and create a happy, peaceful, romantic atmosphere for you two."

She gestured toward the long wall opposite the bed. "*2:29* will go there, centered and perfectly lit. The two companion pieces will hang on either side. What do you think?"

"What I've always thought: you're a genius. Can I keep the shroud?"

Megan nodded approvingly. "Dramatic. Definitely staying. But the frame? No. We'll replace it with something sculpted and timeless—walnut, maybe a wrought-iron canopy. A piece that looks like it belongs behind one of those elegant shutters, with just a whisper of faded teal and ochre in the pillows or drapes. It'll echo the painting without trying too hard."

Bobbi applauded softly, her voice warm. "That sounds perfect."

Megan beamed. "This won't just be a bedroom, Bobbi. It's your happily-ever-after Italian hideaway. And when we go shopping, you're telling me everything, starting from the very beginning."

Before they emerged from the bedroom, Bobbi grabbed Megan's arm and quietly asked her, "What are those weird talking vegetables in Cassie's room?"

Megan raised an eyebrow at her and asked, "You've never seen *VeggieTales*?"

Bobbi just shook her head, still holding Megan's arm.

"It's a cartoon that teaches Biblical stories to kids," Megan explained.

"Oh ..." Bobbi had a look of epiphany on her face. "I really need to get caught up on all manners of religion in this house."

When they made it back to the living room, Bobbi gave BR an affectionate hug while Megan showed him the VR rendering of the redesigned master suite.

"That's fantastic," he said, clearly impressed. "Trish said to tell you both to head to my study. We're converting it into your private office."

"Why?" Bobbi asked.

"Because you'll need a quiet room for virtual consults, patient files, a place to lock up your medical bag. I'm so proud of your career; I want to make sure I'm being supportive, especially now that you'll be farther from the clinic."

Megan smiled as Bobbi tilted her head and mouthed, "*Mister Perfect.*"

"Before you head out shopping," BR added, "there's someone you need to meet."

After reviewing the plans for her new office, Bobbi joined BR upstairs to meet Sam Halifax, his longtime friend and head of the law firm that oversaw all of BR's companies. Bobbi had met him twice and liked his easygoing, polished manner. At breakfast, he had made it clear how thrilled he was for her.

After pleasantries, he led her to a conference room. Waiting inside was Juliana Tricocci.

"She's the attorney who handled Cassie's adoption. I've asked her to go over a few things with you. If you like her, she can be your lawyer." BR handed her a file folder then reached into his pocket and gave Bobbi a folded dollar bill.

"What's this for?" she asked, amused.

"Give it to her, and then come downstairs when you're done."

"And what'll *you* be doing?" she teased. "Everyone in your orbit seems to be working at warp speed to make this move happen."

"I'm flying to the Himalayas to find a guru who can explain how you didn't know your best friend was my interior designer."

"Someone who can explain Megan? You may be gone a while," she quipped, shaking her head.

She turned to Juliana. "Nice to meet you."

"It's a pleasure, Dr. Wyatt," Juliana said, offering her hand. "This'll only take five minutes. Is that all right? Can I get you anything?"

"Call me Bobbi," she replied, shaking her hand firmly.

"I'm Juliana. Let's sit."

BR deeply believed in fostering a culture of cooperation. Even when negotiating contracts, he approached everything as a meeting of the minds—never confrontational, always collaborative. The conference room reflected that ethos— muted colors, soft textures, with couches and chairs clearly chosen for conversation, not confrontation. Bobbi guessed Megan had designed the space to mirror his instinct for harmony over hierarchy.

"Juliana, can you explain why I need a lawyer?" Bobbi asked once they sat.

"Do you have one?"

"No. The clinic has counsel. I've used them a few times for paperwork, like when I bought my house."

"That's great. And it's about to change," Juliana said with a warm, professional tone. "You're marrying a billionaire. That makes you a target. We don't need to decide anything today, but there are a few things we'll want to look at."

"Shoot."

"Let's start with malpractice insurance. Do you know your coverage limit?"

Bobbi shook her head. "No clue. It's a standard policy through the clinic. I've never had a claim."

"Excellent, but it's worth reviewing. Sam says you're a phenomenal doctor, but you've probably seen colleagues get hit with nuisance lawsuits. Once people know who you're married to, they may see dollar signs, even if you've done nothing wrong."

Bobbi sat up straighter. "I hadn't thought about that."

"Also, I understand BR is adopting your daughter, Samantha, and you're adopting Cassie?"

"Yes, Sami's my daughter."

"I can handle all the paperwork. I know Cassie's background, but I'll need to ask whether Sami's biological father could potentially interfere, whether he might try to claim custody or cause you problems when he finds out who you married."

Bobbi's stomach clenched. She handed over the dollar. "This makes you my lawyer, right?"

The lawyer nodded and tucked it away. "You have full confidentiality."

In a tone that brooked no room for doubt, Bobbi said, "Sami's biological father doesn't know she exists. He's never been part of my life or hers."

Juliana wisely asked nothing further. "Understood. We'll talk more later to ensure everything is buttoned up legally. My job's to protect you—and both kids—completely."

"Good."

"There are a few other things we'll want to go over, eventually. For now, just promise me you won't sign anything legal without me reviewing it."

"Deal. BR asked me to give you this folder."

Juliana flipped it open and scanned the documents, making a few notes on her legal pad.

"This is all in order. Here's how we'll work together: I'll review any documents, provide a summary, an opinion, and the next steps, and then carry out whatever you decide. This is an amendment to BR's will." She held up the file folder. "If you sign, as of today, if anything happens to him before you're married, you'd have full custody of Cassie and access to unlimited financial resources to support her."

Bobbi's eyes flicked over the wording, her breath ragged. It was one thing to share a home, another to plan a life … but this was deeper. This was BR saying, *Right now, this instant, you're the one I trust with my child.* Bobbi didn't speak; she signed.

"The second document adds you to his personal credit card account. You're not legally liable for anything, just authorized to use the cards. There's one in your name, issued this morning."

"Easy." Bobbi laughed and signed.

346

"I'll make copies of everything for you." Juliana handed over the new credit card. "You can start using this immediately. Just so you're aware, the credit limit is one million dollars."

Bobbi did a double-take. "That's a *limit*?"

Juliana smiled. "Welcome to the BR Bradford household."

~~~

Bobbi came downstairs and stepped straight into a home makeover tornado. BR was nowhere to be seen, but the carpet had already vanished from Sami's room, and BR's office was halfway packed under Mrs. Lincoln's laser-focused supervision. Mrs. Smith stood by the doorway, directing a cleaning crew poised to swoop in the moment the space was cleared. BR's security team loitered with practiced ease, eyes scanning for anyone bold enough to snap a picture or pocket a souvenir. Meanwhile, Trish and Megan were everywhere—measuring, capturing VR images, Trish scribbling notes as Megan fired off ideas like she was running a design sprint.

Bobbi blinked, taking it all in. "I was upstairs for fifteen minutes. Did I miss a time-lapse montage and a Coffee Corner IV drip?"

Megan laughed but didn't break stride.

Bobbi stepped closer and lowered her voice. "Megan, I need five minutes. Bedroom. Just us."

Megan nodded, already sensing the shift. "Trish, call Casa di Pietra in the Bronx; make sure everything on their site is in stock and ready to be cut and installed by tomorrow."

Bobbi raised an eyebrow. "Casa di Pietra? House of Stone?"

Megan smirked. "Only the best Italian marble for your palazzo, Principessa."

Bobbi smirked back. "It's a bedroom, not a Tuscan villa."

"Not yet," Megan said, already heading for the hall.

Behind closed doors, Bobbi and Megan exhaled, looked at each other, and burst out laughing at the sheer absurdity of the morning.

Finally, Bobbi asked, "What's the agenda for the day?"

Megan pulled out her JadePad.

Bobbi studied it before saying, "Will you kill me if I add two more errands?" She then told her about the credit card.

Megan plucked the credit card from Bobbi and squealed. Then she snorted at what Bobbi said. "Bobbi, shame on you. When have I *ever* complained about shopping with you? Especially with an unlimited credit card? What do you need?"

"BR's taking me to a fancy restaurant tonight to celebrate our engagement. I need a spectacular dress. We'll probably end up with our first engagement photos tonight. I want to look dazzling for him."

The redhead's golden eyes sparkled. "You won't believe this. I looked up the artist from that painting—Marianna Remi? She's been touted as an up-and-coming talent in fashion design for the last two years. Painting's just always been her passion. Her first U.S. collection's about to launch, and there's a boutique in SoHo doing private previews. I've seen a few early pieces—I'm obsessed. Her eye is extraordinary, and you in one of her dresses? Showstopper. This could be your full-circle fashion moment."

"That's unbelievable!"

Bobbi's expression shifted, and she lowered her voice. "Megan, I'm mortified to say this out loud, but *you* know everything in my closet. Every pretty thing I own, you either picked out or helped me choose. I've got a million sports bras and everyday underwear, but my lingerie game is … pretty weak."

"*Weak*?" Megan scoffed. "It's nonexistent. You've never needed 'little things' to have every man in the room trying to follow you home. You'd look sexy in a burlap sack. Why is this coming up now?"

Bobbi buried her face in her hands. "BR's never seen me in my underwear. Not even a one-piece, let alone a bikini. I don't want to disappoint him."

Megan stared, stunned. "Wait—*what*? You've been together for two months, and you obviously slept here last night. Are you telling me you haven't …?"

Bobbi shook her head without lifting it from her hands.

Megan gave a low whistle. "Wow. Okay. Want me to take you to that sexy lingerie boutique?"

Bobbi peeked through her fingers. "Desperately."

"We have *so* much to talk about," Megan said as she jumped to her feet, fully energized. "He gave you a credit card with a million-dollar limit, and he's never seen you in a bikini? We're fixing that. First, we find a swimsuit so hot it might set off the smoke detector. Then we get you a knockout, low-cut Marianna Remi dress for your fancy engagement dinner. After that, lingerie so sexy he'll never know what hit him." She laughed, already pulling up her phone. "And if we time it right, bang trim, mani-pedi, and you're home in time to knock his socks off. Give me two minutes to reroute us. Trish will handle everything here."

Bobbi smiled. "Megan, what would I do without you?"

"Fortunately, you'll never have to find out."

CHAPTER THIRTY-FIVE: THE WHIRLWIND
BR

The elevator doors opened, and Bobbi and Megan swept into the penthouse like a couture hurricane. Garment bags and sleek shopping totes swung from their arms—some from luxury makeup counters and high-end shoe stores BR recognized, others from elegant boutiques he didn't, including one tiny bag with satin ribbon and a name he couldn't pronounce, which he suspected had something to do with lingerie. A few boxes were tied with bows, and one bag had what looked suspiciously like a marble tile sample sticking out. He had no idea what half of it was, but judging by their energy, it had been a wildly successful mission.

"Make room; it's about to get glamorous in here," Megan called to BR with a wave, already moving furniture to clear space for an impromptu photo shoot. Bobbi was halfway to the bedroom when Megan added, "Let me know when you want me to check your makeup."

Bobbi shot her a grin over her shoulder. "Ten minutes."

Megan soon disappeared into the bedroom, carrying a makeup bag.

BR froze, unsure whether to pace or play it cool.

A few minutes later, Megan reappeared, eyes gleaming. "Ready?" Before BR could answer, she turned slightly toward the hallway and called, "Bobbi, you're on."

Bobbi stepped into view.

For a second, BR forgot how to breathe.

The dress was a rich sapphire blue—deep enough to echo the diamond in her engagement ring and vibrant enough to highlight the gold of its setting. It hugged her curves like liquid silk. The neckline plunged asymmetrically, revealing a bold view of her cleavage. A thigh-high slit revealed the endless line of her legs, sheer stockings catching the light. Her heels were high, strappy, and unapologetically feminine. She'd gone for the "wow factor" and nailed it.

Her long, lustrous hair had been styled in loose, shining waves that tumbled down her back. She usually wore it down only in their most intimate moments, when she was relaxed, unguarded. Seeing it styled like this, intentional and dazzling, took BR's breath away.

Megan's makeup makeover was flawless: a whisper of gold at the eyes—subtle, luminous, and perfectly echoing the rare Italian gold of her ring—and a slightly dramatic touch of rose lit up her lips.

Bobbi turned slightly toward Megan and cooed, "Good call on the dress. I think he's about to hyperventilate."

"Well, if your fiancé passes out, luckily for him, he's got a doctor nearby. You can try mouth-to-mouth ... but with how you look in that dress, I'm not convinced that'll help him recover."

BR could barely focus. "I'm not entirely sure I'm going to make it through dinner," he muttered, making Bobbi's smile somehow grow even brighter.

Bobbi didn't miss a beat. "That's how I felt the night you took me to dinner at The Red Dragonfly."

He almost laughed—almost. That night had completely upended each of their life plans in the best, most improbable way.

It had brought them here.

BR barely noticed as Megan buzzed around them, a blur of motion and velvet camera angles, pausing only to adjust a curtain or direct Bobbi's pose. "This light is insane," she murmured. "It's perfect. The glow from Broadway behind you, the skyline kissing her hair. Okay, Bobbi, left hand on his chest. Show off the rock. You're going to break the internet," Megan chirped. "All right, I'm good. I'll send the best pictures to both of you. Go get engaged again."

As the elevator descended, Bobbi reached over and adjusted BR's lapel with a smile. "You good?" she asked softly.

"Define good," he murmured, still reeling from how overwhelmingly sexy his always-gorgeous fiancée looked tonight.

She gave him a winsome look and slipped her arm through his.

"Have you given any thought to how we want to handle the engagement announcement?" he asked.

Bobbi hesitated. "Yeah. And I keep going back and forth."

"We could just tell friends. Plan a super small, private wedding. Keep it low-key and see how long we can hold the line," he offered, though even he didn't believe it would work.

Bobbi nodded. "Except ... when I walk into the clinic Monday morning with this ring on my finger, people will ask who I'm marrying. It won't stay quiet."

He looked at her gently. "I don't want you to feel ambushed. Once it's out there, it's out there. People might try to take your picture at work. Or follow you. That's not fair to you or your patients. And it could cause problems for Sami."

"I know, but ..." She looked down then back up with a smile that hit him square in the chest. "I feel amazing tonight. And if we do it on our terms—with a couple of beautiful photos, a short press release, and a simple announcement in *The Times*—then maybe it's easier. Dignified. Romantic. Controlled. If it's public knowledge, there won't be any need for sneaky photos."

BR nodded slowly. "Option two, then."

"Option two."

The car was already waiting. Ronnie opened the door, and BR let her go first, watching her gracefully slide in.

Not too long later, they pulled up in front of a low-lit, impossibly elegant building tucked discreetly between two limestone façades. There was no sign, just a bronze plaque beside the door that read "*Élan 11*" in narrow serifed letters and a doorman who recognized BR at once.

Inside, Élan 11 was a dignified retreat. Whispered conversations. Candlelight instead of overheads. Waitstaff who moved like shadows. The room was filled with people who were serious about fine dining *and* never posted photos of their food.

BR was used to attention when he walked into a room but, for once, people weren't looking at him.

As Bobbi stepped in beside him, the soft buzz of conversation dipped then swelled again into a low murmur. BR glanced sideways. She didn't seem to notice the eyes on her. Or maybe she did and just didn't care. Her sapphire dress shimmered beneath the golden sconces. Her hair caught the light.

The maître d' appeared—polished, discreet—and led them to a secluded table with a perfect view of the room. BR pulled out her chair himself. The flicker of a candle caught her ring, sending sparks of blue and gold dancing across the tablecloth.

In a quiet voice, the maître d' asked, "Mr. Bradford, Mr. Compton from ESPN asked if he could come over and say hello."

Turning to Bobbi, BR nodded. "This isn't a celebrity grip-and-grin. He's a major sportscaster for ESPN. Before that, he was GM of the Chicago Cubs. He and I sponsor a charity that builds baseball diamonds in underserved neighborhoods and raises money for the Negro Leagues Baseball Museum. I promise it'll just take a moment."

Clay Compton had grown up in poverty in Mississippi but graduated with honors from Dartmouth before making it to the major leagues. BR stood to greet him.

"Clay, may I introduce Dr. Bobbi Wyatt?"

As they shook hands, a server approached with an expensive bottle of Franciacorta—the elite Italian alternative to champagne—and a chilled bottle of Pellegrino.

"Compliments of the management," the server said, uncorking the bottle.

Clay smiled then looked apologetic. "I'm sorry. It looks like I've interrupted a celebration. BR, I'll call you. We've got exciting news about the KC project. Dr. Wyatt, it was a pleasure."

Bobbi accepted his regards with a warm smile then turned her focus back to BR. "He seems lovely."

"He is. But tonight, I just want to talk about us. So ... when would you like to get married?"

"I'm not sure. But can we talk about our honeymoon first? I need something romantic to think about, something that's not the chaos back at the penthouse or the stress of planning a wedding."

Even in the middle of a candlelit restaurant, BR felt the Bobbi Bubble wrap around them. "Do we even need to discuss it? We'll honeymoon in Italy. We have to find our street, the one from *2:29*."

Her eyes lit up. "Can we take the kids to Italy someday? I want to do all the touristy things with them. But, for our honeymoon, I want it to be just us. Maybe Tuscany? Or the Amalfi Coast? I think you'll like how I look in a bikini."

"You're fully dressed right now, and I can barely handle it. Don't get me started on bikinis." He grinned. "Tuscany or Amalfi? Let's do both. We'll land in Rome, find our street, spend a week in Tuscany, and a week on the coast. But we have to kiss under the Bridge of Sighs in Venice."

Bobbi sighed, dreamy and content. Then her expression shifted. She turned her head sharply as her eyes swept the room. "BR ... something's wrong."

She spotted Clay Compton hunched forward at a table three spots over, his hand pressed to his chest. A ragged cough broke the silence, dry and strained. Then another. Then nothing.

The woman beside him—he recognized her now, Kaela Merritt, the Olympic snowboarder—put her hand on his back. "Clay? Are you okay?"

Compton made a choking sound—wet, desperate—and then slipped sideways in his chair.

Bobbi was already sprinting toward him.

~~~

Bobbi

She caught part of his fall, breaking it with her arms, but the sudden shift caused the heel of her beautiful new shoe to snap off. Bobbi stumbled forward, one knee slamming into the carpet, tearing her stocking on the chair leg.

"Call 911!" she barked. "Bring me your AED—now." She was already rolling him onto his side. "He's not getting air."

Her voice dropped as she checked his pulse—thready. Slowing.

"Full obstruction," she said sharply. "Possible loss of perfusion. He's about to go into cardiac arrest. I need help lifting him—*now*."

A former football player, one of the ESPN crew, rushed over. Together, they got Clay upright enough for Bobbi to slide behind him. The sudden shift scraped her knee, but she didn't flinch.

The slit in her skirt gave way with an audible rip as she braced herself and wrapped her arms around his midsection. She thrust once, twice.

Nothing.

She locked her arms again. A third thrust.

Still nothing.

Her heart pounded. Clay wasn't getting oxygen. She could feel time slipping. They were seconds away from a crash.

She planted her feet, clenched tighter, and thrust again.

With a violent gasp, Clay coughed and began to breathe.

Bobbi quickly moved to face him, steadying him. "Clay, I'm Dr. Wyatt. Remember? Look at me. Can you breathe?"

He nodded weakly, eyes glassy. Then, without warning, he lurched forward to thank her ... and vomited straight down the front of her dress.

The mess splattered across her chest, dripping into the neckline, soaking through. A splash hit her hair, which had come loose in the chaos.

The restaurant went silent.

Bobbi sat back on her heels, covered in vomit, hair tangled, dress and nylons ripped, but composed. The romantic haze of the evening was gone, but she was still every inch a doctor.

Clay moaned, horrified. "Oh God. I'm so sorry."

She quickly rechecked his vitals. Pupils. Breathing sounds. Reassured.

A new light flooded the restaurant. A police car had pulled up to the curb, lights spinning. Two officers hurried in.

One of the cops glanced at the table and did a double-take. "Wait a second—this is the ESPN crew, isn't it?"

An ashen server said, "Yeah. That's Clay Compton. And that woman just saved his life."

The officer turned to her. "Miss, that was—"

"*Doctor*," she said gently, wiping her face with a linen napkin. "It's Dr. Wyatt."

Another squad car arrived, followed by a pair of paramedics.

Bobbi calmly explained the situation, scooting back to let them take over. One medic knelt with a stethoscope. The other fit an oxygen mask and checked Clay's pulse.

"We're taking him in," one of them said. "We want a full cardiac workup."

Kaela Merritt stepped forward, lifting her voice to be heard by the diners. "He's going to be okay. And for the record, this is Dr. Bobbi Wyatt. She saved his life before the rest of us even realized what was happening."

A hush fell. Then everyone stood and applauded. Loud. Sustained. Grateful.

BR was standing, clapping the loudest.

Bobbi exhaled loudly, still kneeling, vomit down her dress and hair in disarray. She removed her broken shoes and continued to wipe her face and hair with the linen napkin.

A manager rushed over, pale and rattled. "Everyone, we're so sorry, but we have to end dinner service. Health protocol. The area's contaminated."

A young bartender arrived at Bobbi's side. She handed over a neatly folded black server uniform. "It's clean, and there's a private washroom this way," she said softly, already helping Bobbi up and leading her through a side door.

Bobbi locked the washroom door and leaned over the sink, bracing her elbows on the counter. "Jesus," she whispered. "That was close."

Then she laughed—harder than she meant to. "Did I just pray?" she questioned aloud. "What's BR doing to me?" She looked up at her reflection and laughed ruefully—hair tangled and wet, makeup smeared, vomit down the front of her ruined dress.

The smile lingered as she turned on the tap. She splashed water on her face, wiped off the last of her makeup, and rinsed the worst of the mess out of her hair. Once it was clean enough, she finger-combed it out quickly and efficiently.

Her dress was ruined. So was the spectacular new bra. She tossed the shredded silk stockings into the trash, carefully slipped out of the dress, wiping herself down again, and then slid into the crisp server uniform.

No shoes, wet hair, bare-faced, but her patient was alive. Somewhere, Dr. Sam would be proud.

She exhaled, composed herself, and then stepped back into the dining room, fingers brushing her engagement ring.

The diners were filtering out. BR was still at their table, talking with the manager.

Bobbi walked toward him, highly aware she was braless, her once-stunning dress folded in a discreet bag the bartender had provided.

BR stood to greet her.

She gestured to her outfit as she approached then stubbed her toe—hard. Nevertheless, she reached the table with a casual smile, as if nothing had happened.

"So ... where were we? You were promising me a kiss under the Bridge of Sighs?"

He pulled her into his arms. "I'm marrying Wonder Woman."

She laughed into his chest. "Wonder Woman's a brunette."

"Details," he murmured before lifting her hand to kiss her ring.

Bobbi looked down, sheepish. "I have no shoes."

He smiled. "Ronnie's bringing the car around." Then, before she could protest, he scooped her into his arms—bare feet, loose hair, no bra, server uniform, and all—and carried her straight through the restaurant like a groom crossing the threshold.

Outside, drizzle shimmered in the streetlights. A few diners, waiting for their cars, stepped aside and applauded.

One discreet camera flash went off at just the right moment—her arms wrapped around his neck, her face radiant, hair tousled, the ring glinting faintly in the light. It was a moment of quiet triumph and pure love.

By the time they reached the waiting car, the photo was already online. The lighting. The angle. The expression. They looked like the iconic scene from *The Bodyguard*—Kevin Costner carrying Whitney Houston out of danger. Except, this time, the beautiful woman wasn't the one being saved—*she* was the hero. The guardian.

In the back seat, Bobbi groaned. "All I want is to get back to the penthouse, take the longest shower of my life, and possibly barbecue that bra."

"It died a hero," he said sweetly.

Then she froze. "Wait—BR, your shoulder. You carried me!"

He blinked. "No pain."

She leaned over and kissed his shoulder gently. "You're healed."

He reached for her hand. "*You* healed me."

Her breath caught. "You should give Rex a bonus."

He tapped his JadePhone. "Done."

She glanced at him. "What were you talking to the manager about while I was changing?"

BR hesitated. "Nothing important."

She raised an eyebrow.

He sighed. "I asked how many people were on shift—servers, bartenders, cooks. I didn't want anyone missing out on their tips or wages, so ... I took care of it."

Bobbi looked at him with quiet admiration then curled into his side. "I like where we're going."

He stroked her arm and smiled. "The penthouse?"

"Yeah," she murmured. "That, too. But I meant I like where *we're* going."

Then her phone lit up. She answered. "Hi, Daddy."

"Dr. Daughter, you're the lead story on SportsCenter! ESPN just showed a clip of you saving Clay Compton! Your mother and I are so proud of you! What are you wearing in that picture of BR carrying you?"

She closed her eyes. "It's a long story. I'll tell you everything tomorrow. I'm okay."

As soon as she hung up, her phone dinged again. This time, it was Gina texting.

OMG, you are trending number one on every social media!

Gina forwarded a link from *TMZ*:

BR Bradford's Hero Bombshell Fiancée

And another from the *New York Post*:

Blonde, Brilliant, Badass—BR's Mystery Fiancée Saves ESPN Legend in Midtown Meltdown

BR's phone buzzed, too. He glanced at the screen. "It's Bree."

He listened for a moment then nodded. "Got it. Make sure the focus stays on Bobbi, not me." He put the call on speaker.

Bree's voice came through clear. "Bobbi, how're you holding up? We're all so proud of you."

"This is overwhelming. What do I do?"

"We've got you," Bree said. "I have Liz coordinating with the PR and social media teams to keep our response consistent. Nothing goes out without your say-so. Every talk show is calling. The networks, radio stations, papers, they all want interviews with you. Oprah called personally. ESPN wants to feature you. *People* magazine is offering the cover. Just tell us what you want."

"No interviews. No talk shows, even though my mother idolizes Oprah. I just did my job. A doctor's job is to provide care, whether she's in a dress or scrubs. On Monday, I'm going back to work."

BR looked at her with quiet pride, completely in her corner.

Liz joined the call. "Three clear pictures are making the rounds. You look fantastic. The first two show you trying to save Clay Compton—focused, beautiful, in control. The third is BR carrying you out. The diners are applauding. Your hair's down, your face glowing. It radiates confidence, love, and happiness. Nothing embarrassing here—quite the opposite. Outsider's honor."

Bobbi exhaled. If Liz said it, she believed it.

"One more thing," Liz added. "Megan sent Chrissy and me her five favorite photos for the wedding announcement. Oh, Bobbi, you look spectacular. That'll be the narrative in two more days—a happy couple getting married."

Just then, Sami got through. "Mom, you're a *hero*!" she yelled. Her pride made Bobbi's heart swell. "All my friends are calling me."

"Sami, baby, just be careful who you talk to, okay? I'm not giving any interviews. And you still need to brush your teeth, do your homework, and get some sleep. We've got a big weekend coming up."

Bobbi could practically hear Sami's eyeroll.

A few minutes later, Bree and Liz called back.

"The media loves what you said about doing your job," Bree told her. "That's our official response—it's already circulating with the press."

The black car rolled to a smooth stop in the private garage beneath the hotel. Megan was already there, waiting, arms crossed, holding a sleek pair of black flats in one hand.

"Nice going, Bobbi. I leave you alone for two hours, and you save a life instead of that gorgeous dress. Where *are* your priorities?"

"Hi, Megan," Bobbi said weakly.

Megan held out the shoes. "I grabbed these from your closet. Put them on before the staff thinks BR's dating a runaway cult member."

Bobbi slipped them on with a grateful sigh. "How'd you know we were back?"

"Please. We still track each other's phones. And when *People* sent a breaking news alert saying my best friend saved

ESPN's star while wearing my eyeliner, I knew you'd need backup."

Bobbi hugged her tight. "Oh, Megan, I was so scared. He was about to crash. I'm sorry about the dress." Her whisper was too soft for BR to hear.

"I love you," Megan whispered back. "You're a damn hero. Also, I'm stealing that server shirt. You make it look good."

BR joined them, having just wrapped up one last call. "Thanks for everything, Megan. Why are you still here?"

"I got special lights for the paintings. The carpenter and electrician just finished the install. I wanted it all set before you got home. I thought I had plenty of time ... before my best friend came home early after saving a life in couture."

Everyone laughed.

"Good night, you two," Megan said. "Have fun. I'll see you first thing in the morning, Bobbi. We've got a busy day tomorrow."

CHAPTER THIRTY-SIX: 2:29

BR

"Sweetheart, I need to call my mom. She was with the moving girls today and wanted to give me an update. And I'm sure she's excited about tonight. I also got a text from Dr. Thibodeau, and I really need to call her. While I do, can you check in on Cassie? Just make sure she's okay?"

BR stepped away to call Anna Maria.

She answered on the first ring. "Unc! We saw it on Instagram. Bobbi's amazing."

"She really is."

"We're so excited about your engagement! Gina and I are having lunch next week, but we were texting when the news broke. She said, 'That's my cousin!' and I said, 'That's my aunt Bobbi!' Cassie couldn't ask for a better mother."

"We both feel terrible that you and Siobhán found out about our engagement from the news," BR said. "We were planning to tell you ourselves this morning."

"You mean a little thing like Bobbi heroically saving a man's life threw off your schedule?" Anna Maria teased. "I think you get a pass. And not to burst your balloon, but ... Gina already told me! We were texting about your engagement when the news broke. She wrote, 'That's my cousin!' and I wrote back, 'That's my aunt Bobbi!'"

She laughed softly. "Don't worry; Siobhán and I made sure Cassie didn't catch on. But we're both so excited for you. And our Cassie couldn't ask for a better mother."

He heard Anna Maria sniffle as she relayed the moment to Siobhán.

"I promise. The little angel's already asleep. How about I carry her up in the morning so her mother can wake her?"

"Perfect. Love you."

"I love you, Unc."

BR made one last call. Bree and Liz were still at the office, handling the most critical inquiries. His director of communication had the social media and PR teams under control.

Bree sounded like she always did—calm, organized, and in charge. "The networks, major sites, and press outlets are handling this beautifully. The focus is on Bobbi's heroic quick thinking, with a lot of positive attention on the Clay Compton angle. And, of course, your surprise engagement. Since Bobbi's nearly invisible on social media, the only photos circulating are her LinkedIn headshot and a couple of clinic portraits. Depending on how she feels, this could become a great platform to inspire girls to pursue medicine. We fed the team. Transport is getting them home safely. I already thanked them for you."

"You're the best. I'm turning off my phone for the night. Thanks for everything."

BR lit the candles that Megan had discreetly placed in the bedroom. The paintings were covered and awaiting Bobbi's unveiling. The new carpeting and paint had transformed BR's utilitarian bedroom into a beautiful space.

Bobbi was finishing the last of her calls in the living room. She motioned for him to sit down beside her.

"I'm *so* disappointed. I planned the sexiest lingerie seduction for our first time. We may have to wait another day or two. Please don't be mad at me."

He dismissed the comment with a shake of his head and a wave of his hand.

"Sweetheart, do you mind if we just jump in the shower and then go to sleep?"

"Want me to carry you in?"

Bobbi bit her lip and blushed. "I kind of do."

She was so busy nuzzling his neck that BR didn't think she looked around the redecorated bedroom. The bathroom looked the same; tomorrow would be the big day for the renovation.

He watched as Bobbi turned on the shower, making sure the sprays were strong and the water was hot. Then, without a word, she took off the server uniform and her panties. For the first time, she stood naked in front of BR.

He undressed quickly, seeming in a daze as he stared at her body. Then, when they stepped into the shower together, he grinned and said, "I get one of my fantasies tonight."

"Seeing me without my clothes on for the first time?" she asked as the steam rose around them.

"Okay, two. *That's* been a fantasy of mine since the night you wore that scorching outfit to Marco's," he said, his voice low. "Still, I've got another fantasy, and I want to live it out *right now.*"

"Sweetie," she said gently, brushing a damp lock of hair from her cheek, "normally, I'd be all over you. But I'm completely exhausted and served as a human barf bag tonight. Can we save your fantasy for another night?"

"Nope. This one can't wait. Turn around."

She craned her neck back at him and raised both eyebrows, but did as she was told.

Then he began—slowly, sensually—washing her hair.

Bobbi's soft moans rose above the sound of the water. "That's one fantasy you can live out every day," she murmured. "That feels incredible."

They kissed beneath the spray, bodies pressed close.

Bobbi gently pulled back and reached for the soap. "My turn."

Bobbi took her time, running her hands over him as the lather slid across his skin. When she reached his chest, she kissed the scars one by one—without comment, without hesitation—just love.

His breath caught. He hadn't expected that. His excitement was unmistakable.

Bobbi looked up at him. "You okay?"

He nodded, silent.

She let her hands drift lower, paused, and then raised her eyebrows with mock seriousness. "So ... when people said you were a huge star, I didn't realize they meant it literally ..."

He laughed, shaking his head. "You're impossible."

"Maybe I'm not that tired after all," she whispered. Then she kissed his shoulder, stepped back into his arms, and rested her head against his chest.

He wrapped her in the towel as they stepped out. "We've waited this long. We've got the rest of our lives."

He lovingly dried her hair with a thick towel.

"I'm so sorry to disappoint you tonight. I'm so relaxed now. All I want to do is sleep in your arms, in *our* bed. Let's unveil the paintings and sleep deep in the bubble tonight. Is that okay?"

They walked into their bedroom, a sanctuary lit only by candles. In one day, the room, and their lives, had been transformed.

BR turned on the gallery lights above all three paintings as Bobbi padded to the closet, wrapped in a thick towel. Moments later, she reappeared in one of his crisp blue dress shirts, sleeves rolled, hem barely brushing her thighs. Her hair was damp, her legs bare, and her eyes glowed with something more than candlelight.

"You're gonna kill me, Wyatt," he said quietly.

She smiled. "Not yet. First, we have something to see." Bobbi removed the coverings from the two smaller paintings and audibly choked up, remembering their beauty and significance. BR could feel her heart pounding as he held her.

Then, with a deep breath, she turned to the largest canvas. Gently, she lifted the black cloth from *2:29*. They stood together in front of it.

BR turned to face her. "I love you, Bobbi," he said softly. "My life changed that night at Fortuna's, when we met. Everything started right there."

Behind him, *2:29* began to shimmer. The colors grew deeper. The edges softened. The scene seemed to ripple, as if the surface was water and the world inside was calling them back.

Only Bobbi saw it but, sensing a shift, BR asked, "What's happening?"

"Trust me?" she asked in return, already knowing the answer, and reached for his hand. "It looks like I get my fantasy tonight," she said, her voice soft but certain. "The first time we make love … is going to be in Italy. Come with me."

He nodded.

Together, they stepped into the painting, and Bobbi showed him the apartment for rent.

Look for *Bobbi's Blondes*, coming soon.

ABOUT THE AUTHOR

S. R. Bradford is an award-winning motivational speaker, historian, and writer whose work celebrates leadership, resilience, and personal empowerment. A former National Teacher of the Year and recipient of the Golden Apple Award, Bradford's presentations—often described as *"dramatic, entertaining, and powerful"*—have been featured on *The Today Show*, *CNN*, and in *The New York Times*.

Bradford is a devoted parent and passionate advocate for animal rescue, sharing life with a much-loved rescue dog named Ace. When not writing or speaking, Bradford can often be found volunteering, reading, or enjoying the magic of Broadway.

Bradford holds degrees from Goddard College and DePaul University, with postgraduate coursework at Northwestern University. *The Bobbi Blend* is Bradford's debut novel and the beginning of a new journey in fiction.

S. R. Bradford lives in the Midwest, where writing, speaking, and exploring new stories remain at the heart of S.R.'s work. *The Bobbi Blend* marks the beginning of a new chapter in a career dedicated to the power of words to educate, entertain, and connect.

S. R. Bradford is the pen name of a presidential and congressional award-winning historian and speaker.

Find S.R. Bradford here:

TheBobbiBooks@proton.me
https://thebobbibooks.com
https://www.instagram.com/thebobbibooks

www.ingramcontent.com/pod-product-compliance
Lightning Source LLC
Chambersburg PA
CBHW030625250626
47154CB00006B/1921